Praise for THE SCAM

"Janet Evanovich and Lee Goldberg are an amazing team. Her dry, but witty, humor and his influence on a nonstop, super-sizzling plot makes their fourth book in the Fox and O'Hare series their best yet."
—Fredericksburg *Free Lance-Star*

"Evanovich . . . and Goldberg . . . are a perfect matchup for light, over-the-top reading entertainment."
—*bookreporter*

Praise for THE JOB

"Even if you can't always tell the good guys from the bad guys, there's no doubt who'll come out on top when the Fox is in the hen house."
—*Kirkus Reviews*

Praise for THE CHASE

"Readers familiar with Evanovich's novels will love this series, and hopefully there will be more adventures by this writing duo."
—Associated Press

"Great fun, with plenty of twists and action."

—*The Sacramento Bee*

"A fast and entertaining read . . . If you are looking to an entertaining tale, you would be hard-pressed to find one better than this page-turner."

—*Examiner.com*

"*The Chase* . . . is a polished little diamond with facets that may remind readers at different times of James Bond, *Ocean's Eleven* and *The A-Team*. Their secret ingredient is a winning sense of humor that informs both their prose and their decision-making. Like their con-artist hero Nicolas Fox, Evanovich and Goldberg have made charm their most important weapon."

—Milwaukee *Journal Sentinel*

"A comfy seriocomic caper just right for beach reading."

—*Kirkus Reviews*

Praise for THE HEIST

"*The Heist* is the perfect title to carry on a trip to the beach. The laugh-out-loud humor that readers expect from Evanovich is in full force, and Goldberg's crafty and elaborate writing is prominent. . . . Everyone will be eager for the next book in the series."

—Associated Press

"The action is fast paced and the writing is first rate, making *The Heist* an excellent choice for vacation reading."

—*Huntington News Network*

"After she catches him red-handed (almost literally—he just stole a diamond called the Crimson Teardrop), an FBI agent and a high-stakes con artist team up to thwart similar crimes. They are attractive. They will spar, which may mask romantic feelings. A breezy read."

—*San Antonio Express-News*

"Sparks fly."

—*Fort Worth Star-Telegram*

"Hang on as the action in this caper races around the globe, producing situations that are vintage Evanovich—both dangerous and hilariously absurd!"

—*RT Book Reviews*

Evanovich readers cite humor and sense of family among the reasons for reading her books, and I concur wholeheartedly."

—*BookPage*

"The dialogue's snappy . . . the pace is quick. . . . Evanovich's great gift is an ability to create situations zany enough to provoke bursts of laughter."

—*The Philadelphia Inquirer*

"The things Evanovich does so well—family angst, sweet eroticism, stealth shopping, that stunning mix of terror and hilarity—are . . . better than ever."

—*Booklist* (starred review)

"Evanovich comes up a winner."

—*Orlando Sentinel*

"Evanovich writes a hilarious book . . . with lots of scary moments and an exciting climax. . . . First rate."

—*Record Courier*

"Expect a good time."

—*New York Daily News*

BY JANET EVANOVICH

THE STEPHANIE PLUM NOVELS

One for the Money	*Lean Mean Thirteen*
Two for the Dough	*Fearless Fourteen*
Three to Get Deadly	*Finger Lickin' Fifteen*
Four to Score	*Sizzling Sixteen*
High Five	*Smokin' Seventeen*
Hot Six	*Explosive Eighteen*
Seven Up	*Notorious Nineteen*
Hard Eight	*Takedown Twenty*
To the Nines	*Top Secret Twenty-One*
Ten Big Ones	*Tricky Twenty-Two*
Eleven on Top	*Turbo Twenty-Three*
Twelve Sharp	

THE FOX AND O'HARE NOVELS WITH LEE GOLDBERG

The Heist	*The Scam*
The Chase	*The Pursuit*
The Job	

KNIGHT AND MOON

Curious Minds (with Phoef Sutton)

THE LIZZY AND DIESEL NOVELS

Wicked Appetite	*Wicked Charms* (with Phoef
Wicked Business	Sutton)

THE BETWEEN THE NUMBERS STORIES

Visions of Sugar Plums	*Plum Lucky*
Plum Lovin'	*Plum Spooky*

THE ALEXANDRA BARNABY NOVELS

Metro Girl	*Troublemaker* (graphic novel)
Motor Mouth	

NONFICTION

How I Write

THE PURSUIT

A FOX AND O'HARE NOVEL

JANET EVANOVICH

AND LEE GOLDBERG

BANTAM BOOKS NEW YORK

The Pursuit is a work of fiction. Names, characters, places,
and incidents are the products of the authors' imaginations or are used
fictitiously. Any resemblance to actual events, locales,
or persons, living or dead, is entirely coincidental.

2017 Bantam Books Mass Market Edition

Published in the United States by Bantam Books,
an imprint of Random House, a division of
Penguin Random House LLC, New York.

BANTAM BOOKS and the HOUSE colophon are registered
trademarks of Penguin Random House LLC.

Originally published in hardcover in the United States by
Bantam Books, an imprint of Random House,
a division of Penguin Random House LLC, in 2016.

ISBN 978-0-553-39279-1
Ebook ISBN 987-0-553-39278-4

Cover design: Carlos Beltrán
Cover illustration: Ray Lundgren

Printed in the United States of America

randomhousebooks.com

2 4 6 8 9 7 5 3 1

Bantam Books mass market edition: March 2017

ACKNOWLEDGMENTS

We'd like to thank Dr. D. P. Lyle, cataphile extraordinaire Gilles Thomas, and Alan Blinken, former U.S. ambassador to Belgium, for sharing their expertise with us.

THE PURSUIT

1

Nicolas Fox, infamous con artist and thief, woke up in a coffin. His ability to stay calm was partially due to the lingering effects of the tranquilizer shot he'd been given eighteen hours earlier, in Honolulu. It was also due to his belief that if his abductors had really wanted him dead, he would already be dead instead of napping in a high-end casket. Especially after he had thrown one of the kidnappers through a glass coffee table and tried to choke another with a kukui nut lei. So despite the dire nature of his present situation, Nick was optimistic about his future.

He lifted the heavy lid of his coffin and sat up to find himself in a bank vault. Concrete walls were lined with hundreds of safe-deposit boxes. The ceiling was low, outfitted with strips of fluorescent lights. The floor was white tile. A twelve-inch-thick steel door was ajar, as was an iron-barred gate that opened into the vault.

It took Nick only a second to realize that it was all fake. The iron bars of the gate were PVC pipes that had been painted black. The wall of safe-deposit boxes was a large photograph. The floor was linoleum, the steel door made of painted Styrofoam. It was the equivalent of a movie set. Someone was training for a heist and Nick had a good idea which vault they were planning to hit—the basement diamond vault located in the Executive Merchants Building in Antwerp, Belgium.

A man walked onto the set. He was dressed like a fashion-conscious Angel of Death in a black turtleneck sweater, black jeans, and black loafers. He was in his fifties, but had the athletic build of someone thirty years younger. It was his strikingly angular face, and the thinning, pockmarked skin glued like yellowing wallpaper to his sharp cheekbones, that betrayed his age.

Nick had never formally met the man, but he remembered him from Hawaii. He had led the abduction team. He spoke excellent English with a slight accent. Nick knew he was Balkan.

The man tossed Nick a cold bottle of mineral water. Nick caught the bottle and noted that it was Valvert, a Belgian brand. Nick was pretty certain he wasn't in Hawaii anymore.

"How are you feeling?" the man asked.

Nick took a long drink before he replied. "I

suppose traveling to Belgium in a coffin is better than flying coach these days. At least I was able to lie flat."

"And sleep like the dead."

"The afterlife looks surprisingly like the diamond vault in the Executive Merchants Building in Antwerp," Nick said.

"You're very good."

"I'm assuming that's why I'm here and not buried in this coffin."

"For the time being," the man said.

FBI Special Agent Kate O'Hare closed and locked the door on the high-end Oahu beach house. Her maverick partner Nick Fox had rented the house, and last night he'd disappeared. His red Ferrari was still parked in the driveway. His blood was also left behind. Okay, maybe it wasn't *his* blood, but it was *someone's* blood. And the blood trail led to the front door. Not such a shocker since a lot of people probably wanted to kill Fox. He was a world-class thief, con man, and an international fugitive. For the past couple years he'd been secretly working with Kate to take down bad guys that the FBI couldn't touch. Not that he was doing it out of the goodness of his heart. It was either help the feds or go to jail for a very long time.

And lucky me, Kate thought. I got stuck with him. Not only was she stuck with him, but she was also sort of hot for him. Could it possibly get any worse?

The beach house was at the end of a cul-de-sac. Houses to either side were hidden behind gates and tropical hedges. The sound of the surf was a constant murmur in the distance.

Kate walked down the driveway and cut across to one of the neighboring houses. She rang the bell and pulled the FBI badge case from her pocket. She flipped it open beside her head for the benefit of whoever looked through the peephole. The home-owner would see a blue-eyed woman in the vicinity of thirty with a slim, athletic build, her brown hair currently cut in a rakish, chin-length bob that not only met FBI requirements but also was practical. Her hair didn't require much care and didn't give an assailant a lot to grab in a fight. She wore a white permanent press polyester shirt, skinny jeans, a holstered Glock clipped to her belt, and a thin-bladed knife in a sheath just above her ankle.

The door was opened by a short woman in her midfifties wearing a purple halter top, colorful floral shorts, and flip-flops. She was more charred than tanned, her skin like tree bark. She held a Bloody Mary in her left hand, her long, polished fingernails as red as her drink.

"Do we really have to do this again?" the woman asked.

"Again?"

"Just because I signed a petition demanding to see a president's birth certificate doesn't mean I'm going to take a shot at him from my bathroom window while he's bodysurfing. When's he coming?"

"I'm not here about a presidential visit, ma'am. I'm investigating a possible crime that occurred next door."

"You'll have to narrow it down. Crimes occur there all the time. It's party central. That's why I have a camera aimed at the house. It's so I have proof of the drunken tourists who drive over my grass, vomit on my flowers, and let their kids pee on my palms. But does anybody care? No."

This brought a smile to Kate's face. The woman had security cameras. And one of them was aimed at the beach house Nick had rented. This was good.

"I'd like to look at the footage," Kate said.

"Hallelujah! You know how long I've been waiting for someone with a badge to ask me that?"

Kate edged past her and tried not to scrape herself on the lava-rock wall in the process. The woman closed the door, opened a coat closet behind her, and swept aside some windbreakers on hangers to reveal a shelf holding a DVR, a flat-screen monitor, a keyboard, and a mouse.

"Ta-da," the woman said. She turned on the monitor and typed in a password. The image on the screen was divided into six squares showing different angles of her property. One angle was a clear view of the rental house, and she clicked on the feed to expand it to full screen. "You can rewind using the backspace key. I got this at Costco. Great, isn't it?"

"Wonderful," Kate said.

"Can I get you a Bloody Mary?"

"Sure," Kate said. She didn't want a Bloody Mary, but it was the easiest way to get rid of the woman.

It took Kate only a few seconds to scan through the footage on the DVR and find what she wanted. Yesterday, late afternoon, a Ford Explorer drove up to the beach house, and four men got out. They drew guns and fanned out around the house. Kate could tell from the way they moved and handled their weapons that they were trained soldiers, just like her. This was a professional strike team. And yet they didn't try to disguise their faces.

Moments later, Nick emerged from the house, his hands zip-tied behind his back, a gun held to his head by a man with a pockmarked face. Nick was six feet tall, brown-haired and brown-eyed, and even now, in this dangerous situation, he moved with the relaxed grace of a man confident in his ability to take care of himself. She was relieved to see that Nick was alive and uninjured, but she still felt a pang of anxiety in her chest. He was far from safe. Behind Nick and his captor, two other men carried out a third man who was covered with blood, his clothes shredded. A glass coffee table had been shattered in Nick's rented house. She suspected this bloody guy was the unfortunate missile that had destroyed the coffee table.

The pockmarked man shoved Nick into the backseat of the Explorer while the two other men opened the rear door, hefted their injured comrade inside like a sandbag, and slammed the door closed. The men piled into the car and drove away, giving Kate a good view of the license plate. That sloppiness intrigued her.

The woman returned with a fresh drink in each hand and held one out to Kate. Kate's drink had a big pineapple wedge on the rim. "Here's your Bloody Mary."

"Sorry, I have to pass. I can't drink on the job." Kate unplugged the DVR and tucked it under one arm. The last thing she wanted was new footage of Nick Fox, one of the FBI's Ten Most Wanted fugitives, floating around. "I'm going to need to take this with me as evidence. Is that okay with you?"

"Be my guest."

"It might be a while before you get it back. In the

meantime, I'll have a forceful talk with the owners of the rental house about taking responsibility for the bad behavior of their tenants."

She'd also return to the beach house later tonight to clean up the blood and take Nick's suitcase, clothes, and toiletries. She wanted to be the only law enforcement agent on Nick's trail.

"Thank you so much," the woman said. "Bring back the DVR when you're off-duty, and I'll make you the best Bloody Mary you've ever had."

"Deal," Kate said. She'd never be back, but she'd make sure the woman got a new DVR.

Kate got into her Jeep, took out her cellphone, and found the phone number for the duty agent at the FBI field office in Honolulu. She identified herself and asked the agent to run the Explorer's license plate for her. The response was almost immediate. The car was registered to the same airport-based car rental agency as her Jeep. That was great news, because she knew that most rental car companies tracked their cars, either with GPS units or theft prevention devices that, in some cases, could even be used to remotely disable the vehicle. She thanked the duty agent and called the rental company.

"This is FBI Special Agent Kate O'Hare. You rented a Jeep to me yesterday afternoon. I need you to ping the locator on a Ford Explorer of yours with the following license plate number and tell me where I can find it. I'll be stopping by shortly with identification, and I'd appreciate it if you had the information ready for me."

The Ford Explorer was parked under a broken streetlight where Lagoon Drive came to a dead end against the eastern fence of the Honolulu International Airport runway. The road got its name from the Ke'ehi Lagoon that ran the length of its south side and faced Waikiki. On the north side of the road was a line of general aviation terminals, cargo carriers, and tour operators. It was a remote spot and was virtually deserted, the silence occasionally broken by jetliners, fat with tourists, coming in for landing.

Kate drove up to the SUV slowly and parked. She got out of the Jeep, drew her weapon, and approached the Explorer. Abandoned and empty. No surprise there. There was blood all over the cargo area, along with glass shards, soiled gauze, and torn wrappers from bandages and other medical supplies. She holstered her gun, went back to the Jeep, and retrieved her go bag. It contained everything she needed for a few days in the field, including clothes, extra ammo, rubber gloves, and an evidence-collection kit. She took the rubber gloves and kit and returned to the SUV.

It bothered her that whoever had snatched Nick

didn't feel it necessary to properly dispose of the Explorer. It suggested that they were either stupid or already out of the country. She didn't think they were stupid. She meticulously searched the SUV and found a Walgreens receipt and a disposable cellphone. The cellphone had been wedged into a cranny by the back wheel well. It could have been in the wheel well for weeks or months, or it could have fallen out of the injured guy's pocket when they tossed him into the cargo area. Kate dropped the phone and the receipt into the evidence bag. If every person called from the phone was also using a throwaway phone, it created a completely closed network. If she lucked out and the phone belonged to the injured guy and he had made at least one call to a nondisposable phone, she had a lead.

If the phone didn't give her anything, she'd have the fingerprints she was going to lift from the car, the photos of the bad guys she was going to pull from the DVR and the security camera at Walgreens, and the list she was going to get of every private jet or cargo plane that had departed the airport in the last twenty-four hours.

2

"Why don't you stretch your legs?" the pockmarked man said to Nick, with a sweeping wave of his hand to express his generosity. "What can you tell me about this vault?"

"Just some useless trivia," Nick said.

Nick got up stiffly, cracked his back, and began walking slowly around the set, shaking his arms to get the blood flowing again. Still wearing a red aloha shirt with a surfboard motif, khaki shorts, and flip-flops on his otherwise bare feet, Nick stood in colorful, casual contrast to his host.

"Indulge me," the man said.

"The building was constructed in the mid-1970s and is occupied exclusively by individual diamond merchants who store their inventory in safe-deposit boxes in the vault, which is two floors underground."

As Nick spoke and continued circling the room, three more men and one woman came in to listen.

11

The men had the demeanor of thugs. The woman was young, graceful, and stunning, with natural blond hair and emerald green eyes. She would have looked elegant even if she'd been wearing a garbage bag instead of Gucci.

"The vault door weighs three tons, has a lock with a hundred million possible combinations, and can withstand twelve hours of sustained drilling, not that it would ever happen, since it's protected by an embedded seismic alarm that will go off the moment the drill bit touches the steel. Even if you could get the vault door open, it's protected by a magnetic field." Nick pointed to a plate on the door that aligned with another, matching, plate on the wall. "If the field between the door and the wall is broken, the alarm goes off at the police substation, which is only half a block away."

"That's true at night," the man said. "But during business hours, the vault is wide open so the merchants can get to their diamonds."

Nick nodded his head. "But the interior gate remains locked. It's opened remotely by security guards stationed in a command center upstairs who watch from a video camera mounted outside the vault door. After hours, opening this gate requires a special key that is impossible to duplicate."

"The bars could easily be cut with a torch."

Nick reached up and tapped a matchbox-sized unit

on the ceiling. "Sure they could, but that's not an option. The vault is also protected by a light detector as well as a combination heat and motion sensor."

"So you don't come through the door," the man said. "You tunnel in."

"The room temperature is maintained at sixty degrees Fahrenheit at all times," Nick said. "An increase of more than five degrees in the ambient room temperature will trigger the alarm." Then he added: "Oh, and there are also seismic sensors in the floor and the walls to prevent tunneling your way in."

The man nodded, impressed. "You've studied this vault before."

"It would be professional negligence if I hadn't. I could lose my license to steal." Nick winked at the woman then looked back at the man. "Frankly, I'm surprised you're even interested in this. It's not your style. You're more of a smash-and-grab guy."

"You know who I am?"

"It's not a big secret. Your face is on the wall of every law enforcement agency from Stockholm to Perth. You're Dragan Kovic, leader of the Road Runners, an international gang of diamond thieves who've pulled dozens of jewelry store robberies across twenty different countries in the last decade, stealing two hundred million dollars' worth of diamonds."

"Closer to two hundred and fifty million," Dragan said. "But who's counting?"

"Your gang's trademark is driving a vehicle, often an Audi, through a storefront. You've also used a FedEx truck, a bulldozer, an ice cream truck, a motorhome, a cement truck, and my personal favorite from your repertoire, a police car. Then you smash the display cases with pickaxes, grab the diamonds, and speed off. You're in and out of the stores in four minutes and out of the country within two hours." Nick pointed to the vault door. "But this is different. You can't drive an Audi through that."

"That's why you're here," Dragan said. "There's at least five hundred million dollars' worth of diamonds in that vault, and we've already got clients lined up, waiting impatiently for the stones. You're the only one with the skills to get us inside. It's taken us more than a year to find you, and we're running out of time to pull off the job."

Things weren't adding up for Nick. Why would Dragan be interested in a heist that he knew was beyond his team's skill level? He had been doing the same routine for the past ten years. Why change now? Nick was about to pose the question when a fifth man limped onto the set. His face was covered with stitches, making him resemble a scarecrow stuffed into loose-fitting Versace sweats instead of burlap sacks. His flat eyes looked like they'd been ripped from a doll and glued onto his face. It was the guy who'd attacked Nick in Hawaii, and been tossed through the coffee table.

The scarecrow made eye contact with Nick, did his best to ball his meaty hands into fists, and took a step forward. Dragan cut him off, placing a halting hand on his chest.

"Easy, Zarko," Dragan said. "You can't blame a man for defending himself."

"I don't blame," Zarko said, staring at Nick. "I kill."

"How did you find me when the FBI, Interpol, and just about everybody else on earth with a badge hasn't been able to?" Nick asked.

"They would have much more success finding crooks if they were crooks themselves," Dragan said.

The deputy director of the FBI had come to the same conclusion. That was why Nick was now secretly teamed up with Kate.

"We found the forger in Hong Kong who made the 'Nick Sweet' passport you've been using lately," Dragan said. "He's done a few of ours, too. He was an excellent craftsman."

" 'Was'?"

"Sadly it took some persuasion to convince him to help us find you . . . persuasion which unfortunately left him incapable of forgery or tying his shoes again.

However, in the end he was quite generous with his information."

Nick sighed and shook his head in disappointment. "I'm a thief. Instead of abducting me and threatening me, did it ever occur to you to just politely invite me to participate in one of the biggest diamond heists in history?"

"I like leverage," Dragan said.

"Five hundred million dollars in diamonds is plenty of incentive for me," Nick said.

"That's our money."

"Minus my fifteen percent commission as a creative consultant."

"I'm not used to negotiating," Dragan said. "I'm used to taking what I want."

Nick turned to the blond woman. "I assume you've rented offices in the building, posing as a diamond merchant."

She smiled, like a child witnessing a magic trick. "How did you know that it was me occupying the office and not Borko, Dusko, or Vinko?" She gestured to the other men in the room besides Dragan and Zarko.

"The Road Runners always use a beautiful, seemingly rich woman to case the jewelry stores that they're planning to hit, often months in advance," Nick said. "Why would it be any different now that the target is a vault?"

Her smile widened. "You think I'm beautiful?"

Dragan rolled his eyes. "Litija's been a tenant in the building for nearly a year. She can go in and out as she pleases during business hours."

"I have an empty office where I do nothing but sit and watch *House Hunters International* and *Love It or List It* from America on my laptop," she said. "I have a safe-deposit box in the vault that I visit at least twice a day, though all that's in it is some makeup."

"But it's thanks to her that we've learned every detail of their security system," Dragan said, "and were able to construct this accurate re-creation of the vault to try to devise a way in."

"Impressive, but overkill. Getting in is easy," Nick said.

Litija was skeptical. "You just told us all of the reasons why it can't be done."

"Let me kill him," Zarko said.

Nick looked at one of the remaining men, who'd said nothing so far, and had a face only a turtle could love. "What's your opinion?"

"I think we spent too much on your coffin. When Zarko is done with you, it will be easier to bury you in bags."

"I'm sorry I asked," Nick said. "What about you, Litija?"

"I'd really like to see you do it, because you're

cute, funny, and are the only person besides Tom Selleck who has ever looked good in that outfit," she said, gesturing to his aloha shirt and shorts. "But I don't believe that you can."

Nick turned to Dragan. "I guess you didn't share my résumé with them."

"I don't ask for advice on my decisions," Dragan said.

"I'm relieved to hear it, considering the consensus of the room. So let's make a deal, shall we? Think of me as a willing and eager participant. I'll even overlook how you got me here."

"Very gracious of you," Dragan said. "It's been a pleasure watching you try to turn this situation to your advantage. I can see why you're a world-class con man, but it also makes me worry that I'm being swindled. So here's my one and only offer. You will remain as our guest. If you get us into that vault and out safely with the diamonds, we'll give you a ten percent cut. But if anything goes wrong, you die. How does that sound?"

"Fifteen percent would sound better," Nick said. "But I'm in."

"Excellent," Dragan said. "What do you need?"

"A car, for starters," Nick said.

"Cars are not a problem. That's how all of our robberies begin."

"I thought you'd appreciate being in your comfort zone."

"What kind of car would you like?"

"One that can fit in Litija's purse," Nick said.

Kate's dad, Jake O'Hare, was in shorts and flip-flops when Kate handed him his boarding pass.

"I'm going to Antwerp and I might need help," Kate said. "We have just enough time to get to the airport."

"Andy's not going to like this," Jake said. "We have a one o'clock tee time."

"Since when would you rather play golf than execute an unlawful extraction?"

"You didn't tell me the part about the unlawful extraction," Jake said. "The answer is never."

Kate had grown up as an Army brat, following her father around the world while he performed "extraordinary renditions" with his Special Forces unit. He was retired now, living with Kate's sister in Calabasas, enjoying the good life and missing the old one.

"Are you traveling in those clothes?" Jake asked. "They look like you slept in them. Not that I mind, but the TSA might pull you out of line thinking you're a vagrant."

Kate looked down at herself and smoothed out a

wrinkle in her navy blazer. She hadn't slept in the clothes, but they weren't exactly fresh either. She'd kicked through the dirty laundry on her floor this morning and chosen some clothes that looked the freshest.

"I just rolled in from Hawaii and didn't have a lot of time to put myself together," she said. Not to mention she wasn't all that good at the whole pretty-girl thing. She didn't have time. It wasn't a priority. She had no clue where to begin. Her father had taught her forty-seven ways to disable a man with a toothpick before she was nine years old, but he hadn't exactly been a fashionista role model. And clearly she was lacking the hair and makeup gene.

The ten-story Executive Merchants Building was a major repository of the world's wealth. The building looked like just another 1970s-era concrete and glass box, a place somebody might go to have a cavity filled, a car insured, or a tax return completed. The complete absence of style was the style. The only ornamentation on the building was its array of big, boxy surveillance cameras.

The main entrance was on the southern side of Schupstraat, one of three narrow streets that comprised the "special security zone" in the heart of Antwerp's diamond district and Jewish quarter.

The three streets, Rijfstraat, Hoveniersstraat, and Schupstraat, formed a rigid "S" that began on the northeast corner of the district and ended on the southwest edge. Both ends of the "S" were closed to free-flowing vehicle traffic by retractable steel columns in the pavement that were lowered after vehicles passed police inspection at adjacent kiosks and then raised again after the inspected cars entered the secure zone.

On a Thursday at 11 A.M., three days after Nick's abduction, Litija walked into the Executive Merchants Building. She sashayed through the marble-paneled lobby and blew a playful kiss to the elderly guard who sat in the control center behind a thick window of bulletproof glass. He waved back at her with a friendly smile as she approached the turnstile that controlled access to the first-floor offices, the elevators, and the stairwell. Litija swiped her tenant ID card over a scanner and walked through the turnstile as it unlocked.

She bypassed the elevator and took the stairwell. She paused on the landing just inside the door for a moment, listening for voices and looking around to make sure she was alone. There were no cameras in the stairwell. No footfalls of anyone else climbing the stairs.

She hurried down to the next landing, crouched beside an air vent near the floor, and took a screwdriver out of her purse. She quickly unscrewed the grill, reached into her purse again, and pulled out a radio-controlled red Lamborghini with a tiny camera taped on top of it.

Litija placed the car into the vent, and it sped off.

3

Nick and Dragan sat in the back of a panel van parked directly across the intersection from the police kiosk on the southwest corner of Schupstraat and Lange Herentalsestraat, which also happened to be the northwest edge of the Executive Merchants Building. Borko and Vinko were in the front seats, trying very hard to look anywhere but at the uniformed, heavily armed officers they were facing.

"Do we really have to park here?" Borko asked.

"Any further away and we wouldn't have a signal," Nick said. He used a joystick to steer the Lamborghini while watching the camera's view on an iPad that sat on his lap.

"But we're parked right outside the building we're going to rob," Vinko said. "The police can see us and our van."

"Relax," Nick said. "A thief planning to rob that

building would have to be insane to sit here to do his recon."

Dragan gave him a hard look. "You're reading my mind."

"That's what makes this spot the safest place to be," Nick said. "Besides, the police aren't on the lookout for thieves plotting to break in. Everybody knows it's impossible. The police are for show." Nick steered the Lamborghini past several air vents and around a tight corner. "How long have the guards worked in the building?"

"One guy just got his thirty-year pin. The others have been here nearly as long."

"That proves my point," Nick said. "They've stayed so long because it's a very cushy job. Nobody has tried to break in to the vault since the day the building opened, and they know that nobody ever will."

Nick parked the Lamborghini at the end of an air vent that gave their camera a view down into the vault foyer. They could see the open vault door and the closed gate. Something caught Nick's eye. He zoomed in on a door a few feet from the vault.

"You don't have that door on your set," he said.

"Because it's a supply closet," Dragan said. "We aren't interested in stealing toilet paper and file folders."

Litija came in, and Nick adjusted the camera view

to a wider angle. She walked past the open vault door, stood in front of the inner gate, then turned to wave at the security camera and the guards watching in the control room. It looked like she was waving at Nick and Dragan.

"The security camera that's mounted outside the vault is only watched during business hours, when the door is open," Nick said. "But at night and on weekends, there's nobody watching the monitors. The feed is recorded and taped over every thirty days. In fact, there isn't a single guard in the building after hours. Do you know why?"

"Because a break-in is impossible," Dragan said.

"You're catching on," Nick said.

Litija was buzzed through by the guards upstairs. She pushed the unlocked gate to let herself in and stumbled a moment after the gate swung closed behind her. She dropped her purse in the process and crouched down to pick it up.

"When the vault is open during the day, the heat and motion sensor is deactivated, of course, or everyone who walks in would set off the alarm," Nick said. "More important, to protect the privacy of the tenants and the contents of their safe-deposit boxes, there aren't any cameras in the vault."

So nobody saw Litija take a tiny bottle of hairspray from her purse and spritz the combination heat and motion sensor, coating the surface with a thin, milky film. She got up, tugged on her miniskirt, and presumably went to her safe-deposit box, disappearing entirely from view.

A few moments later, Litija walked out of the vault again, closed the gate behind her, and, before she left, offered a parting wave to everyone who was watching.

"That takes care of the heat and motion detector," Nick said. "In the morning, our camera will be parked right here, so we'll be able to see the building manager enter the combination and open the vault. Then we can do it, too."

"We're still using a car to open the vault," Dragan said. "I love it."

"You have a reputation to maintain."

"You have style, Nick, I'll give you that." Dragan pointed to the magnetic plate on the vault door and the matching one on the jamb beside it. "But the instant we open the vault door, we'll break the magnetic field, setting off the alarm in the police station. And if we cut the power to the magnets, that will activate the alarm, too."

"Don't worry," Nick said. "I've got that covered."

"How?"

"If I tell you now, it would ruin the surprise."

Nick was sharing details only as they were needed so Dragan couldn't proceed without him. It was a way to extend his life expectancy for as long as possible. He figured if he hung in there long enough, Kate would track him down and rescue him. He'd been under constant watch and hadn't been able to contact her, but he knew she was like a dog with a bone when she had a job to do. And right now, like it or not, her job was to retrieve him. He was government property.

"What about the gate?" Dragan asked. "It can only be opened with a key that can't be duplicated."

Nick smiled. "We'll rely upon human nature for that."

While Nick and Dragan were parked on Lange Herentalsestraat, Kate O'Hare and her father were standing on Schupstraat, outside the Executive Merchants Building. They were lost amid the stream of tourists, police officers, and bearded men in yarmulkes carrying attaché cases full of diamonds chained to their wrists.

Kate had identified the men who grabbed Nick by running their pictures and fingerprints through FBI databases. She had pinpointed their location when she gleaned a non-cell number from the throwaway phone. The call had been to an office in the Executive Merchants Building. The number was no longer in service, but it was a credible enough lead to get Kate and her father on a plane to Antwerp, the medieval

Belgian port city that was home to 80 percent of the world's trade in rough diamonds. Their first stop was Stadspark, a triangular park in the city center, where they picked up two Glocks and plenty of ammo that an arms-dealing friend of Jake's had hidden for them in a prearranged spot. From there they went to Schupstraat.

Kate's phone rang and she recognized the number as coming from the Federal Building in West Los Angeles where she was currently based.

"O'Hare," Kate said.

"Hey, Katie Bug. It's Cosmo Uno. Whatcha doin'? What's shakin'? Haven't seen you in forever. Heard you zipped in here and zipped out. Like you were here for a nanosecond, right? And I must have blinked and missed you. Bummer, right? Am I right?"

Kate stared at her phone. Cosmo Uno was the annoying idiot in the cubicle next to her. He was shorter than her, single and desperate, slicked his hair up with what looked like goose grease, and was a foot jiggler. All day long when she was in her cubicle she could hear him jiggling his foot.

"Why are you calling me?" Kate asked him. "And how did you get my number?"

"You're gonna love this. Wait until I tell you. Like I thought I was the luckiest guy in the building to get the cubicle next to you, and now we're working together."

"*What?*"

"That's over the moon, right? I mean, we're practically partners. Do you love it? I love it."

Good thing she wasn't in the building, Kate thought, because she'd have to shoot him.

"See, here's the thing," Cosmo said. "Jessup thought it would be a good idea if you had someone to help you keep track of expenses."

Kate narrowed her eyes. "Un-hunh."

"So I'm going to be your expense guy. For instance, there's an item we just received for a rental car in Hawaii. That's a mistake, right?"

"I'm busy," Kate said. "Good talking to you."

She disconnected, turned to her father, and pointed at the building directly in front of them.

"The office that one of the Road Runners called on the throwaway was in this building," Kate said. "A building, incidentally, with a vault that holds a fortune in diamonds."

"A vault that's impossible to break in to," Jake said, holding up the Antwerp guidebook he'd bought so they'd look like tourists. "Rick Steves says so right here."

"That's one mystery solved," Kate said. "Now we know why a gang of international diamond thieves kidnapped Nick."

"We don't actually *know*," Jake said.

"Okay, we *think* we know."

"Good enough for me," Jake said. "What's the plan?"

"We'll get a room at the hotel across the street." Kate pointed in the general direction of Lange Herentalsestraat, where, unbeknownst to her, Nick had been sitting in a panel van only a few minutes earlier. "Then we'll watch for an opportunity to rescue Nick. We need to be ready to take it when it comes."

"I'll call my friend who left the guns for us in the park," Jake said. "He can get us a rocket launcher."

"We don't need a rocket launcher."

"Sure we do," Jake said. "Nothing creates opportunity like a rocket-propelled explosive."

"It would also create an international incident. I'm going to be in enough trouble as it is."

Kate hadn't informed her bosses, Special Agent in Charge Carl Jessup or Deputy Director Fletcher Bolton, that Nick had been taken, or that she was pursuing him to a foreign country. She couldn't take the risk that they wouldn't let her go.

"Not if we don't get caught," Jake said.

"We aren't blowing up anything, Dad. Whatever we do will have to be quick and quiet."

"We're dealing with the same thieves who drove a bulldozer through a jewelry store in Saint-Tropez in broad daylight and escaped in a speedboat," Jake said. "So this might end quick, but it won't end quiet."

Kate's phone rang again. Same L.A. number. "Oh for the love of Pete," Kate said, opening the connection. "Now what?"

"You haven't filed your form S-Q-zero-zero-niner," Cosmo said.

"I'm pretty sure I filed that," Kate said, having no idea what he was talking about.

"We can't find it."

"If you call me again I'll have you killed," Kate said. "I can do it. I know people."

And she disconnected.

4

Shortly after 1 A.M. on Saturday, a panel van drove up to the Executive Merchants Building's underground parking garage on Lange Herentalsestraat, half a block down from the police kiosk at the intersection with Schupstraat.

Nick was one of five men in the back of the van. Zarko, Vinko, Borko, and Dusko were on the team. Dragan was not. They were all dressed in regular street clothes.

Zarko took a remote control out of his pocket, aimed it at the garage door, and pressed a button. The garage door rolled open. Even before they'd kidnapped Nick, the Road Runners had easily captured the frequency of the forty-year-old garage door system and programmed a remote to match it. It was easy because there were fifty-seven videos on YouTube that explained how to do it. There were no videos that explained how to get into the vault and bypass the multiple alarm systems.

Nick and the four men spilled out of the van carrying duffel bags. They ducked under the garage door, and the last one, Zarko, closed it behind them. The van drove off, made a U-turn, and parked half a block down with the headlights off. The driver was sticking around as their lookout.

"They're inside," Kate told her father on her disposable cellphone. She stood in the shadowed alcove of a closed falafel joint on the west side of Lange Herentalsestraat, midway between the garage and the parked van where the driver was watching for signs of trouble. She cupped the phone in her hands so it wouldn't emit any light. "One of the men is definitely Nick."

"It's dark out and you're twenty yards away," Jake said from a car parked up the street, just above the intersection with Schupstraat and the police kiosk. "How can you be sure it's him?"

"I know how he moves."

He moved like a panther. She'd had the crazy urge to run out the instant she saw him, but Kate remained very still. She didn't want to attract the attention of the driver in the parked van.

"Now what?" Jake asked.

It was a good question. She hated the idea of sitting there while one of the biggest heists in history was pulled off right in front of her. But her top priority was Nick. For a moment she considered overpowering the driver in the van and either taking his place or putting a gun to his head to get him to do as she wanted, but there were too many ways that scenario could go wrong.

"We wait," she said.

In the garage, the five thieves put on night vision goggles. Vinko went up to the locked door that led into the building and ran Litija's tenant ID over the scanner. The door unlocked. Vinko bent down, stuck a rubber wedge under the door to keep it open, and the men headed down the main corridor. When they reached the lobby, Borko went off to deactivate the DVR in the control center while Nick and the three other men took the stairs down to the vault.

They walked out of the stairwell into the foyer that faced the imposing vault door. Nick unzipped one of the tote bags he carried and removed a suction cup tool commonly used to carry heavy panes of glass. There was a vacuum-tab suction cup on either end of the horizontal handle. Nick placed one suction cup against the magnetic plate on the vault door, the other on the matching plate beside it, and pulled back the locking tabs. The suction cups held. He used an electric screwdriver to unscrew the magnetic plate from the doorjamb.

Nick pocketed the screws and looked at Zarko, who stood in front of the vault door, bouncing on his heels, anxious to get started. The stitched cuts on Zarko's face were swollen and red. Nick thought he should probably see a doctor about that.

"You can open the vault now," Nick said. "But very slowly."

Zarko entered the combination, turned the three-pronged spindle wheel to retract the locking pins, and pulled the heavy door open. As he did, the magnetic plate on the jamb came away with the door, dragging wires out of the wall socket. Nick stared at the magnetic plate. If it fell, they were finished. But the suction cup device kept the two plates together, maintaining the magnetic field as if the door was still closed.

Nick watched closely to make sure the wires didn't break. He waited until the door was open just wide enough for a man to enter the vault by slipping under the taut wires that were attached to the magnetic plate.

"Stop," he said.

Zarko did. Now the iron gate was all that separated them from a bank of safe-deposit boxes filled with millions in diamonds.

Zarko bounced on his feet again and tipped his head toward the gate. "How do we open it?"

The other three Road Runners looked at Nick too, eager to see what he'd do next.

"With a paper clip," Nick said.

Nick reached into his pocket. He held up a paper clip between his index finger and thumb for them to admire. The four men stared blankly at him.

"Trust me," Nick said. "Best tool ever designed by man."

Nick unbent the paper clip into a straight wire, went to the supply closet door, and effortlessly picked the deadbolt lock. He opened the door, reached inside the closet, and came out holding a bizarre four-sided key that looked both ancient and magical. The thieves stared, astounded.

"How did you know it would be in there?" Dusko asked.

"Human nature." Nick slipped past the open vault door to get to the gate. "There's only one key and the guards don't want to lose it. They also want it handy if something ever goes wrong with the remote locking mechanism. So they hung the key in the closet. I'm sure it wasn't kept here to start with, but it's probably been there for at least a decade or two."

"Morons," Zarko said.

Nick slid the key into the gate's lock. "That's what

happens when the same security people do a job for forty years without any incidents. They get lazy."

He opened the gate and slipped the key into his pocket as a souvenir. He reached up and stuck a piece of black electrical tape over the light sensor on the ceiling. He pulled off his night vision goggles.

"You can turn on the lights now," Nick said.

Zarko hit him from behind with a lead sap, once to get him down, and once more to keep him there.

Kate was still standing in the dark alcove, leaning her back against the front door of the falafel joint, when she saw the garage door roll open at the Executive Merchants Building and the van begin to slowly drive up the street.

She called her father. "They're coming out."

Jake started his car but kept his headlights off. "I'm ready."

When the van passed Kate's hiding place, she bolted across the street and ducked behind a car that was parked close to the garage. The van stopped in front of the open garage. Four men carrying heavy duffel bags dashed out of the garage and jumped into the van. Nick wasn't one of them.

Damn!

"Follow the van," Kate said into her phone.

"Don't lose those men and the diamonds. Ram them and call the police if you have to."

"Where are you going?"

"To find Nick. He didn't come out."

She stuck the phone into her pocket and got ready to move. The van drove off. The garage door started to come down. Kate raced for the garage, dove to the ground, and rolled under the descending door an instant before it closed.

And this is why I don't spend a lot of time ironing my clothes, she thought, getting to her feet, noticing that the knee was ripped out on her jeans.

The door to the building was wedged open. Kate ran inside to the lobby, went straight for the stairs, and took them down to the bottom floor. The vault door was open, with some kind of suction tool stuck to the front and wires dangling from the wall. She ducked under the wires and into the vault. Nick was on the floor sprawled motionless among hundreds of mangled safe-deposit boxes, loose cash and papers, assorted jewelry, gold bars, silver coins, and scattered diamonds.

Kate dropped to her knees beside him and quickly scanned his body for injuries. Blood matted the side of his head, but he was breathing, and his eyes were fluttering open.

"Nick? It's Kate. Can you hear me? Nick!"

He winced as he regained consciousness. "Crashing

headache," he said. "Blurred vision. Think I see an angel." He managed a small smile. "You found me."

"I swore to you a long time ago that I'd never let you get away."

"I didn't think I'd ever be thankful for that," he said.

Kate helped Nick up, sitting him against the wall for support. "You have a concussion. We should take this slowly. I don't think the police know about what just went down yet."

She surveyed the pile in the center of the vault. "There's got to be millions of dollars' worth of jewelry, diamonds, and cash that they left behind."

"It was an embarrassment of riches. They only took the very best and left when they had as much as they could carry. Not that I saw what happened. They took me out before the action started."

"You're lucky they didn't kill you."

Nick blinked hard, trying to focus his vision. "I'm no good to them dead. They wanted me to get caught to distract the police and buy them time to get away."

"They weren't afraid you'd talk?"

"What could I possibly tell the police that they don't already know?"

Kate gestured to the bank of safe-deposit boxes. Most of the slots had been forced open, but there were still at least a third of them that hadn't been touched. "How did they decide which boxes to break open?"

Nick's head was starting to clear a bit. "No idea. I wasn't involved in that part of the planning stage."

Kate's phone vibrated in her pocket. She retrieved her phone and answered it. "Where are you, Dad?"

"Still parked on the street."

Nick squinted at her. "You brought your dad?"

"I told you to follow the thieves!" Kate said to Jake.

"I don't care about them or the diamonds," Jake said. "I care about you. You have two minutes, maybe less. The police are swarming the place. I bet now you wish I'd gotten that rocket launcher."

"Get out of here and burn your phone."

She split open her own phone, removed the micro SIM card, and swallowed it.

Nick stared at her in disbelief. "Did you just eat your SIM card?"

"I don't want anyone finding it. The phone is a disposable, and to my knowledge I didn't make any traceable calls, but better safe than sorry." She dropped the phone onto the floor, smashed it under her foot, and kicked the debris away. "The police are coming. Something must have triggered the alarm."

Nick had a sinking realization. He moved aside and glanced with dread behind him. He'd been leaning against the heat and motion sensor and had wiped the hairspray off it with his back.

"You have to arrest me," he said to Kate.

"Think again. Get up, we'll find a way out." She reached for him but he resisted, grabbing her wrists to get her attention.

"There's only one way out of this vault," Nick said.

"You'll find another," she said. "You're Nick Fox. That's what you do."

"Not this time. You have to arrest me. If you don't, we'll both go to prison. You need to get in touch with Jessup. Find out what was in this vault. I'm thinking it might have contained more than diamonds."

They could hear a rumbling upstairs, like a herd of cattle running through the halls. The police were in the building. They had only a few seconds left.

Kate took out her gun and tossed it onto the pile of stuff the thieves had left behind. "Lie facedown on the floor."

"You're so hot when you take charge," Nick said.

Nick lay facedown on the floor, and Kate straddled him. She pinned one of his arms behind him, reached into her coat pocket with her free hand, and whipped out her badge just as a half dozen police officers spilled into the vault, their guns drawn.

"I'm Special Agent Kate O'Hare, Federal Bureau of Investigation," she said. "This man is mine."

5

Kate sat in an interrogation room that was just like every other one she'd ever been in. It had the same cinder block walls, the same piss-yellow fluorescent light, and the same dirty mirror that hid whoever was watching. The only difference was that this time she was the suspect being questioned.

Chief Inspector Amelie Janssen sat across the table from her with notepad and pen. The detective's shoulder-length hair had a just-got-out-of-bed wave to it. Probably because she'd just gotten out of bed. It was 4 A.M.

"I can't count all the laws that you've broken," Janssen said. "If it were up to me, you'd be in handcuffs and ankle chains like any other common crook. But it's not my decision. It's up to the general commissioner, and she's waiting to hear from the prime minister's office, which is demanding an explanation from the U.S. ambassador in Brussels."

"I captured an international fugitive who is wanted in a dozen countries, including this one," Kate said. "So instead of complaining, you should be congratulating me."

"You're right. Where are my manners?" Janssen said. "Congratulations on helping the Road Runners pull off the biggest diamond heist in the history of Belgium."

"I had nothing to do with that."

"You certainly didn't do anything to stop it. As far as I'm concerned, you're an accessory after the fact."

"I apprehended the man responsible for the crime," Kate said. "Or have you forgotten that?"

"While the rest of the Road Runners got away with the diamonds," Janssen said. "If you'd told us you were here and what you were doing, we could have staked out the building and captured them all in the act."

"I didn't know there was going to be a robbery."

"Okay." Janssen leaned back in her seat again. "So explain to me how you ended up in the vault with Nicolas Fox."

Kate had learned from Nick that the best lies were the ones that stuck as close to the truth as possible. So she followed his advice.

"There were rumors for months that Fox had joined the Road Runners. So when I heard that Dragan Kovic and several members of his gang were spotted

43

last week in Honolulu, I got on the first flight out there to see if they'd left any tracks," Kate said. "They did. I found out where Dragan went to rent a car, then used the GPS records for the vehicle to retrace his movements for the few hours that he was on the island. That led me to the store where his gang bought their disposable phones, which have unique identifying numbers. With that information, and some help from a friend at the NSA, I was able to pull the call records. There was only one call off the island."

"To the Executive Merchants Building," Janssen said.

"You got it."

"You should have notified us at that point."

"I didn't have anything," Kate said.

"You had enough to go on to fly here and watch the building, hoping you'd spot Fox or a Road Runner who could lead you to him."

"Yes, but it was an outrageous long shot. I didn't even tell my bosses what I was doing. I just cashed in some vacation time and booked a flight."

Janssen sighed and made a note to herself on the pad. Kate tried to read it upside-down, but it was in Flemish. "What happened next?"

"Jet lag," Kate said.

"I don't understand."

"I was sitting in a dark alcove across the street from the building and I fell asleep."

"You're kidding me."

"I wish I was, because it's humiliating. But I'd barely slept for the last week and I'd been watching the building all day. I was exhausted. When I woke up, a van was pulling away and the garage door was closing. It didn't feel right so I made a run for it."

"You could have gone to the police instead. They were right up the street."

"I am the police," Kate said.

"Not here."

"It's who I am everywhere, and since I only had a split second to act, my reflexes took over. I managed to roll under the garage door right before it closed," Kate said. "I took the stairs down to the vault and discovered that the three-ton door was wide open. I was sure that the vault had been emptied, that the thieves were long gone, and that I'd slept through the heist. I lowered my guard, which is how Fox got the jump on me when I went into the vault. We fought and I won."

Janssen stopped taking notes and set her pen down. "What was Fox doing there?"

"I assume that he was double-crossed and left behind," Kate said. "Maybe we'll find out, and get a lead on the missing diamonds, when you stop wasting valuable time questioning me and we begin interrogating him."

"You aren't getting near him," Janssen said. "You're out of this."

"He's my prisoner."

"You have no authority here to arrest anybody. You can stand in line to extradite him with all of the law enforcement agencies in Europe. That is, after he's released from our prison, in thirty years."

There was a knock on the other side of the mirror. Janssen threw a glance at the mirror and saw her own irritated expression reflected back at her.

"Stay here." Janssen gathered up her notebook and pen and left the room.

Kate thought she'd given a good performance. Her story unfolded like a farce but it would be very hard for Janssen to prove it wasn't the truth. However, it was just the beginning. The U.S. State Department, Justice Department, and the FBI would demand answers too, and probably her badge, if not her head.

Janssen came back in and held the door open. "You can go, but you can't leave Antwerp. We're holding on to your passport and your badge until we decide what to do with you."

Kate stood up. "What about Nicolas Fox?"

"He's not your problem anymore."

. . .

Kate stepped out of the monolithic police station into the Saturday morning sun. She walked up the street, past coffeehouses and upscale clothing shops, with no particular destination in mind.

She was emotionally numb. She'd come to Antwerp to save Nick, and instead she'd put him in prison. There was a time, not so long ago, when she would have celebrated his capture. Instead, she was already thinking about how she was going to manage to get Nick free.

She caught a glimpse of a familiar figure reflected in a shop window. It was Jake. She didn't turn to acknowledge him. He'd approach her when he was certain nobody else was on her tail. She wanted to be sure too. So now her wandering had intent.

She crossed the Groenplaats, a large plaza ringed by cafés and bars, and headed for the Cathedral of Our Lady, a Gothic monument to failed dreams that had taken two hundred years to build and yet was still incomplete. The cathedral was supposed to have had two matching four-hundred-foot towers. But in the 495 years since the church opened its doors, only one tower had been finished, and could be seen all over the city, while the other tower remained uncompleted and half as tall.

To reach the cathedral's entrance, Kate had to go

down a narrow cobblestone street, a bottleneck of restaurants, coffeehouses, and Leonidas chocolate shops, all crammed tightly together and stuck to the side of the church like barnacles. At the base of the cathedral's unfinished tower was a sculpture of four stonemasons at work. She stopped to look at the sculpture, not to wonder if it was a critical statement about the glacial pace of construction, but to see if the bottleneck had revealed anyone shadowing her. It hadn't. Her father walked past her and went inside the church.

Kate followed him and discovered that the church charged admission. Her father hadn't lost any of his edge, she thought. Paying for a ticket and going through the turnstile presented an obstacle that would flush out anybody following them. She paid her six euros, walked through the turnstile, and entered the vast nave with its impressive vaulted ceiling.

At the base of each pillar holding up the church were altars to the various craft and professional guilds that had been leaders of the community in ancient times. The altarpieces were large paintings by Flemish masters. The paintings depicted guild members demonstrating their particular trades.

She stood in front of the altarpiece for the fencing guild, which had once served as Antwerp's de facto police force. It was a painting of Saint Michael, the guardian of paradise, and his army of angels battling a seven-headed dragon and a legion of naked man-beasts with what looked like monster masks over their crotches.

"Those are some nasty codpieces," Kate said in a voice slightly louder than a whisper.

Her father pretended to take pictures of the nave with his cellphone. "They sure are. Codpieces are uncomfortable enough to wear without fangs and horns on 'em."

"I'm not going to ask how you know that," she said.

"What happened in the vault?" Jake asked.

"I was caught in the act of arresting Nick. I told the police that I'd tracked him here from Hawaii and stumbled into the heist."

"I'm glad you were able to smooth-talk your way out of jail. I was already making plans to help you."

"What did you have in mind?"

"I was going to do what any sensible father would in a situation like this," Jake said.

"You started looking for a good criminal lawyer?"

"I ordered explosives from my buddy in Amsterdam."

She looked at him. "*That's* what you consider the sensible thing? Blowing a hole in the police station and mounting a jailbreak?"

"Of course not. That would be insane."

"Then what were the explosives for?"

"I was going to ambush the armored police van carrying you to court on Monday morning and blast open the doors to set you free."

"At least that won't be necessary now." Kate took a seat in the row of pews behind him and lowered her head.

"The plan is still on," Jake said, snapping some more photos. "Now we can use them to bust Nick out. We've got forty-eight hours to work on the details and steal the necessary vehicles. A garbage truck and two motorcycles should do it."

Good grief, Kate thought. I'm going to steal two motorcycles and a garbage truck! As if she hadn't already broken enough laws. She pressed her lips together and made the sign of the cross.

"What are you doing?" Jake asked. "We're Presbyterian."

"The agreement Nick had with the FBI was that if he was ever caught by the police, anywhere in the world, our operation was over and he'd be on his own."

"I didn't agree to that," Jake said. "Besides, he's my friend and you love him. That's more than enough for me."

Love him, she thought. Jeez Louise. That's wrong on so many levels.

"I don't . . . you know," she said to her dad.

"What?"

"The *L* word."

"Love?"

"Yes. The *L* word and *Nicolas Fox* shouldn't be said in the same sentence. Especially not out loud."

Jake gave his head a small shake. "How would you describe your relationship with him?"

"Reluctant partners," Kate said.

"Okay, I'll buy that. What else?"

"I guess I think he's hot."

"Too much information," Jake said. He got up with his back to her, and left a disposable phone behind on the pew. "Get some rest. Call me when you're ready."

6

Kate walked back to her hotel. She needed some sleep to clear her head. She needed to make sure that whatever the plan, her dad wouldn't end up in a Belgian jail too.

She went to her room, found her iPhone, and left her boss, Carl Jessup, a voicemail that said only "What was in the vault?"

Kate flopped facedown on the bed fully clothed and fell asleep almost instantly. It felt like she'd closed her eyes for only a second when she was awakened by the electronic trill of her iPhone. The time on the clock radio, next to her phone, was 3 P.M., and the caller ID on her phone read "Jessup."

Kate grabbed the phone. "O'Hare," she said.

"How much of the story that you told the Belgian police is true?" her boss asked. His Kentucky drawl was disarmingly low-key. It was as if he was casually asking about the weather, or the price of turnips, and not about an international incident that was likely to end Kate's career with the FBI.

"Ninety percent," she said. "What I left out was that Nick was kidnapped by the Road Runners to pull off the heist and that I came here to rescue him."

"Then you did the right thing going to Antwerp without telling me," Jessup said. "You gave us plausible deniability."

"That was the idea."

"I sincerely doubt that."

"How much trouble am I in?" she asked.

"That depends on if you get caught," Jessup said.

"I think they bought my story."

"I'm not talking about that," Jessup said. "I'm talking about you breaking Nicolas Fox out of jail."

"Excuse me?" Kate could feel beads of panicked sweat appearing on her upper lip. How did Jessup know she was planning a jailbreak?

"I'm expecting the Belgians to throw you out of the country within forty-eight hours, so you don't have much time to free Nick, and you need to do it without hurting anyone. If you get caught, we'll say it was a desperate act by a crazy FBI agent who fell in love with the man she was chasing."

It wasn't that far from the truth, but even if Jessup knew it he wouldn't sanction a jailbreak for it. There had to be another reason.

"I can't believe you're asking me to do this, sir. I expected you to tear my head off and order me to forget about Nick."

"I would have, and I'd still like to, but we believe one of the safe-deposit boxes in that vault contained a vial of smallpox," Jessup said. "Now the Road Runners have it. The smallpox was probably their target all along."

"How is that possible? Smallpox was eradicated decades ago, and the only samples that exist are at the CDC in Atlanta and a lab in Russia."

"Yes, that's been the general assumption."

"'Assumption'?"

"Well, it's not like somebody went around to every lab in the world and verified that each smallpox sample ever collected was destroyed. However, since nobody has been infected in forty years, the accepted belief is that the virus was wiped out and the only samples of the virus are secured."

"You're telling me that isn't true."

"In the early 1990s, a Soviet defector revealed to MI5 that the Russians were secretly developing a super-virulent strain of smallpox, in blatant violation of international agreements, through a civilian drug company called Biopreparat. After that came out, the U.S. and NATO threatened an all-out bioweapons arms race, so the Soviets caved, ended the program, and destroyed the smallpox."

"But not all of it," Kate said.

"They were in the midst of complying with international demands when the Soviet Union collapsed and descended into chaos. One of the bioweapons scientists, Sergei Andropov, fled Moscow with a vial of smallpox in his pocket to sell to the highest bidder. Sergei settled in Antwerp, where his cousin Yuri Baskin was a diamond merchant. But before Sergei could make a deal with anyone, he was killed in a car accident. The vial was never found."

"But you think Sergei gave it to Yuri," Kate said, "who stashed it in his safe-deposit box in the Executive Merchants Building vault and was afraid to touch it after his cousin's suspicious death."

"It was only a theory before, but now we're certain that's what happened," Jessup said. "The Belgian police found some of Sergei's research notes from Biopreparat on the floor of the vault along with a cigar-sized metal container that could be used to store a vial."

"How could the smallpox virus still be alive after all these years?" Kate asked, though she wasn't sure *alive* was the right word.

"The temperature in the vault was kept at a constant sixty degrees," Jessup said. "Even if the temperature wasn't controlled, we know the virus could still survive. A forty-five-year-old vial of smallpox was found two years ago in Washington,

D.C., by a custodian. It was in a cardboard box in an unlocked closet at the National Institutes of Health. Testing of the sample at the CDC revealed it was still viable."

Kate was wide awake now. "That's frightening."

"Not as much as Dragan Kovic selling smallpox to ISIS or some rogue nation and what they might do with it. Smallpox is the deadliest virus humanity has ever known. It killed three hundred million people in the twentieth century alone. All you have to do is inhale one microscopic particle and you're infected. You become a walking chemical weapon that infects everyone within a ten-foot radius."

"Nobody is vaccinated for smallpox anymore," Kate said. "Most of the population has no immunity. The virus could spread at light-speed through a major city."

"That's the nightmare scenario," Jessup said. "You need to break Nick out of custody. Then the two of you have to retrieve that vial, find out what it was going to be used for, and stop the plot, whatever the hell it is."

"Yes, sir."

"And stop threatening to kill Cosmo."

Kate disconnected and set her iPhone on the bedside table. She reached down to her purse on the floor, dug around for the new disposable phone that her father had given her in the church, and hit the preprogrammed key that dialed his cell. He answered on the first ring.

"Jake O'Hare, Man of Action."

"I'm ready," Kate said.

Early Sunday morning, Kate put on her sweats and jogged into Stadspark, which had once been the site of a Spanish fort. She dashed across the footbridge, over a duck pond that had been part of the fort's moat, and then followed a paved trail as it snaked into a canopy of trees and bushes. She stopped at a stack of stones that appeared to have once been a man-made waterfall but that was dry and weedy now.

She made sure she was alone before retrieving blasting caps and a small brick of C4 plastic explosive that had been hidden there the night before by her father's buddy the arms dealer. She stuffed the goodies into her hidden running belt, jogged out of the park, and went shopping for duct tape, a razor blade, paper clips, and another disposable phone. The Meir, Antwerp's main shopping street, was lined with renovated medieval buildings shoulder to shoulder with modern re-creations. Every two feet there seemed be another Leonidas chocolate café, the Starbucks of Belgium. The Leonidas cafés were inescapable, so she surrendered and got herself a hot chocolate.

. . .

Kate was halfway across her hotel lobby when she was stopped by a paunchy forty-something man in a rumpled business suit. He had the bloated belly and pained expression of a man who'd been constipated for days, perhaps even months.

"Miss O'Hare?" the man asked, sizing Kate up from a computer-generated picture of her that he held in his hand.

Career bureaucrat, Kate thought, smiling politely. American. No doubt clogged up with schnitzel.

"Conrad Plitt," he said. "I'm attached to the U.S. embassy in Brussels."

"I was expecting to see an FBI legat," Kate said, referring to the FBI legal attachés at U.S. embassies who worked with local law enforcement agencies on cases involving American interests.

"Sorry to dash your hopes, but sending an FBI agent here to deal with this muck-up would only worsen an already terrible situation," Plitt said. "It would imply to the Belgians that the FBI had prior knowledge of your actions or that they tacitly approve of your conduct. We can't have that. Besides, the FBI has notoriously poor diplomatic skills, which you've profoundly demonstrated already."

She might have been offended by his comment if it hadn't been totally true. Not to mention she was standing there holding the makings of a bomb in a grocery bag.

"What happens now?" she asked.

"My job is to convince the Belgians that despite your unorthodox and inappropriate conduct you're a hero and that the apprehension of Nicolas Fox is a win for everybody. If I can do that, I deserve the Nobel Peace Prize. The first step is for you to offer the Belgian authorities your total and unconditional cooperation with their investigation."

"I'd be glad to do that, but they've made it clear they don't want me involved."

"They still don't," Plitt said. "But Nicolas Fox does. He refuses to talk to anybody but you."

"He's playing with us," Chief Inspector Amelie Janssen said, clearly not pleased with the way things were proceeding.

"Of course he is," Kate said. "What did you expect?"

Kate was standing in an observation room, looking out at Nicolas Fox. He was sitting at an interrogation table, and he was wearing an orange jumpsuit, his wrists in handcuffs and his ankles in chains. And yet, he not only appeared relaxed and content, but somehow managed with his posture to make the hard, stiff chair seem incredibly comfortable. There was a time when his cool attitude would have irritated Kate as much as it obviously irked Janssen. Now Kate found it reassuring to see him in control of himself and his environment.

She hoped she appeared equally in control. If she did appear equally in control she thought it would be an acting miracle because she didn't *feel* in control. What she felt was *sick*. Not exactly on the verge of throwing up but moving in that direction. She was making a maximum effort to put up a hard-ass front. She'd decided on a role. She'd rehearsed her lines. She'd put some Imodium in her purse just in case.

Jeez Louise, she thought. This isn't my *thing*. I'm good at enforcing the law, not breaking the law. How did I get into this *mess*? She narrowed her eyes at Fox. It's *him,* she thought. It's my stupid obsession with Nicolas Fox.

"Are you okay?" Janssen asked Kate. "Your face is flushed."

"I'm fine," Kate said. "I'm just *angry.* I *hate* this guy."

Not far from the truth. She hated him. She liked him. She hated him. She liked him. And she especially hated him because he looked so damn good in his jumpsuit. It was just wrong, wrong, wrong.

Kate flipped through several pages of inventory itemizing everything that was stolen from the vault, with the notable exception of the vial of smallpox.

"He's a con man," Kate said. "Manipulating people is what he does for fun and profit."

"That's why it was a huge mistake for my bosses to give in to his demand that we bring you in. I warned them not to do it, but although they have badges, they are politicians, not police."

"Were you getting anywhere with him?"

"No, but now that you're here, it completely undercuts my authority in the interrogation. He'll think that he's the one in charge now. It won't be easy getting back the upper hand."

Kate put a paper clip on the papers. "If you want him to give you information, you're going to have to play his game."

Kate walked out of the observation room and into the hallway, where a uniformed guard stood outside the interrogation room door. Janssen nodded her approval at the officer, and he opened the door for Kate.

She strode into the interrogation room, sat down at the table, slipped the paper clip off the papers, and made a show of examining them. Everything Kate and Nick were about to say and do was for Janssen's benefit. But Kate also had a message to convey to Nick and a delivery to make.

"You're looking good," Kate said.

"Orange is my color."

"I'm referring to the handcuffs," Kate said. "You were born to wear them."

"They're a bit snug."

She looked up from her papers. "You're facing a long prison stretch, and once you get out there are a dozen countries lined up to lock you away again."

"I've always been a popular guy."

"It seems you weren't that popular with the Road Runners. They double-crossed you and got away with hundreds of millions in diamonds. That's got to hurt."

"I pulled off the biggest heist in Belgian history," Nick said. "Making history is not a bad way to end a career."

"You can thank your so-called friends for your grand finale. Tell me where they are and what they're doing with the diamonds. Maybe you can do a little less time. Where do we find Dragan Kovic?"

"Haven't you heard about honor among thieves?"

"They betrayed you."

Nick shrugged. "Not all thieves have honor."

Kate leaned forward. "I'm offering you your only chance for vengeance against the people who put you here."

"You put me here. Not talking is how I get my revenge." Nick leaned forward too. "Your screwups led to the success of the biggest diamond heist in Belgian history. You'll probably lose your badge."

Kate gathered up her papers, leaned back in her seat, and shook her head in disappointment.

"My job is done anyway. I vowed that I'd never let you get away, and I meant it." She got up and went to the door, pausing for a moment to take one more look at him before leaving. "Remember that on Monday morning when you're on your way to prison."

She walked out, satisfied that she'd delivered her message to Nick and more. Now Nick knew that she'd be making her move on Monday morning and, while they were nearly nose to nose over the table, he'd taken the paper clip she'd brought for him.

Janssen met Kate in the hall. "That was a waste of time."

"I wouldn't say that. I got him talking."

"But he didn't say anything," Janssen said.

"The man loves to hear his own voice. He'll give me something next time, and then something more after that, just to keep the conversation going. Before it's over, he'll give up the gang."

"There won't be another meeting." Janssen held out a plane ticket. "You're on the eleven A.M. flight Monday to Heathrow with a connecting flight to Los Angeles."

Kate didn't take the ticket. "I'm the only one he'll talk to and the only one with a shot at breaking him."

63

"While you are somewhere over the Atlantic, there will be a press conference here announcing the arrest by Belgian police of international fugitive Nicolas Fox, the mastermind behind the vault robbery. We'll thank the FBI for providing crucial resources, and that will be the end of U.S. involvement in our ongoing investigation and manhunt."

Plitt had done his job with surprising speed, Kate thought. Maybe he deserved a Nobel Prize after all. She took the ticket from Janssen.

"This is a mistake."

"Bon voyage, Agent O'Hare," Janssen said. "A police officer will be waiting at your hotel at nine A.M. to escort you to the airport."

With those words, Amelie Janssen officially set the timer ticking on Nicolas Fox's escape.

7

At 6:45 A.M. on Monday, Kate left her hotel for her morning run in a tank top, jogging shorts, and a running belt full of explosives.

She jogged a block west into Stadspark and quickly veered off the paved trails into a thicket of bushes where her father had stashed a gym bag that contained a loose black sweat suit, a black balaclava, and gloves. She pulled the clothes on over her own. The size and dark color of the sweats had been chosen to obscure her figure and allow her to pass for a man. Kate put the balaclava on her head, rolled up the face mask to form a rim across her brow, then dashed back out onto the path and out of the park.

Kate jogged up Bourlastraat and slowed to a walk as she approached Leopoldplaats, where four streets intersected around a statue of King Leopold on horseback. There was a lattice of electric cables overhead that powered the trams that crisscrossed

up into the van and sat on one of the two metal benches. The only window was the mesh-covered porthole into the front crew cab. One of the officers secured Nick with a seatbelt and shut the thick rear door, locking it from the outside.

The two officers climbed into the front, which had special windows designed to withstand the impact of rocks and other hard objects typically thrown at cops in riot situations. But they weren't heading into a riot. This was just a routine prisoner transport, one of many they did each day, and they had no reason for concern. So after they drove off, neither one of the officers glanced over their shoulders into the porthole to see what Nick was up to. If they had, they might have seen him spit a paper clip into his hands.

Nick figured the trip to the new Palace of Justice near the banks of the Schelde River would take twenty minutes at most. They would travel east on a street that changed names four times, then southwest on a wide tree-lined boulevard that changed its name five times and then followed the path of the walls that once ringed the ancient city. The Palace of Justice's distinctive roofline, evoking the masts and sails of the ships that once traveled the river, made it look like the police were delivering prisoners for a cruise instead of a jail sentence. But Nick knew the van wouldn't be reaching its destination this morning and, being an experienced criminal, he had a pretty good idea where Kate would be making her move.

He easily unlocked his handcuffs and chains with the paper clip and braced himself for action as the van rolled into Leopoldplaats.

Kate pulled the balaclava's mask down over her face as the paddy wagon entered the plaza from the west. The garbage truck charged out of the northbound street like a freight train, T-boned the paddy wagon on the passenger side, and bulldozed it into the wide stone base of the King Leopold statue.

The two dazed but uninjured police officers were trapped in the crew cab. The driver's side door was pinned against the statue while the passenger side was smashed against the huge grill of the garbage truck, which was driven by Jake, his face hidden behind a balaclava.

Kate ran to the back of the paddy wagon and took the explosive out of her belt. The bomb looked like a cellphone and spark plugs wrapped in white Silly Putty. She hammered the door with her fist, then stuck the bomb to the door, right on top of the locking mechanism.

"Cover your ears and hit the floor," she said in her most manly impersonation. "And pray we didn't use too much C4."

Nick immediately flattened himself facedown between the benches and pressed his hands against his ears. He hoped any shrapnel from the door would pass over his head.

The two officers heard the warning too, and kicked at the windshield with their feet, but it was futile. The glass was designed to withstand much worse abuse. Jake ducked down under the dashboard of his truck.

Kate ran back the way she came, and as she did, she hit a key on the cellphone in her pocket that auto-dialed the phone that was wrapped in the C4. The bomb exploded like a thunderclap, the sound echoing off the buildings in the plaza.

Nick sat up, his ears ringing, and saw daylight through the jagged, smoking hole in the steel door where the locking mechanism had been. He pushed the door open and jumped into the street. He saw a figure in black running away, assumed it was Kate, and was about to follow her when someone grabbed his arm and he heard a familiar voice.

"Your ride is this way," Jake said, gesturing to the two motorcycles parked across the street.

"Thanks for coming," Nick said.

"My pleasure. Nothing beats a jailbreak for fun and wholesome father-daughter bonding." Jake glanced

JANET EVANOVICH AND LEE GOLDBERG

back at the two furious officers. One of them was already on the radio, calling for backup. "We've got to go."

They dashed across the street and jumped onto the motorcycles. Jake took off first across the plaza and Nick followed his lead just as a tram passed behind them, blocking the officers from seeing which way they went.

Nick looked for Kate as they sped away, but she was gone.

Kate didn't have a lot of time. The police were coming to the hotel in less than an hour to escort her to the airport. She ran back to the park and into some bushes, removed her black clothes, covered them with dirt and leaves, and dashed out onto the trail again in her original jogging attire.

She returned to the hotel at 8:15 covered in sweat. She smiled politely at the man at the front desk as she caught her breath at the elevator.

Jake led Nick into an underground garage a few blocks away from Leopoldplaats. They rode their motorcycles down two levels to a stolen Renault that Jake had parked there. There was a set of clothes for Nick folded neatly on the backseat. He quickly changed out of his orange jumpsuit into a polo shirt, jeans, and running shoes. Jake handed him the car keys, five hundred euros, a disposable phone, and a pair of Ray-Ban sunglasses.

"Is there anything else you need?" Jake asked, pulling off his balaclava.

"This is more than enough. In fact, it's too much." Nick tossed the car keys back to Jake. "I can find my own way out of the city."

"Are you sure?" Jake said.

"Evading capture isn't much of a challenge now that Europe has open borders," Nick said. "The only way a fugitive can get caught these days is if he gives himself up."

Nick shook Jake's hand, slipped the Ray-Bans onto his face, and sauntered casually to the stairwell.

Kate showered, changed into a T-shirt and jeans, grabbed her go bag, and got down to the lobby promptly at nine. No airport escort in sight. She heard sirens and honking horns coming from the street and the rumble of helicopters flying low overhead. Nick's explosive escape and the police response had created a traffic nightmare throughout the city.

She found a couch that had a view of the door and the street beyond, picked up a day-old issue of *USA*

Today from the coffee table, and flipped through it while she waited patiently for her escort to arrive.

Her iPhone rang at 10 A.M.

"Hey, Katie Bug," Cosmo said. "Where are you? I bet you're out of country, right? That's so cool. You're like James Bond only you're a girl. Did you see him in *Spectre*? Man, I loved when he blew up that building in the beginning. And then did you see the part where he kicked the guy out of the helicopter? I want to kick a guy out of a helicopter someday. That would be so cool, right? Did you ever kick someone out of a helicopter?"

"I'm kind of busy right now, Cosmo."

"I know. I know. I hate to bother you, but Jessup needs your form HB7757Q."

"I thought you needed SQ009?"

"That one too. HB7757Q is for hotel rooms exceeding your allowed per diem. You probably don't have anything to put on that one, right? I mean, how much could you spend on a room? I stayed at a Hampton Inn once and I got free breakfast. It was awesome. I could fill these out for you if you want. You could just give me the info and I could fill out the forms. I could go to wherever you are or you could come here. If it's after hours you could come to my house. I know how to make Swedish meatballs in a toaster oven and I have some apricot schnapps."

"Yeah, that sounds good, but I don't think I can do any of that right now."

"Or we could just have mixed nuts. I get them in bulk at Costco."

Kate disconnected. She felt very righteous because she hadn't threatened to shoot him.

A white Opel Astra pulled up in front of the hotel, and Amelie Janssen emerged. The chief inspector had a grim expression on her face and walked into the lobby like someone facing a triple root canal followed by a colonoscopy. Kate stood up, grabbed her bag, and met Janssen at the door.

"This is a surprise," Kate said. "I was expecting a rookie cop and a ride to the airport in the backseat of a filthy patrol car."

"That was the plan," Janssen said, "but there was an incident this morning and I wanted you to hear about it from me personally."

"What kind of incident?"

Janssen put her hands on her hips, instinctively staking her position and bracing herself for the unpleasant experience to come. "Fox escaped."

Kate swore, turned her back to Janssen, and took a few steps away, putting some distance between her and the chief inspector while presumably getting a grip on her anger. The truth was that Kate didn't have much faith in her acting skills and was afraid her performance would ring false eye to eye. The truth was, she was struggling not to smile. Kate took a deep breath and faced Janssen again. Now if Kate wasn't showing her rage, Janssen would chalk it up to admirable self-control.

"How did it happen?" Kate asked, her words clipped, her voice flat.

"The prisoner transport vehicle carrying Fox to court was rammed by a garbage truck. Two assailants blasted open the transport with explosives. Fox and the assailants escaped on motorcycles. Nobody was hurt, and the whole thing was over in two minutes. It was a professional job, crude in its simplicity, but executed with precision."

"Another Road Runner smash-and-grab, only this time they took Fox instead of diamonds," Kate said, stepping up to Janssen again. "It's right out of their playbook."

"So it is, and that means they've already split up and will be out of the country within a few hours, if they aren't already. But we'll launch an intense manhunt for Fox anyway and notify international authorities to be on high alert."

"That explains why Fox wouldn't give me anything on the Road Runners," Kate said. "It wasn't about honor. He knew they'd be coming back for him."

8

The most wanted man in Belgium wasn't thinking about who might be pursuing him. He was enjoying a croissant, a selection of fresh fruit, a yogurt, and a hot cup of coffee in his leather seat in the first-class compartment of the Thalys high-speed train to Paris. He'd arrive at Gare du Nord station in forty minutes. This, Nicolas Fox thought, was the civilized way to break out of jail.

He wasn't worried about being spotted by any police officers that might be waiting to greet the train. The authorities were frantically searching for a fugitive, and he didn't look like one. A person's appearance, Nick had learned, was as much about attitude as facial features and build. The Ray-Bans and the relaxed, unhurried gait of a man preoccupied by the email on his phone were all he'd need to become essentially invisible. He would blend into the crowd on the train platform and let the stream of humanity carry him out into the city.

Nick sipped his coffee, settled back in his seat, and fantasized about what his reunion with Kate O'Hare would be like. He wouldn't mind if they were both naked.

Kate flew to Heathrow Airport in London but intentionally missed her connecting flight to Los Angeles. She wasn't going to leave Europe until Dragan Kovic was out of business, and she and Nick had recovered the smallpox.

She hadn't heard from Nick yet, but before she'd left Antwerp, she received a text from her father in Amsterdam. He was boarding a flight to Los Angeles. His successful escape gave Kate some peace of mind and some assurance that Nick had also got out of Belgium safely.

Kate's idea of airport shopping was Sunglass Hut and See's Candies, so she was surprised to discover Caviar House & Prunier as she walked through the terminal. She was wondering how many people cracked open a $400 tin of fish eggs for an in-flight snack, when her cellphone vibrated, announcing the receipt of a text message. It was a street address in Bois-le-Roi, France, from "Dr. Richard Kimble," the hero of the classic TV series *The Fugitive*. Nick was safe and waiting for her.

She looked up the address on Google Maps and booked the first available flight to Paris. Ninety minutes later, she arrived at Charles de Gaulle Airport, where she rented a compact Citroën with a stick shift and drove the seventy-five kilometers south to Bois-le-Roi.

It was nightfall by the time she reached the tiny village, located where the dense Fontainebleau forest met a bend in the Seine. The streets were narrow, potholed, and uneven. Her car bumped along past old homes made of stone, their windows bordered with heavy shutters that had protected the inhabitants over the centuries against harsh weather and even harsher invaders.

Kate passed through the village and continued down a road that was little more than a rutted path. It ended at a property ringed by a low, rough wall cobbled together out of sharp jutting rocks and bricks and mortar. She drove through the open gate, her tires crunching on the loose gravel, and gaped at the house in front of her. Low-slung and sprawling, it was mostly stone with a leaf-strewn, sagging tiled roof. Smoke curled out of the two lopsided chimneys, and flickering candlelight glowed behind the windows.

Kate thought the picture would be complete if the Seven Dwarfs were standing in front of the house the plaza every few minutes. She stopped and pressed her back against the wall of the 150-year-old three-story stone building that occupied the corner. The building had a tower with a dome shaped like a wizard's hat and topped with a spire that looked to her like a boa constrictor that had swallowed a basketball. It was why Kate had picked that spot to wait. Nobody glancing in her direction would notice her with all of that Gothic gaudiness screaming for attention.

She surveyed the scene. Most of the cafés and shops that ringed the plaza hadn't yet opened. The vehicle traffic was light in all directions, and only a few people were on the streets. On the south side of the plaza, a huge garbage truck idled at the corner of a side street, facing the plaza and alongside a parking area for bikes, scooters, and motorcycles. An especially observant passerby might have noticed that two of the motorcycles, parked side-by-side, had keys in their ignitions.

The trap was set. Now all they needed was the mouse.

At that moment, a handcuffed and ankle-chained Nicolas Fox was led out of the back door of the police station by two uniformed police officers and guided into the back of a paddy wagon. Nick climbed singing "Heigh-ho, heigh-ho!" It was a house that belonged in a children's storybook. It was cozy and warm and inviting.

The front door opened and Nick stepped out. He was casually dressed in a cable-knit sweater and khaki slacks. Classic attire for the country gentleman welcoming a visitor to his bucolic home.

Kate got out of the car and walked toward him. The fairy-tale image of the Seven Dwarfs faded and was replaced with the Big Bad Wolf luring Little Red Riding Hood into his lair.

"You're the woman of my dreams," Nick said.

"I bet you say that to every woman who breaks you out of jail."

"Only the FBI agents."

"I feel like I've given myself completely to the dark side."

"Not completely," he said, "but I have plans to finish the process."

"Do those plans involve a glass of wine?" Kate asked.

"I have an excellent burgundy."

Kate shucked her jacket and took the glass of wine from Nick. "I hadn't expected to find you in a country cottage. I've always thought of you as more black glass and chrome."

Nick looked around. "It's a pleasant refuge. It's actually one of my favorite places."

Kate tasted the wine. "Is this home?"

He settled his hands at her waist and pulled her close. "Home is an elusive concept for me." He took her glass, set it on an end table, and kissed her. The first kiss was feather light. The second lingered. The third kiss was full-on passion. When they broke from the third kiss, Kate was unbuttoned and missing her underwear.

"So soft," Nick murmured, his hand on her breast.

Not so much him, Kate thought. He was the opposite of soft. He was . . . holy moly.

Kate had no idea what time it was when she awoke next to Nick in the huge four-poster bed, only that it was a new day. A gentle breeze drifted through the half-open windows, rustling the curtains and carrying with it the woodsy scent of the forest.

She sat up and looked at the white plastered walls, the hardwood floors, the thick, rough-hewn wood beams across the ceiling, and the collection of meticulously detailed ships in bottles displayed on shelves around the room.

"What is this place?" she asked.

"Just one of my little European hideaways."

"How many do you have?"

"I try not to keep much cash in banks. I know how easily they can be broken into. So I put most of my money into real estate. It's hard to steal a house, though I've done it."

"I'm sure there's nothing you haven't stolen." She picked up a ship in a bottle off the nightstand and examined the elaborate galleon. "Did you steal this as well?"

"My neighbor's hobby is making those, and he can't stop. His home is full of them so he gives them away to everybody in town. The rest end up here. I don't mind. He looks after the house and the Jag for me while I'm away."

She put the bottle back on the nightstand. " 'The Jag'?"

"I've got a restored 1966 Jaguar E-Type convertible in the barn."

"Of course you do."

"If you're nice to me I'll take you for a ride."

"I have to be nice *again*?"

He kissed her bare shoulder. "If you want to go for a ride."

Being *nice* to Nick was now at the top of Kate's list of favorite things. It was even ahead of parachuting out of a plane. Being *nice* to him had rewards for her that could only be described in terms of volcanic eruptions.

"Okay," Kate said, "but we have to speed it up. We have work to do."

"Honey, you can't put a time limit on perfection.

And it's too late to recover the diamonds, if that's what you're thinking. The loot was split up immediately after the heist, and the diamonds are being recut, so they'll be unidentifiable. Most of them will end up back in Antwerp soon, bartered and sold by the same merchants that they were stolen from."

"It's not about the diamonds," Kate said. "You were right. That wasn't what Dragan was really after. It was a vial of smallpox. We have orders from Jessup to find Dragan Kovic, recover the smallpox, and discover what he's plotting."

"That's serious," Nick said, taking a lingering look under the bed linens at Kate. "Give me ten minutes, tops."

"Deal."

Kate dug into her breakfast of hot chocolate, fresh croissants, and cheese. "That ran longer than ten minutes."

"Not my bad," Nick said. "I could have been done in *three* minutes."

"I had a concentration problem. My mind kept wandering back to how we're going to find Dragan."

"Finding Dragan is going to be easy. After a job, most of his gang goes back to their home turf in Serbia, and he hides out in Italy. That's where he does all his business and where the corrupt authorities, under the finger of the Naples and Turin mafia, protect him. I know that he's somewhere on the Amalfi Coast, so that's where we'll go and make ourselves obvious."

"What will you do when you meet him?"

"Offer to join the Road Runners, of course," Nick said. "Working on the inside is the only way we'll find out what happened to the smallpox and why he wanted it."

"What makes you think he'll take you back?"

"It's either that or he'll kill me."

"And if *that's* what he decides to do?"

"You'll stop him," Nick said. "That's your role in this charade. You'll be my bodyguard, partner in thieving, and sex therapist."

"Works for me," Kate said.

Nick and Kate arrived in Sorrento, Italy, that night. It had been a five-hour journey to get there. It took one hour to drive by limousine from Bois-le-Roi to the airport, two hours to fly by private jet to Naples, and finally forty minutes by yacht to cross Naples Bay. The yacht was graciously provided by the Hotel Vittorio Sorrentum, the world-class five-star resort where Nick had booked a suite with bay views.

Sorrento was an ancient resort town perched high atop the peninsula's sheer cliffs and squeezed between craggy mountains and a deep gorge. The temperate Mediterranean climate, combined with a unique location that was easy to defend and hard to attack, made Sorrento the perfect getaway for the wealthy, the powerful, and the detested of ancient Greece and the Roman Empire. It was a place where they could sip *limoncello*, gorge on pasta, and engage in their favorite debaucheries without worrying too much about their own safety. Dragan Kovic's presence here proved that was still the case.

The Hotel Vittorio Sorrentum, where Nick and Kate were staying, was two hundred years old and built atop the ruins of a Roman emperor's villa. The hotel was perched on the edge of a high cliff overlooking Naples Bay, the yacht harbor, and the swimming docks below. Their suite had elaborate frescoes on the ceiling, was furnished with antiques, and had a long veranda facing the moonlit sea. Two shot glasses filled with ice-cold *limoncello*, Sorrento's famous lemon liqueur, were waiting for them on a silver tray on the dining table when they came in.

"Criminy," Kate said. "What did this cost? Couldn't you have just gotten a room? Did we really need a suite with a view? How am I going to explain this to Jessup? What am I going to do about form HB7757Q?"

"Tell Jessup the suite came with complimentary *limoncello*."

Kate knocked back her *limoncello*. "The Hampton Inn gives you free breakfast."

"I don't think there's a Hampton Inn in Sorrento."

"Just saying."

Kate looked out the window at Mount Vesuvius in the distance. "Do you think Dragan has heard you're here?"

"He knew before we arrived. I registered in the hotel under my last alias, Nick Sweet, the one Dragan used to find me in Hawaii."

"Then he'll know that you want to be found."

"We're playing a game. The next move is his. Let's stretch our legs and take a walk through town."

"Let me get my tourist essentials and we'll go."

Kate removed a Glock and a combat knife from her suitcase. Nick had acquired them for her from his disreputable sources before they left France.

She put the wrinkled blue blazer on over her blouse to hide her gun and slipped the knife into an ankle sheath.

Nick was wearing a perfectly ironed white linen shirt and tan slacks.

"Nice shirt," Kate said.

He tugged on one of his sleeves. "Handmade by Jean Philippe, Singapore."

Kate tugged on her blazer sleeve. "T.J.Maxx, Tarzana."

They took the elevator down to the lobby, walked

through the lush flower garden, and emerged onto Piazza Tasso, the town square that spanned the deep gorge that for centuries cleaved Sorrento in half. The plaza was defined by a bright yellow baroque church, cafés, and bars with crowded outdoor seating. Corso Italia, Sorrento's central thoroughfare, was closed off to vehicle traffic at nightfall and was jam-packed with people out for a stroll.

Nick and Kate slipped into the flow of people moving down the brightly lit street past clothing stores, gelato shops, and the occasional British pub catering to the annual contingent of rowdy U.K. tourists. There was a party atmosphere on the boulevard but, as exuberant and alcohol-fueled as it was, it felt to Kate more like a kid's birthday celebration at Chuck E. Cheese's than Mardi Gras in New Orleans. The only danger she sensed came from two men who'd been following them since they'd left the hotel.

"Let me show you the old town," Nick said, making an abrupt turn down an alley, not much wider than a footpath. The alley led to Via San Cesareo, a pedestrian-only street that was barely wide enough for two lines of people walking single file in each direction.

Kate could smell garlic, lemon, fish, cooking fat, and leather as they passed the open restaurants and shops. The scent of sweat, tobacco, sunscreen, and perfume came off the crush of people.

"This was the site of the original walled city, built by the Greeks centuries before the birth of Christ," Nick said. "The buildings are tall and the streets are intentionally narrow to keep people in the shadows and cool in the heat."

Everywhere she looked, there was someone selling fresh *limoncello* and countless other lemon-infused products, from candy and soap to candles and lipstick. There were also shops selling tiles, sandals, paintings, leather bags, pottery, and other handmade goods. All produced by tired artisans who were right there, hunched over their worktables, as if to prove everything was locally made.

Some people a few steps ahead stopped to sample the *limoncello* being offered by two rival shopkeepers on opposite sides of the street, causing a foot traffic jam that pushed Kate up against Nick's back for a moment.

"It's a pickpocket's dream here," Kate said.

"Not a bad place for an ambush or a stabbing, either."

"You saw the men behind us," she said.

"There were two more walking toward us before we came down here," Nick said. "They are probably waiting in one of the alleys coming up."

"You led us into a trap."

"I thought I was leading *them* into one." Nick looked over his shoulder at her. "Or was I mistaken?"

She smiled at him. "You're not. Go into that leather store on your left and head to the back."

They passed the warring *limoncello* merchants and entered a tiny shop stuffed with handmade leather goods. Hundreds of purses, handbags, belts, and satchels hung from the ceiling and walls. In the back of the store, surrounded by scraps of leather, an old man was sewing a handbag.

Kate backed into a cranny beside the door while Nick moved further into the store, pretending to admire a messenger bag. She took a belt off the wall, looped it through its buckle to create a choke collar, and waited.

A moment later, one of their pursuers stepped in. She dropped the belt loop over his head, cinched it tight around his neck, and yanked him back against her. He began to struggle, but abruptly stopped when he felt the sharp tip of her knife against his spine.

"If I jam my knife between these vertebrae, I'll cut the nerves that control your lungs. You'll suffocate from a stab wound," she whispered into his ear. "At least I think so. I've never had a chance to try it. But I'm eager to see if it works."

Hard to tell if the man understood English. Good to see that he understood the seriousness of the knife at his back.

Nick stepped up, removed the gun that the man

had half-tucked into his pants, and aimed it at the doorway as the second man came inside.

"Good evening," Nick said. "Come in and join us."

The second man saw the situation his partner was in, and the gun aimed at his own gut, and raised his hands.

"Drop your gun in a handbag," Nick said. The man did as he was told, dropping the gun into the nearest open purse. "Now, gentlemen, do you speak English?"

They nodded yes.

"What was the plan this evening?" Nick asked them.

"We were told to bring you to see Mr. Kovic," the man in the doorway said, speaking with a thick Serbian accent. "For a friendly talk."

Kate tugged on the belt, tightening it around her prisoner's neck. "What about the two men waiting up ahead? What were they going to do?"

"Box you in so we could take you down to the car on Via Accademia. That's all. Nobody was supposed to get hurt."

"Tell Dragan I'd be glad to talk with him," Nick said. "He's warmly invited for breakfast tomorrow on the terrace of my hotel. Say around eight?"

"He won't like this," the man in the doorway said.

"Tell him the lemon tarts are excellent," Nick said.

Kate removed the belt and stepped back.

Nick kept his gun on the men as they left, then he dropped it into the purse with the second man's gun. Kate slipped her knife back into her ankle sheath, and Nick carried the purse up to the old man, who was still working on his bag. The old man was unperturbed, as if incidents like this happened in his store every day.

"We'd like this purse, please," Nick said.

"That will be a hundred euros," the old man said.

"The price tag says fifty," Nick said.

"That's the price of a purse," the old man said. "Gun totes are more expensive."

Nick paid him the hundred euros and they left the store.

9

Nick and Kate had dinner in their suite. Smoked red sea bream with a salty cinnamon brioche as an appetizer, followed by seaweed pasta with Venus clams, sea urchins, and chives as their entrée, and warm lemon cake with a lemon sorbet for dessert. They finished their meal with the obligatory icy shots of *limoncello*.

"The seaweed and sea urchins were okay," Kate said, "but they're never going to replace mac and cheese."

Nick sat back and watched Kate. "No matter where you go, you are who you are. You're willing to try new things but more often than not you return to your cultural roots. I like that about you."

"And you're the opposite," Kate said. "You embrace your environment. You're a human chameleon. It's impressive, but sometimes I wonder if you've lost yourself. When you're playing a role, are you standing on the outside looking in, or have you become that person and kicked Nick to the curb?"

"Some of both," Nick said. "When I'm in a con I'm outside, looking in. When I'm in my French country house I'm enjoying that part of me."

"And which one is the seaweed and sea urchin Nick?"

"I like them. I have an adventuresome palate."

Kate thought his adventuresome palate was at least partly responsible for their new sexual relationship. Like seaweed and sea urchin, he would continue to enjoy her when their paths crossed, but she couldn't see him settling for the monotony of monogamy. And she couldn't see herself justifying the relationship once this assignment was completed. She had serious feelings for Nick, but in the end he was a felon and she was the FBI.

In the morning they showered, dressed, and went down to the lobby restaurant for breakfast on the wide terrace that jutted out over the cliff. The low stone wall along the edge of the terrace was adorned every few feet with marble busts of ripped men and voluptuous women. Perhaps the busts were an incentive, Kate thought, to encourage guests to take it easy at the buffet.

Nick selected a table facing west, giving them

a view across the gorge to Sorrento, the bay, and the villas along the mountainous peninsula. Kate, being Nick's bodyguard, sat with her back to the view, preferring to keep her eye on the hotel and anybody who came out to the terrace. She was the first to see Litija stroll toward them like she was on a fashion show runway. Litija was wearing a wide-brimmed red sun hat, enormous round sunglasses, a white skintight dress with bracelet sleeves and a very short skirt that Kate thought could use a couple more inches of material.

Litija came up behind Nick and bent down to kiss his cheek. "Nick, you devil. Who let you out?"

"She did." Nick tipped his head to Kate and stood up to pull out a chair for Litija. "I'd be under lock and key if it wasn't for Kate."

"Proving once again that behind every great man is a resourceful woman," Litija said, offering her hand to Kate as she sat down. "I am Litija."

Kate shook her hand. "So, does this mean Dragan has you to thank for his success?"

"I wouldn't be that presumptuous." Litija smiled, plucked a grape from the fruit bowl, and popped it into her mouth. "He has lots of women. I'm just here having a little vacation after spending months in dreary Antwerp."

"Will he be joining us?" Nick asked.

"Don't be ridiculous," Litija said. "He can't take

the risk of being seen in public with you. You're a wanted man."

"So is he," Nick said.

"But he didn't just escape from Belgian police custody. You're the most wanted man in Europe right now."

"He put me in that situation."

Litija took another grape. "That's something you two can discuss at his villa. It's beautiful, right on the coast. His boat is waiting to take us there."

"I don't think that's a wise idea, based on the welcome we got last night," Nick said.

"That was an unfortunate misunderstanding. Dragan is a careful man and all he wanted to do was invite you over for a drink," Litija said. "His overly cautious approach can sometimes come across as unintentionally rude."

"At least it was more polite than kidnapping Nick at gunpoint and shipping him overseas in a coffin," Kate said.

"That's true!" Litija laughed and wagged a finger at Kate. "I like the way you think. But I wouldn't talk to Dragan like that. He doesn't have a great sense of humor."

"I'd really like to avoid another journey in a coffin, especially one that lasts an eternity," Nick said. "That's why I'd prefer meeting him in daylight in a public place."

"You won't be in any danger at Dragan's villa," Litija said. "If you're worried, bring your weapons. You can have a gun in each hand and a knife in your teeth if that makes you feel better. Nobody will take them away from you."

"I can guarantee that," Kate said.

"That's what I've heard," Litija said, then turned back to Nick. "So, really, Dragan is the one who should be concerned about his safety, not you. What possible reason can you have for not accepting his invitation now?"

"None at all," Nick said. "Shall we go?"

"He can wait." Litija reached for a croissant. "I haven't had breakfast and I love the *sfogliatelle* here. Have you ordered a bottle of champagne yet?"

"Coming right up," Nick said, and waved to the waiter.

Kate didn't know what the heck a *sfogliatelle* was but she suspected it would be expensive. And champagne. *Ka-ching!* She hoped there was a lot of space for itemizing on form HB7757Q.

Dragan's fifty-foot open-air yacht was classically Italian in its styling, rich in polished mahogany and supple leather, with the sculpted lines of a sports car and the iconic aura of a movie star. The pilot and deckhand, nautically dressed in jaunty blue sailor caps and white Paul & Shark polos and shorts, were the two men that Nick and Kate had confronted the previous night. If the men held a grudge, they didn't show it, though they definitely seemed uncomfortable in their uniforms.

Kate thought they looked like they were auditioning for jobs at Disney World, all suited up in Mr. Smee outfits.

The men seated Nick, Kate, and Litija on board, untethered the lines from the dock, and steered the boat out of the marina. They maneuvered past the anchored yachts and around the coming-and-going ferries that served Naples, Capri, and the resort towns further south along the Amalfi Coast.

"This is the scenic route to Dragan's villa," Litija said as they cruised past Marina Grande, a fishing village nestled in a cove below Sorrento. "It's also the most direct. For centuries, the only way to get to his villa was by foot or by donkey. Can you see me on a donkey?"

They headed south on the choppy turquoise sea with the high jagged cliffs and rocky coves of the Sorrento peninsula on their left and the mountainous island of Capri on their right. The edge of the peninsula was largely undeveloped, covered in chestnut trees and scrub, too steep and rough in most places for anything but the occasional stone watchtower, a vestige of the time when pirates and invaders were a constant threat, and observers sent out smoke signals to warn of imminent attacks.

There was no doubt in Kate's mind that one or two of the towers were still manned. Dragan's men would be watching, sending back the modern-day version of a smoke signal alerting Dragan of anyone venturing into his territory.

The boat veered toward a sharp gorge. As they got closer, she could see that the gorge created a small cove hidden behind two tall rock formations that looked like stone fists rising up from the sea.

The water inside the cove was calm and lapped on a pebbled beach that gave way to a stacked rock sea wall and wooden dock. The ruins of an old village built in the bedrock reminded Kate of caves, and she was fascinated with the elaborate Moorish façades.

Above the village, she could see terraces and tunnels cut into the cliff face. Steep, winding steps led up to a large stone building on a craggy point. The building was an architectural Frankenstein that combined the ruins of a church, a fortress, and a villa with a long sea-facing terrace and battlements along the precipice. It would be a long walk up, and Kate was looking forward to seeing Litija attempt it in her five-inch stiletto heels.

Nick looked at the cliff face. "Chairlift?" he asked.

"Better than that," Litija said. "There's an elevator."

She led them along the sea wall to one of the buildings embedded in the hillside. They took a few steps inside, where an elevator was cut into the rock. Litija pressed the call button, and the door slid open.

"This shaft has been here for centuries," Litija said. "I can't remember what for. There are all kinds of passages and shafts here. But Dragan stuck an elevator in this one, which is a good thing, because with these heels, I'd never be able to climb a thousand limestone steps."

Damn, Kate thought. She'd been ready to race the bitch.

The three of them stepped into the elevator, which was large enough for six, and Kate thought it went up faster and smoother than the one in the Federal Building in Los Angeles. Apparently, international diamond thieves could afford better contractors than the U.S. government.

Kate brushed her jacket back and put her hand on her gun just in case there was an unwelcoming welcome committee. Litija noticed and smiled.

"A Glock 27. Nice. I prefer the Sig Sauer P239," Litija said. "But there's nowhere to hide it on this dress."

"You could put it under your hat," Kate said.

"That's where I keep my garrote," she said.

The elevator stopped and the doors opened onto the terrace. Kate was expecting a militaristic vibe, something in keeping with a fugitive criminal's stronghold. What she saw instead could have been a five-star resort. There were a dozen chaise lounges facing the sea. A deep blue lap pool hugged the hillside and was fed by a little waterfall. A long arched colonnade draped in blooming bougainvillea led to the villa. Dragan Kovic, dressed in all black, looked out of place in his colorful surroundings.

Dragan stood at the edge of the terrace beside a mounted telescope aimed at Capri. He wore a linen Nehru jacket open over a silk T-shirt, skinny jeans, and loafers.

"Nick, it's so good to see you," Dragan said. "Congratulations on your remarkable escape, though I think you owe your inspiration to us."

"If not my inspiration," Nick said, "certainly my motivation."

"Did you come here to kill me?"

"I'm not a killer," Nick said.

Dragan looked over at Kate. "No, but I suspect she is."

Kate had her eyes on the man beside Dragan. He looked like he'd shaved his face with an outboard motor and was regarding her as if she were livestock on an auction block.

"I can be," Kate said. "If I'm provoked."

Dragan followed her gaze. "Zarko and I will be on our best behavior."

"I wish that had been your attitude on the diamond heist," Nick said. "Instead, you double-crossed me, cheated me out of my share, and left me to take the fall."

"I heard that you put yourself in that position," Dragan said.

"How could I have possibly done that?"

"Zarko told me that you tried to escape with some diamonds while the men were preoccupied breaking open the safe-deposit boxes."

"That's what he did." Zarko looked Nick in the eye as he lied. "So I put him down. He may have just been sneaking off, but I think it was more than that. He wanted payback for snatching him in Hawaii. He was going to slip away with some diamonds and trip a silent alarm so we'd get caught. If I hadn't stopped him, your best men would be in jail and you'd be the humiliated victim of one of his famous cons."

"Turning my own heist against me and walking away richer for it," Dragan said. "That sounds like a trademark Nick Fox con to me."

"I admit I wasn't thrilled about being kidnapped, but I have too much pride in my work to sabotage a chance to pull off the biggest heist in Belgian history," Nick said. "By breaking into that vault, I did something everybody thought was impossible. Having that feather in my cap is worth more to me than a pocket full of diamonds. More important, I would never double-cross my crew, even one that kidnapped me. I have my reputation to consider."

Dragan glanced at Zarko. "He makes a good point."

"Of course he does, he's a con man," Zarko said. "He'll turn any situation to his advantage with fast talk. Look how he went from being your hostage to being a partner in the heist."

Litija laughed and stretched out on a chaise lounge. "He's got you there, Nick. That was slick."

"There's a lot to think about," Dragan said. "But we'll sort it out to everyone's satisfaction before the day is done, I promise you. In the meantime, I hope you'll make yourselves at home here at Villa Spintria."

"Is this a brothel?" Nick asked.

Dragan cocked his head, clearly amused. "Why would you say a thing like that?"

"Because *spintriae* were ancient Roman coins that depicted an astonishing variety of sex acts and were used to pay prostitutes."

"I'm impressed, though I suppose when it comes to money, even coinage as rare as *spintriae,* you would know about it," Dragan said. "This place has been many things, including a monastery and a fortress. During the restoration of the property, barn, and orchards, we unearthed some *spintriae*. Perhaps they spilled from the pocket of a soldier or were a prized possession of a lecherous monk. We'll never know."

"They're adorable," Litija said, pulling a necklace from under her collar. There was a spintria coin dangling from the gold chain.

Adorable was not the adjective Kate would have used to describe the position, or the sex act, that the woman and two men were demonstrating on the coin.

Nick leaned down to Litija's chest for a closer look at the coin. "If the U.S. Treasury put that on coins instead of dead presidents, coin collecting would become every boy's favorite hobby."

"What you may not know is that *spintriae* is also what Roman emperor Tiberius called the men and women he brought to his villa on Capri to pleasure him," Dragan said. "Those who didn't please him got tossed off a three-hundred-meter cliff to the sea. That spot became known as the Salto di Tiberio, the Tiberius Drop. You can see it from here. Come take a look."

He patted the telescope, which was beside a squared opening in the low wall where a cannon once stood. The opening made Kate nervous, given the topic of Dragan's little speech. But if Nick was concerned, he didn't act that way. He walked up to the telescope and peered through it. Kate kept her hand on her gun, ready to shoot Dragan if he made a move on Nick.

"There's not much to see," Nick said. "Just some crumbling walls."

"It was magnificent in its day," Dragan said. "I wanted to re-create the splendor of his villa and his pursuit of pleasure, without the debauchery."

Zarko snorted. "Where's the fun in that?"

Dragan shoved Zarko over the wall.

The sudden, violent action took them all by surprise. One second Zarko was standing there, and the next he was gone. Litija bolted up from her chaise lounge in shock. Kate drew her gun out of reflex. Nick took a slight step back from the wall, but otherwise kept his calm.

No one was more surprised than Zarko, who was so astonished to be plunging to certain death that he didn't start screaming until an instant before hitting the rocks below.

"But I did like the Tiberius Drop," Dragan said in a matter-of-fact way. "So all of that considered, Villa Spintria seemed like a fitting name for this place. I hope that answers your question, Nick, and resolves some of our issues."

Nick peeked over the edge at the rocks below. "It's a step in the right direction."

"I'm glad to hear it," Dragan said. He walked over to Litija, took her trembling hand in his own, then turned to Nick and Kate with a gracious smile. "Come with us. I'll show you around."

Dragan ignored Kate's gun and strolled toward the flower-draped colonnade. Nick joined Kate and tapped her right arm.

"I think you can put that away now," he whispered. "It's impolite."

Kate holstered the gun but kept her hand near it. "He just murdered a man in cold blood."

"It's a good sign," Nick said.

"Because it wasn't you?"

"It means he needs me more than he needed Zarko."

"So we're in," Kate said. "But in for what?"

10

Dragan led them around to the east side of the villa to show them the view of his acres of lemon trees. A centuries-old stone farmhouse, serving as his processing plant, was located in the middle of the orchard.

"Villa Spintria is not just my vacation getaway," Dragan said. "It's a business. We make *limoncello* here that's sold throughout Italy. It has a unique flavor that comes only from our lemons thanks to the enchanted spot where they are grown."

There wasn't anything enchanting about the spot where Zarko had stood, Kate thought, or where he'd landed.

"The business is a legitimate front for laundering your money," Nick said.

"It's more than that. I like to see the trees on the hillside, to smell the lemony scent sweetening the sea breeze, and to enjoy a *limoncello* after my meals. It makes Italy a totally immersive experience for me. But the business also explains what we're doing out here if anyone is curious."

"And it explains why you have armed guards walking the property," Kate said. She couldn't see the boundaries of his land, but she did notice the sentries in the turrets atop the villa.

"We don't want anyone stealing our lemons," Dragan said.

"You can't be too careful," Nick said. "There are thieves everywhere."

Dragan led them to the villa, and they entered a large room with a barrel dome ceiling painted in gold leaf. Kate thought the room might have been the refectory of the former monastery. There were open windows facing the hills to the east and the sea to the west. It created a pleasant cross breeze that carried the sweet, salty scent that Dragan liked so much. Kate liked it, too. There was something naturally relaxing about it, offsetting the fact that a man had just died.

Dragan motioned for them to sit on one of the two couches on either side of a table where a pitcher of chilled lemonade and several glasses had been set out on a silver platter.

"I assume you didn't just come here to settle a dispute," Dragan said. "You would like to collect your share of the Antwerp heist, which I'm glad to give you. But what if I could offer you that and so much more?"

"I'm listening," Nick said, taking a seat on a couch facing the sea.

Kate sat beside Nick, and Litija poured lemonade into the glasses. Kate noticed Litija's hand was still trembling. Obviously the lemony sea breeze wasn't doing much for her.

"You can let your money ride, so to speak, and add it to your share of the biggest robbery we've ever attempted," Dragan said, sitting on the couch facing them and the lemon groves beyond. "Perhaps the biggest ever attempted by anyone."

"That's quite a boast," Nick said, taking a sip of lemonade. "But you'll have to be more specific."

Dragan glanced at Kate, then back at Nick. "I'd like to be, but first I have to know that I can trust you, that I have your complete loyalty."

"Shouldn't I be the one concerned about that after what happened to me in Hawaii and Belgium?"

"That's what I mean," Dragan said. "I need to know if that lingering resentment is something I should be worried about before I bring you into the big caper."

"And before I get involved with you again," Nick said, "I need to know that I won't be double-crossed."

"I have a solution that should reassure both of us," Dragan said. "I have a diamond heist planned for tomorrow afternoon in Paris. It's a modest job that has been in the works for months. Zarko was going to be the lead man. But now that he's unexpectedly dropped out, I find myself a man short. I'd like you to take his place. If the job goes well, then I'll bring you into the big caper."

"And if I'm not interested in either one?" Nick asked.

"I'll give you your share of the Antwerp heist now, and you'll go on your merry way," Dragan said.

Nick took another sip of lemonade while he pretended to contemplate his options. But Kate knew there was nothing to think about. He had to say yes if they were going to infiltrate Dragan's organization and find out what had happened to the smallpox vial.

"You wouldn't be offering me 'the big caper' unless you desperately needed my unique expertise to pull it off. So I'll do this job tomorrow on two conditions," Nick said. "First, I get Zarko's share of the Paris heist on top of what you already owe me, regardless of whether I decide to stick around afterward."

"Agreed," Dragan said.

"Second, Kate comes along, too," Nick said. "I need someone in the crew I can trust to watch my back."

Dragan studied Kate. "How do I know she's up to the task?"

"I broke Nick out of police custody," Kate said. "I planned it and executed it within forty-eight hours of his arrest. I think that speaks for itself about my capabilities and experience."

"I only work with the best," Nick said to Dragan. "In fact, as far as I'm concerned, this job tomorrow is *your* audition. I expect to see precision and professionalism at every level, or I'm out."

"There he goes," Litija said. "Turning it around on you again, Dragan. I've never met anyone so slick."

"Neither have I," Dragan said. "Nick is one of a kind, and he continues to prove it, which is as irritating as it is impressive." He shifted his gaze to Kate. "You're in, but your share will come out of Nick's pocket."

"I don't care whose pocket it comes from as long as it ends up in mine," Kate said.

"Then it's settled. You'll both be staying here tonight and traveling with us to Paris by private plane tomorrow morning," Dragan said. "I've already taken the liberty of checking you out of the hotel and having your things brought here."

"You were pretty sure of yourself," Nick said.

"I'm a hard man to say no to," Dragan said.

Kate was hoping that if Dragan had checked them out he also took care of the bill. God knows what the champagne and *sfogliatelle* cost.

. . .

Dragan left Litija behind in the refectory and took Nick and Kate into a windowless room decorated with framed antique maps on the walls and an antique floor globe in one corner.

"This is a remnant of the old fortress and served as the commander's map room. It's where he planned tactics and strategy," Dragan said. "I use it for the same purpose. I stare at the ceiling and hope for inspiration."

Kate looked up. The ceiling was covered with a fresco of the heavens and the Greek gods that commanded them. She was about to look away when something caught her eye, and she did a double take. The illustration of Zeus, the god of gods, had Dragan's face, pockmarks and all. What a lunatic, she thought.

He walked over to an architect's model of a building that was displayed on a table in the center of the room. "Do you recognize this?"

It was an octagonal building with an open square in the middle. A street ran through the middle of the square, and there was a tall, slender box standing upright in the center. The box had a drawing of a column that had a statue of a Roman Caesar on top. There was another box that had been cut to fit over a portion of the building on one corner of the model.

Nick bent down and studied the model. "Place Vendôme."

"You know Paris," Dragan said.

"I know where the best jewelry stores in the world are," Nick said. "You aren't seriously considering hitting them?"

"Why not? It's a great score, and the location is perfect. There's only one way in and out." Dragan pointed to the street that ran through the middle of the octagon. "Rue de la Paix. The buildings on either side of the square are continuous and essentially form two walls. That makes it easy for us to control the flow of traffic."

"It also makes it easy for the police to box you in," Kate said.

"That's not going to happen," Dragan said in a dismissive tone that did not invite argument.

"Is this going to be another smash-and-grab?" Nick asked.

"You make it sound so crude," Dragan said. "But yes, it is."

"I see two problems. The biggest one is right here, next door to the Ritz hotel." Nick pointed to the building next to the one covered with the box. "That's the Ministry of Justice, which runs the nation's courts and prison system. There are police officers armed with automatic weapons inside and outside the building at all times. They can show up at any of the jewelry stores within the plaza in seconds."

"Set that quibble aside for now," Dragan said. "What's the other problem?"

"After your smash-and-grab on the Champs-Élysées, the city installed solid steel pillars a couple feet apart to prevent cars from leaving the street and smashing through the storefronts. They run all along the inner circumference of the octagon."

"Ordinarily, those pillars would be an impediment, but not now. We have a once-in-a-lifetime window of opportunity. The Colonne Vendôme and the Ritz are currently being renovated. They are entirely covered in scaffolding and hidden behind decorative shrouds." Dragan tapped the slender box in the center of the square and then the one covering the building in the corner. "Usually, it's an open square, but now there are plywood fencing and trucks around the base of the *colonne* and construction workers everywhere."

Nick smiled. "And you've had your men working among the construction crew for months."

"Indeed I have. At four o'clock tomorrow, several of our construction workers will place the ends of two parallel scaffold platforms on two of the steel pillars in front of Boucheron jewelers at the northeast corner of place Vendôme and rue de la Paix."

Nick nodded, getting the picture. "Transforming

the pillars from obstacles into an inclined ramp for a speeding Audi."

"*Your* speeding Audi," Dragan said. "You and Kate will go airborne and crash through the front window of the store. You will get out, smash the display cases with hammers, steal the jewels, and exit on foot to rue de la Paix, where two motorcycles will be waiting for you both to make your escape. While you are doing all of that, the same sequence of events will be happening at the opposite end of the square, at the Bulgari store on the western corner of place Vendôme and rue de la Paix, with another set of thieves."

"Two robberies at once?" Nick said. "Isn't that pushing your luck?"

"We'll never get an opportunity like this again to strike place Vendôme," Dragan said. "We'd be fools not to take full advantage of it."

Nick tapped the Ministry of Justice building. "And what about this building full of police? You haven't explained how you are going to deal with that quibble."

"No, I haven't. It's not necessary for you to know those details. It's a separate operation. But let me give you some peace of mind. There are construction office trailers, stacked on top of each other, that have created a temporary four-story building in front of the Ritz that significantly blocks the view of Boucheron from the police officers stationed at the front door of the Ministry of Justice," Dragan said. "The scaffolding, scrim, and plywood fencing around the Colonne Vendôme blocks their view of Bulgari, too, not that you should be concerned about what is happening there, either."

"The police may not see the robberies go down, but they are certainly going to hear them," Kate said. "They can get across the square while we're still smashing display cases and seal up the two ends of the street, boxing us in. It will be like shooting fish in a barrel. How are you going to stop that?"

"All you need to know is that we will," Dragan said. His voice was sharp. It was clear he didn't like the questioning. "There is no point in cluttering your head with irrelevant information. I want you concentrating on your jobs. I don't want you distracted thinking about what someone else is supposed to do. That would jeopardize the entire operation. You have enough to think about as it is and a strict timetable to follow."

"He's right, Kate," Nick said. "We'll do our parts and trust that everyone else is doing theirs."

"So you're in?" Dragan asked.

Nick smiled. "Like you said, it's a once-in-a-lifetime opportunity."

More diamond robberies, Kate thought. I'm going

to spend the rest of my life in jail and then I'm going to burn in hell.

They spent the next hour going over the exact details and timing of the robbery, their escape, and their rendezvous afterward with Dragan, who would not be participating in the crime. The fact that he'd be sitting it out really bothered Kate. It meant that Dragan would be avoiding all the risk and, if things went bad, he'd be able to walk away and go right back to business.

"Now that we have the details straight, you are free to enjoy my property," Dragan said. "A light lunch will be set on the patio. You can help yourself to refreshments. Your guest suite is just down the hall."

11

Dragan left Kate and Nick and was on his way to his first-floor office when he ran across Litija sitting on a couch, drinking *limoncello* from the bottle.

"I don't understand you, Dragan," she said in their native Serbian.

"Good. If I was easily understood, I'd also be predictable. I'd be imprisoned or dead by now."

"*You* told Zarko to leave Nick behind in the vault. You wanted Nick to become the focus of the police investigation and distract them from you. When you lied about it to Nick today, Zarko backed up your story with more lies." She took a swig from the half-empty bottle. "You rewarded Zarko by pushing him off a cliff to protect your lie from ever being revealed."

Dragan pitied her. She was a versatile operative, able to go undercover to lay the groundwork for a heist, or use her body to seduce a useful person of either sex, or participate as a pinch hitter in any aspect of the robbery itself. But as effective as she was, she lacked imagination, a chess player's ability to see several moves ahead. She would never become more than she was today, a pawn in someone else's game. *His game*. He didn't like explaining himself to anyone, but he saw it would be necessary if he wanted to keep her.

"You are mistaken, Litija, about why I did it. I made a strategic decision to achieve our objectives. I hadn't counted on Nick escaping, but since fate stepped in and brought him to me I decided he would be an asset. Zarko and Nick would never have worked well together, and I needed the skills that Nick has more than those that Zarko possessed. The only asset Zarko retained was the benefit I could derive from his death. It sent a message to Nick that I was clearing the path for him to join us. So I sacrificed Zarko for the mission."

This was all true. But Dragan had also been eager to try out his Tiberius Drop. Zarko happened to be standing in the right spot, and Dragan had almost no impulse control. He didn't see the need to share any of that with Litija.

"You see no value in loyalty," Litija said. "Everyone is expendable to you. You sacrificed Zarko, a fellow Serbian, a man who had loyally served you for years. You have no heart."

It was a good thing they weren't outside standing on the terrace when she'd said that, or she would have experienced the Tiberius Drop herself. Dragan had zero tolerance for criticism. He supposed he could break her neck, but that would require more effort than he was willing to expend right now. And finding her replacement would be tedious. It would take weeks of interviews, watching candidates demonstrate weapons skills, watching them in hand-to-hand combat with his men, watching them fuck his entire staff, including ugly old toothless Maria, who tended the garden and smelled like dead fish. A shiver of revulsion ripped through him at the memory of Litija with Maria. He had to give it to her. The girl had stamina. And as if all that wasn't exhausting enough, he would have to personally test out the few women who survived. He didn't have the time right now to go through that, so he ignored the insult and answered the underlying question.

"Nick is brilliant, but he doesn't always work alone," Dragan said. "He often assembles a highly skilled crew for his jobs, and individually they're nearly as good as he is. Until his escape, I didn't know that his crew had any lasting allegiance to him. Now we not only get Nick, but his people, too, to help us on the next phase of our plan, assuming that he passes the place Vendôme test first. We'll be able to accomplish our near-term and long-term objectives much sooner, and with a greater chance of success, than we could have without him."

Nick and Kate left the house and walked to the far edge of the pool to stand by the waterfall where they couldn't be overheard.

"Airborne?" Kate said. "Are you kidding me? We're going airborne and then we're going to crash through a storefront and smash jewelry cases with a hammer. What is this, Hollywood? That stuff only happens in movies. They use stunt drivers and fake storefronts. People don't actually do this stuff. It isn't done!"

"I think I can do it," Nick said.

"Think? That indicates doubt. That's right next to I *don't* think I can do it. I want no part of this ridiculous scheme. I'm not robbing a jewelry store in place Vendôme."

"It could be fun," Nick said, grinning at Kate. "Flying through the air, smashing into stuff."

"Seriously?"

Nick shook his head. "No. When I pull a heist I make sure there's no danger to innocent bystanders, and for the most part I only con people who deserve it. This is not something I would ever choose to do. I'm participating in this because there's a lot at stake. We've been tasked to get the smallpox vial, and that's what we're going to do."

"If we get caught, it will create an international scandal, and we'll lose our best chance at stopping Dragan. He'll go underground. We won't know what he's done with the smallpox until people somewhere start dying horrible deaths."

"We won't get caught," Nick said.

"How do you know?"

"Because Dragan and his crew are great at this."

"You say that like you admire him."

"I appreciate his skills," Nick said. "He's a criminal mastermind."

"He's a homicidal psychopath."

"That's definitely a character flaw, but he's exceptionally good at what he does. His robberies look like quickly improvised smash-and-grabs. But the truth is they are the result of careful preparation, undercover work, and split-second timing. Dragan has the patience to play the long game. There aren't many people in this business who do."

"You're willing to play the long game," Kate said. "On the surface you seem like a spontaneous kind of guy, but you actually have a lot of patience."

"You noticed."

"Hard not to."

"You're referring to my expertise as a master criminal, right?"

"Of course."

Nick grinned and Kate grinned back.

"There are other times when patience comes in handy," Nick said.

"Are you bragging?" Kate asked.

"Just saying."

Place Vendôme, originally called place Louis le Grand, was built in 1699 as a luxury townhouse development for the rich. That's what it was until one day in 1792, during the French Revolution, when nine aristocrats got their heads cut off and stuck on spikes in the middle of the square. Overnight the neighborhood became place des Piques (Place of Spikes) and a popular setting for public executions. It took another hundred years before the square got its new name and once again became an enclave for the rich, not only as a place to live, but more important for the job at hand, to spend outrageous amounts of money on precious jewels.

At exactly 3:57 P.M. on Thursday Nicolas Fox drove a black Audi A4 into place Vendôme. Kate O'Hare sat in the passenger seat thinking about all of those heads on spikes and how hers could soon be on one, too, figuratively speaking. The Boucheron jewelry store was directly ahead. The Ministry of Justice was to their left, and there were four police officers armed with M16s standing outside and even more of them inside. This was an extremely dangerous heist, and they were entrusting their escape, and possibly their lives, to the Road Runners and their ability to stop the police from responding. Kate didn't like putting her safety into anyone's hands but her own.

At the same moment that Nick drove into place Vendôme, an identical Audi with two Road Runners inside entered the square from the opposite end of rue de la Paix and headed in their direction. The two cars passed without seeing each other because the sheathed scaffolding and plywood fencing around the 144-foot-tall Colonne Vendôme in the center of the plaza blocked opposing traffic from view.

"I ambushed a police transport on Monday to rescue a crook and here I am on Thursday, robbing a jewelry store," Kate said. She and Nick were buckled tight into their seats and wore matching crash helmets with tinted visors that obscured their faces. "They didn't train us for this at Quantico."

"That's why the FBI needs me to catch people like me. Sometimes you have to commit crimes to prevent bigger crimes," Nick said. "The curriculum at Quantico needs to be changed. They should invite us in to teach."

The very thought gave Kate a queasy stomach.

Ahead of them, four construction workers emerged

JANET EVANOVICH AND LEE GOLDBERG

from behind the *colonne*'s fence, crossed the street, and laid the ends of two scaffold platforms down on the small steel pillars that stuck out from the sidewalk in front of Boucheron.

"I'll be sure to mention the change in curriculum when I testify in my defense," Kate said. "Maybe I can get the charges against me reduced."

"Keep that positive attitude," Nick said. He floored the gas pedal and pressed the horn to warn anyone in the store about what was coming.

The four construction workers scrambled out of the way an instant before the Audi hit the improvised ramp.

Kate's heart stuttered as the car went airborne and headed straight for the elegant limestone façade of the jewelry store, with its large windows and ornamental columns. The building looked monumental and foreboding, daring them to do what the centuries, revolutions, and wars seemingly could not—break down the walls.

Even though she knew the front end of the car had been structurally reinforced for the collision, all of her instincts told her that driving into anything at high speed was suicide. It didn't help that she also knew that the Audi's air bags were disabled. She placed her gloved hands flat on the dashboard and braced for impact.

The Audi blasted through the window in an

explosion of glass, plaster, and limestone, smashed through a display case in a spray of diamonds and splintered wood, and came to a stop in the center of the store.

Kate opened her eyes, relieved that she was conscious and in one piece. The windshield was shattered. She could hear alarms ringing. She drew her gun, unbuckled her seatbelt, and got out of the car. Dust was settling like snow. Four store employees were backed up against the far wall in terror. The guard, dressed in a suit like a secret service agent, was rising from the floor near the door and reaching for the gun in his shoulder holster in the same motion.

"Don't do it," Kate said, aiming her gun at his forehead. "Drop the gun and kick it under the car." He did as he was told and she gestured to him to join the others against the wall.

Nick smashed display cases with a pickax, scooped up the diamonds, and dumped them into an open backpack that he wore on his chest instead of his back. Kate kept the five employees covered and glanced at the watch on her wrist.

By her estimate, unless something incredible was done, they had less than thirty seconds before the police officers from the Ministry of Justice took them down.

. . .

A few moments before the two Audis crashed into the two jewelry stores, two large dump trucks full of rubble that had been parked beside the *colonne* simultaneously pulled out into the rue de la Paix and turned across it, blocking the street and sealing off the plaza from traffic. The drivers leaped out of their trucks and ran away as their vehicles emptied their loads into the street.

At that same instant, a dozen police officers poured out from the Ministry of Justice and ran across the plaza toward the jewelry stores on the two ends of rue de la Paix. That was when a series of carefully timed small explosions started going off like a sequence of fireworks. The blasts released the massive scaffolding around the *colonne,* which unpeeled itself like a giant banana. The poles and scrim tumbled to the plaza and forced the police officers to scramble back to avoid being crushed.

It was in the midst of that smoke, chaos, and destruction that Nick and Kate ran out of the jewelry store, jumped onto two motorcycles parked on rue de la Paix, and sped northwest toward place de l'Opéra, one of the busiest and most crowded intersections in Paris. Seven streets branched off the plaza outside of the grand gilded Paris opera house, creating an enormous churn of man and machine.

They snaked through the traffic, making a hard right onto rue du Quatre-Septembre, then a sharp left onto a narrow one-way street. They came to a sudden stop at the intersection with the broad boulevard des Italiens, where there was a long line of motorcycles parked on the sidewalk in front of the Gaumont Opéra multiplex movie theater. Nick and Kate parked their motorcycles with the others, left their keys in the ignitions to encourage theft, and went to the ticket window. They were ten minutes early for the 4:15 showing of the latest *Mission Impossible* movie.

Nick removed his helmet, holding it at an angle that obscured the view of the ticket window security camera. Kate took her helmet off as well, her back to another camera pointed at the entrance to the theater.

"*Deux billets pour* Mission Impossible, *s'il vous plaît,*" Nick said, passing some euros through the slot to the female cashier. She passed back two tickets. Nick and Kate entered the theater and immediately split up to go to the restrooms.

As Kate went into the women's room, Litija emerged from one of the four stalls, leaving a large Galeries Lafayette shopping bag and a purse behind. Kate went into that stall and closed the door while Litija washed her hands at the sink.

She set her helmet on the floor, unzipped her jumpsuit, and opened the shopping bag, which held a sundress and flip-flops. She quickly changed into the new clothes and stuffed her helmet, gloves, and jumpsuit into the bag. Kate dropped the Glock in the purse, hung the strap on her shoulder, and walked out.

Litija took the shopping bag and left without saying a word. Kate approached the mirror and checked to see if, in her professional opinion as an FBI agent, she looked like someone who'd just robbed a jewelry store.

The dress and the flip-flops said *no*. The expression of horror said *yes*. She forced herself to relax and smile. For the greater good, she thought, checking her watch. It was 4:09. In one minute, the sold-out 2 P.M. showing of *La Dernière Vie,* a World War I epic and the most popular movie of the week in France, would be letting out.

She knew that Nick was in the men's room changing his clothes and handing off the diamonds to the Road Runner who'd been waiting for him just like Litija had been waiting for her. Those two Road Runners would dispose of the two thieves' jumpsuits and helmets and then transport the diamonds to the next person in the relay race to get the loot out of the country as fast as possible.

Kate took a pair of large sunglasses out of the purse, put them on, and walked out of the bathroom just as the audience for *La Dernière Vie* spilled out of one of the auditoriums. She slipped into the middle of the exiting crowd and so did Nick, who now wore a lightweight gray hoodie, jeans, and tennis shoes. He came up beside Kate and put on a pair of Ray-Bans as he stepped into the sunshine outside.

"*Formidable,*" Nick said, referring to the film they'd supposedly just seen. "*Marion Cotillard était incroyable.*"

"*Oui,*" Kate said. That was the extent of her French, and she had no idea who Marion Cotillard was. Inspector Clouseau was the only French character she knew, and a Brit had played him.

Nick took her hand and together they turned right on boulevard des Italiens toward place de l'Opéra. Traffic was gridlocked. The air was alive with the sound of sirens and horns. There was a palpable, urgent energy on the streets. Something had happened. Kate picked up a word here and there from the people they passed.

"*Diamants!*" "*Voleurs!*" "*Place Vendôme!*"

When they reached place de l'Opéra, everyone was looking down rue de la Paix toward the helicopters and smoke in the sky over place Vendôme. Nobody had any reason at all to notice Nick and Kate, who darted across the street and took the stairs down to the metro station.

There was a southbound train arriving as they reached the tracks, and they took it. They didn't care which line it was. The more transfers they had to make between metro lines to their destination, the better it was. It would be harder to follow their tracks. Nick and Kate settled into a seat. It wasn't until that moment that Kate felt that they'd made their escape.

"It's a shame we couldn't stay for *Mission Impossible*," Nick said. "We probably missed an exciting heist."

12

After two metro transfers, Nick and Kate got off at the Mouton-Duvernet station and climbed the stairs to the street. They emerged on avenue du Général Leclerc beneath a distinctive green cast-iron archway and a *Métropolitain* sign written in a florid art nouveau script that screamed "You're in Paris!"

They were in the heart of the fourteenth arrondissement, a neighborhood known primarily for the massive Montparnasse Cemetery crammed with ornate tombs and for the fifty-nine-story office tower that rose over it like an enormous black headstone.

Nick and Kate walked a half block south on avenue du Général Leclerc, then turned right on rue Brézin, a one-lane street that ran only a single block from east to west. They were just another anonymous, unremarkable couple out for an evening stroll on a street lined with apartment buildings and a wide assortment of shops. Nick gestured across the street

JANET EVANOVICH AND LEE GOLDBERG

to Picard, a store with a giant snowflake in the window.

"That's a grocery store made just for you," Nick said. "All it sells is frozen food."

"You say that like it's a bad thing," Kate said. "I'm too busy chasing bad guys to cook."

"That's why restaurants were created," Nick said.

"I go to restaurants."

"I'm talking about the kind without a drive-through window."

"They're too slow and overpriced," Kate said. "Speaking of food, should we pick up something at Picard's to heat up for dinner?"

"I'd rather turn myself in to the police and eat whatever the jail is serving."

"You're too snooty about food," Kate said.

Nick smiled. "I can see this is going to be a major stumbling block in our relationship."

"We have a relationship?"

"You haven't noticed?" Nick asked.

"I hadn't given it a name."

"*Relationship* is a broad term. It can mean most anything."

"What does it mean to you?"

"In our case? Partner, lover, pain in the ass."

Kate nodded in agreement. "That covers it."

They took rue Brézin to its end at a T-intersection with avenue du Maine. It was just a half block shy of the spot where five other streets hit the wide tree-lined boulevard from various angles, creating a whirlpool of traffic.

Nick and Kate's destination was a six-story apartment building directly across from rue Brézin on the wedge-shaped corner of avenue du Maine and rue Severo. The building looked like the bow of a ship, heading due north through a sea of cars to the Montparnasse office tower. On the ground floor, there was a pharmacy and a business that sold coffins and headstones. Kate pointed to the plush coffin in the window as they approached the door to the apartment building.

"I wonder if Dragan gets a discount on those," Kate said.

Nick waved a digital key over the scanner beside the door, unlocking it. "He probably owns the shop."

They entered a lobby facing another locked door, this one made of glass, allowing them to see the spiral staircase in the foyer that led up to the apartments. Nick waved his key over the scanner beside the list of apartment buzzers, and they heard the telltale click of the second door unlocking.

The building was hundreds of years old and was in relatively good shape, but the spiral staircase that led up to the apartments was too tightly wound to fit even a tiny elevator. So they climbed the stairs to the sixth-floor apartment where they were meeting

Dragan Kovic. It was a long climb up on wooden steps bowed from centuries of use. Kate couldn't imagine living there and having to lug groceries, or anything else, up those stairs every day. But then maybe this was how French women stayed thin. That and smoking instead of eating.

The creaking steps announced their arrival long before they got to the sixth floor. The door to the apartment was partly open. They stepped inside a large room that was unfurnished and painted bright white. The ceilings were trimmed with elaborate crown moldings, cornices, and rosettes, the walls with half-height wainscoting. Against all that whiteness, black-clad Dragan Kovic stood out dramatically, as if he were illuminated from every angle. He sat in one of three folding chairs in the center of the living room, a bay window behind him overlooking the busy street below.

"Did we pass the audition?" Dragan asked.

"You did," Nick said, closing the door behind them. "Your team was precise, disciplined, and professional. I'm very impressed."

"Likewise," Dragan said. "You were briefed on the plan only last night and yet, without any prior location scouting or dry runs, you performed flawlessly. I commend you."

"I take it the other team got away safely," Kate said.

"They did. And the ten million dollars in diamonds we acquired from the two robberies are already being dispersed for cutting and resale," Dragan said. He then shifted his attention to Nick. "So now you are at a crossroads. You are free to leave with your share of this robbery and the one in Antwerp. You are also welcome to join us in our biggest endeavor. But if you agree to participate, there is no backing out. I need your decision now."

"The way I see it, you and I are the best at what we do, but together, we could reach heights neither one of us could on our own," Nick said. "So yes, I'm in, for the challenge as much as the profits."

Dragan shifted his gaze to Kate. "And you?"

"I go where he goes," Kate said. "I'm good, but I need direction."

"I admire a person who has an objective view of their own skills," Dragan said, "as well as their limitations."

"There's one more thing we have to settle," Nick said. "I won't go into another heist blind, like the Antwerp job. Before I sign on, I need to know what the objectives really are."

"I don't understand what you mean," Dragan said.

Nick sighed with disappointment. "Our partnership hasn't even started yet and already you're lying to me. I know about the vial of smallpox."

Dragan jerked at the mention of the deadly virus. It was as if he'd been given a small electric shock.

"How did you know about the vial?" Dragan asked.

"Because I am very, very good at what I do," Nick said.

"That's not an acceptable answer."

The two men were staring at each other eye to eye, so neither of them noticed Kate slip her hand into her purse and grab her gun. She'd be ready if things quickly went bad.

"I've had my eye on that vault for years and I've tried to learn as much as I could about what was in those safe-deposit boxes," Nick said. "Before the police grabbed me in the vault, I noticed that box number 773 was open and on the floor next to me. That box belongs to diamond merchant Yuri Baskin. His cousin was Soviet bioweapons expert Sergei Andropov, who died in Antwerp before he could sell a vial of smallpox he'd smuggled out of Russia. The vial was never found. It's been assumed for decades that the vial was in Yuri's box. If it was, I've got to ask myself, 'What does a diamond thief want with one of the most lethal viruses on earth?'"

Dragan continued to stare at Nick for a long moment before coming to a decision. "If I tell you, and then you decide to walk away from this, I'll have to kill you."

Nick laughed. "You'll kill me *now* if I walk away, so what have you got to lose? I was a dead man the moment I admitted that I knew about the smallpox."

Dragan flicked his gaze toward Kate for a moment. Long enough to notice the Glock pointed at him. Then focused back on Nick and smiled. "I'm not so sure about that. You like to take big risks with your life."

"That's what makes life fun," he said.

"Please sit down," Dragan said. "I have a story to tell you."

Dragan took a cigar out of his pocket and lit it with a match.

"Does it have a happy ending?" Nick asked as he took a seat on a folding chair.

Kate remained standing, only slightly more relaxed, gun still in hand. She was dealing with a guy who'd had someone paint him as Zeus on the ceiling of his office. She thought either he had a sense of humor or else he was majorly nuts. She was going with the latter.

"That will be up to you," Dragan said and blew a puff of smoke in his direction.

"In February 1972, a Yugoslavian went on a pilgrimage to Mecca and came back to Kosovo infected with smallpox. He had no idea that he was infected, of course, and since he'd recently been vaccinated, he only developed a slight rash and therefore didn't see a doctor for treatment. He infected eleven people, just by being near them," Dragan said. "One was a teacher who spread the virus to thirty-eight more people, mostly the doctors, nurses, and patients in the three hospitals in three different cities where he was treated and misdiagnosed. In his final days, the teacher's eyes turned black. His skin broke out in blood blisters and split open. His internal organs disintegrated and blood poured out from every orifice in his body. That's because smallpox destroys the membranes that hold the body together, inside and out. It's like decomposing alive. A horrible, agonizing way to die."

Dragan spoke in a detached way, a distant observer of a long-ago event. But as the story got bloodier, he leaned forward, his arms on his knees, bringing himself closer to his guests as he became more engaged. He flicked some ashes on the floor and continued.

"It takes two weeks after someone is exposed to smallpox before doctors can detect it or someone shows symptoms. But by then, it's too late. The sick are already highly infectious, spreading the virus to anyone within ten feet," Dragan said. "So the epidemic moves in waves, with the number of sick growing exponentially. The only way to stop it is to quarantine the sick and vaccinate everyone else. So that is what the government did. The army sealed off entire towns. Public gatherings were banned across the nation. Ten thousand people suspected of being infected were herded up and quarantined in apartment buildings encircled by barbed wire and armed soldiers. Eighteen million people were vaccinated. The epidemic was over in eight weeks. In the end, only about two hundred people were infected and thirty-five died. It could have been much worse."

"Were you in Yugoslavia at the time?" Nick asked.

"I was nine years old." Dragan pointed to his pockmarked face with his cigar. "That is how I got my lovely complexion. The lasting, parting kiss of smallpox to those it has abandoned. Ever since then, I've been enchanted by that demon."

"I'd think after what you've been through, you wouldn't want anything to do with smallpox," Kate said.

"I'm immune now to her charms, but I remain in awe of her deadly power. I've finally found a way to harness that power for myself," Dragan said. "I think that's always been my destiny."

"I'm a thief and a con man," Nick said. "Not a salesman. If that's what you are hoping to get from me, I'm afraid I wouldn't know where to even begin looking for a smallpox buyer."

"I have no intention of selling smallpox to anyone. I used half of the money that we've earned from our heists, prior to the Antwerp job, to recruit scientists and build a state-of-the-art weapons lab to develop

137

my own cache of weaponized smallpox. What I was lacking until now was a start-up sample to work from."

"If you don't intend to sell the smallpox," Kate said, "why build a lab to create more of it?"

"Because I want to unleash smallpox on an American city."

"What will you gain?" Nick asked.

"I want to cash in on the massive drop in the stock market that is sure to follow the 'terrorist attack.'"

"That's where the rest of your money is going," Nick said. "You're going to invest two hundred million dollars on Wall Street betting against the market. It's a safe bet, because you'll know exactly when the market is going to plunge."

"That's right," Dragan said.

Nick let out a slow whistle of admiration. "You'll make *billions*."

"*We* will." Dragan stood up, excited, practically evangelizing now. "It will be the greatest score of our lives, perhaps the greatest in the history of crime. The riches we will reap almost defy imagination."

But that financial windfall would be earned on the deaths of thousands of people, Kate thought. Nobody in the United States is vaccinated for smallpox anymore and, as a result, there weren't tens of millions of vaccines on hand to inoculate the population of a major city. The epidemic would rage a lot longer, and claim more lives, than it had in Yugoslavia more than forty years ago. It would be a catastrophe of epic proportions.

She was tempted to shoot Dragan right now, or at the very least arrest him, and bring the plot to an end before it could get started. But that wouldn't get the smallpox sample back or prevent others in his organization from moving forward with his plans without him.

"It's a brilliant scheme," Nick said. "But I still don't see why you need me."

"As it turns out, the smallpox sample we acquired from Antwerp is small. My scientists are working with it even as we speak but it will take time to get the quantity I need. If I had a second sample the process would go much more quickly."

"I have no idea where to find that," Nick said.

"I do," Dragan said. "Everyone thinks that only two samples exist, one in America and one in Russia. The truth is, there are many unrecorded samples that were collected back when smallpox was widespread. Those samples are secretly stored and studied in government, institutional, and private high-security biolabs located in several countries. One of them happens to be a mile from this apartment."

"You want me to steal it for you," Nick said.

"Or I'll kill you."

Dragan made it sound like a joke, but they all

knew that it wasn't. He appeared to be alone but there were almost certainly armed men inside and outside the building awaiting his word on whether to let Nick and Kate leave alive.

"Well, that makes it an easy decision," Nick said. "I'll steal the smallpox, but I want forty percent of the profits from the stock market gamble."

Dragan laughed. "You're a very amusing man. I'll give you your share of the Antwerp and Paris heists and you can bet that against the market yourself. You'll do extremely well."

"I'll definitely be doing that," Nick said. "In addition to my forty percent."

"You're being ridiculous. You don't deserve forty percent."

"I deserve more, but I'm being generous. Without me, you won't have the smallpox you need to make the investment pay off. This isn't a heist you can accomplish with one of your glorified smash-and-grabs."

"So I'll kill you and find someone else with the expertise to steal the smallpox for me."

Kate's grip tightened on her gun, and she steeled herself for action. Dragan didn't appear to be armed. Nick didn't look worried at all.

"You wouldn't have kidnapped me for the Antwerp job if there was somebody else," Nick said. "But let's say that there is someone out there. How many years will it take to find him? And what if you're wrong, and he's not another Nicolas Fox? You could lose the millions you've sunk into the scheme already. Are you really willing to take that gamble?"

Dragan pondered his cigar for a moment, took a long drag, savoring it, then blew out the smoke. "What makes you so sure that you'll be able to break into the lab and steal the smallpox?"

"Because I'm the best," Nick said. "We both know it."

"Fine," Dragan said. "You can have ten percent."

"Forty," Nick said.

"Fifteen."

"Forty."

"Fifteen," Dragan said. "And that's my final offer."

"If I am going to do this, we're going to be partners."

"If you don't do this, you're going to be dead."

Nick waved off the comment as if it was meaningless and not the genuine threat that Kate knew it was.

"I'm showing you my respect, and acknowledging the considerable investment you've already made, by giving you sixty percent instead of insisting on fifty-fifty," Nick said. "I get forty percent. Or you can execute us now."

Kate raised her gun and pointed it at Dragan's head. "He can try."

That's when she noticed the red dot of a sniper's targeting laser on Nick's forehead and another on her chest. There were snipers on the building across the street. Nick was aware of the targeting dots, too, but he ignored them.

"Make up your mind," Nick said. "I'm hungry. Robbing jewelry stores gives me an appetite."

Dragan sat down, perhaps to give his snipers a clean shot, or to rest while he considered the offer. After a minute that felt to Kate like forever, he finally smiled, leaned forward, and offered his hand to Nick.

"Sixty-forty," Dragan said.

"You have yourself a deal," Nick said and they shook hands.

"The lab is within the sprawling Institut National pour la Recherche sur les Maladies Infectieuses complex on rue Denfert-Rochereau," Dragan said. "Walking distance from this apartment, which you will be using as your base of operations. The challenge isn't just breaking into the lab, but safely acquiring the sample and transporting it. One mistake and lots of people will die."

"Don't tell me you're worried about the loss of human life," Kate said.

"Of course not. I'm worried about it occurring before I place my bets on the table," Dragan said. "Not only wouldn't I profit from the accident, but a smallpox epidemic in Paris would put authorities worldwide on heightened alert. It might even prompt mass vaccinations, which would severely dilute the impact of a future attack."

"I value my life and my future earning potential too highly to allow that to happen," Nick said. "We'll take all of the necessary precautions."

"I'll give you all of the manpower, cash, and resources that you need to do this right," Dragan said. "Just give me a shopping list."

"I'll do that," Nick said. "But I'll also have to bring in people of my own who have specialized skills and who I can depend upon."

"Can you trust them not to talk?" Dragan said.

"As much as you trust your people," Nick said. "But they'll be freelancers and they won't know the big picture, only the immediate objective, so you won't have to kill them afterward."

"You're beginning to understand me," Dragan said.

"I know you can play the long game, but I'll say this anyway so there's no misunderstanding," Nick said. "You need to be patient. It's going to take me some time to case the institute, come up with a plan, recruit my people, and set the stage for the robbery."

"Are we talking weeks or months?"

"I won't know until I have a plan," Nick said. "But I get bored easily, so figure on weeks."

"Litija will move you into the apartment tonight."

Dragan passed a card to Nick. "You can reach her at this number. She can reach me."

Once again, Kate noted, Dragan was keeping a safe distance from the operation. Nick pocketed the card and stood up.

"Send my share of the two robberies to my Cayman Island account," Nick said. "I'll give you the number. I won't do anything for you until I see those dollars in my account."

"Where are you going?" Dragan asked.

"I thought I'd take a stroll to place Denfert-Rochereau," Nick said. "And see the lay of the land."

"I'll send your money, but don't think about running out on me," Dragan said. "Or I'll torture and kill both of you."

Nick shook his head. "You can't go ten minutes without making a threat, can you?"

"It's called leadership," Dragan said. "Stay in touch."

13

Nick and Kate walked back across avenue du Maine and along rue Brézin. Kate didn't speak until they were heading up toward the Mouton-Duvernet metro station.

"What possessed you to tell Dragan that you knew about the smallpox?" Kate asked.

"I wanted to hurry things along."

"You could have hurried us into graves."

"It worked, didn't it? He told us his whole, twisted plan."

"I wanted to shoot him in the head."

"Has anyone ever talked with you about anger management?"

"Yes," she said. "That's why I *didn't* shoot him. But he still has to be stopped."

"He will be," Nick said.

"I could alert Jessup right now so he can organize a multi-agency raid on Dragan's place in Sorrento."

"Wouldn't do us any good," Nick said. "We don't know where he's going from here. Even if he does go back to Sorrento, you don't know if his lab is there, and his sources in Italian law enforcement will tip him off about the raid. He'll escape, you'll confiscate a bunch of lemons, and lose your best chance to stop his scheme."

"So what do you suggest we do?"

"We steal the smallpox for him," Nick said. "Or at least make him believe that we have."

"I get it," she said. "You're going to switch the real smallpox with a harmless vial of something else."

"I don't know what I am going to do. But you've heard the phrase *Follow the money,* right?"

"It's a tried-and-true method of investigation. It almost always leads to the heart of any criminal conspiracy."

"We're going to use the same approach. Only we're going to 'Follow the pox' to find his lab and the virus that he's already got."

They walked past the Mouton-Duvernet station and up to place Denfert-Rochereau. Here seven streets converged in a plaza around a bronze sculpture of a proud lion the size of a bus.

"That's the Lion of Belfort, a bronze replica by Frédéric-Auguste Bartholdi of his monumental sandstone sculpture in the hills above Belfort, a village near the German border," Nick said. "Bartholdi is perhaps best known for the Statue of Liberty. The lion honors French Colonel Denfert-Rochereau, who defended Belfort 'like a lion' against a Prussian siege for a hundred days in 1870 even though he was vastly outnumbered."

"Why do you know so much about some random sculpture?"

"I've thought about stealing it," Nick said.

"Why would you want to do that?" Kate said. "It's huge, it weighs tons, and it's right in the middle of a busy intersection. It's impossible to steal."

"That's why I want to," Nick said. "Maybe we can do it at the same time that we steal the smallpox."

"Steal the lion another day," Kate said. "Let's keep this simple. Relatively speaking."

Nick's cellphone chirped. He took it out of his pocket and glanced at it. "Our millions have arrived. Dragan may be a homicidal lunatic, but he pays his bills promptly."

"That's his one virtue," Kate said.

"He also produces an excellent *limoncello*."

They crossed the plaza, where avenue du Général Leclerc became the tree-lined place Denfert-Rochereau, and continued walking up the west side of the street.

There was a florist on the corner, and then a nail salon, a furniture store, and an empty storefront, boarded up and available for rent. Beyond that was a block of beautifully renovated four-story buildings. It took a moment for Kate to realize they weren't individual buildings nor were they old. It was actually a recently constructed, single structure more than a half block long with multiple old-style façades that gave the impression of being several different buildings. But even that view was deceptive. It was actually a long wall with offices on top. The windows on the ground floor were barred and there were no doors to the street, just a guard-gated archway midway down the block leading to a motor court and more buildings beyond. There was a plaque written in French on the wall. Nick read it and gave Kate a translated summary.

"This was the site of the Saint Vincent de Paul Hospital for Children, the Home for Young Blind Girls, and other medical institutions. The original chapel is still here, but the rest has become the National Research Institute for Infectious Diseases." Nick stepped back from the wall and gave it, and the gate, a quick once-over. "It can't be any harder to break into than the Antwerp diamond vault."

"Perhaps," Kate said. "But diamonds can't kill you."

Nick and Kate took the metro from the place Denfert-Rochereau to Gare de Lyon train station, and from there they took a commuter train for the half-hour journey to Bois-le-Roi. They walked the two miles from the train station to Nick's house in silence, lost in their own thoughts.

Kate trudged through the door, slumped against the wall, and closed her eyes. "Stick a fork in me."

Nick leaned into her. His hands were at her hips and his lips skimmed across hers. "I'm feeling romantic."

"Ommigod," Kate said, more groan than spoken word. "What are you, Superman? How can you possibly be feeling romantic? I'm so tired I can't feel my fingertips."

"No problem. I'll help you get to the bedroom, and then all you have to do is lay there."

"Fine," Kate said. "Don't wake me when it's over."

"Okay, but you'll be sorry if you sleep through this. I have some new moves."

"Maybe I just need coffee."

"Good idea," Nick said. "You get comfortable and I'll whip up a double espresso."

Kate opened her eyes and stretched. She was alone. A shaft of light peeked from between the drapes and spotlighted the pillow where Nick should have been. She touched his side of the bed. It was cold. He hadn't been in bed for hours ... if at all. She checked her iPhone on the nightstand for the time. It was a little after 6 A.M. Kate slipped out from under the heavy comforter and padded barefoot into the living room.

Nick was working at his laptop and making notes by hand on a yellow legal pad. There was an open Paris map, a half-empty pot of coffee, and a crinkled-up Toblerone wrapper beside the laptop.

"What are you doing?" Kate asked.

"Plotting a crime."

"You never came to bed."

"No. You instantly fell asleep so I drank the coffee and came in here to work. I couldn't stop thinking about stealing the smallpox. There was too much I didn't know. So I started doing some research. The institute comprises half a dozen buildings. They are patrolled 24/7 by armed security guards and covered by hundreds of cameras, inside and out. Every door is locked, and they require a card key to open, even the broom closets and bathrooms."

"That's not surprising." Kate went into the kitchen to make fresh coffee. The kitchen had a cast-iron stove, a farmhouse sink, butcher-block countertops, and a coffee maker so elaborate that Kate thought it might be capable of cold fusion. It was too daunting to even think about using it. What was the point of having a rustic old kitchen if he was going to put that appliance on the counter?

"There's more," Nick said. "To get to the biocontainment labs, you not only need a card key, but you have to pass a fingerprint scan and retina scan at every stage. There are at least eight doors to pass through before you finally get to a seat in front of a microscope."

"Do you have any instant coffee?" Kate asked.

"I have rat poison," he said. "It's probably tastier. I'll make you an espresso in a minute."

Kate opened the refrigerator and surveyed the contents while Nick continued his briefing.

"The labs are also under constant video surveillance and are protected by an array of high-tech gizmos, including motion detectors and infrared sensors," Nick said. "I was wrong. A biocontainment lab is even better protected than a diamond vault."

"You like a challenge," Kate said.

The refrigerator was filled with various cheeses, several paper-wrapped packages of butcher-sliced meat, a packet of smoked salmon, and some eggs. There were grapes, mushrooms, carrots, asparagus, and green peppers in the drawers. It all looked like too much work for breakfast. She'd have traded it all for Folgers crystals and Cocoa Krispies.

"But I've got some good news," Nick said.

She closed the refrigerator and looked back at him. "You have Cap'n Crunch?"

"The labs have independent air flow and exhaust systems separate from the rest of the building to keep any viruses from escaping. As an extra precaution, the labs are all underground and practically encased in concrete."

She gave up on food and drink, took a seat in a chair beside him. "Why is that good news?"

"Because the metro, the sewer, the city aqueduct, and the catacombs all run under the place Denfert-Rochereau."

"The 'catacombs'?"

"Abandoned limestone quarries under the city that are filled with the bones of millions of dead Parisians that were unearthed from cemeteries over the centuries," Nick said. "Part of it is a popular tourist attraction."

"My God."

"They used to give boat tours of the sewers, too."

"Makes me wonder what Paris Disneyland is like."

"The point is, the ground underneath the institute is a maze of tunnels. We can dig our way into the lab."

"Do you know where to find the lab and the smallpox?"

"Nope, that's top secret. The institute isn't supposed to have smallpox. We'll never find out where it is."

"I'm sure you'll come up with a way to find it," Kate said. "In the meantime, I'll run into town and get us some Pop-Tarts."

"They don't have Pop-Tarts here," Nick said. "They have fresh croissants and baguettes."

"You really are out in the boonies. It's a good thing Paris is only a thirty-minute train ride away."

"I thought you were giving up the microwave for me."

"I never said that and, besides, you don't microwave Pop-Tarts," Kate said. "How can you be a criminal mastermind and not know that? They are a tasty toaster treat."

"Forget about Pop-Tarts," Nick said. "I've got the plot all worked out. It doesn't matter where the lab is, or where they keep the smallpox, because we don't need to know any of that to pull off this heist."

"Maybe I'm tired, and in desperate need of caffeine and sugar, but I think I'm missing something," Kate said. "How can we break into a lab and steal the smallpox if we don't know where the lab or the smallpox are?"

"Because we're not tunneling into the lab." Nick pulled over his Paris map and circled a building next door to the institute on avenue Denfert-Rochereau. "We're going to tunnel in here."

Kate looked at the map. The building wasn't labeled. "What's in there?"

"It was a terrible Indian restaurant for a while," Nick said. "Before that it was a travel agency. Now it's vacant and available for rent. But soon there's going to be a world-class level-four biocontainment lab in the basement."

Now it was all becoming clear to Kate, and she couldn't help smiling at the beauty of the con. "We're going to break into a fake lab and steal fake smallpox."

"That's the idea," he said.

"It's so wonderfully simple." How did he come up with that so fast? It was one of the things about him that used to aggravate the hell out of her when she was trying to arrest him.

"It's not quite as simple as it sounds," he said. "To succeed, we have to pull off a dangerous balancing act that could go wrong in a thousand different ways."

"Creating the fake lab is the kind of thing we've done before," Kate said. "We've got a crew we know can do it."

"The trick isn't building the set, it's making the Road Runners, a group of very smart professional thieves, believe that they're tunneling into the real lab and that the smallpox is genuine," Nick said.

"The heist needs to feel completely authentic in every way. Not just the work itself, but the palpable risk, the ever-present sense of danger. We have to create a totally immersive physical and emotional experience. One false note and it's over."

"So where do we start?"

"With omelets and espresso."

14

Uber driver Gaëlle Rochon was on her way to pick up a couple at the Parc des Buttes-Chaumont. She thought this was a charming name for what was once an abandoned limestone quarry used as a garbage dump and a pit for dead horses. In 1867, the putrid site was transformed into a popular Paris park, a romantic landscape painting come to life with a faux Roman temple atop a lushly landscaped, dramatic peak on a mountain in the center of an artificial lake. When Gaëlle looked at that lake, she imagined the dead horses floating just below the surface.

Of course, she'd always been more interested in what lay beneath Paris, and in the city's past rather than its present. It was her father's fault. The widower had spent his life as an *égoutier,* a worker in the sewers, pushing muck along the channels with his ever-present *rabot,* a pole with an angled paddle at the end. On nights and weekends, he and his beloved precocious daughter explored the secret world of the catacombs. When her father died five years ago, she followed his final wishes and scattered his ashes in the ossuary beneath place Denfert-Rochereau. Now, when she wasn't driving the streets of Paris, she spent every free moment wandering the two hundred miles of forbidden catacombs beneath them, the sewers, subways, canals, quarries, and crypts that made up the underworld. She was twenty-seven years old, five foot three, blond, and slim. Maintaining her weight was important for crawling through some of the tight tunnels between chambers without getting stuck.

She knew her way around Paris much better from below than she did from above, except when it came to the nineteenth arrondissement, where Parc des Buttes-Chaumont was located. This was her neighborhood, and this Uber pickup was her first of the day. She pulled up to the park's entry gate at place Armand Carrel in her rented Peugeot 508 sedan and got out to greet her clients.

Gaëlle wore a gray pantsuit and an open-collared white shirt so that she looked more like a personal chauffeur than a taxi driver.

The stylish young couple, obviously Americans, immediately double-checked her identity from her photo and the make of the car that popped up on the Uber app on the man's iPhone. She opened the back door of the Peugeot for them in the meantime.

"Good afternoon," she said. "Where can I take you?"

"*Au Vieux Campeur, 48 rue des Écoles, s'il vous plait,*" the man said.

"*Oui, monsieur.*" He got extra points from Gaëlle for having a perfect French accent.

She knew Au Vieux Campeur well. It was a sporting goods shop that sold a lot of the equipment that *cataphiles* like her needed to explore the underground. The store was in the heart of Saint-Germain on the Left Bank, which was great news, because getting there would take the couple past a lot of Paris highlights, like the Pompidou Centre and Notre Dame, and that usually led to a more generous tip. She got behind the wheel and headed west on rue Armand Carrel.

"My name is Nick, and this is Kate," the man said in English.

"Nice to meet you," Gaëlle said.

"We're thrilled to meet you, too, Gaëlle," Kate said. "We're looking forward to you showing us around after we do some shopping."

"Are you interested in a city tour?" Gaëlle asked them.

"Definitely," Kate said.

"I can show you the sites, but I have to warn you, I'm not a tour guide," Gaëlle said. "You'll get better details from your guidebook."

"Not for the catacombs," Nick said. "We'd like to see what lies beneath Paris."

She eyed him suspiciously in her rearview mirror. Who were these two? How did they know she was a *cataphile*?

"There's a tour of *les catacombes* ossuary at place Denfert-Rochereau," she said. "I can drop you off out front. Tickets are twelve euro. I can pick you up at the exit on rue Rémy Dumoncel when your tour is over."

"We want to see more than the bones," Kate said. "We'd like to get a feel for the catacombs as a whole, the entire network of subways, sewers, quarry galleries, and access tunnels under Denfert-Rochereau."

"What makes you think I know anything about that?" Gaëlle asked.

"Because you were practically raised down there, and the sewer workers are like your family," Kate said. "That's why the police and the agents of the Inspection Générale des Carrières turn a blind eye to your trespassing. Anybody else who spent as much time down there as you do would have been put in jail or bankrupted with fines by now."

It was obvious to Gaëlle now that it was no coincidence they'd ordered an Uber pickup at Buttes-Chaumont Park. They knew she'd be the closest Uber car because they knew that's where she lived.

They were waiting for her. That creeped her out big-time.

"How do you know who I am?" she asked. "Who are you?"

"Two fun-loving, adventurous people who are very curious about the underground," Nick said. "And who have the resources to find the best person in Paris to be our guide."

"We're sorry if you feel we've invaded your privacy," Kate said. "We meant no offense or harm. We'll make up for it by paying you your day fare plus a thousand euros to take us on a guided tour of the underground."

The money was definitely enticing, but she couldn't shake the uncomfortable feeling that came from these two Americans knowing so much about her.

"I don't have the gear for it, and neither do you," Gaëlle said.

"That's why we're heading to Au Vieux Campeur," Nick said. "We'll buy whatever is needed for ourselves and for you. So you'll also be getting brand-new spelunking gear out of this on top of what we're paying you."

The deal was getting better every minute, but even so, it felt wrong, like she was betraying something sacred. The catacombs were her sanctuary.

"If you're looking for a place to take that unique Paris selfie that nobody else has to show off to your

Facebook friends, then forget it," Gaëlle said. "The real catacombs, not the cleaned-up, well-lit portion that's open to the public, are not a tourist attraction. It is a very special place that needs to be respected."

"We'll treat it like a church," Nick said.

"It's also rough and dangerous down there. There are no bathrooms, drinking fountains, or places to get a latte. The air can be dusty and foul. You'll have to crawl through some tight spaces, wade through raw sewage, and walk through unstable caverns that could collapse at any time. If you're the slightest bit claustrophobic, you will be entering hell," Gaëlle said. "It's a rugged wilderness. It's not a walk in the park."

"We can handle ourselves," Kate said.

Gaëlle glanced back at Kate and Nick and appraised them. They were fit, and there was a steely confidence in Kate's eyes. Gaëlle believed they could take care of themselves. Even so, she didn't like it.

"The spiders down there are as big as your hand and have a nasty bite," Gaëlle said. "The rats aren't afraid of people and will attack if they feel cornered. There's rat feces and urine everywhere and, if it gets in an open wound, it can kill you."

"And yet, you love it underground," Kate said.

"The catacombs are left over from underground quarrying for limestone that began in the thirteenth century and didn't end until 1860. For centuries, people have worked or sought refuge in the catacombs. There's sketches, murals, carvings, and graffiti from the Prussian war, the storming of the Bastille, the German occupation during World War II, the riots of the 1960s, every historical event you can think of and some you never heard about."

"It's a natural museum," Nick said.

"It's much more than that," Gaëlle said. "There's also the bones of six million Parisians down there, nearly three times the living population of Paris. Maybe their ghosts are there too, and that's what makes the silence so profound. It's an escape from everything, true peace. There are places so quiet, it feels as if you've escaped from your body and merged with the earth and everybody who has ever walked on it. The past is alive down there in ways no museum could ever be."

"Now you know why we picked you as our guide," Nick said. "Do we have a deal?"

"If I see you take a single selfie," Gaëlle said, "I'll smash your phone with a rock."

line built by Napoleon the Third. It followed the walls that once encircled Paris," Gaëlle said, leading them over a bridge. "It was basically abandoned in 1934, but the tunnels, stations, and tracks all still exist."

On the other end of the bridge, the cyclone fencing had been cut, creating a flap that could be pushed open. Gaëlle crouched down and climbed through. Kate and Nick followed. Gaëlle led them down the chipped concrete steps that ran alongside the graffiti-covered footings of the bridge to the tracks below.

"There are many levels to the underground," Gaëlle said as they walked along the tracks. "The sewers, aqueducts, and metro lines are closest to the surface at thirty to fifty feet below. There are some church crypts, utility tunnels, and underground garages that go just as deep. The limestone quarries and ossuaries are fifty to ninety feet below the streets and are interconnected by Inspection Générale des Carrières, or IGC, access tunnels. The IGC monitors the below-ground quarries for public hazards like extraordinary contamination or possible collapse."

The embankment seemed to get deeper as they walked, and the streets above began to fade away in the upper periphery of Kate's vision. The weedy, rusty tracks and the overgrown plants on either side of her made it easy to imagine they were in a postapocalyptic world where nature had taken back everything that man had built. As they neared the mouth of a railway tunnel, Kate realized that there were no longer any buildings around, only trees and dense shrubs, and that the street noise was nearly gone.

"Where are we?" she asked.

"Parc Montsouris," Gaëlle said and stopped in front of the railroad tunnel. "Time to suit up."

She unzipped her backpack and put on her gloves, helmet, and kneepads. Nick and Kate did the same.

Gaëlle flicked her helmet light on and walked into the dark tunnel. The walls were covered with graffiti, and the air was heavy with the stench of urine and stale beer. The floor of the tunnel was littered with mattresses and discarded cans and bottles. Midway down the tunnel, Gaëlle stopped in front of a piece of plywood wedged up against the wall near her feet.

"There are many ways into the catacombs. You can get in through basements, parking garages, metro tunnels, sewer lines, and manholes. We are already forty feet below street level here, so this saved us a descent." She slid the plywood aside to reveal a jagged hole cut into the stone, barely large enough for a person to fit through. "Go in feetfirst and drag your pack in behind you. Watch your head when you get up."

She took a rag from her pocket and tied it in a knot around her neck.

"What's that for?" Kate asked.

"Habit and tradition," Gaëlle said. "The sewer men began wearing these knotted rags centuries ago to protect themselves from the biting spiders that can drop on them. But mostly I do it because I'd feel naked without it under there."

Terrific, Kate thought. Biting spiders. How fun was that?

Gaëlle climbed in, followed by Nick and then Kate. It was a tight fit, opening to a passage that was barely three feet high. They walked in a crouch for about twenty yards, their helmets scraping against the stones sticking out of the ceiling, before they reached an intersection with another corridor where they could stand upright. The walls in this corridor were a mix of carved rock and stacked stone reinforcement.

Gaëlle stopped and pointed to an engraved plate in the wall that read *Avenue d'Orleans*. "In many places, the names of the streets above are engraved in the walls."

"By whom?" Nick asked.

"Miners, sewer workers, smugglers, resistance fighters, the IGC doing inspections, or just somebody handy with a hammer and pick," Gaëlle said. "You'll find signs here going back centuries. This is an old one. Avenue d'Orleans was changed in 1948 to avenue du Général Leclerc. It's easy to find your way around in the sewers. For every street in Paris, there is a matching sewer underneath, right down to the street signs on the corners."

They entered a corridor with knee-high water and sloshed through it for a while until they reached some dry tunnels that spilled out into a series of larger caverns, all covered with artwork. Sculpted gargoyles peered out at them from one cavern. In another, limestone pillars sculpted to look like people holding up the earth.

"How often do the police patrol down here?" Nick asked.

"Police patrols are limited," Gaëlle said. "And there's a lot of ground to cover. Since the Paris terrorist attacks, the police are less interested in writing tickets for trespassing than making sure nobody puts a bomb under the Louvre. So they tend to patrol under important buildings now."

"Can we turn off the lights?" Kate asked. "I'd like to see the darkness and hear the silence."

They turned their helmet lights off and then the lanterns. The blackness that came was the most complete Kate had ever experienced. The only sound she heard was their breathing.

They turned their lights back on and Gaëlle led them out of the cavern, down a long, low corridor, and across another gallery and into one of the many tunnels. She stopped in front of a chest-high hole cut in the wall. The hole was about the size of a doggy door. When they emerged on the other side of the hole they were standing in a river of dry human bones that rose as high as Kate's ankle. The floor of the entire corridor, as far as their headlamps could reveal, was covered with bones.

"You get used to it," Gaëlle said, heading on down the tunnel. "After a while, you forget they are bones."

Kate and Nick followed Gaëlle out of the ossuary, up a ladder of iron rungs embedded in the wall, to another level. This was a more modern passage, finished in smooth concrete and lined with all kinds of pipes, wires, and electrical conduits.

"This is a telecom and utility corridor," Gaëlle said. "Built about thirty years ago, but workmen are always down here, adding new lines for cable television, high-speed Internet, whatever. You'll also find cables like these running through some of the ossuaries."

"In case the dead want to check their email," Nick said. "Or binge on *The Walking Dead*."

"I've done both," Gaëlle said.

"I thought you came down here for the solitude," Kate said.

"Not always," Gaëlle said. "Sometimes I just want to relax, watch a movie, and really crank up the sound, so I bring down my laptop and hijack a movie off one of the cables. The acoustics down here are great."

"You're not worried about anyone hearing you?" Nick asked.

"We're under thirty feet or more of limestone. You could bring a band down here for a concert and nobody will hear a thing."

They went down several intersecting utility corridors, some of them lit by lights on the walls, until they came to a door that looked like a watertight hatch from a submarine. Gaëlle spun the wheel, opened the heavy door, and they stepped into a wide, arched chamber with a river of sewage running down the center. The smell wasn't as a bad as Kate had expected. It wasn't much worse than a men's locker room. A blue plaque with white letters on the wall read *Boulevard Saint-Jacques*.

"This is one of the sewer lines," Gaëlle said. "The sewer men walk along the side paths with paddle tools to move the muck along. Or a bunch of men will drag a sluice boat through the center channel with ropes to do the job. The work hasn't really changed in centuries."

They walked along the concrete banks, which were dimly lit every few feet by industrial lights on the wall. Gaëlle pointed out the huge pipes above them that carried freshwater and a series of tubes that used to be part of the post office's vast abandoned pneumatic network for delivering letters to buildings by compressed air.

They crossed a bridge over the sewer channel to a ladder built into the wall that went up about twenty feet into a circular shaft. Kate looked up and saw a pinhole of sunlight streaming through a manhole cover.

Gaëlle climbed up the shaft, moved the manhole cover aside, and they were bathed with sunlight and blasted with noise. Kate and Nick followed Gaëlle up and found themselves standing on the sidewalk of boulevard Saint-Jacques, facing place Denfert-Rochereau and the Lion of Belfort. Kate had to squint and hold a hand up to shade her eyes. The sunlight seemed unusually harsh after the pitch-darkness of the underground.

"I brought you up here because this spot is unique," Gaëlle said and pointed to the train station across the street. "That's the regional rapid transit system line, the RER. There's also a metro station here, a subway line, the sewers, an aqueduct, utility corridors, and, below it all, the catacombs. All the levels of the underground world come together here. It also used to be the entrance to Paris. It's a short walk back to the car from here, or we can go through the sewer instead."

Kate wanted the fresh air but the sewer would

give them more privacy for the conversation they still needed to have. "Let's take the sewer."

Gaëlle seemed surprised by the answer, but shrugged and headed back into the manhole. "As you wish."

Kate followed her down, and Nick brought up the rear, sliding the manhole cover back into place behind them. They walked alongside Gaëlle on the concrete banks to the sewer underneath place Denfert-Rochereau, then crossed a metal bridge to follow the line that ran under avenue du Général Leclerc.

"We didn't ask you to show us the underground out of idle curiosity or for the unusual experience," Kate said.

"I assumed there was more to it," Gaëlle said.

"Nick and I are operatives for an international private security company, and we've been hired to prevent a biological attack on the United States. The group that's planning this attack intends to steal the killer virus for their weapon from a basement lab at the Institut National pour la Recherche sur les Maladies Infectieuses."

"On Denfert-Rochereau," Gaëlle said, putting the pieces together. "They're going to dig their way in."

"They are and they aren't," Nick said. "We've infiltrated the group to trick them into breaking into a fake lab in the basement of another building on the same street. We need you to help us fool them."

"What could I do?" she asked.

"You'd be their guide. You'd lead them to the dig site by a different route each day, supposedly to avoid attracting attention, but really just to confuse them," Nick said. "We could also switch out some of the street signs underground to add to their confusion."

"After what we've experienced today," Kate said, "I don't think confusing them is going to be that hard."

"If what you are saying is true," Gaëlle said, "why is a private security firm stopping this terrorist attack and not the police? Who hired you?"

"We can't tell you who our client is," Kate said. "But I can say that we're often hired because we can ignore laws, jurisdictions, and national borders that restrict the ability of law enforcement agencies and governments to do their jobs."

"We aren't accountable to taxpayers, either, and have very deep pockets," Nick said. "We'll pay you a hundred thousand euros to help us."

Gaëlle stopped and stared at him. "How much?"

"One hundred thousand euros."

She kept staring at him. "*Mon Dieu. Vraiment?*"

"*Oui,*" Nick replied.

"Before you get seduced by the money," Kate said, "you need to know that what we are asking you to do is extremely dangerous. You'll be undercover among killers. We'll be there with you, and we'll do our best to protect you, but we can't guarantee your safety."

Gaëlle narrowed her eyes. "How do I know you're who you say you are?"

"You don't," Kate said. "You'd have to trust us."

"Two complete strangers that I just met," Gaëlle said. "Telling a pretty fantastical story."

"That's right," Kate said.

"But once you're involved, you'll see the inner workings of the con and the time, effort, and expense that's going into it," Nick said. "It will be immediately clear to you that we couldn't be doing anything else except what we say we are."

"There will also be nothing stopping you at any time from walking away or going to the police or telling the bad guys who we are," Kate said. "So the trust works both ways. We'll be trusting you with our lives and those of our team."

"You have other people involved in this?" Gaëlle said.

"People we've recruited for their special skills," Kate said. "Just like you."

Gaëlle thought about it for a long moment. "I haven't done much with my life. I just drive people around and wander through dark tunnels, lost in the past or myself. What good has it been? What have I achieved? If I can use that experience to save lives, then everything I've done up until now has actually meant something. So yes, I'll help you, and I'll take your money, too."

Nick shook her hand. "Welcome to the team."

others steered clear of him. Huck was an average-looking forty-four-year-old man, slightly pudgy and perhaps a little too pale, wearing a ragged Musée de Florentiny T-shirt with a faded picture of Rembrandt's *Old Man Eating Bread by Candlelight* on the back. So he fit right in. The place was full of hipsters in fashionably vintage clothes and stylishly torn jeans.

After twelve years employed as a sewer engineer for Hydro-Québec, Huck had acquired a faint, but persistent, *l'air du poop* that wouldn't go away, no matter how much he showered nor how many gallons of Old Spice that he put on. It was also why he hadn't been laid in six years, except for a merciful prostitute who'd had a raging head cold.

It was a sad, pitiful situation that would have destroyed the self-respect of most men. But Huck Moseby wasn't most men. He took strength from the secret knowledge that he was a criminal genius. A few years ago, he'd committed the biggest robbery in Canadian history, tunneling into the Musée de Florentiny from the sewer to steal their entire collection of masterworks. Problem was there were two other robbers, a man and woman in ski masks, who coincidentally were already in the museum stealing the Rembrandts. The couple wouldn't let him have a Rembrandt or anything else, sending him back into his hole at gunpoint with only a Musée de Florentiny T-shirt to show for his brilliance and months of toil. The other thieves got the paintings, the glory, and even the credit for tunneling in, though he had no idea how they'd actually entered the museum. The paintings were recovered, but the two thieves were never caught.

It was because of that life-defining event that he wore the T-shirt almost constantly and wouldn't buy a new one even though they were still sold, in a variety of sizes and colors, at the Musée de Florentiny gift shop. The T-shirt was his armor against the indignities he had to endure each day.

He was taking a bite out of his thick sandwich when an attractive couple in their thirties sat down across from him at the table. He chewed and silently counted off the five seconds it usually took for his scent to travel across a tabletop and for the couple to awkwardly depart. Ten seconds passed, and they were still sitting there, perusing their menus while presumably awash in his *odor d'égout*.

"I've never seen a Jewish deli with a menu in French," the man said.

"I guess you aren't as worldly as you think you are," the woman said.

Huck felt a strange chill. There was something both sexy and familiar about her voice.

"We never got around to visiting this place on our last trip to Montreal," the man said.

"We were in a bit of a hurry," the woman said, and abruptly met Huck's gaze, startling him.

He'd never seen her face, but he was certain that he'd looked into those striking blue eyes before.

"Please tell me you've washed that shirt since we gave it to you," Kate said to Huck.

Huck dropped his sandwich on his plate and felt his heart drop along with it. *It was them.* The thieves who'd robbed the museum of their Rembrandts and him of his glory.

"It's you," Huck said, knowing the words were lame the moment he'd said them. "The two thieves who stole those paintings from me."

"They weren't yours," Kate said, "though they might have been if you'd got the drop on us instead of us getting the drop on you."

"It just wasn't your lucky day," Nick said.

"It wasn't fair," Huck said. "You got the Rembrandts. You could have let me take a Matisse or a Renoir. You were leaving them behind anyway."

"We were on our way out and wanted to make a clean getaway," Kate said. "We couldn't take the risk that you'd accidentally activate an alarm or otherwise alert the authorities."

"But you're right," Nick said. "It wasn't very gracious of us. We've been troubled by it ever since."

"Really?" Huck said.

He was flattered that they'd given him any thought

at all. Somehow, it made him seem part of the fraternity of master thieves. But then he reminded himself of how they'd humiliated him and quickly changed his tone and demeanor.

"Troubled?" Huck said. "Is that how you felt rolling in your millions while I slept in this crummy T-shirt?"

Kate's eyebrows inched up. "You sleep in that shirt?"

"Figuratively speaking. The point is, I thought there was supposed to be honor among thieves, and you two showed none."

"You're right," Nick said. "We disrespected you. That's why we're here, to make amends."

"Are you going to give me a million or two?" Huck asked and picked up his pickle. "If not, you can shove this pickle up your ass and leave."

"We want to make it up to you by bringing you in on a heist that requires your unique expertise," Nick said.

The man who'd stolen the Rembrandts from the Musée de Florentiny was coming to Huck Moseby for his expertise. That was even better than a million dollars. It confirmed everything Huck believed about himself and that had sustained him for so long. He really was a criminal genius.

Huck leaned forward and whispered, "What's the caper?"

Kate leaned toward him and instantly thought better of it. He really did smell bad. "Are you familiar with the Road Runners?"

Of course he was. "They are international diamond thieves, maybe the best in the world."

"We're working with them, but we're going after something more valuable than diamonds," Kate said. "We're stealing a biological agent from a high-security research lab in central Paris. We're tunneling into the lab through the sewers. It's extremely dangerous and if we're caught, we'll be spending our lives in a French prison."

"That's why we need Huck Moseby," Nick said. "You're a professional sewer engineer, an experienced excavator, a world-class thief, and you can pass as French. You were born for this job."

Huck was still reeling from being called a world-class thief. He went deaf and numb for a moment. He didn't listen to what else Nick had said, but after that clear acknowledgment of his talent, he was on board for anything.

"What is it you need me to do?" Huck asked.

"Lead the excavation team and get us inside the lab," Nick said. "You're the best sewer man in the game."

He had a reputation? He was in the game? He was THE BEST? Why hadn't anyone told him? That knowledge, that recognition, would have made the last few years so much different. Somebody should have sent him a certificate or something.

Huck leaned even closer, almost upending the table. He wanted to be sure he was hearing this right and not having a delusional episode. "Let me get this straight. You want me to go to Paris and lead the Road Runners in a dig through the sewers into a high-security laboratory."

"That's right," Nick said, leaning back. "And we'll pay you a hundred thousand dollars to do it."

Huck took a deep swig of his cherry soda, wishing that it was something stronger, even though alcohol gave him tremendous gas.

He couldn't believe what he'd just heard. The people who'd pulled off the biggest robbery in Canadian history wanted to pay him $100,000 to lead the best thieves on earth in a subterranean heist in the most magnificent sewer in the world. It was all he could do not to cry with joy. But that wouldn't be fitting behavior for a world-class thief. So instead he cleared his throat, sat back, and pondered his soft drink can as if he were actually struggling with the decision.

"Who will I be working for?" Huck asked.

"Me," Nick said.

"Who are you?"

"I'm Nicolas Fox and this is my associate, Kate. You get us inside and we'll do the rest."

Huck's jaw dropped, and he covered up his shock

by reaching for his sandwich as if he'd opened his mouth to prepare for a bite. He took a mouthful of smoked meat and used the chewing time to get a grip. Nicolas Fox was a legend. Huck was going to be among the greats.

"You'll be calling the shots underground," Nick said. "You know sewers and excavation and we don't. You'll be working with a local expert on the Paris underground. She will be your number two."

A woman in the sewer. This job was getting better every second. He nodded as he chewed and tried to swallow.

"Your crew will be as many Road Runners as you think are necessary," Nick said. "These are smash-and-grab guys, not diggers, so you'll have to show them the ropes. We'll all be meeting in Paris in seven days for a recon. After that, you'll give me a list of what you need, we'll get it, and then we'll go to work."

"Assuming you're interested, of course," Kate said. "We'd completely understand if you're not. You could die of old age in a French prison that makes Devil's Island look like Club Med."

Huck swallowed, and picked a piece of meat out of his front teeth. He didn't want to appear too eager in front of Nicolas Fox.

"I've got a number of ambitious capers in the

cooker here that I can put on hold," Huck said, "but not for a hundred grand."

"How much do you want?"

He was the best sewer man in the game and deserved compensation commensurate with his talent, but he didn't want to let this dream slip through his fingers. "One hundred and twenty-five thousand, all expenses paid, and first-class airfare."

"You drive a hard bargain," Nick said.

"I'm a hard man," Huck said.

He actually was. All this talk of his expertise was better than Viagra, not that he needed it or had any opportunity to put the results to work. But that would change now that he was a master thief. Women would sense his magnificence and flock to him.

Nick glanced at Kate. She gave him a slight nod. Nick smiled and held his hand out to Huck.

"We have a deal," Nick said and got up. "We'll be in touch."

They walked out and Huck was alone again at an empty table, left to wonder if it had all been a figment of his imagination.

"I'm still not comfortable with this," Kate said as they left Huck in Schwartz's and walked down boulevard Saint-Laurent to their rented Porsche Cayenne parked a block away.

"Yes, I know. I noticed how hard you were trying to dissuade him."

"Huck doesn't realize it, but, when we first met him, we saved him from a life of crime and likely imprisonment. Now we've sucked him back into it."

"Not if we don't arrest him," Nick said.

"But we're paying him to commit a crime."

"We're paying everybody in our crew to do that."

"But they are doing it for the right reasons."

"We can't tell Huck that we're conning the Road Runners to prevent a terrorist attack," Nick said. "Huck has to believe in what he's doing to convince the Road Runners that this is real. He's a key part of creating that authenticity I was talking about."

"Is that why you told him who you are?"

"The Road Runners know who I am, that means he has to as well. Besides, it also bolsters our position with Dragan and the Road Runners. He can attest that you and I pulled off the biggest heist in Canadian history."

"We told Gaëlle Rochon about the con."

"Because we need her to confuse the Road Runners underground so they won't figure out they aren't actually digging underneath the institute," Nick said. "She wouldn't have helped if she thought we were real thieves, and Huck won't help us if he knows that we aren't."

"He might have for the money and the thrill."

"Maybe, but it's too risky. It goes back to the authenticity we're trying to create. The Road Runners have to believe that Gaëlle knows her way through the underworld, and that it's as much of a maze as we say it is," Nick said. "That will come through naturally. It doesn't require her to act. Huck can't act. He could barely stop himself from crying when we offered him the job. If Huck knew he wasn't really digging into a real lab, he'd show it. By us not telling Huck, his enthusiasm and determination will be real."

"Okay, but what happens if Huck comes back here after this is over, convinced that he's 'the best sewer man in the game' and starts looking for a museum to rob?"

"He'll be so terrified by the way this heist ultimately turns out that he'll never want to commit a crime again," Nick said. "He'll thank God that he got out alive and with his hundred and twenty-five thousand dollars."

"I hope you're right," Kate said as they reached their car. "Because I don't want his next heist and his eventual imprisonment on my conscience."

"Let's just survive this job first," Nick said, unlocking the car and walking around to the driver's side.

"Good point."

"If I'm wrong about Huck, I promise you that we'll come up with a way to scare him straight."

"You also need to talk to Gaëlle and caution her against talking to Huck."

They got into the car and headed for the airport, where they had a private jet waiting to take them to Los Angeles.

17

Boyd Capwell ran across an open field in Ojai, California. He was being pursued by half a dozen bug-eyed bald women in halter tops and cutoffs. The women were running with their arms outstretched and their gnarled hands clawing at the air in front of them as if it might bring Boyd closer to their drooling, wide-open, shrieking mouths.

He was racing for the forest and freedom when more of the mutant women poured out from between the trees like a tidal wave, screeching their insane, lusty cry as they charged toward him. There was no place for him to go. He was surrounded.

Boyd dropped to his knees, a beaten man, and looked up to the sky. Tears streamed down his chiseled anchorman's face, his fists were balled up with rage.

"Why, God, why? What have I done to deserve your pitiless wrath?"

The sky rumbled, as if God were clearing his throat to speak, and out of the blue heavens came the Hellcopter. An airborne gunship that looked like a flying great white shark sheathed in cannons, machine guns, harpoons, and missiles.

The Hellcopter swooped down low, its machine guns spitting hot death, mowing down the mutant women. Boyd stood up to face the Hellcopter as it landed. The pilot's door opened and out came Willie Owens, boobs first. Her enormous breasts strained against a tight, nearly transparent white T-shirt. Besides the double-D silicone boobs, collagen-plumped lips, and peroxide blond hair, there was nothing mutant about the woman in the Daisy Duke shorts and pumps. She was all woman and proud of it.

Willie strutted up to Boyd, tore open his shirt, buttons flying, and appraised his body, which wasn't bad for a guy in his forties who didn't exercise.

"Finally, a real man," she said.

"Finally, a real woman," he said.

He reached for her breasts, and she kicked him in the knee.

"Cut!" Boyd yelled, clutching his knee.

Nick Fox turned to Chet Kershaw, a big bear of a man in his early forties with a professional makeup bag slung over his shoulder. Nick and Chet were standing together out in a field, under a tent that covered a bank of monitors. The monitors showed various angles on the action. Kate O'Hare and Tom Underhill, an African American man in his thirties with a tool belt around his waist, were in the tent, too. Tom was holding a remote control joystick to pilot a drone with a tiny GoPro camera attached to it. They were watching the live stream of the GoPro's video on one of the monitors.

"Was that kick in the script?" Nick asked.

"Nope," Chet said.

Chet was the last in a family dynasty of Hollywood makeup artists and special effects masters adept at all the live, "on set" magic in front of the cameras that was now primarily done digitally in postproduction.

"That was my favorite part," Kate said.

"Mine, too," Tom said, landing the drone beside the tent.

Tom's day job was making inventive playhouses, tree houses, and other fanciful structures. He'd retrofitted the old helicopter, which Nick had acquired for a past scam, into a fake Hellcopter combat vehicle for this film.

Willie marched over to them, Boyd trailing after her, limping. She was a fifty-something single Texan with a natural affinity and dangerous zeal for driving or piloting just about anything on land, sea, or air with a motor.

Joe Morey was right behind them, a Steadicam rig strapped to his upper body to hold a digital camera.

He was an electronic security and alarm systems expert who excelled in hidden video and audio surveillance.

"Why did you kick me?" Boyd yelled at her. "You killed the emotion of the scene."

"Because you tried to cop a feel," Willie said. "That's not going to happen."

"I wasn't 'copping a feel,'" Boyd said. "My character was reaching out to touch the humanity that he thought he'd lost."

"It was you using this movie as an excuse to feel me up," Willie said. "Something you've wanted to do for years."

"It's acting," Boyd said. "Didn't you read the script?"

"Which you wrote so you could touch my tits."

"Which I wrote to showcase your talent as a pilot, Chet's talent as a makeup and visual effects artist, Tom's talent as an imagineer, Joe's talent with cameras and sound, and my skills as triple-threat multi-hyphenate writer, actor, and director." Boyd looked back at Joe, who seemed startled to be seen. "Why are you still shooting? Didn't you hear me say 'cut'?"

"This is for the behind-the-scenes documentary," Joe said.

"Turn it off," Boyd said, then called back to the two dozen barely dressed, bloodied mutant women in the field. "Take five, but stay where you are. We're going to do a pickup on that last bit of dialogue, and we don't want to screw up the background continuity."

"What are you guys shooting here?" Nick asked.

"A short film we can use as an industry calling card," Chet said. "We'll post it on YouTube, Vimeo, IMDb, places like that. It's what you've got to do to get jobs in Hollywood these days."

"We've all done our best work with you two," Boyd said. "But we can't exactly use you as a reference or show our reel, can we?"

"I see your point," Nick said and turned to Joe. "I didn't know that you had Hollywood aspirations."

"I don't," Joe said. "I'm a single, hot-blooded man and I know my way around cameras and mikes. When Boyd told me he needed a camera and sound guy, and that there'd be a dozen strippers running around half-naked in front of me, how could I say no?"

"I see what you mean," Nick said.

Kate looked out at the women lounging in the field, smoking cigarettes, checking their emails, and snapping selfies. "They're strippers?"

"Who else would play these parts?" Willie said.

"This production must have cost a fortune," Nick said.

"You've paid us a fortune," Boyd said. "Unfortunately, we can't count on you for future employment. Work with you is unpredictable at best, and we've got our muses to serve. So we've reinvested some of our earnings in our own potential."

"I'm surprised you're doing another zombie flick," Nick said to Chet. "I thought you were tired of the genre."

"Those aren't zombies," Chet said.

"They sure look like hungry zombies to me," Kate said.

"It's lust," Chet said. "They don't want to eat Boyd. They want to screw him."

"Good grief," Kate said. "Why would they all want to do that?"

"My character is the last man on earth," Boyd said. "Germ warfare has turned people into sex-crazed mutants. The mutant men are sterile but the women are not. They need me, the last real man, to repopulate our planet and keep our race from going extinct."

"Of course they do," Kate said. "So what's stopping you from giving all those women what they want?"

"They're hideous," Boyd said. "I can't mate with them."

"Because of their appearance?" Kate said.

"Would you want the next evolution of the human race to look like that?" Boyd said. "My character is a reluctant Adam searching for a still human, still hot, postapocalyptic Eve."

Willie raised her hand. "That's me."

"So if you understand that," Boyd said, "why did you ruin the dramatic and emotional payoff to the whole story?"

"You mean the money shot?" Willie said.

"I mean the passionate salvation of the human race."

"Funny you should bring that up," Nick said. "That's kind of why we're here."

"I didn't think this was just a friendly visit," Tom said. "But aren't you being a bit melodramatic?"

"Unfortunately, he's not," Kate said. They were out of earshot of the strippers, but she lowered her voice to a near whisper as an extra precaution. "We need your help to prevent a biological attack on an American city by overseas terrorists."

"Wait a sec," Joe said. "Isn't that a job for Homeland Security, the CIA, or the U.S. military, and not some high-end private security firm?"

Chet laughed at Joe. "You honestly believe that's who they work for? These two go around the world taking down supercriminals. Have you ever thought about the money that they spend on the cons and thefts we've done together? It's millions of dollars. Who could their clients possibly be to pay that bill?

That's why I've always figured that they're really working off the books for some U.S. acronym."

"I've never cared," Willie said. "I like the fast cars and the money."

"It doesn't matter to me who they are working for," Tom said. "What matters is that I can trust them, that they're doing the right thing, and that we've put a stop to some very bad people doing very bad things." He turned to Kate. "You can count me in on this."

"I appreciate that," Kate said. "But you don't even know what the assignment is yet, what the risks are, or what we are paying. You have a family to think about."

"That's right, I do," Tom said. "That's why if there's anything I can do to stop that biological attack from happening, I will do it and I won't take a dime for it, either."

"You'll do it for God and country," Boyd said. "That's powerful motivation for a character. I know, because that's my character's motivation today."

"Your motivation today is vanity and booty," Willie said. "You've cast yourself as the last man on earth that every woman wants to screw."

"Who is saving his precious seed for your character out of his profound love for God and country," Boyd said to her, then looked back at Kate. "The point I'm trying to make is that I'm in for whatever part you want me to play in this life-or-death drama. I am an American and this country 'tis of thee."

"I'm in, too," Willie said. "Because I like kicking ass and this sounds like some ass that needs kicking."

Chet raised his hand. "Count me in."

"Me, too," Joe said.

18

A n hour later, after the movie was wrapped with Boyd's Adam and Willie's Eve locked in an embrace, they all reconvened in the barn. Boyd, Willie, Chet, Tom, and Joe sat on picnic table benches while Nick and Kate stood in front of them and briefed them on the broad strokes of the new project.

"You and Nick are such complex, conflict-ridden characters," Boyd said. "I've definitely got to play Nick in the movie."

"Wouldn't you rather play yourself?" Nick asked.

"Leonardo DiCaprio will want that part," Boyd said. "So will George Clooney, but I think he's too old to do me justice."

"Sofía Vergara without the accent would do a decent job as me," Willie said. "But she'd need to get a boob job."

"Her boobs are enormous," Chet said.

"Not enough," Willie said.

"I'll settle for any of the Hemsworths," Joe said. "I'm a dead ringer for all three of them."

"Hopefully, there will never be a movie, because if this story ever comes out, we'll all end up in jail," Kate said.

"But the FBI would get us out, right?" Tom said.

Joe gave his head a small shake. "I'm sure it's CIA."

"You're all wrong," Boyd said. "It's the Men in Black."

"No one is going to get us out of jail," Kate said.

She hoped that wasn't true, but there was no guarantee anyone could help them if things went wrong.

"Tell us about this biological attack," Boyd said. "And how my character is going to save a city."

"We've infiltrated a gang of international diamond thieves called the Road Runners," Kate said. "The group is made up almost entirely of ex-Serbian soldiers and led by a lunatic named Dragan Kovic."

"A very smart and cautious lunatic," Nick said. "They've made over four hundred million dollars from their robberies as of this week and have never been caught."

"Now we know what they were doing with all of that money," Kate said. "They've been developing a biological weapon that they will use to attack an American city. They plan to weaponize smallpox."

"My God," Tom said. "That's inhuman."

"They already have a smallpox sample, but it's not quite good enough for their purposes," Nick said. "So they want Kate and me to steal a smallpox sample for them from a research institute in Paris."

"We need to find Dragan's lab, retrieve the smallpox sample they already have, and stop them from pulling off their attack," Kate said.

"Stealing the smallpox in Paris is how we're going to do it," Nick said. "We're going to use a tracking device to follow the stolen virus back to Dragan's lab and shut them down for good."

"Aren't you taking an enormous risk?" Joe said. "What if you lose track of the smallpox and they get away with it?"

"Eliminating the risk is where the con comes in," Nick said. He looked at Chet and Tom. "You two are going to build a fake biolab in the basement of an empty storefront on the same street as the real lab."

"The Road Runners will break into a fake lab and steal fake smallpox," Kate said. "The vial itself will be the tracking device that leads us to Dragan's lab. Nick and I will be part of the Road Runners crew tunneling into the institute to steal the virus."

"We've also recruited two other people," Nick said. "Gaëlle Rochon, an expert on the Paris underground, who will be aware that it's a con, and Huck Moseby, an experienced sewer worker and tunnel digger, who won't be."

"Gaëlle's job is to lead the Road Runners around in circles so they don't know they are digging into the wrong building," Kate said. "Huck's job is to supervise the dig into the lab to steal the virus."

"I can get photos and blueprints of a real biolab," Tom said. "Building the fake lab should be easy. The critical issue is how real it has to be, and that depends on whether the Road Runners will be in the room or only seeing it on-screen."

"Same goes for dressing the lab with scientific equipment and props," Chet said. "How much of it has to actually work?"

"I will be the only one entering the lab where the smallpox is supposedly kept," Nick said. "The others won't go any further than the room that leads to it. That's the room we are going to dig into from below. So everything just has to look and sound good."

"Getting the necessary props and equipment, and making them all look like they are working, is not a problem, either," Chet said.

"In that case, if everybody kicks in to help on the construction, I can have the lab set built in a week," Tom said.

"I can dress it up as we go," Chet said.

Joe jerked a thumb at himself. "Where do I fit in?"

Nick turned to him. "We're going to recruit you

as part of the Road Runner team to compromise and control the institute's security systems."

"Your cover will be easy to remember," Kate said. "You're going to be you. Not your real name, or your real past, but you'll be demonstrating your real skills."

"I can handle that, but I still don't get what I'll be doing," Joe said. "There is no security system for me to disable because we aren't really breaking into the institute."

"Your job is to create the illusion that we are," Nick said. "Early on in the job, you will tap into the institute's actual video surveillance system and integrate our fake lab's video feed into it for our robbers to see on a monitor that we'll set up underground for them. That will convince them of our make-believe world. On the day we break into the fake lab, you'll put on a convincing show of disabling the nonexistent alarm systems."

"No problemo," Joe said.

"I'm not sure you understand the danger you're going to be in," Kate said, concerned by his enthusiasm. "You're going to be undercover with us among the thieves. You won't be on the dig, you'll be in a van or someplace else nearby. But you will be living and working with the Road Runners while straddling both sides of the operation, the break-in and the con. That's a dangerous balance to maintain. If they catch you, they will kill you."

"I get it, don't worry," Joe said. "I'll create fake software interfaces for my computer screen so even if they have a guy sitting next to me in the van, he won't be clued in to what I am doing."

"Smart move," Nick said. "Because Dragan will probably have someone with you so they can keep an eye on us."

"I only have one question," Joe said. "What are we going to be seeing on the video feed from the fake lab?"

"The scientists at work," Nick said, "and the extraordinary precautions they take as they handle and study the viruses."

"We're going to be those scientists?" Boyd asked.

"You, Willie, Chet, and Tom," Kate said. "Everybody is doing double duty on this job."

"But, Boyd, as the only professional actor among us, this crucial aspect of the con is going to rest on your shoulders," Nick said. "You need to create the world that we're breaking into. We need to feel, through the performances of your cast, how dangerous the job is for these scientists and how seriously they take the risks."

"Who are the characters?" Boyd asked. "What are their backstories? What do they want out of their lives? What personal dramas are playing out through their lab work?"

"We're counting on you to improvise that," Nick said. "It's basically a silent movie, so don't worry about dialogue. But your laboratory technique has to be absolutely accurate. I'll get you training videos. Everything depends on the authenticity of the performances you create on that set."

"It won't be the first time," Boyd said. "I was a background doctor on several episodes of *Grey's Anatomy.* I silently conferred with nurses and other doctors, comforted the loved ones of critically ill patients, and walked urgently down hallways on my way to save lives while Patrick Dempsey and Ellen Pompeo belabored their dialogue in the foreground."

"What am I driving?" Willie asked. "Because you certainly didn't bring me into this for my acting ability."

"Once the fake smallpox is on the move, you'll be driving or piloting whatever vehicles we need to follow it," Nick said. "You'll have cars, a plane, and a boat on tap. Dragan's lab could be anywhere in Europe."

"This is the critical endgame," Kate said. "If we don't find Dragan's lab and retrieve the smallpox, people will die."

Conversation stopped at the sound of a car driving

up. The engine cut off. A door slammed shut. Footsteps approached.

Cosmo Uno peered into the barn. "Knock, knock!" he said. "Am I interrupting? What are you doing? Are you making a movie? It looks like you're making a movie. Like you have movie equipment. Is this a wrap party? Am I too late?"

"Ommigod," Kate said.

Nick looked over at Kate. "Do you know him?"

"Cosmo Uno," Kate said. "He works in the cubicle next to me."

"What cubicle would that be?" Willie asked. "Pee-wee's playhouse?"

"Hah, I get that a lot," Cosmo said. "I look like Pee-wee Herman, right? Except he has better clothes. I don't know how he gets his clothes to fit him like that. They're all so tight. Where does he hide his gun, right?"

Nick turned his back to Uno and faced Kate. "If he recognizes me I'll have to kill him."

"If you kill him I'll be your sex slave," Kate said. "I'll do *anything*. I'll learn how to make an omelet, I swear."

"Promises, promises," Nick said. "Get him out of here."

Kate turned Cosmo around and steered him toward the door. "How did you find me?" she asked him.

"I pinged your cellphone and got lucky. I figured it was the perfect time for us to get together and fill out your GS205."

"Are you kidding me? A GS205?"

"I brought an extra pen."

Willie tagged after Kate and Cosmo, draped an arm over Cosmo's shoulders, and pressed her breast into him. "Honey, what's a GS205? Do I need one?"

"It itemizes civilian damages incurred during an active investigation," Cosmo said.

"I don't have any of those," Kate said.

"According to accounting you destroyed multiple cars, a fast food burger joint, a multimillion-dollar high-rise condo in London, a couple boats . . ."

"I have to itemize that?" Kate asked, mentally going through a laundry list that included the jewelry store, armored police van, a couple private residences, some "borrowed" planes, and the DVR that she still hadn't replaced.

"It's all in the manual," Cosmo said. "I have a copy in my briefcase here. Do you know there are a bunch of ladies with bald heads in the parking lot? I think they're smoking dope. One of them said she would give me a tug for five. That's a good price, right? I think she liked me."

"Does our boss know you're here?" Kate asked.

"Maybe not here precisely, but he could find me

if he wanted to because I came in a company car and they all have transponders."

"Damn," Kate said. "I was never able to get a company car. How'd *you* get one?"

"I filled out form BBB704ZX," Cosmo said.

"What kind of car is it?" Willie asked.

"It's white," Cosmo said.

Willie looked toward the open barn door. "Can I drive it?"

"No," Cosmo said. "Only people who have filled out the appropriate requisition can drive that car."

Willie leaned in, and Cosmo instinctively looked down at the triple-D nipple that was smashed against his chest.

"I'd really like to see your white car," Willie said. "I'd be *very* grateful."

"We aren't allowed to accept gratuities," Cosmo said, his eyes going a little glazed.

"Just a look," Willie said.

Cosmo was still focused on the nipple. "A look?"

Willie slipped her hand into Cosmo's pants pocket, Cosmo gave a gasp, and Willie pulled out his keys.

"Follow me," Willie said to Cosmo. "I'm going to take us for a ride."

"Maybe a *little* ride," Cosmo said, "but you'll have to fill out pedestrian form WA33."

Willie led Cosmo out of the barn, and there was the sound of car doors slamming shut. The engine turned over, and Willie spun the tires, sending gravel flying against the barn wall. The car flew past the open barn door like white lightning, and Kate heard Cosmo screaming.

"Eeeeeeeeeeeee!"

"He's from Homeland Security, right?" Chet said.

Kate did a grimace. "Meeting adjourned."

19

Jake O'Hare lived with Kate's younger sister, Megan, her husband, Roger, and their two kids in a hilltop gated community of Spanish Mediterranean–style homes in Calabasas, California. The community was located about an hour south of Ojai on the southwestern edge of the San Fernando Valley.

Megan's house had two detached two-car garages in the front. One of the garages had been converted into a *casita* for Jake with a bedroom, a bathroom, and a living room with a kitchenette.

Kate parked her Crown Vic, a used cop car that she bought at a police auction, behind Megan's new Mercedes C-Class, the Calabasas Corolla. Her arrival excited the family's Jack Russell terrier, who announced her by barking, jumping, and scratching frantically at the windowed front door.

Megan scooped up the dog and opened the door

as Kate approached. "The peripatetic daughter returns."

"'Peripatetic'?" Kate kissed her sister on the cheek, petted the dog's head, and stepped inside the house. "What's that mean?"

"It means you're constantly traveling and rarely around," Megan said, closing the door. She was three years younger than Kate, two inches taller, and a few pounds heavier. She wore a long, loose T-shirt with tight leggings and short Ugg sheepskin boots. "*Peripatetic* is one of Sara's vocabulary words at school this week. We're supposed to amalgamate them into our daily conversation to enrich our family discourse."

Megan's daughter, Sara, was nine years old, and Tyler, her son, was seven. They both went to an elementary school where Megan was president of the PTA.

"Is *amalgamate* also one of this week's words?" Kate asked.

"And also *discourse*. Pretty smooth how I worked them all in, isn't it?" Megan said, leading Kate into the kitchen. "To keep Sara sharp, we're using all of her vocabulary words in regular conversation until her big test at the end of the month."

"You're a very supportive mother," Kate said. "Where are the kids?"

Megan set the dog down. "They're in the backyard,

playing with their grandpa before they do their homework. He's peripatetic, too. He's always traveling to some reunion for ex-military guys. But I think it's just a cover."

"For what?" Kate asked, trying to sound innocent.

"Mercenary work. He comes home way too happy."

"Maybe he really enjoys reliving old times with his buddies."

"I'm sure he does," Megan said. "By shooting people and blowing things up in some third-world country. And while we're on it, you're looking pretty happy too. Things must be going well with 'Bob.' "

" 'Bob'?"

"The forbidden office romance you were contemplating last month. You obviously jumped right into it. You have the skin tone of a woman who is getting laid."

Kate held her arms out in front of her and examined her skin. "There's a skin tone for that?"

Megan held her arm out beside Kate's. "It's this one. Ever since I got my tubes tied, Roger and I can't keep our hands off each other."

"I didn't know you got your tubes tied."

"You would if you followed me on Twitter, friended me on Facebook, or kept up with my Instagram. I tweeted, updated my status, and sent out photos on my way to the operating room."

"That's why I'm not on social media. People are way too open about their private lives. I don't need to see pictures of what somebody had for lunch or hear about how difficult their last bowel movement was or see on a map where they were when either one happened."

"In today's world, if you aren't on social media, you don't exist," Megan said. "You might as well be living in a cave or a monastery."

"I prefer to pick up the phone and talk," Kate said.

"You don't do that, either," Megan said. "Probably because you're too busy with Bob?"

"I should say hello to Dad and the kids," Kate said, heading for the sliding glass door to the backyard.

"You're running away from the subject," Megan said.

"As fast as I can," Kate said and stepped outside. Megan's backyard overlooked the Calabasas Country Club golf course and the San Fernando Valley. There was a lap pool, a built-in barbecue, and a brown lawn that was slowly dying under the state-mandated water rationing brought on by the drought.

Sara and Tyler were splashing around in the pool, and Jake was watching from a lawn chair.

"Ah," he said. "Here's the peripatetic daughter."

"Sticks and stones," Kate said, pulling a chair up next to Jake. "I could use some help."

"Does it involve a rocket launcher?"

"Possibly."

"I'm there."

Kate gave her father a quick briefing on the con that she and Nick were going to mount in Paris.

"Nick and I will be on the inside with the Road Runners," Kate said. "I need someone on the outside, watching our backs and protecting our crew in case things go wrong."

"I can get some guys for that," Jake said. "I'll need a couple hundred thousand dollars for salaries, weapons, and surveillance equipment."

"It's going to be more than a babysitting job," Kate said. "The tracking device on the stolen vial of fake virus will lead us to Dragan's lair and the real virus. But once we find it, we may not have time to wait for Jessup to organize and deploy a strike team. We might have to take down Dragan and the Road Runners ourselves. That won't be easy. They are Serbian Army Special Forces veterans, and they will be very well-armed."

"I've been up against worse," Jake said. "If you want to make it a challenge, ask me to overthrow a country, too, while we're at it."

"You were younger when you were doing that."

"You think I've lost my edge?"

She shook her head no. "What I'm saying is that you did your time and came out in one piece. Now you're free to play golf, teach hand-to-hand combat to your grandchildren, and help your daughter break a thief out of a foreign prison. It's a dream retirement. You don't have to go up against a small army of trained killers anymore."

"Dragan Kovic intends to attack the United States of America with a biological weapon," Jake said. "I would be honored to die preventing that bastard from succeeding, and so would the guys I'm going to bring in on this. It's a much better way to go than sitting in a recliner watching *Matlock* and waiting for a nurse to change your diaper."

"Is that what you're afraid of?" Kate asked.

"It's one of the few things that truly terrify me."

"What are the others?"

"Outliving you." Jake looked back at Megan, who was wrapping towels around Sara and Tyler. "Or them." He thought for a beat. "And there's a lady handing out samples of cocktail wieners at Costco on Saturdays who scares the bejeezus out of me."

Kate stayed at Megan's for the rest of the afternoon but left before dinner. She drove to West Los Angeles to brief Jessup in his office at the Federal Building.

It was a twenty-mile trip that took her over an hour in bumper-to-bumper freeway traffic.

"It's a good thing we broke Nick out of jail again or we never would have known about this," Jessup said after listening to Kate's report.

"Was that decision weighing on you?"

"Like an elephant threw a saddle on me, hopped on my back, and told me to giddyup."

"That's a vivid picture."

"Not as vivid as thousands of people dying of smallpox on the streets of New York City," Jessup said. "That one is going to haunt me. We'll keep an eye out for anyone making significant investments against the market. That way we'll know if an attack is imminent."

"I hope it won't come to that," Kate said.

"Me too. I may have to go to my AA meetings twice a week until this is over to stay sober," Jessup said. "So recover the smallpox fast, get the hell out, and call me when it's done. I'll arrange for the safe pickup or disposal of the virus."

"What about Dragan and the Road Runners?" Kate said. "We need to take them down."

"Not if it's going to jeopardize the mission. The priority is stopping the bioweapon from being made or deployed. Anything else can wait."

"You can apprehend them at the same time the strike team hits the lab," Kate said.

"I can't convince the Justice Department, the Pentagon, or European authorities to authorize a military or law enforcement strike against the lab, in whatever country it ends up being in, without giving them solid evidence to justify the action," Jessup said. "I don't see how I can do that without revealing our covert operation. If I do that, they won't buy the smallpox story anyway, because the FBI will have zero credibility and I'll be in jail. Do you understand what I'm saying to you?"

"The cavalry won't be coming to our rescue."

"I'm sorry, Kate."

"Don't be, sir. I knew before I came here that you'd tell me that," Kate said. "We'll work with what we have."

"I feel like I'm sending you and Nick on a suicide mission."

"Good," Kate said. "Because if I survive, I'm asking for a raise and a company car."

"You'd have to fill out a requisition for the car," Jessup said. "It isn't worth it."

Kate went to the door and peeked outside.

"Is there a problem?" Jessup asked.

"Cosmo Uno."

"He's a good man," Jessup said. "You need him."

"Isn't it bad enough you stuck me with Nick Fox?"

"This is different. This is about paperwork. You aren't filing the necessary reports."

"I always give you a full report."

"About your covert operations with Nick. But you've fallen way behind on your routine paperwork as an FBI special agent and that could start drawing unwanted attention. The last thing we need is anyone in D.C. scrutinizing your activity because you've become sloppy with your paperwork. Be happy you have Cosmo Uno helping you out. It could keep us both out of prison."

"He's in his cubicle, isn't he?" Kate asked.

"Probably."

Kate stepped out of the office and very quietly crept down the hall. She took a circuitous route to the elevator and was almost in the clear when she heard Cosmo calling her.

"Katie! Holy cow, I can't believe it's you. I almost missed you. I bet you came in to see me. Am I right?"

Kate took off at a flat run, bypassed the elevator, and took the stairs three at a time. Cosmo was a flight of stairs behind her.

"Wait for me!" he yelled. "Did you get an emergency call? Are you gonna use your Kojak light? Do you have one? I can get you one. I can fill out form GS4781 and requisition a light for you."

Kate burst out of the stairwell, sprinted the rest of the way to her car, and took off. She stopped at a light and looked around. No Cosmo. She was in the clear.

I used to be by the book too, she thought. Although she had to admit she was never great with paperwork.

Boyd, Willie, Joe, Chet, and Tom left for Paris with Nick and Kate on a private jet out of LAX early the next morning. The in-flight entertainment was industrial videos of level-four biocontainment labs that played on the cabin's various flat screens.

The first video they watched together was a tour of a lab from the point of view of scientists entering and going to work. The scientists entered the labs through an air lock leading to a locker room, where they undressed. From there they walked naked through another air lock into the dressing room, where they put on cotton scrubs, socks, and surgical gloves. They taped the gloves and socks to their scrubs, then went through another air lock into a room that had a dozen bulky white positive pressure suits hanging from the walls and coiled blue air hoses dangling from the ceiling.

Each positive pressure suit had a huge clear wraparound visor and built-in gloves but otherwise resembled a cross between an astronaut's moonwalk suit and a wetsuit. Air nozzles with a snap coupling at the end hung like tails from each pressure suit. Once the scientists were suited up, they put on rubber boots, grabbed one of the coiled hoses from the ceiling, and snapped them to their air nozzles. The hoses rapidly inflated the suits and puffed them up.

"They look like balloons with people inside," Willie said.

"More like the Stay Puft Marshmallow Man from *Ghostbusters,*" Joe said.

"What's the point of inflating the suits like that?" Willie asked.

"If the suit gets punctured," Kate said, "air is forced out instead of sucked in, blowing out the pathogen and buying you some time to get into decontamination before you can get infected."

Kate had some understanding of dealing with deadly viruses. Her military training had prepared her for chemical warfare situations on the battlefield.

"In those suits, it will be difficult to convey our stories through body language," Boyd said. "But thanks to those large visors, we'll be able to express a lot of emotion and narrative with our faces."

"We're going to be silently squirting liquids into pipettes and squinting at viruses through microscopes," Chet said. "Where's the drama in that?"

"Because there's a small tribe in Africa that is going to be wiped out if we can't discover which variation of bird flu jumped from their chickens into their children," Boyd said. "Not just the people but an entire culture are hanging in the balance. So yes, there's drama."

"Can that actually happen?" Tom asked. "Can a chicken sneeze and infect you with something?"

"Do chickens sneeze?" Joe asked.

"Who cares?" Chet said. "We won't be talking and we're going to be in those white suits. Nobody is going to know what's going on."

"They will know the emotion," Boyd said.

Once the suits were inflated, the scientists in the video unhooked the hoses, walked through another air lock, and entered the lab, where they immediately connected their pressure suits again to coiled air hoses that hung from the ceilings.

The lab was filled with workstations, biosafety cabinets, incubators, microscopes, and centrifuges for working with pathogens, freezers for storing the pathogens, and autoclaves for sterilizing equipment. There were also cameras in every corner to allow for constant surveillance.

The scientists filed in one by one, and each went to a workstation. When a scientist walked as far as a hose could go, he unlatched the hose from his suit, set the hose on a hook overhead, then walked to the next station or piece of equipment and attached himself to a new hose there.

There was an adjacent control room, where people could observe the scientists at work and interact with them. It was separated from the lab by a large, super-thick window and an air lock. The observers could see images from the microscopes and the readouts from other devices in the lab on their computer screens.

"The scientists in the lab are isolated physically from everybody else, but they are connected to the outside world electronically," Nick said. "The surveillance footage and the readouts from their equipment can be shared over a secure web connection to scientists within the building and all over the world. They call it the Biosecurity Collaboration Platform."

"I call it an open invitation to hack into the entire system," Joe said. "They might as well have a sign out front that says 'C'mon in, everybody is welcome!' "

"What are those blue suits hanging in the control room?" Chet asked, pointing to suits similar to the pressure suits but not nearly as bulky. "I saw some in the balloon-suit room, too."

"In case the positive pressure suit system fails, or there is some other emergency, those are protective suits with their own battery-operated air-purifying respirators attached," Nick said. "The battery has a four-to-six-hour charge."

"What happens if you're in one of those white balloon suits and have an itch?" Willie said. "Or need to pee?"

"You have to leave the lab and go through decontamination," Kate said. "You're about to see that process now."

To exit the lab, the scientists went through an air lock into a shower room, where their pressure suits were doused for eight minutes with decontamination chemicals. From there, they went through another air lock back into the suit room. They climbed out of the pressure suits, went through an air lock into another changing room, stripped out of their scrubs, gloves, and socks and stuffed everything into a biohazard hamper, and then went naked into another shower room. After showering, they went through an air lock back into the locker room to get dressed in their street clothes.

"How much of that do we need to build?" Tom asked.

"The lab and the control room," Nick said. "We're going to tunnel in through the control room wall. I'll enter the lab through the control room air lock, retrieve the virus from a refrigeration unit in the lab, and off we go."

"You're not going to put on a balloon suit or one of those blue ones?" Willie asked.

"I'm stealing the vial, not opening it," Nick said.

"Be careful," Boyd said. "A horrific lab accident in the Congo left me impotent and destroyed my marriage. Six other colleagues weren't so lucky."

"You know the virus is fake, right?" Kate said. "There is no actual danger."

"That's the careless attitude that gets people killed," Boyd said. "Do you want those deaths, and the shattered lives of their loved ones, on your conscience? I know a man blinded by a deadly lab accident. Now the only thing he sees are the people that he lost."

"Oh God," Willie said. "He's in character already."

"We all need to prepare," Nick said. "The sooner the better. There are more instructional videos on board that you can watch. I've also got books on lab procedure and blueprints of typical biolabs for you to study. Let's get to it. We land in Paris in ten hours . . ."

"That's where Dr. Lyle Fairbanks will find his redemption," Boyd said. "Or lose his soul."

20

Gaëlle Rochon picked them up at the airport the next morning. Introductions were made all around, and she drove them in a rented van to the storefront that Nick had leased on avenue Denfert-Rochereau.

The Indian restaurant that had last occupied the property, and all of its fixtures and furniture, were long gone, but the space still smelled of curry and grease. The windows were covered with cardboard, and there was a thick layer of dust on the hardwood floor.

"There's a large apartment on the second floor," Kate said. "That's where you'll be staying. You'll find cots and furniture up there. While you're out and about on the street, if any neighbors ask what you're doing, tell them we're turning this place into an American-style diner. You're the design team that was brought in from America to do it."

"How do we explain the medical equipment?" Chet asked.

"Say that a clinic of some kind is going in upstairs, but you really don't know much about it," Kate said.

Nick turned to Chet, Tom, and Joe. "Use this floor any way you need to make the set in the basement work."

"Let's take a look downstairs," Tom said.

Nick led the way to the back of the room and a wide flight of stairs to the basement.

"The kitchen was downstairs," he said as they went down the stairs. "So it's a big space with all the utilities you'll need already routed in."

The walls were covered with subway tiles, and the floor was concrete. There were lots of open holes in the walls and floors with pipes sticking out and exposed wiring where kitchen appliances once were.

Tom nodded to himself as he walked the perimeter of the room. "I can work with this. I'll use the existing walls as much as possible and keep demolition to a minimum."

"Give Gaëlle a list of everything you need that can be purchased legally and for cash," Nick said. "I'll get the rest."

"I made up a list on the plane of the laboratory equipment that I need." Chet handed the list to Nick. "Basically it's everything you saw in that lab, along with some compressors and fans to run the air hoses."

Joe tapped the floor with his foot. "I'd like a look underground. I want to see what cable, telecom, and other utility lines I can tap."

"I'd like to go, too," Chet said. "I need to see the street signs in the sewer and catacombs so I can create convincing fakes."

"I'll be glad to give you both a tour," Gaëlle said. "There are jumpsuits, helmets, and boots upstairs for you. We can go whenever you're ready. One of my favorite manholes is right down the street."

"Welcome to Paris," Willie said.

They spent the next week building the lab, working in shifts under Tom's direction. They also helped Chet with the tedious task of running all the necessary wires, A/V cables, and air supply lines that were needed to operate the lights, positive pressure suit air hoses, surveillance cameras, and scientific equipment. The set was capped with a fake ceiling to hold the lights and the hoses. Two of the actual basement walls were incorporated into the control room, but the rest of the lab was made with fake walls.

The interior walls of the control room and the lab were elaborately tiled, painted, and decorated.

But the opposite side, visible only from the outside of the set, were naked plywood and two-by-fours, like the framing of a house without drywall. The fake walls were propped up with wooden braces bolted into the concrete floor. The air lock doors, with the exception of the one between the control room and the lab, opened to the empty basement. The portion of the basement walls visible through the portholes in the lab's air lock doors were painted to imply the room beyond.

"It's as convincing as the hospital set on *Grey's Anatomy*," Boyd declared on the night the set was completed.

The next morning at 9:00, after a last tour of the set, everyone but Nick, Kate, Gaëlle, and Joe got into their positive pressure suits and prepared to do a rehearsal. Joe sat at a console on the first floor and faced two keyboards and four flat-screen monitors aligned in a row.

"There are discreet green lights inside and outside the lab set to let the cast know when the cameras are live," Joe said. "That way they only have to act when we know that someone is watching."

"Let's see the surveillance feed from the real institute," Kate said.

"Breaking into their website was ridiculously easy," Joe said. He tapped a few keys and one of his screens filled with dozens of thumbnail mini-screens showing corridors, labs, parking lots, conference rooms, and offices within the institute. "I'm also hardwired into their surveillance system as a backup. I could probably shut down their alarms and hijack control of their air locks for real if I wanted to."

"It's a good thing we're fake thieves," Kate said. "When this is over, remind me to have a serious talk with their security people."

"Show me our lab," Nick said.

Joe tapped another key, and the empty lab appeared on another screen.

"Can you pull up the surveillance feed from one of their real labs and see how it compares to ours?" Nick asked.

"Sure," Joe said.

An instant later, the image on the screen split, the real lab showing up on the left, their empty set on the right. In the real lab, half a dozen scientists in their white inflated positive pressure suits were diligently at work.

"*Formidable,*" Gaëlle said. "There is no difference."

"Re-creating an empty room is easy," Nick said. "It's the acting that matters. Let's start the show."

Joe hit a button on another console. Suddenly the fans, compressors, and other equipment mounted on the first floor roared loudly to life to pump air into the hoses in the basement set to inflate the positive pressure suits. He pressed a second button that turned on the green light for the actors. That was their call to action.

Boyd, Willie, Chet, and Tom lumbered into the lab one by one, unhooked their air hoses, and moved to their workstations or elsewhere in the room before hooking up to a nearby air hose again. They all seemed to move around the lab with purpose, retrieving samples, putting others away, examining things under microscopes, carefully squirting liquids into pipettes, and putting vials into the centrifuge.

"That's as dull as the real lab work," Gaëlle said. "If there's a story there, I'm missing it."

"That's because we can't see much of their faces from these high angles," Joe said. "Their expressions are lost."

"Don't tell Boyd that," Kate said. "He'll demand close-ups."

"What matters to me is that they are coming across as real lab workers," Nick said. "Let's keep it going for a few more minutes. We don't know how long they will have to perform at any given time. I want to be sure they can sustain it for a while."

On the set, Boyd approached Willie, who was at a microscope, examining a slide. The microscope itself didn't actually work. The magnified image on her monitor was part of a preprogrammed show generated by the computer. He hunched down and looked over her shoulder.

"That's the pathogen that rendered me impotent," he said.

"This is going to be the elbow that renders you impotent if you don't stop crowding me."

"That's not your line," Boyd said. "It's 'You're more of a man now than you ever were, Dr. Fairbanks. You sure as hell aren't impotent when it comes to saving lives.'"

"If I say that, I'll throw up in this suit, which could kill me," Willie said. "I could drown in my own puke."

"The line underscores the sacrifices we make and the ultimate nobility of what we do here," Boyd said. "Do you have a better line that achieves the same thing?"

"Nobody can hear what we say. It's a silent movie."

"Some of the greatest films in the history of cinema were silent," Boyd said. "It's the performance that matters."

"Are you insecure about your virility?"

"That line doesn't work," Boyd said.

"It's a genuine question. You've written two scripts now that are focused on glorifying your tiddlywink. You're obsessed with yourself."

"That's ironic coming from a woman who inflated her breasts like one of these suits."

She tried to elbow him, but couldn't move fast enough with her arm in an inflated sleeve. He easily dodged it.

"Now we have some drama and nobody had to hear a word," Boyd said. "I think I've proved my point."

Proud of himself, Boyd walked away from her toward Chet at another workstation, stretching his air hose taut. He disconnected it but forgot to set it in a hook before letting go. The hose snapped back like a whip, sweeping vials off countertops and whacking Willie out of her seat. A hiss of air came from her suit.

"Congratulations," Chet said. "You've just contaminated the entire lab and probably killed Willie."

"Now I see the story," Gaëlle said. "Willie can't stand him."

"Cut," Nick said with a sigh.

Joe hit the button turning off the green light and shutting down the air system that was inflating their suits.

"Can I talk to them?" Nick asked.

Joe hit a button on a console and pointed to the monitor. "Go ahead, there's a mike embedded in the monitor. They'll all hear you."

JANET EVANOVICH AND LEE GOLDBERG

"You started off great but then you forgot to follow lab procedure," Nick said. "Trying to elbow a fellow scientist in the groin is a definite no-no in a room full of toxic viruses, Willie. It may not be a written rule, but I think it's generally understood."

"Let's review," Kate said. "Never let go of a taut air hose, Boyd. Always hook it up and make sure it's secure before moving on and connecting to another one. You've seen now what can happen if a hose flies around. A mistake like that could kill people in a real lab but, more important, it will kill me, Nick, and Gaëlle in the real world."

"This was only our first rehearsal," Boyd said. "We are just beginning to find our characters and get comfortable in this space. It's all part of the artistic process."

"You have two days, three at the most, to get it down before showtime," Nick said. "We're picking up Huck Moseby at the airport in two hours."

"That's our checkered flag," Kate said. "The con begins today."

Whenever Huck Moseby dreamed of Paris, it was never about strolling the Champs-Élysées or climbing the Eiffel Tower, or riding an excursion boat along the Seine at sunset, or enjoying a coffee and tart at a sidewalk café. His dream was to visit the sewers, the

Shangri-la of waste disposal systems, the inspiration for such literary masterpieces as *The Phantom of the Opera* and *Les Misérables*. There was a time when the Paris sewers were appreciated. In the late 1800s, the rich and powerful would dress up in their finest clothes to tour the sewers on fancy gaslit gondolas to see for themselves the technological and engineering marvel that was the pride of Paris. Far too few people in the world today, in Huck's opinion, realized that the sewers were what truly made Paris the City of Light.

He was thinking about that as he arrived at Charles de Gaulle Airport. Nick, Kate, and a beautiful young blond woman were waiting for him outside customs.

"How was your flight?" Nick asked.

The flight had been seven hours of sheer bliss for Huck. He'd flown Air France first-class, where he was pampered like never before in his life. He was going to forever treasure the faux-leather case of toiletries, the airplane socks, and the eye mask that he'd been given.

"It was great," Huck said. "I'm rested and ready to go."

"I'm glad to hear that," Nick said. "This is Gaëlle Rochon, our guide to the Paris underground. She will be your right-hand man from here on out."

"It's a pleasure to meet you," Gaëlle said to him in French. "I've heard so much about you from Nick."

"Likewise," Huck replied in French. "I am eager to see the sewers."

"I am eager to show them to you," Gaëlle said. "And to learn how they differ from yours in Montreal."

"You've worked in the sewers?"

"No, but my father, my grandfather, and my great-grandfather were all sewer men," Gaëlle said. "The sewer is like my second home. You'll probably find this ridiculous, but sometimes I think I am more comfortable there."

Huck felt color coming into his pale cheeks. He was in love. "I don't think it's ridiculous," he said. "I feel the same way."

"Would you like us to take you to your hotel to rest up?" Kate asked. "Or perhaps get you something to eat?"

"I'm here to work," Huck said. "Show me the blueprints of the lab, a map of the streets, and take me to the sewers."

"It's nice to work with a pro," Nick said.

21

Gaëlle drove them to a side street off avenue du Général Leclerc that was three blocks south of place Denfert-Rochereau. She parked behind a white van with a distinctive SAP logo representing the Section de l'Assainissement de Paris, the city sewer utility. It was a van that Nick had purchased and Chet had painted to look like the real thing.

They got out of the car and got into the van, where Gaëlle presented Huck with a set of genuine SAP overalls, boots, helmet, and the spade-like tool for sluicing sewage. Huck held the tool reverently, as if it were Excalibur.

"This is the Stradivarius of sewer tools," Huck said. "I never thought I'd hold one of these."

"You can have it," Gaëlle said, slowly wrapping a rag around her neck to prepare for her descent.

"It's an honor," Huck said, breathlessly watching her knot her rag as if she were doing a striptease.

He pulled a rag of his own out of his pocket and put it around his neck.

"You came prepared," Gaëlle said, watching him tie his knot.

"I'm a sewer man," Huck said. "And a Frenchman."

"*Québécois,*" Gaëlle said.

"Are we really so different?"

"I don't know yet," she said. "But I'm looking forward to finding out."

Kate rolled her eyes at Nick, and Nick smiled back.

"I've put the site plan of the Institut National pour la Recherche sur les Maladies Infectieuses and blueprints of the lab building in your bag with your flashlights and other equipment," Nick said to Huck.

Nick had put a lot of effort into having the blueprints forged and the site plans altered to misdirect Huck so he wouldn't know that they would actually be digging into the basement of a building outside of the institute's property. Probably unnecessary, Nick thought. Huck wasn't going to see much past Gaëlle.

"You're not coming with us?" Huck asked, unable to hide his delight that he and Gaëlle would have the sewers to themselves.

"We've been down there already," Kate said. "We know the general spot where we'll be digging. We'd just be in your way while you figure out the technical details."

"Scout the sewer, review the plans at your hotel,

then let us know at breakfast tomorrow how long the dig will take, how many men you'll need, and what equipment is required to do the job right," Nick said. "Demand the best tools and don't worry about the cost. Money is no object."

Nick and Kate opened the back of the van, got out, slid the door closed behind them, and headed down the street toward the intersection with avenue du Général Leclerc.

"A match made in heaven," Nick said.

"No kidding. Huck should be paying *us*."

Nick took his phone out of his pocket. "Time to call Litija and get this robbery started."

"Before you call Litija and we end up undercover again with the Road Runners, I'd like to know that Dad and his guys are out there watching. I don't know why we haven't heard from him yet." She took out her own phone and dialed his number.

"Are you sure you want to call now?" Nick said. "It's four in the morning in L.A."

"He's an early riser."

"Howdy-do," Jake said.

"You sound awfully chipper for so early in the morning," Kate said.

"I'm always chipper. Give me a second. I need to flush the *toilette*."

"You're talking to me on the toilet?"

"*In* the *toilette*," Jake said. "I really had to go after

235

all the running around you did this morning. But don't worry, I had eyes on you while I was inside."

"What are you talking about? Where are you?"

Nick tapped her on the shoulder and glanced across the street. She followed his gaze and saw Jake stepping out of a *sanisette,* a cylindrical gray hut on the sidewalk with the word *toilette* written on the side above a map of the neighborhood. There were hundreds of *sanisettes* throughout Paris and they were not only a place to relieve yourself but to find out where you were. The door to the public bathroom slid closed behind Jake like an elevator and the chemical self-cleaning cycle began inside.

Jake strolled down the street, not visually acknowledging her, continuing to talk on the phone.

"We've been here for the last three days," Jake said.

Kate walked with Nick, parallel to Jake, as they all headed toward place Denfert-Rochereau. "Who is 'we'?"

"Walter Wurzel is on the rooftop of the building behind me. He's had you in his scope while I was in the *toilette.* Best sniper there is."

He'd also taught Kate how to shoot a rifle when she was nine and they were all stationed on Guam. But she knew time had taken its toll on him.

"Does he still have cataracts?"

"That was years ago, and even half-blind he can still shoot the ears off a butterfly."

As if to prove it, a laser-targeting dot appeared on Nick's chest.

Nick looked down at the dot. "Friend or foe?" he asked.

Kate smiled. "It's Walter Wurzel saying hello."

Nick had met Walter in Kentucky a few years back on the Carter Grove scam. He'd proven that he was still a good shot on that job, and he'd had one eye patched at the time.

"Who else is on the team?" Kate asked Jake.

"You're being tracked on foot by Antoine Killian, not that you'd ever know it," Jake said. "He's a founding veteran of the Brigade des Forces Spéciales Terre, the French special ops, and he's the living definition of stealth. He's invisible unless he wants to be seen. He blends into the shadows."

Kate was so caught up in talking to her dad that she nearly collided head-on with a morbidly obese man wearing a beret, a tent-sized overcoat, and smoking a huge cigar.

"That was Antoine," Jake said.

Kate glanced over her shoulder to see Antoine tip his hat to her from behind. He took up nearly the whole sidewalk. She looked back at her dad as she spoke into the phone.

JANET EVANOVICH AND LEE GOLDBERG

"He must be four hundred pounds. How can he possibly disappear into the shadows?"

"Do you see him now?"

Kate whirled around again. Antoine was gone. He must have ducked into a building or a car, but he'd done it with surprising speed and agility, even for someone who didn't measure his weight on an industrial scale.

"Impressive," she said.

"I've brought in Robin Mannering, formerly of the British Army's Special Reconnaissance Regiment," Jake said. "He's an expert driver, cold-blooded assassin, speaks five languages, and is irresistible to women. We call him the lady killer. He could always seduce a woman close to the enemy into telling us all their secrets. That's him parked in the Alfa Romeo convertible."

The car was at the curb right in front of them. The smiling old man at the wheel had a spray-on tan, capped teeth, and was wearing a toupee. His face was pulled so tight that the double chin above his cravat might once have been his scrotum.

"What's he do these days?" Kate asked.

"Seduces the wives and lovers of heads of state for MI6," Jake said. "The man is a legend."

Nick leaned close to Kate and whispered, "I think the man we just passed is wearing one of William Shatner's old toupees and Mr. Ed's teeth."

"Please tell me this isn't all you've got," Kate said to her father.

"I have a dozen American commandos on standby in Kaiserslautern, Germany. They are armed and equipped for any situation on land or sea," Jake said. "They can immediately deploy to almost anywhere in Europe within two hours."

Kate stopped walking. "Because they're stationed at Ramstein Air Base. Are you telling me you've got active duty soldiers involved in this?"

"They aren't on active duty, at least not officially. Let's just say they're enterprising young men who are ready to handle situations that fall outside the boundaries of usual U.S. military jurisdiction. They're the guys I trained to replace me and my team when we retired."

"They're doing black ops for the Pentagon and the CIA?" Kate asked.

"They wish they were. They're bored out of their minds in Kaiserslautern. Regime change and extraordinary renditions have really slowed down under this administration. So they could use some excitement."

"They could get court-martialed for helping us," Kate said. "If they don't get killed first."

"Who do you think will be deployed for this mission if Jessup is able to push the button? These guys. So they're in either way. Besides, nobody is going to slap their hands for thwarting a terrorist attack on America in their free time. It's their job," Jake said. "It's not like they got drunk one weekend and deposed a dictator for fun."

"You've done that?"

"Let's just say there's a capital in deepest, darkest Africa where you'll find a guano-covered statue of a soldier who looks a lot like your old man," Jake said. "Bottom line, you're in good hands."

"I know that. Keep a close eye on our people. I'll let you know when the virus is on the move." Kate hung up and looked at Nick. "Dad has our backs."

"I never doubted it for a second. It's showtime." Nick took out his phone and dialed Litija.

Dragan Kovic knew five minutes into Nick's presentation in the apartment on avenue du Maine that he'd made the right decision bringing the master thief into his scheme. Nick made the impossible seem ridiculously easy.

"The labs are primarily designed to keep viruses from getting out, not to keep people from getting in," Nick said at the outset, flanked by his team of Kate, Joe, Gaëlle, and Huck. "The institute has some very elaborate security measures, but they made one key mistake. They built their basement lab in the middle of a honeycomb of tunnels that have existed for centuries. We're simply going to stroll into one of those tunnels, dig a hole into the lab, take what we want, and be on our way."

"During the dig, I'll be in a van on the street and hardwired into the institute's security system," Joe said. "I'll disable the alarms as soon as Nick enters the lab, and I'll hijack the video feed so the guards will see an empty room."

Huck told Dragan it would take at least twelve hours using a $12,000 Hilti DD 500-CA diamond coring rig to tunnel into the lab from within a municipal utility shaft full of electric, fiber-optic, cable, and telecom lines that ran parallel to the basement.

They would have to cut through six inches of concrete, twenty feet of limestone, and finally sixteen inches of heavily rebar-reinforced concrete to create a tunnel just large enough for a man with a pack to crawl through, a *chatière* as Gaëlle called it, a pet door.

"We'll tap the electric lines and plumbing lines that run through the tunnel to power the coring rig," Huck said. "We'll have a second coring rig and a small, portable generator as backups in case the rig fails or we lose power."

"What we need from you are five men," Nick said to Dragan. "Three of them will be underground to help with the drilling and removal of the extracted cores, which can weigh over two hundred pounds."

"The other two will be up on the street, acting as lookouts to alert Joe if there's trouble or any police activity," Kate said. "He'll tip us off. We won't have any radio or cellular signal in that part of the underground. We'll communicate with Joe using a single phone that's hardwired into a telecom line that runs through the shaft. We won't be able to hear a thing with that drill going, so I'll be manning it and we'll install a flashing light to tell us when a call is coming in."

Kate's job, as far as Dragan could tell, was to watch Nick's back. The only equipment that still had to be acquired were the diamond core drills, the track, an air blower to clear exhaust fumes, a backup generator, and three trucks painted to look like sewer and telephone utility vehicles. He could easily acquire all of that within a day.

Dragan was staring at an iPad that Joe, the alarm and video expert, had given him. Joe had already hacked into the institute's surveillance system, and Dragan was watching the lab in real time. He had the sense that the scientists were working on something highly critical today, and that the man in charge was riding them to quickly produce results.

"I think this woman wants to kill her boss," Dragan said, pointing to his iPad screen. "You can see it in her body language."

Litija looked over his shoulder. "That suit doesn't

do anything for her figure. You can't tell she has a body at all."

"See how the man in charge keeps looking at the wall clock," Dragan said. "They are racing against time on something."

"Or maybe he just wants to go to lunch," Litija said.

Dragan handed the iPad back to Joe. "Very impressive."

"Joe still has work to do," Nick said. "He has to do the hardwiring he talked about. We'll do that, and the underground prep work, on Friday night disguised as utility workers. We begin the dig on Saturday afternoon, and finish in the predawn hours on Sunday. I'll stroll into the lab, pick up the sample, place it in a secure, temperature-controlled container, and bring it up to the street."

"We'll take it from there," Litija said.

"And then what happens?" Kate asked.

"We celebrate our success," Dragan said, well aware it wasn't the answer Kate was fishing for. "I have to commend you all on your brilliant planning."

The expertise and swift action that Nick brought to the scheme was beyond Dragan's wildest expectations. Now the smallpox outbreak in Los Angeles could happen within a few weeks instead of months or years. Zarko's death was definitely a worthwhile sacrifice.

"My men will arrive tonight," Dragan said. "You'll have the equipment and vehicles you requested by the end of the day tomorrow. You'll all be working out of this apartment until the job is complete. Litija will see to anything else that you might need."

Dragan would talk to her later to work out the details of transporting the smallpox to his lab. He gestured to Nick to join him by the front door of the apartment, away from the others.

"I want Litija in the van with Joe so she can keep an eye on everything," Dragan said.

"You mean on me," Nick said.

"She will work with the lookouts and be an extra set of eyes on the institute security cameras," Dragan said. "Her job will be to keep you safe and assure the success of the robbery."

"Kate thinks that's her job."

"It's her job underground and Litija's job above."

"I've always wanted two women to stay on top of me," Nick said. "When do I begin betting my savings against the market?"

"On Monday," Dragan said. "The attack will happen in six weeks or so in Los Angeles."

"Why L.A.?"

"It's Hollywood. Celebrities are America's royalty. It will be much more terrifying to see the bodies of famous people than complete strangers. On top of that we kill two for the price of one."

"I don't understand," Nick said.

"When a famous actor dies, so do the beloved characters that he plays. But it gets even better than that."

"We'll kill some adorable puppies, too?"

"We won't just be killing actors, but the hopes and dreams embodied in the movies they made. That's certain to terrify and depress the market worldwide, not just in the U.S. We'll be sure to short a lot of entertainment industry stocks."

"You've really thought this out," Nick said.

"And you're making it all possible," Dragan said, clapping Nick on the back. "You're even better at this than you say you are."

"I don't like to brag," Nick said and rejoined his team.

Nick and his people were very talented, and if this wasn't going to be Dragan's final crime, maybe he wouldn't have decided to have them executed immediately after the robbery. He was already feeling a twinge of regret as he left the apartment, and they weren't even dead yet. Dragan went down the spiral staircase and thought about his decision.

If he spared them, could he take the risk that one of them might talk before or after the smallpox outbreak in L.A.? No, of course he couldn't, and he was angry at himself for even considering the notion. It was ridiculous and stupid. Did he feel anything for the thousands of people, perhaps *tens of thousands,* who would perish in Los Angeles? Absolutely not. So what difference did a few more corpses make?

None at all.

Dragan stepped outside, walked across the sidewalk, and got into his black Maserati GranTurismo Sport parked at the curb. It was a good thing that he was becoming a billionaire and retiring soon, he thought. He was beginning to get soft.

22

There were three snipers watching Dragan drive off on avenue du Maine. Two of the snipers were Road Runners in a sixth-floor apartment in the building directly across the street. Their names were Daca and Stefan, and their job was to protect Dragan while he was in the apartment. Now that Dragan was gone, Daca and Stefan began dismantling their weapons and packing up.

The third sniper, on the rooftop of the same building, was Walter "Eagle Eye" Wurzel. He'd also had his eye on Dragan while Jake O'Hare, standing beside him with binoculars, watched the others in the room. Walter and Jake knew about the two snipers on the floor below them and would stay on the rooftop until Antoine Killian, in the shadows somewhere on the street, alerted them that they were gone.

"I hope I don't regret that I didn't kill Dragan

when I had the shot," Walter said, lifting his eye from the scope as the Maserati drove off.

He wore large square-rimmed glasses with thick lenses balanced on a bulbous nose covered with red squiggly capillaries. The glasses magnified his eyes and made them look unnaturally large. He lay on his stomach, the rifle balanced on a tiny tripod.

"If you'd killed Dragan," Jake said, "the snipers would have killed Nick and Kate."

"Maybe, but you're talking about saving two people instead of thousands," Walter said. "At a certain point, we may have to choose between our team and our mission."

"There is no choice," Jake said. "I believe in Kate and Nick, but if their con fails, we take down Dragan and stop the attack, no matter what."

"Let's pray it never comes to that," Walter said. "In the meantime, do we have any croissants left?"

Jake reached for the bag next to him and looked inside. "One chocolate and one butter."

"I'll take 'em both," Walter said. "I'm hypoglycemic. My vision gets blurry when my blood sugar crashes."

On Saturday afternoon, Kate parked a sewer department van on boulevard Raspail. It was just north of place Denfert-Rochereau, beside a bus stop shelter that had a large advertisement featuring

Johannes Vermeer's painting *Girl with a Pearl Earring*. The ad read *Atelier Vermeer. Apprenez à peindre comme les ancien maîtres. Copies de tableaux.* It was the first thing Nick saw when he emerged from the rear of the van wearing a sewer worker's jumpsuit. "Vermeer Workshop. Learn to paint like the masters. Copy the paintings."

He figured that spotting an advertisement for a school that taught art forgery, at the outset of faking the robbery of a level-four biolab, was probably a very good omen.

He walked to the manhole and used a crowbar-like tool to remove the cover while Road Runners Dusko, Vinko, and Borko unfolded a chest-high yellow canvas pedestrian barricade around the opening. The four men transferred the equipment from the van to the manhole and down into the sewer while Kate remained in the driver's seat with the engine running and watched for trouble. This was the first time they'd entered the sewers so close to the institute and place Denfert-Rochereau, a high-traffic area for cars and pedestrians. Being so visible was a necessary risk, since it was the largest manhole close to where they'd be digging, making it the best place to deliver the heavy equipment. But it was also the moment when they were the most likely to attract unwanted attention.

Once they were done, Nick disassembled the tripod

while Dusko and Vinko removed the barricade and put it back in the van. Then the two Serbians went down into the sewer to join Borko. Nick followed them in, slid the manhole cover back into place, and Kate drove off. The operation had taken less than ten minutes.

In the sewer, each man picked up a piece of equipment, and Gaëlle led them single file through several IGC access tunnels to the lighted utility corridor where they would be working. The corridor was about six feet high and six feet wide, and the concrete ceiling and walls were lined with scores of pipes and conduits.

There was a big *X* written chest-high on the wall where they would be drilling three twelve-inch circular shafts, one right next to another, in a tight cluster to create one tubular tunnel large enough for a man to crawl through.

Vinko placed the diamond coring tool on the track. Dusko attached the coring bit and water line to the machine. Borko plugged the rig into the electric line. Nick powered up a twelve-inch flat-screen TV that Joe had mounted on the wall and that was hardwired into the institute's video surveillance feed. Several angles on the lab came up on-screen. There were four scientists working in their inflated suits.

"They are putting in some overtime," Nick said.

Vinko came up beside him and looked at the screen. "Is that a problem?"

"No. They can't hear us digging and will be long gone by the time we punch through the wall at two or three in the morning."

Vinko watched them working with their pipettes of plague for a moment.

"I'm glad you're going into that room and not me," Vinko said. "The air is full of death."

"The room will be clean when I go in," Nick said. "It'll be a lot more sanitary than the sewer we just walked through."

Huck took out the tablet device that operated the computerized coring tool and typed in some data. "I'm ready."

Nick shut off the monitor. Everyone put on their goggles and ear protectors. Huck tapped a key on the tablet, starting the drill. The diamond core bit began spinning, the water-moistened circular face cutting into the concrete with a noise amplified so much by the confines of the tunnel that it became a physical sensation. The men shook with the sound, and the wall wept slurry under the spinning bit as the core driller made its slow progress.

A panel van from Orange, the French telecom company, was parked on a nearby side street that ran along the ivy-covered walls on the southeastern edge of Montparnasse Cemetery. Litija and Joe were sitting in the back of the van at a console watching two monitors.

One monitor showed dozens of thumbnails representing the views of all security cameras inside and outside the institute. The other monitor showed a full-screen picture of the lab they'd be breaking into.

Litija closely watched the scientists in the lab to see if any of them appeared to notice the sound or rumble of the drilling outside their walls. Nothing seemed to break the concentration of the scientists on their experiments. The only thing she sensed was the urgency and seriousness of their work. She glanced at the other monitor. Nothing out of the ordinary was happening elsewhere at the institute either.

"So far so good," Joe said, looking to her for agreement. But she didn't give it to him.

She picked up the radio and called her lookouts.

"Daca, what do you see?" she asked in Serbian.

He was stationed atop a building that overlooked place Denfert-Rochereau so he'd be able to see any police vehicles approaching from any of the intersecting boulevards.

"*Ništa se dešava,*" he replied. Nothing is happening.

"Stefan, what do you see?" she asked.

He was positioned atop a building one block further north, where avenue Denfert-Rochereau intersected with place Ernest Dennis. Between the two men, she'd know if authorities were coming from any direction.

"*Isti*," he replied. The same.

Litija set the radio down and gave Joe the nod he was looking for.

"So far so good," she said.

That was true for now. But she knew with absolute certainty that it wouldn't last.

By midnight, Huck had drilled through the limestone and was close to cutting his first hole into the concrete wall of the laboratory. In the hours leading up to that, Nick and the three Road Runners had lugged a dozen cylindrical cores of solid concrete and limestone out of the utility corridor and into the sewer, lining them up along the wall. Nick and Vinko had just brought out the last two limestone cores and were drenched with sweat.

"Here you are, working for Dragan Kovic, the man who kidnapped and then betrayed you," Vinko said to Nick. "That makes no sense to me."

"Dragan didn't betray me," Nick said. "Zarko did."

"We both know that's not true. Zarko always followed orders. He took a fall for you."

"A very long one."

Vinko got in Nick's face. "Zarko and I grew up in the same village. We served side by side in the war. He was like a brother to me. He's not a punch line for a smart-ass remark."

"I didn't push him off the cliff. If you have a problem, it's with Dragan, not me."

Vinko shook his head and poked Nick's chest hard with his finger. "Dragan did it for you."

Kate stepped out of the adjoining IGC tunnel. "Huck is about to punch through into the lab. Do you guys want to be there for it or is it interrupting your tea time?"

"We're on our way," Nick said.

Vinko walked away, brushing past Kate into the tunnel. She turned to Nick.

"Do we have a problem?" she asked.

"No, but Dragan might." Nick rubbed his chest. He was lucky he didn't have a collapsed lung. "Tossing Zarko off a cliff probably wasn't a great move for employee morale."

They made their way back to the utility corridor. Huck was crouched outside the four-foot-diameter opening and held the tablet controller for the diamond core driller. The core driller was twenty-two feet further down and digging through the concrete wall of the lab under remote control.

A brownish slurry, from the water that kept the

drill bit wet, spilled out onto the floor. Dusko was trying to suck up as much slurry as he could with a workshop vacuum.

"We're close," Huck said. "Any second now."

Nick turned on the monitor, showing several views of the empty lab. One angle showed the back wall of the control room. Kate, Borko, Vinko, and Gaëlle huddled closely around Nick for the big moment.

The first thing they saw was a circular seam opening up in the wall, then water seeping through. An instant later, the diamond-serrated edge of the core bit cut through, looking like the wide open mouth of a metal snake that had just swallowed a huge chunk of concrete. They were in.

The drilling went very fast after that. The remaining two bores were cut in less than two hours, making the hole wide enough for a man with a pack to crawl through. The drilling tool was removed and the track was pulled up. It was time for Nick to go inside. He picked up the small backpack that contained the titanium case for the vial of smallpox and went to the mouth of the tunnel.

"Good luck," Kate said.

"The hard part is already over," Nick said.

He gave her a smile, their eyes met and held for a long moment, and he crawled inside.

In the van, Litija and Joe sat at their console and stared at the image of the empty control room and the hole in the wall. Nick crawled out, his white SAP jumpsuit smeared with wet slurry, and wiped his gloved hands on his suit.

They watched him take off the muddy work gloves, set them on the counter, and pull out a pair of white surgical gloves from his pocket. He put the rubber gloves on, took off his backpack, and removed the container for the vial from inside the backpack. His lips were pursed and he seemed to be moving to a jaunty beat.

"Is he whistling?" Litija asked.

"It's 'Whistle While You Work,'" Joe said. "From *Snow White.*"

"How do you know?"

Because Joe could hear him. Now that Nick was in the basement of the storefront, the signal from his earbuds wasn't blocked anymore by tons of limestone and concrete. Nick could hear Joe and Litija, too. But, of course, Litija didn't know that.

"That's what he always whistles when he goes in solo on a break-in," Joe said.

Nick looked up at the camera and pointed to the keypad that operated the air lock.

"Yeah, yeah, I'm unlocking it," Joe said and began typing furiously on the keyboard.

The air lock door opened and Nick stepped inside. Only his face was visible through the porthole window. Joe switched the image on the monitor to a view from a camera inside the lab.

Nick stepped out of the air lock and, still whistling, made his merry way across the lab to the freezer that contained the deadly virus.

"That, ladies and gentlemen, is a natural thespian in action," Boyd said, pointing at the TV. Willie and Tom were in the storefront with him. They were a floor above the lab set, sitting in folding chairs and watching the con unfold on their screen. Chet was down in the basement, outside the set with his tool belt on, ready to spring into action if there was a technical problem.

"Notice how effortlessly Nick expresses his relaxation as well as the joy he derives from his work," Boyd continued. "That is body-language acting. His entire character comes through."

Nick looked up at the camera, pointed to the keypad on the freezer, and whistled some more while he waited for Joe to release the locking mechanism.

"That is Nick being Nick," Willie said. "He's just having fun."

"People thought the same thing about James Garner, Jimmy Stewart, and Spencer Tracy," Boyd said. "The great actors make acting look easy, as if they are just playing themselves. You're forgetting that this is not a real robbery. That's Nick acting like a thief who is enjoying himself."

"But it is a real con," Tom said. "I think he likes that even more than stealing stuff."

"Because it involves acting," Boyd said.

The keypad of the freezer flashed green and Nick opened the door. A fog of frost escaped, dissipated, and revealed the rows of vials inside, each presumably containing a deadly virus.

"Look, he's stopped whistling," Boyd said. "That's because he's staring into the gaping maw of rampant pestilence, misery, and doom. The chill he's feeling on his face might as well be the fingers of Death stroking his cheek. He's learned so much from me."

Nick set his box down on a nearby counter, opened it up, then slowly reached into the freezer for a vial.

23

Something on the monitor caught Litija's eye. She nudged Joe and pointed to Nick.

"What is that on his back?"

"Dirt," Joe said.

"No, no, the black thing," she said. "I think it's moving."

Joe tapped his mouse and the camera zoomed in on the black dot. It was a big, black spider and it was crawling between Nick's shoulder blades toward his neck.

"That's a spider," she said. "We've got to warn him."

"How?" Joe said, knowing that Nick could hear every word they were saying. "Besides, what harm could it do?"

Litija picked up the phone. But it was too late.

As Nick turned to place the smallpox vial in the

container, the spider went over his collar and down his bare neck. And bit him.

Nick winced at the sting and reflexively reached for his back with both hands, dropping the vial of smallpox.

The vial hit the floor and shattered.

Everyone in the utility tunnel stared in horror at the screen. Nick was still reaching for the spider, and hadn't realized yet what had happened.

"The spider just killed him," Vinko said, the edges of his mouth curling into a smile.

Nick will live, Kate thought, but the con, and all the work they'd put into it, was dead. She swore, ducked into the opening, and started crawling for the lab.

Vinko looked at the others. "What's she going to do? Read him his last rites?"

Litija couldn't believe what she was seeing and, at that same instant, neither could Nick, who spotted the broken vial on the floor. The full impact of what it obviously meant slammed him. He was infected with smallpox. Nick staggered back from the broken vial, shaking his head, seemingly unwilling to accept the inescapable truth—that he was a dead man.

This changed everything for Litija. All of the plans she'd made would die with him. She couldn't let this happen. There had to be a way to salvage this for herself.

And then, as if Nick were reading her thoughts, he looked up into the camera and right at her. She could almost see his mind working, desperately searching for a way out of this.

Save yourself, Litija thought. Save me.

She saw Kate crawl out of the hole into the control room. Her first thought was that Kate was crazy to expose herself to the virus, then Litija remembered that the lab had an independent air system and there was an air lock between the two rooms.

Kate knocked on the control room window to get Nick's attention.

In the few seconds that it had taken Kate to crawl from the utility corridor to the control room, she'd figured it out. Nick was a world-class thief and a master con man. And yet, he'd been foiled by a spider . . . a very photogenic spider, one with a Boyd Capwell sense of drama and a Hitchcockian sense of timing.

Nick approached the window with an appropriately shell-shocked expression on his face.

Kate got close to the glass and whispered, "You

jerk. You changed the game plan and you didn't tell me."

Kate knew he could hear her through the earbuds they were both wearing, and she wanted to be quiet in case anybody else came through the opening behind her.

"That's cruel," Nick said. "You're not showing a lot of sympathy for my dire predicament."

"The spider was no accident," Kate said. "It's not even a real spider, is it?"

"It's a tiny robot Chet made for me," Nick said. "I put it on my back in the air lock and he operated it by remote control from outside the set."

"You did this so Dragan will have to take you to his lab to harvest the virus. You've made yourself the smallpox sample," Kate said.

"I'm also the tracking device. I swallowed it as I was crawling in. There's another one in my biohazard suit." He tipped his head to the three emergency protective suits hanging on the wall behind Kate. "It's like one of those."

She didn't look behind her. "So you also had Chet create a working bioprotection suit for you, too. Very thorough. You planned to do this from the start and hid it from me. I really thought you trusted me."

"I do."

"You have a strange way of showing it."

"There wasn't time to tell you. I couldn't shake the feeling that you, me, Gaëlle, and Huck weren't going to make it out of the sewers alive. The broken vial was a last-minute decision that will ensure we all make it to the street, where there is protection," Nick said.

"Once Dragan realizes that you're not really infected, he'll kill you."

"I'm responsible for Dragan having the smallpox that he's already got. If this attack happens, all those deaths are on me. I made it possible. I couldn't live with that. This way, I guarantee that I will have a chance to stop him."

She couldn't fault him for having a conscience. In fact, it was nice to know that he did. But it didn't make her any less angry or any less afraid for his safety.

"It's suicide," Kate said. "You idiot."

"Where's your optimism?"

"I prefer being realistic."

"You'll rescue me before anything bad happens," Nick said.

"Don't be so sure. I was too late in Antwerp."

"You made up for it later."

"That'll be hard for me to do if you're dead."

"I think you're missing the point here," he said. "I'm trusting you with my life. How much more could I trust you than that?"

Kate squinched her eyes shut. "Ugh!"

Litija squinted at the screen. "It looks like they are saying goodbye."

Joe shook his head. "I think Nick is up to something."

"How can you tell?"

Because he'd heard their conversation. "He's got that sparkle in his eye."

It was true, he did. Or maybe Joe just imagined it.

"You can see a sparkle?" she asked.

"Can't you?"

The phone rang. Joe hit a switch, putting the call from the tunnel on the speaker.

"Nick is the smallpox sample now," Kate said.

It took a second for Litija to wrap her head around that. At first what Kate said made no sense at all to her, and then she realized it was brilliant. Things could move forward exactly as Litija had planned. The only difference was that now the box carrying the virus wasn't titanium, it was flesh and blood.

"How is he getting out of the lab without infecting everyone?" Litija asked.

"He'll strip out of his clothes and put himself in an impermeable vinyl suit like the blue ones hanging in the control room," Kate said. "The suits have independent air purifying respirators that operate on a battery with a six-hour charge. But there's one thing he needs to know first. Does Dragan have the smallpox vaccine? If Nick can get it within the next seventy-two hours, he has a chance."

"Yes, of course he does," Litija said, though she had no idea if Dragan did or not and she didn't care. It was the only answer Nick wanted to hear so that's what she gave Kate.

"Gaëlle will lead the others out of here and up to the street," Kate said. "I'll bring Nick to the manhole on rue Boissonade. Have the sewer utility van waiting to roll."

Rue Boissonade was a good choice, Litija thought. It was a residential side street that ran along the northern perimeter of the institute, on the other side of the block from avenue Denfert-Rochereau. There was little chance of any cars or pedestrians there at this time of the morning, and there would be few, if any, surveillance cameras. Daca and Stefan wouldn't be able to see them, but the two snipers could still watch the major cross streets and give her plenty of warning if the police were coming.

"There's one thing *I* need to know first," Litija said. "What happens if he tears his suit going through the little tunnel you just dug? He could infect us all."

"I'll tape up any tears."

"Won't you get infected?" Litija didn't care about Kate's health. What she was worried about was Kate starting an outbreak herself in Paris and ruining everything.

"I was vaccinated for smallpox in the military," Kate said. "It was part of our preparation for chemical warfare."

"Okay," Litija said. "Give the phone to Vinko."

Vinko got on the line and they had a quick discussion in Serbian. Litija told him that Nick was now the virus but that everything else was to go exactly as planned. When she was done, she caught Joe staring at her suspiciously.

"Why weren't you talking in English?" he asked.

"He's not very good at English and I wanted to make absolutely sure there were no misunderstandings," Litija said. "Or people could die."

It made sense to him. Joe nodded his approval. "Starting with us."

Definitely, she thought.

Nick went through an air lock in the back of the lab that presumably led to the room where scientists donned their positive pressure suits. Instead, he walked off the set into the basement where Chet was waiting for him with the blue biohazard suit on a hanger. There was an open bottle of red wine and a plate of cheese, prosciutto, and grapes on a table for Nick, too.

"Well played," Chet said.

"The real credit goes to that spider of yours," Nick said, unzipping his sewer worker's jumpsuit and stepping out of it wearing only a T-shirt and Calvins. "You ought to sell it as a novelty item. It would go over big with little boys eager to scare their sisters and mothers."

"Too late. You can buy radio-controlled spiders for twenty dollars on the Internet," Chet said, scooping his spider from the floor. "This one costs two grand. It's left over from a movie I worked on. So is this biohazard suit. It only looks and sounds like the real thing. It's not actually impermeable, and the respirator doesn't purify the air you're breathing or exhaling."

"I'll try not to wear it around anyone infected with a real virus." Nick popped a few cubes of cheese in his mouth and poured himself a generous glass of wine, which he drank like water. "Okay, let's do this."

Boyd, Willie, and Tom came down the stairs as Chet was helping Nick into the suit. It looked like something an astronaut might wear for a moonwalk except with a huge transparent hood instead of a helmet.

"That was a brilliant performance," Boyd said.

"I thought I overacted and made the bite look more like a gunshot," Nick said, stepping into rubber boots with his suit-covered feet.

"You had to. It was a silent movie," Boyd said. "Every gesture and emotion has to be exaggerated to make up for the lack of dialogue. But you conveyed the abject horror perfectly. It really felt like you were doomed."

"Because he might be," Willie said. "Kate's right, Nick. You're an idiot. Making yourself the virus was a dumb move."

"I admire what he's doing," Tom said. "He's risking his life for one chance to save thousands of Americans. It's noble."

"Be sure to put that in his eulogy," Willie said. "It'll bring everyone to tears."

"You're almost as bad as Kate," Nick said.

Nick taped his boots to his ankles with duct tape. He got up and headed for the air lock. "You all did great work, as usual. Willie, you'd better get in your car, we'll be going soon."

"I won't lose you," Willie said, heading back up the stairs.

"Once we're gone," Nick said, "the rest of you get out of here and take the first flight back to Los Angeles."

Nick gave everyone a thumbs-up and walked through the fake air lock into the lab.

"You can find me in Miami," Boyd said. "I'm not going anywhere near Los Angeles until I hear how this turns out."

"That makes two of us," Chet said.

"Three," Tom said. "I'm meeting my family in Walla Walla."

Kate was already in the control room holding a roll of duct tape when Nick entered the lab. He walked across the lab to the air lock and stepped inside. The door closed behind him. He waited for the green light that indicated the air had been sucked out of the tiny room and new air pumped in. It was all for show, of course, none of that was actually happening, but they had a lie to sell if anyone was watching.

The green light went on and Nick stepped out. He modeled the suit for her.

"How do I look?"

"Very stylish," she said. "I'll go through the tunnel first and wait for you on the other side. I'll check you out for tears and tape up any that I see."

"You'll get infected," Nick said.

"I've been vaccinated."

"No, you haven't."

"How would you know?"

"I would have seen the scar," he said.

"You must have missed it."

"I gave you a very thorough examination," Nick said. "I can map every freckle."

"I don't think I am going to be in any *real* danger of infection, do you? I'll see you on the other side of the tunnel," she said and crawled inside.

He waited a moment, then carefully crawled in after her. It was a tight fit, but the diamond core driller had left the walls fairly smooth, and he went slowly. When he got to the end, she helped him out of the hole and checked his suit out for punctures or tears.

She tore off a few pieces of duct tape, putting one on each knee and another on his back, where the shape of the respirator stuck out like a backpack under the suit.

"Were there some rips?" Nick asked.

"I don't think so. I covered the scratches just to be on the safe side," she said. "Follow me."

They walked single file down the corridor, through an IGC access tunnel, and then into the sewer. A sign on the wall read *rue Boissonade*. They reached the ladder to the manhole and Kate climbed up first, pushing the manhole cover up and sliding it aside. She climbed out into the predawn darkness and saw the SAP truck parked at the curb under a street lamp. Litija was in the driver's seat. The three Road Runners, Gaëlle, and Huck were standing a safe distance away on the sidewalk behind the van, as if Nick might explode and they didn't want to get hit by the shrapnel.

Kate climbed out and waved Vinko over. "Help me ease Nick out of here."

Vinko looked like he'd rather have a hot coffee enema, but he came over anyway.

As Nick slowly emerged, they each took one of his arms and gently eased him out of the manhole, careful to make sure his suit cleared the opening without scraping it. The instant Nick was out, Vinko joined Borko and Dusko behind Gaëlle and Huck. It was like the three Road Runners were using Gaëlle and Huck as human shields.

Kate led Nick to the back of the van and opened the doors for him. Nick stepped inside the empty cargo area. Once he was settled on a bench, Kate started to climb in, too.

"What do you think you're doing?" Litija said, turning in her seat to look at them.

"I'm going with you," Kate said.

"No, you're not." Litija lifted a Sig Sauer P239 off her lap and aimed it at Kate. "Get out."

"It's okay, Kate," Nick said. "I don't need your protection anymore. I think I'm way past that now."

"I thought I was more than protection to you," she said.

"You thought wrong," Nick said. "Good luck to you."

"I'm not the one who is going to need it."

Kate stepped out and slammed the door closed behind her. Litija set her gun down on the passenger seat.

"Put on your seatbelt," Litija said. "We don't want any accidents."

24

Kate watched the van drive away before turning to face Gaëlle and Huck and the three Road Runners.

The Road Runners had guns drawn, and Gaëlle and Huck had eyes wide with fear. Dusko moved a short distance from the group and aimed his gun at Kate.

"You really don't want to do this," Kate said to the men.

"It's not a question of what we want," Vinko said. "We follow orders."

Kate stared him down. "I'd reconsider if I were you. If you don't lower those guns, you'll be killed. We have protection."

"You don't look protected to me," Vinko said.

She stayed stoic. "You're making a mistake."

Vinko and Borko aimed. So did Dusko.

Huck took Gaëlle's hand. Gaëlle squeezed it hard and they both closed their eyes. What they heard next sounded like two sandbags hitting the ground. It took a second for Gaëlle and Huck to realize that they weren't shot. They turned around and saw that Vinko and Borko were dead on the ground, both shot in the head.

Kate didn't hear or see the shots, but knew she had Walter, up on a rooftop somewhere, to thank for saving Gaëlle and Huck. She looked at Dusko now. He stood very still, eyes wide, and then toppled face-first to the ground, a knife in his back. Antoine Killian stood a few feet behind Dusko. Kate had no idea how the enormous man had got there or where he'd come from so fast.

"*Merci,*" Kate said to him.

He nodded and offered her a polite smile. "*Je vous en prie.*"

She assumed it was French for "You're welcome" or "No problem." Antoine stepped up, pulled his knife out of Dusko's back, and wiped the blood off on the dead man's jumpsuit.

A black BMW 7 Series sedan slinked around the corner behind Gaëlle and Huck and glided smoothly to a stop beside Kate. Willie was at the wheel and lowered the passenger window to speak with her.

"I've got a strong tracking signal on Nick," Willie said, holding up a tablet device that was plugged into the car's USB port. "They're crossing the intersection of boulevard Saint-Michel and boulevard Saint-Germain."

Kate turned to Gaëlle and Huck, both of whom looked shell-shocked. "It's all over. You're both safe now. Thank you for everything you've done. Now get out of here fast and maybe go on a vacation for a few weeks."

She got into the BMW, and it sped away.

It wasn't until the car was gone that Huck Moseby realized that the fat man who'd stabbed Dusko had disappeared. Now he and Gaëlle were alone with three corpses. Huck didn't know what had just happened or who the fat man was or who the woman in the car was or who the hell had shot Vinko and Borko. All he knew for sure was that he'd barely escaped death and that Gaëlle was holding his hand.

He looked at her and thought she was the most beautiful woman he'd ever seen. She was literally the woman of his dreams. It was hard to believe that she actually existed.

"If you'll have me," he said in French, "I will devote my life to making you happy."

She smiled. "You have a deal."

They kissed softly and then walked away, still holding hands.

"The first time we met," Nick said, buckled in tight in the back of the van, "I'd just emerged from a coffin in a fake diamond vault in Belgium. Now here I am in a hazmat suit, infected with smallpox, and we're driving through the streets of Paris in a sewer van. Who would have imagined that?"

"You lead a wild, exciting life," Litija said.

"You do, too."

"But it's been much more profitable for you than me."

"It doesn't seem like it at the moment," Nick said.

"I'm sure you've been in situations as bad as this." She glanced at him in the rearview mirror. "How many times have you had a gun to your head or a knife to your throat?"

"This is different. I can talk myself out of those situations."

"I've seen you do it and it was amazing, especially the way you played Dragan. Nobody has ever done that before. It's not just what you say, it's also the outrageous risks you take at the same time. You've inspired me."

"Really?" Nick said. "To do what?"

"You'll see," she said.

She remained silent as they headed north through central Paris, along much of the same scenic route that Gaëlle had taken with Nick and Kate during their Uber ride. They hit the A1 freeway, taking the ramp for Lille/Aéroport Charles de Gaulle/Saint-Denis. Nick figured they were going to an airport to board Dragan's private jet for a trip to another country. Suddenly Litija exited off the freeway and drove into an industrial warehouse district miles away from the airport.

"Are we taking the scenic route?" Nick asked.

Litija ignored him and proceeded through the rotting gates of a sprawling abandoned factory. The cavernous brick buildings had multiple smokestacks and were tangled in the gantries, pipes, and conveyor belts that ran through them, around them, and over them. She drove into one of the buildings, which was the size of an airplane hangar, and stopped the van.

"Where are we, Litija?"

"At a turning point for both of us." Her cellphone rang. She answered it and put it on the speaker. "Hello, Dragan. I've put you on the speaker and am talking to you in English so Nick can hear you, too."

"I'm very sorry about what happened to you, Nick," Dragan said. "But I can assure you of two things. Thanks to your quick thinking, you'll survive and our project can still go forward as we planned. You'll be a very rich man when this is over."

"I like that," Nick said.

JANET EVANOVICH AND LEE GOLDBERG

"In a few minutes, you'll be on my plane and on your way to my lab, where you'll get the best medical care and you can watch our plans take shape while you recuperate."

"Recuperate? I thought I was getting the vaccine."

"You are," Dragan said. "But not immediately. We need to wait for the virus to multiply in your bloodstream so we can extract a potent sample that we can work with."

"You're using me as an incubator?"

"It's not how I would have liked to do things, but you're the one who dropped the vial. So we're turning lemons into *limoncello,* as they say."

"Okay, so what's the delay?" Nick asked. "Why are we sitting in this warehouse?"

"I can answer that," Litija said. "There's been a little change in plans, Dragan. I wanted you to hear Nick so you'd know he was with me and that he's still alive."

"Smallpox doesn't kill instantly," Nick said.

"But I do," she said. "I will kill Nick unless twenty million dollars is wired to my offshore bank account in the next ten minutes."

Litija disconnected the call.

Kate and Willie heard every chilling word through their earbuds as they sped along on the A1 freeway.

This was an unexpected complication they didn't need after one too many complications already.

"How far behind them are we?" Kate asked.

"Five minutes," Willie said.

"Make it two," Kate said.

Willie floored the gas pedal and wove through the cars in front of them like the *Millennium Falcon* flying through an asteroid belt. Kate took out her phone and hit the speed-dial key for her father.

"How close are you, Dad?"

Willie leaned on her horn and drove between two lanes, shearing off the side-view mirrors. "Oops. I guess I should have taken the insurance," she said.

"Ten minutes," Jake said. "But we'll make it five."

"Just sit tight, Nick," Litija said, aiming her Sig Sauer at him. "Once I have the money, I'll leave you here. I'll let Dragan know where to find you when I'm a safe distance away."

"That could take hours, and I don't have a lot of hours to spare."

"It is what it is."

"I have a better idea. It's getting stuffy in here. So I'm going to unzip this suit and get some air unless you put that gun down and start driving."

"If you touch that zipper, I'll shoot you."

"That would be stupid, because if you puncture this suit, you'll be infected with smallpox."

"There are three problems with your threat. The first is that I've been vaccinated against smallpox."

"I don't believe you," Nick said. "So I will call that bluff."

"The second is that I'm a dead woman anyway, because whether you live or die, Dragan will hunt me to the ends of the earth. But with twenty million, I'll have a better chance of outrunning him or at least living very, very well until he finds me."

"That just proves how much you want to live."

"Which brings me to number three. You don't want to die. You'd rather take your chances with the virus than risk a bullet in the head from me. Besides, you've got nothing to lose in this transaction. What do you care if I walk away with twenty million dollars? You're going to be a billionaire."

"Assuming Dragan pays."

"He'll pay," she said. "What's twenty million against billions?"

"You might kill me anyway just to spite Dragan."

"Do I strike you as a spiteful person?"

"Isn't that why you are doing this? Because you're mad that Dragan killed Zarko?"

Litija laughed. "I don't care about Zarko. You met him. He was a slug."

"But you were shaking after Dragan pushed him off the cliff."

"Because it could easily have been me if I'd been standing there," she said. "I'm doing this for the money. I want to be rich and far away from Dragan Kovic. The man is insane, in case you haven't noticed."

"I noticed," Nick said.

"But you still went into business with him. You must be crazy, too." She picked up her phone and checked it. "The money hasn't shown up in my account yet. You've got three minutes."

There was a tap-tap on the driver's side window and Litija went pale. It was Kate, tapping the barrel of her gun against the window.

"Put the gun down or I'll blow your head off," Kate shouted through the glass. She was still in her dirty sewer worker's jumpsuit.

Litija stared at Kate in absolute disbelief. "How did you get here?"

"The same way he did," Kate said, gesturing to the passenger side.

Litija turned. A man in his sixties stood outside the window, and he was also aiming a gun at her. He had the buzz cut, bearing, and hardened gaze of a soldier. She'd underestimated Nick and Kate. They'd had a second team of professional killers watching their backs. Her inability to anticipate this move

JANET EVANOVICH AND LEE GOLDBERG

demonstrated why she'd always been somebody's minion. She wasn't clever enough to lead. It proved to her that this twenty-million-dollar play was her last, best chance at changing her fate.

"*You* drop the gun," Litija said. "And the old man drops his, too, or I will kill Nick right now."

"That would be a mistake," Kate said. "Because I'm your ticket to freedom and happiness."

"How do you imagine that?"

"I'll let you go and tell Dragan that I killed you," Kate said. "You won't have your ransom money, but at least you'll be free and won't have to look over your shoulder for the rest of your life. Or you can shoot Nick and die right now. Your choice."

How did Kate know about the ransom? Was the van wired? Was Nick? The fact that she didn't know the answers to those questions was more humiliating evidence that she was destined to a life of servitude and pocket change, never to leadership and wealth. She glanced at her phone, hoping for a $20 million reprieve from her wretched destiny.

The ten minutes were up. There was no alert from the bank that a transfer had been made, and Dragan hadn't called arguing for more time. He didn't pay, and she had the miserable, crushing realization that he never would. He'd rather sacrifice Nick and put off his scheme indefinitely than let her extort a dime out of him.

282

The bastard.

"You gambled that Dragan's greed was larger than his ego," Nick said. "I could have told you that was a losing bet."

Litija put her gun down on the passenger seat and placed her hands on the steering wheel in surrender.

"You can't blame a girl for trying," she said.

Kate stuck her gun in her jumpsuit and opened the driver's side door. "Come on out."

As Litija stepped out, a jaunty little Alfa Romeo convertible sped into the building and came to a stop behind Kate. The man at the wheel was as jaunty as his car. He had a big smile and wore a herringbone wool driving cap, a red cravat, and a tweed jacket. He was so British he might as well have draped himself in the Union Jack.

"Hello, luv," Robin Mannering said. "Going my way?"

Litija looked at Kate. "Where's he taking me?"

"Out of France," Kate said. "He'll set you up with a passport, credit cards, and some cash, and you're on your way."

"But we'll find a decent cup of tea first," Robin said.

The truth was that he would take her straight to the British Embassy, where she'd be placed under arrest. Her faked death would make Litija the perfect secret informant against the Road Runners and law enforcement's best hope of tracking down the stolen diamonds.

"Why aren't you killing me?" Litija said.

"Because I work for Nicolas Fox and he insists that I only kill in self-defense, never in cold blood," Kate said. "It's a character flaw that will probably cost him his life one day."

"That day will come very soon unless you break that rule with Dragan." Litija got into the car with Robin and they drove off.

Kate climbed into the driver's seat of the van and looked back at Nick, who'd unzipped his hood and pulled it off his head.

"Did you see Litija's double-cross coming?" she asked.

"Nope. I must be losing my touch."

Jake got into the passenger seat and reached over to shake Nick's hand. "Good to see you."

"Likewise," Nick said.

"Your crew is long gone, and Antoine and Walter have cleaned up the mess on the street," Jake said. "The three bodies will never be found."

"Vinko, Borko, and Dusko?" Nick said.

"Walter and Antoine took them out and saved our lives," Kate said. "Your instincts were right."

"What about Dragan's two snipers?" Nick asked.

"They couldn't see what happened from where they were," Jake said. "They were watching avenue

Denfert-Rochereau and I was watching them. They left their positions as soon as they saw Litija drive off in this van. They probably assumed the mission was accomplished and are now on their way out of the country."

"We should be, too." Kate picked up the cellphone, hit the speed dial, and waited. Dragan answered on the first ring.

"Have you come to your senses?" he asked.

"That's hard to do when your brains are splattered on a wall," Kate said. "Litija is dead."

"Well done," Dragan said. "How is Nick?"

Nick spoke up. "Eager to get to you as fast as possible."

"How much time do you have left on your battery, Nick?"

"Maybe five hours," Nick said.

"No worries," Dragan said. "We'll have everything ready for you when you arrive."

Dragan gave Kate directions to the terminal and hung up.

"Wherever Dragan's lab is, we'll be there five hours from now," Kate said to her father. "You'll strike two hours later."

"You mean I'll come and get you," Jake said.

"I mean blow the place up," Kate said. "Reduce it to ash. Make sure Dragan and his virus do not get out."

"That was the old plan," Jake said. "But things

have changed now that you two are going to be inside."

"Not the way I see it," Kate said. "Do you have a set of our earbuds?"

"I do, but I hate wearing them," Jake said. "They are too much like hearing aids. They make me feel old."

"When you're within striking distance, the three of us should be able to communicate with one another," she said.

"See you in seven hours," Jake said, kissed Kate on the cheek, and got out.

Kate drove the van out of the warehouse, past Willie in her BMW and the Renault that Jake had driven, and headed for Charles de Gaulle Airport. Willie and Jake would be close behind them, bound for the private plane that they also had on standby.

"We're in this together again," Nick said.

"We are always in it together, even when we're apart."

"Not to be overly unmanly, but the moment I escaped from you that first time in L.A.," Nick said, "I regretted it two minutes later and was tempted to let you catch me just so we could be together."

She looked at him in the rearview mirror. "Really?"

"Really."

Kate was pretty sure she believed him. "I had no clue."

"Would you have done anything differently if you knew I was enamored with you?"

"No," Kate said. "Zip up your hood, we're almost there."

Damn! He was enamored with her way back then, she thought. It was enough to get her doing a happy dance. She wouldn't, of course, because she was the job. Still, she could happy dance in her mind.

Nick secured himself in the suit again as they reached the general aviation area of the airport and the private terminal. She drove through the gates, escorted by a security officer on a golf cart, onto the tarmac beside the black private jet. She backed up so the rear of the sewer van was as close as possible to the open hatch at the front of the plane. Kate didn't want Nick in his biohazard suit to be visible for long. Fortunately it was dawn on a Sunday and the odds of anybody being around to see him were slim.

Daca and Stefan appeared in the plane's open hatch. She recognized them as the same two men who'd followed them in Sorrento and later took them by boat to Dragan's villa. She got out, held her Glock down at her side, and walked to the back of the van.

"Good morning, gentlemen," she said. "I'd appreciate it if you'd open the van and help Nick into the plane."

"We'd rather that you do it," Daca said.

She shook her head and aimed her gun at them. "I want to see that you're unarmed and I want you out of the plane so I can check it out."

"You can trust us," Stefan said. "We're on the same side."

"Is that why your three buddies just tried to kill me?"

Daca nodded acknowledgment. The two men got out of the plane, and Kate stepped aboard. She quickly checked out the cabin and then watched from the hatch as the men opened the van, helped Nick out, and guided him to a seat on the plane. Kate took a seat near the cockpit, and Daca secured the hatch. They had only about four hours left on Nick's battery.

"Let's go," she said to the pilot. "The clock is ticking."

Kate didn't lower her gun until they'd taken off. She didn't think Daca and Stefan were dumb enough to start a shoot-out in the confines of a pressurized airplane. But she didn't turn her back to them, either.

Daca and Stefan stayed as far away from Nick as they could get, not that it would protect them from infection if he decided to open his suit or if he tore it somehow.

"Could somebody flag down the flight attendant?" Nick asked. "I'd like some peanuts and a Bloody Mary."

25

They landed in Frankfurt, Germany, an hour and fifteen minutes later. The pilots didn't announce their arrival, but Nick recognized the skyline the instant he saw the Trianon, a forty-seven-story office building with an enormous glass diamond that was suspended between three pinnacles at the top.

"I once cracked a safe in that building in broad daylight in front of a room full of executives. I pretended to be an expert hired by the corporate bosses in Berlin to evaluate the company's security measures," Nick said. "I scoffed at the lax security in the Frankfurt office and took the diamond-studded Egyptian antiquities that were in the safe with me to a place where they'd be better protected."

"Your living room?" Kate asked.

"A museum in Egypt," Nick said. "I would have kept them, but they clashed with my recliner."

The plane taxied to a stop a few yards away from a black helicopter.

"You're taking the helicopter the rest of the way," Daca said.

Kate aimed her gun at them. "I want you both to go in the bathroom and shut the door. Don't leave until we're gone."

"Why?" Stefan asked. "Are you afraid we're going to shoot you in the back?"

"Yes," Kate said. "Now get inside. No peeking, or the last thing you'll see is the bullet in your eye."

"I bet you aren't half as tough as you think you are," Daca said.

"How ironic," Kate said. "Vinko expressed the same sentiment to me. Now he's dead."

Stefan and Daca squeezed into the bathroom and closed the door. Nick and Kate got out of the plane and walked quickly to the helicopter.

The only person inside the helicopter was the pilot, who acknowledged them with a nod. Kate helped Nick get up into the chopper, then she climbed in and slid the door shut.

"The other guys won't be joining us," Kate yelled so the pilot could hear her over the sound of the rotor blades. "They got airsick."

The pilot gave them a thumbs-up and they lifted off. They headed southeast across the Main River toward the wooded mountains in the distance. They passed over several picturesque, storybook villages of half-timbered buildings and Gothic towers, and finally over a dense forest.

"That's the Spessart forest down there, home of *Snow White and the Seven Dwarfs*," Nick said.

Kate wouldn't have heard him over the sound of the rotors if it wasn't for the earbuds in their ears.

They came to a valley where a clearing had been cut into the woods. In the center of the clearing was an immaculate lawn and a medieval stone castle surrounded by a moat full of dark water. A gravel road ran alongside the edge of the clearing to a crushed gravel lot where two black Range Rovers were parked.

The castle walls were topped with battlements and so was the circular tower that rose high above the tree line. As the helicopter came in low over the castle, Kate could see four men armed with rifles patrolling the battlements and another man atop the tower scanning the forest with binoculars.

The helicopter landed in the grass in front of the drawbridge, where Dragan Kovic stood to welcome them. Nick and Kate got out of the chopper and walked up to Dragan.

"Welcome to Schloss Gesundheit," Dragan said.

"'Castle Good Health' is a strange name for the place where you're producing smallpox," Nick said.

"We inherited the name," Dragan said as he led

them onto the drawbridge. "The castle was built in the 1400s and was a ruin by the 1880s, inhabited by nomads and bandits. That's when it was rebuilt as a sanitarium for people with horrible diseases. It was the ideal place to exile the poor souls, presumably for their health and well-being, because it was remote and the walls were thick. They even sent lepers here. Schloss Gesundheit closed in the 1950s and was abandoned until I came along. Nobody wanted to get near it."

"I can't imagine why," Kate said.

"The same qualities that made it an attractive sanitarium made it perfect for our needs," Dragan said. "It seemed right to keep the name."

They reached the iron lattice gate that sealed the passageway into the castle. Dragan stopped and held his hand out, palm up, to Kate.

"I'd like to have your gun before we go inside," Dragan said.

"I'm sure you would," Kate said. "But it's not happening."

"We're on the same side."

"That's what your people keep saying," Kate said. "It would be easier to believe if Vinko and your men hadn't tried to execute me and the rest of our crew after Litija drove off with Nick."

"I'm certain that I would have faced the same

firing squad if things had gone as planned and I hadn't been infected," Nick said.

"I had nothing to do with it," Dragan said. "This news comes as a complete shock to me."

Dragan wasn't very convincing, but Kate figured he didn't have to try very hard. He knew Nick wasn't going anywhere.

"That's twice you've double-crossed me after a robbery," Nick said. "I should kill you, but self-preservation and extraordinary wealth mean more to me than revenge."

"Vinko, Dusko, and Borko were obviously in league with Litija," Dragan said. "She tried to double-cross us both."

"If what you say is true," Nick said to Dragan, "then your employees aren't very trustworthy. So I'm sure you can understand why I insist that Kate remain armed. She can protect us both."

"Well, when you put it that way, how can I argue?" Dragan said. "I'm glad to have someone of Kate's proven skills protecting us from further treachery."

Dragan nodded to a camera mounted by the entrance and the gate rose, creaking with age. He led them into a passageway leading to a courtyard with a wishing well in the middle.

Nick pointed up at the arched ceiling of the passageway. "I see you kept the *meurtrières*."

Dragan smiled. "I love charming architectural details like those. Every home should have them."

Kate looked up and saw sunlight spilling through six large holes in the stonework. "What are they for?" she asked.

"They're commonly known as murder holes," Nick said. "They're for pouring cauldrons of boiling water or hot tar on invaders."

"I prefer cauldrons of lye," Dragan said. "It makes cleanup so easy. You just hose what's left of your unwanted guests into the moat."

"Have you had the opportunity?" Kate asked.

"Not yet," he replied. "But you never know when unexpected guests might show up."

Kate did. They'd be coming in four hours, and she'd be sure to warn them not to come in through the front door.

They crossed the courtyard and entered the foyer of the castle. A burly Serbian with a gun in a shoulder holster sat at a console similar to those found in office building lobbies. He had a phone and several screens showing security camera views.

There were three doors off the foyer, and one of them was an air lock. Dragan went to the air lock, held a card key up to the reader on the wall, and they heard the lock open.

"After you, Nick," Dragan said.

Nick stepped into the air lock. After a moment,

the door on the opposite side opened and he stepped into a corridor.

Dragan gestured to the door. "Proceed."

"We'll go in together," Kate said, worried that he could lock her inside and have all the air sucked out. She wasn't sure that was even possible, but she didn't want to find out the hard way.

"It will be a tight fit," Dragan said.

"We'll manage."

"As you wish."

She held the door open for him and, once he was inside, she stepped in behind him. He opened the next door and they joined Nick in the corridor. It was almost identical to the corridors inside the Institut National pour la Recherche sur les Maladies Infectieuses that Kate had seen on the security videos. Same walls, same floor, same hospital ambiance.

There were two air locks, one on each side of the corridor, and three large observation windows that looked in on the labs. Another burly armed guard was also waiting in the corridor, presumably to prevent Kate from taking Dragan hostage and demanding the vaccine for Nick.

She'd toyed with a similar scenario, except that she'd demand the smallpox sample instead of the vaccine. The problem was that she had no idea where the smallpox was or if it had already been used to create new supplies of the pathogen. Even if she did, one of the snipers would probably shoot her and Nick before they could leave the castle. Kate couldn't take any action until she knew where every last microbe of the virus was in the facility and her dad had arrived to back her up.

Dragan gestured to the air lock on their left. "Go through there, Nick. It's laid out just like the institute. Go straight through the locker room, the dressing room, and the suit room, where we have the positive pressure suits. You'll see three air locks, each with a number on them. Take the air lock marked number one. That's the lab that we've had repurposed as your quarters. Remove your suit and all of your clothing. Leave everything on the floor. You'll find new clothes waiting for you."

Nick peered through the window into the lab. Amid the workstations, dangling air hoses, and other equipment, he saw a cot with a set of surgical scrubs, slippers, and a towel laid out on the blanket.

"It's a good thing I'm not bashful," Nick said.

"You can draw the blinds if you want privacy," Dragan said and passed his card key over the reader, opening the air lock.

Nick stepped into the air lock and into the next room. A few moments later, Dragan and Kate saw him come through one of the two air locks in the back of the lab. He unzipped the suit and got out of it, stripped off his T-shirt and briefs, and put on the scrubs. He left the suit and clothes piled on the floor.

The other air lock in the lab opened and two technicians entered in positive pressure suits just like the ones Boyd, Willie, and the others had worn, and attached themselves to the air hoses hanging from the ceiling. They each carried large bags and stuffed his suit and clothes into them, sealed them with zip ties, and carried them out again.

"Everything he wore is going into the incinerators in the basement," Dragan said. "The microbiologists who came in will step into a disinfectant shower in their positive pressure suits, then once they've removed the suits and their undergarments, they will shower themselves. We're very serious about safety protocols here."

Nick walked up to the window, faced them, and pressed the intercom button on the wall. His voice came out over a speaker in the corridor. "What happens now?"

Dragan pressed an intercom button on his side. "Make yourself comfortable and get some rest. If you need anything at all, just press the intercom button here, by the air locks, or at any of the lab stations and a technician will handle it."

"What if I need to use the bathroom?"

"There's a bucket, wet wipes, and a roll of toilet

paper under your cot," Dragan said. "Call for service and the bucket will be taken away."

"Not exactly the Four Seasons, is it?"

Before Dragan could answer, Nick shut the blinds. Dragan released the intercom and frowned.

"Moody, isn't he?"

"He gets that way when he goes without sleep for twenty-four hours, spends twelve hours digging a hole in a sewer, and then gets infected with a virus that will make him spew blood from every orifice."

"Nobody said that becoming a billionaire is easy," Dragan said. "Let me show you to your room. I'm sure you'd like to change and freshen up."

"I'd like a tour first," Kate said. "I won't feel comfortable until I get the lay of the land."

"Your uniform is filthy and you smell like the sewer. Clean up, then we'll have brunch and I'll show you around."

He led her out of the air lock, back to the foyer, past the guard, and through one of the other two heavy wooden doors. This led to another corridor that, unlike the lab area, felt like a castle should. It was entirely stone, rough-hewn on the walls and polished smooth under her feet. All that was missing to complete the authentic ambiance were torches to light their way instead of a series of LEDs in the ceiling. Dragan stopped at one of the doors.

"This was Litija's room," Dragan said. "She was

more or less your size. You can wear her clothes or the scrubs that we've left on the bed. I'll see you in the dining room in an hour. It's straight down the hall and to your right."

She didn't have the hour to spare. She needed time to see the layout, come up with a plan, and then execute it before her dad showed up, guns and rockets blazing.

"Let's make it thirty minutes," she said. "I'm starving."

"Very well," he said and walked down the hall.

26

Dragan wanted to smash Kate's head against the wall until it splattered like a ripe melon. *Nobody* talked to him like that. This wasn't a hotel and he wasn't her bellboy. But instead of acting on his impulse, he'd walked away. It wasn't her gun that had stopped him but some practical considerations. He needed her alive. Nick would remain cooperative as long as he was under the delusion that Kate guaranteed his security and eventual vaccination.

But in two weeks, once Nick was sick enough that a nice, virulent sample of virus could be taken from him, then Dragan would kill Kate and take the time to thoroughly enjoy the experience. Maybe he'd use her to try out the lye. *That* would certainly be entertaining. The thought made him smile. Now he had another good reason to wait.

· · ·

Kate closed the door and surveyed the room. It was a dungeon decorated like a bed-and-breakfast. The four-poster bed and armoire were hand carved, very old, and rich with vintage charm. She went to the window, barely more than a slit in the wall. It looked out over the moat and the lawn, where the helicopter was still sitting. She turned back to the room. There was a set of scrubs neatly folded on the bed, but Kate chose to check out what Litija had in the armoire instead. She couldn't holster her Glock on scrub pants.

"How are you holding up?" Kate asked Nick via the earbud.

Nick put his head in his hands so that Kate could hear him without the cameras in his room seeing him talk. "I'm trying not to fall asleep. I'm in position to take decisive action once you find out exactly where the virus is. It must be in one of the rooms or labs within this biosafety area."

"But it's a high-security area and you don't have the card key."

Kate opened the armoire. It was stuffed with Chanel ready-to-wear. Silk dresses, embroidered blouses, miniskirts, and lambskin slacks that were extremely colorful and meant to stand out. Whatever Kate picked to wear would make her an easy target to spot.

"You're forgetting something," Nick said. "I'm

already past security. Dragan graciously escorted me in."

"But you're locked in a lab."

"Actually, I'm not. The biosafety area is designed to lock people out, not to lock them in. I have complete freedom of movement within these labs, once you tell me where to go."

"You make it sound so easy." Kate grabbed a multicolored silk blouse with a busy design, cream lambskin slacks, and a large black belt and tossed them on the bed. The only shoes in the armoire were high heels, so she decided to stick with the mud-caked boots she'd worn in the sewer. "How am I supposed to find out that information? I don't have time to sneak around."

"Ask Dragan where it is."

She slipped out of her filthy jumpsuit and left it on the floor. "Why would he tell me?"

"Because he likes to show off," Nick said.

"It's one thing to brag about his villa and his castle, but there's no reason for him to tell me what he's done with the smallpox."

"So give him one," Nick said.

She tossed her underwear on the bed and stood naked in the middle of the room. "I'll think about it in the shower."

"I'll think about you taking a shower."

"I'd rather you thought of a plan for destroying the smallpox and escaping," she said.

"I'm on it," he said.

Nick got up from his cot, went to the intercom on the wall, and pressed the button.

"I have needs," Nick said.

"What can I get for you?" a man's voice answered.

"A box of cigars. The best Dragan has. And bring me bottles of vodka, scotch, and rum. The highest proof you've got. I intend to get smashed."

"Completely understandable," the man said.

The dining room was huge with a long table under two elaborate chandeliers that resembled upside-down Christmas trees. A large window overlooked the moat and the forest beyond.

Kate was admiring the chandeliers when she spotted the fresco on the ceiling. It was a copy of Michelangelo's *Creation of Adam* from the Sistine Chapel, with a robed, bearded God reaching out from the heavens to touch the outstretched hand of a lounging, naked Adam. But unlike the original, this Adam had Dragan's pockmarked face and an enormous penis. She was still staring at the disturbing image, not really believing what she was seeing, when Dragan walked into the room.

"What do you think?" Dragan asked.

"I'm surprised that your face is on Adam and not God."

"God doesn't have a dick," Dragan said.

"God doesn't need one," Kate said.

"It's not necessary if you're going to rule the heavens, but it is if you're going to conquer the world," he said. "Metaphorically speaking, of course. That's the point this painting is making."

"I wish I could see that painting," Nick said in Kate's ear.

She almost replied *No, you don't.*

Dragan waved her to a seat at the end of a table that was set with smoked fish, sausages, fruit, and an array of pastries, along with coffee, juice, and water.

"Is that the point of the smallpox, too?" Kate asked. "Metaphorically speaking?"

"I suppose it is," he said.

"To pull off your biological attack, you're going to need someone who can slip into the United States to plant the device. You're going to have a hard time doing that with one of your Serbian Army buddies. But it would be no problem at all for an American citizen born and raised in California. Lucky for you, here I am."

"Brilliant," Nick said. *"I knew you'd come up with something."*

"You would do that for me?"

"I would do it for the twenty million you're going to pay me now and that I'm going to use to bet against the market," Kate said as she chose a croissant and poured herself a cup of coffee.

"That's the same amount Litija demanded as ransom for Nick."

"Yes, I know," Kate said. "Right amount, wrong play. You'll be glad to pay for this."

"You have no qualms about launching a terrorist attack against your own country?"

"My country is wherever I happen to be at any given moment," Kate said. "Right now it's Germany. In a few months, it will be the private island in the Bahamas that I am going to buy with my windfall."

Dragan smiled. "You didn't accompany Nick here to protect him. You came to strike a deal for yourself."

"You've hooked him," Nick said. *"Now slowly reel him in."*

She took a bite of the croissant and almost swooned. It was unbelievably flaky and buttery. She licked her lips and nibbled off another piece.

Dragan rapped his knife against his water glass. *Clang, clang, clang.* "It's just a croissant," he said. "We eat them every day. Can we move forward?"

"Yes, but this is a *really great* croissant," Kate

said. "It's flaky and buttery. How do they get it to taste like this?"

"*Focus!*" Dragan said.

"Jeez," Kate said. "I was enjoying a moment, okay?"

Dragan looked like he was running out of patience, but Kate could hear Nick laughing at his end. She put the croissant down, took a sip of coffee, and dragged herself back to the task at hand.

"Having me around makes Nick feel like he's got some control in this situation, that he'll get his vaccine and his money. But we both know that's a fantasy. You're going to kill me as soon as you can get the virus out of him, and then you're going to let him die naturally because it'll be fun to watch."

"If you know that," Dragan said, "why are you still here? Why haven't you left?"

"Because it won't change anything. I know too much. You've got to kill me. You already tried once, and you'll keep at it until you get it done. I'm giving you a better option, one that benefits both of us. Or I can shoot you now and probably get myself killed trying to get out of here."

She took another sip of coffee and looked at him over the rim of her cup as if they were casually discussing a change in the weather and not her life expectancy.

"I can see why Nick is so fond of you," Dragan

said. "Killers are easy to find but you're almost as good a talker as he is."

"He still thinks he can talk his way out of this," she said.

"He's wrong. However, you make a convincing argument for your life. I won't kill you. I believe you're too valuable a resource to waste."

"I knew you were a man of reason."

He was also a man without a woman now that Litija had got her brains blown out, and he'd gotten hard watching Kate eat her croissant. He thought she might be of short-term use to him.

"We can use the couple weeks or so that we're waiting for Nick to die to figure out the operational details of the attack," he said.

"That's fine, but there's only so much we can accomplish from a castle in Germany," Kate said. "After Nick is dead, and while you're cooking up batches of the virus, I can make a dry run into the U.S. and work out the kinks in the field. Nothing beats boots on the ground. I'll come back with what I've learned and we can fine-tune the plan."

"That's an excellent idea," Dragan said. "Would you like to see how the virus is coming along and the delivery system you'll be using to spread it?"

"Why not?" she said and finished her coffee. "I've got nothing better to do."

Dragan and Kate entered the biosafety corridor as a scientist passed them pushing a cart that carried a box of cigars and bottles of vodka, rum, and whiskey. The scientist went through the air lock with the cart.

"Looks like the reality of the situation is sinking in for Nick," Dragan said.

"It had to happen eventually," Kate said. "Be glad he didn't ask for a gun or a bottle of sleeping pills."

Dragan led her past the closed blinds of Nick's lab window to the next window down the hall. Inside, she saw four men in positive pressure suits diligently engaged in their scientific tasks at various workstations.

"This is our second lab, where we're using an old-school method to grow enough smallpox to create a weapon. You see those chicken eggs?" Dragan pointed to a scientist sitting at a table in front of dozens of eggs resting in a tray that looked like the bottom of an egg carton. The man was using a syringe to inject a milky substance into the eggs. "We inject the virus into live chicken embryos. I won't bore you with the science, because frankly I don't understand it all, but the virus thrives in that goop. What you're looking at is our smallpox production line."

Kate desperately wanted to take a step back from the window. There was something unnerving about being that close to something so unbelievably deadly, no matter how many safety protocols were in place. She watched as another scientist, a Chinese man, took a tray of eggs to an incubator and opened it. There were four other trays in the oven-like machine.

"If you're already producing virus from what you got in Antwerp," she asked, "why did you need to steal another sample?"

"The one from Antwerp was small, and production would have dragged on," Dragan said. "The additional virus we've just acquired will speed things up exponentially. Plus the virus in Nick's system is derived from a more recent, and far deadlier, strain smuggled out of a weapons lab near Novosibirsk, Siberia, by a rogue microbiologist in the late 1990s. The smallpox Nick carries is a chimera."

"What's a chimera?"

"It's from Greek mythology. A fearsome monster made of parts of many different animals. In this case, it's a pathogen composed of more than one deadly virus. The smallpox that Nick is infected with is mixed with Ebola. You could call it 'big pox.' It embodies the worst of smallpox and Ebola. It's one hundred percent fatal and incurable."

"You neglected to mention that detail to us before," she said.

"Oops." Dragan shrugged. "My mistake."

"What was the institute in Paris doing with a smallpox chimera?"

"They're studying it to find a cure," Dragan said.

"In the center of a densely populated city?"

"There are level-four biolabs in major cities all over the world," Dragan said. "The institute is just one of many secretly hired by governments to find cures for the worst possible bioweapons in case an army, a terrorist group, or an enterprising investor like me decides to unleash a plague."

"So how do we do this?" Kate said. "I presume we aren't just going to throw those eggs at people."

"Once the eggs are teeming with new virus, we extract the goop and turn it into an aerosol spray." Dragan led her to the next window. Inside that lab, she saw more workstations and freezers. "This is lab number three, where we will be creating the spray and storing it for the weapon."

"Where's the weapon?"

Dragan reached into his pocket and took out a small breath freshener dispenser. It was roughly the same shape and size as a keychain thumb drive.

"It will look like this, only it will be equipped with a small timer," Dragan said, admiring the device. "It releases a mist of micron-sized virus particles. One of these placed in an inconspicuous spot in an airport terminal will infect thousands of people in just a few minutes and spread 'big pox' all over the globe. But I prefer a more targeted approach."

"That shouldn't be hard to smuggle into the U.S. or to hide in a movie theater or an enclosed shopping mall," Kate said. "But you'd have to prove to me that the timer works before I set one up. One spritz and I'm dead, too."

"We've created some harmless mock-ups that you can test."

"How many scientists do you have here?"

"Six scientists in the labs and two engineers who run the air filtration and decontamination systems."

"Where do the scientists come from?"

"England, China, Russia," he said. "There's no shortage of disillusioned, underpaid, ethically challenged scientists out there who aren't getting the respect or salary they want from their country or their profession."

"How many Road Runners are here?"

"A dozen," he said. "Why do you ask?"

"I'm wondering how many people we have to kill to cover our tracks."

Dragan smiled. He liked her answer. "Then you also have to include the two maintenance workers who run the castle's heating and electrical system."

"That's a lot of killing," Kate said.

"There's enough gasoline stored in this castle to power a small town, not to mention the oxygen tanks in the filtration system," Dragan said. "With a few well-placed explosives, we can kill them all on our way out the door."

"I'm glad we're good buddies now."

"Me, too," Dragan said. In fact, he was getting hard again at the thought.

"I haven't slept in over twenty-four hours. Now that we're friends, I can take a nap without worrying you might slit my throat as I sleep."

"I doubt that you ever sleep without worrying about that," Dragan said, leading her back to the air lock. "I certainly never do."

27

Nick lay on his cot, enjoying a tumbler of scotch and a good Cuban cigar. It was relaxing.

"Even though it's not the smallpox chimera, it's still one hell of a scary virus they're hatching next door," Nick said through Kate's earbud. "It's a good thing I fortified myself with cigars and plenty of strong liquor."

Kate entered her room and closed the door. "This is no time to get drunk," Kate said.

"I meant it literally," Nick said. "Dragan not only escorted me through security, he kindly provided me with matches and an accelerant to set the place on fire."

"Can you do it without infecting yourself and still escape?"

"I certainly hope so." Nick blew smoke rings up at one of the cameras aimed at him. "But I'll need you to knock out the cameras and create a distraction so I am not disturbed."

"I can take care of the cameras," Kate said.

"I'll create the distraction," Jake O'Hare said.

"Dad?" Kate went to the window in her room and looked outside. Everything was the same as before. "Where are you?"

"In the woods," Jake said. "I can see you in your window. You're wearing the perfect camouflage for hiding in a jar of jelly beans."

"You're early," she said.

"The traffic was light," Jake said. "Is that a problem?"

"No, it's not."

"Good, because I've got ten men in the woods and two more in the Apache attack chopper that will be here in ten minutes," Jake said. "I'm aware of two men walking the grounds, four more on the battlements, and one in the tower. How many more are we up against?"

"There's one outside the labs," Nick said.

"And one more at the security desk," Kate said. "I don't know where the others are."

"Perhaps they're manning the cauldrons of lye," Nick said.

"The *what*?" Jake said.

"Just don't come in the front door," Kate said. "It's a trap."

"We won't be coming in at all," Jake said. "There's smallpox in there. The fireworks start in eight minutes."

Kate slipped out of her room, walked down the hall, and passed the security guard at the console. She was heading for the third door off the foyer. It was the only one she hadn't been through yet.

"Halt," the guard said, standing up at the console. "You can't go there."

Kate stopped and turned to face him. "I'm Dragan's very special guest. I can go anywhere I want."

The guard stepped out from behind the console and came toward her. "That's Mr. Kovic's private wing. You can't go there unless you are summoned."

"Maybe I want to surprise him."

"Surprises are forbidden," the guard said.

"Okay, if you say so."

As Kate walked past him, she lashed out at the back of his knee with the flat of her left foot. His knee folded and so did he. As he tumbled, she spun around and kicked him in the jaw, snapping his head back and knocking him unconscious. She took his gun and dragged him back behind the console, where she sat down, studied the switches, and began shutting down systems.

Dragan was pondering his extraordinary good fortune as he sat at his office desk, watching the video feed from the lab where the once great Nicolas Fox was mumbling drunkenly to himself and blowing smoke rings at the ceiling.

The Paris job had gone completely wrong in so many ways and yet, inexplicably, it turned out to be an extraordinary success. Instead of getting a mere vial of smallpox chimera, Dragan had lucked out and acquired an infected man, a living factory of the virus. On top of that, Dragan had also acquired Kate, an American who could easily deliver the viral weapon to Los Angeles. Now he had the means to create a global genocide if it pleased him, either by spreading the virus himself or by selling the means to others. It felt good.

But he was a businessman, not a madman. He gained nothing from a worldwide pandemic except proof of his power and a certain sense of accomplishment. He was content to settle for a few thousand deaths, billions of dollars in profit, and an early retirement. However, it might be time to paint his face on God on the dining room ceiling after all.

He was imagining how that might look when the video screen went dark.

Nick had just finished his tumbler of scotch when Kate spoke in his ear.

"The cameras are down," she said. "Make it quick. I'll be waiting for you outside the main air lock."

Nick got up, set his cigar on the cart with the bottles of liquor, and stripped the bedding off his cot. He stuffed the sheets into the bottom shelf of the cart and wheeled it through the air lock into the suit room, where he was greeted by a bloodcurdling scream of sheer terror.

The scream came from a Chinese scientist who was already in the room, preparing to get into a pressure suit. The scientist scrambled backward so fast that he tripped over his own feet and landed hard on the floor.

"I thought you might like a drink," Nick said, gesturing to the cart. "Whiskey, perhaps?"

"Who are you talking to?" Kate asked in his ear.

The scientist covered his nose and mouth, got to his feet, and rushed into the air lock leading to the showers.

"You'll be seeing him soon enough," Nick said.

Nick put on a pressure suit, attached an air hose

to it, and waited to see if there were any leaks that became obvious when it inflated. Satisfied that his suit was airtight, he detached the hose and pushed his cart through air lock number two and into the lab.

The four scientists were intent on their work and paid no attention to him at first. Nick snapped an air hose to his suit and wheeled the cart up to the incubator. He opened the incubator, picked up the bottle of 140-proof Habitation Clément Rhum Vieux Agricole, and began splashing the eggs with the rum.

One of the scientists behind him stood up from his seat. *"Halt! Arretez! Stop!"*

Nick turned around, his lighted cigar between his gloved fingertips. "Anyone want a smallpox omelet?"

He tossed the cigar into the incubator, igniting the rum in a flash of fire that made an audible *whoosh*.

The scientists got to their feet and stood frozen for a beat, mouths open in shock. Nick picked up the Stolichnaya bottle by the neck and smashed it on the edge of a workstation, splattering 100-proof vodka and glass shards all over a tray of eggs. He held up the jagged edge in front of him.

"One tear in your suit and you're infected with plague," Nick said. "Who wants to take me on?"

Okay, so he wasn't sure if they understood English. He thought they would understand the tone and the gesture.

"Time for Nick's distraction," Jake said. He was deep in shadow in the forest with Willie, who was holding a shoulder-mounted rocket launcher and aiming it for fun at the helicopter on the grass. She started to hand him the weapon when he shook his head. "No, you do it."

"I've never fired a rocket launcher before," she said.

"Then you've been denied one of life's greatest pleasures."

"I've never denied myself any pleasure, and I'm sure as hell not going to start now," she said. "What do I do?"

He handed her a set of earplugs and gave her quick instructions on how to release the safety and fire the rocket.

"A child could do this," she said, took aim, and fired.

The rocket shot out and the backfire from the launcher blasted chunks of bark off the trees behind them. An instant later, the helicopter blew apart, sending rotors flying in all directions.

"Hot damn," Willie said. "That's a rush. What can I blow up next?"

Jake shoved her to the ground just as a barrage of

machine gun fire from the castle shredded the trees and branches above their heads.

Dragan was about to call the security desk to find out what had happened to his video feed when there was an explosion outside, followed by the sound of automatic gunfire from the ramparts above. His radio crackled. A guard spoke in frantic Serbian.

"This is the tower. The helicopter is destroyed. We're under attack."

Dragan grabbed the radio from his desk and spoke into it. "From who? From where?"

"I don't know," the guard said. "The rocket came from the woods in front of the castle. We're returning fire."

Those facts immediately raised a crucial question in Dragan's mind. If everybody's attention was focused on the front of the castle, what was coming from behind?

"Zone four, report," Dragan said, addressing the guard patrolling the southern rampart. "What do you see?"

Some initial crackle came over the line. "I see nothing unusual." There was the sound of the guard gasping in surprise, and the gasp was followed by swearing in three languages, an explosion, and gunfire.

. . .

An Apache helicopter gunship is a fast, lethal, and versatile flying arsenal designed to destroy armored vehicles, bunkers, and buildings. It's typically equipped with thirty-eight Hydra rockets, nineteen on each side of the aircraft, and a 30mm automatic chain gun loaded with 1,200 explosive armor-piercing rounds mounted on its nose. That was what the Zone 4 guard saw heading toward the castle.

The next thing the guard saw was the Apache fire a Hydra rocket that zoomed past him at 2,425 feet per second. So at almost the same instant he was aware of the missile firing it had already slammed into the castle's tower, shearing off the top in an explosion of fire and stone.

A cascade of rubble tumbled into the moat as the Apache streaked past the castle, the guards along the battlements firing at the gunship in futile fury.

The two explosions rocked the lab. Beakers and test tubes fell to the floor, providing enough incentive for the scientists to forget about Nick and rush for the air lock. They bunched up in front of it, only able to go through one at a time in their inflated suits. One of the scientists slapped the emergency alarm button, setting off a shrill siren.

Nick struck a match and tossed it on the vodka-soaked eggs. The tray of eggs went up in flames. There was a notebook on the table. He tore the notebook in half and tossed some of the pages into the incubator and the others onto the tray to keep the fires going.

He opened the freezer, doused everything with whiskey, struck a match, and set the contents on fire. He reached for the nearest air hose and sprayed oxygen on the fire, fanning the flames.

There was one last thing to do. Nick yanked the bedsheets off the cart, draped them over some of the workstations, splashed the remaining whiskey on everything, and then tossed a few lit matches on top. The sheets ignited.

Kate sat impatiently at the security console, waiting for Nick. She could hear the gunfire, even over the wail of the alarm, and could feel the rumble of the Apache passing overhead. There was a lot of action going on and she was sitting it out. The guard on the floor began to regain consciousness so she kicked him in the head, more out of frustration than her legitimate need to keep him down.

One by one, beginning with the terrified Chinese guy, the scientists ran out of the air lock, through the foyer, and across the rubble-strewn courtyard in a mad flight out of the castle. Even two guards ran past Kate without giving her a second look. They were all rats leaving a sinking ship. But where was the king of the rats?

Kate hadn't seen Dragan since the grand tour, and that concerned her. As far as she knew, there was only one way out of the castle, and he hadn't come out yet. Where was he? She was tempted to hunt him down, but she didn't want to leave Nick unprotected in his escape.

"Hurry up, Nick," she said.

"My work is done," he said. "I'm on my way out."

28

The Apache gunship swooped around the castle, raking the battlements with its armor-piercing bullets, obliterating the parapet and killing two guards who tumbled into the moat. A handful of people with their hands raised in surrender spilled out of the castle and ran for the woods.

Jake grabbed his radio to relay orders to the strike team. "Apprehend those people when they reach the woods. Nobody gets away."

The Apache came back around and fired two Hydra missiles into the castle walls, blasting huge holes in them. One of the missiles hit something extremely flammable, perhaps propane or gasoline, Jake didn't know what, but it set off a chain reaction of explosions that moved like a blazing zipper along the eastern wall. It looked to him like the choreographed sequence of blasts used to demolish a building. That wasn't supposed to happen yet, not while Nick and his daughter were still inside.

"The castle is coming down," Jake yelled, hoping Kate and Nick could hear him on their earbuds. "Get the hell out of there now!"

Kate got the warning just as she saw Dragan dash across the courtyard from some unseen doorway and climb into the wishing well.

"Oh crap," she said. "Dragan is getting away."

"Go after him," Nick said.

"I'm not leaving you."

"I'm right behind you," he said. "Don't let him escape!"

Kate grabbed her gun and ran to the courtyard. The castle walls were cracking, huge slabs of stone tumbling down as the fissures widened and spread. She climbed over the rim of the wishing well and set her foot on the first rung of a ladder that descended thirty feet down the shaft.

"The wishing well is an escape tunnel," she said. "I'm going in after him."

It was true that Nick was behind Kate. Saying he was *right* behind her had been a stretch. He couldn't leave his area without decontaminating his suit first or he could infect himself and others.

He left the lab and stood in the chemical showers in his pressure suit, thinking it was like standing in a car wash during an earthquake. Disinfectant spray doused him from every angle, thoroughly drenching his suit, while the floors and walls shook. Cracks rippled across the walls, popping off tiles. He could hear the explosions deep in the bowels of the building.

"It sounds like you're in a shower, Nick," Jake said. "Tell me you didn't stop to clean up."

"I couldn't leave like this."

"You're going to be buried alive. Get out of there. You've only got seconds left."

He hoped he'd been in the decontamination showers long enough. But it was either go now or die. Nick peeled off the suit, ran out of the showers, through the locker room, and out into the corridor. The labs were engulfed in flames, and the windows were beginning to rupture, spider-webbing with cracks. He hurried through the main air lock and into the foyer.

Bits of stone were raining down on the entryway as he stepped out. He looked out at the courtyard. The castle's front wall had collapsed like a sand castle kicked by a petulant child, smashing the wishing well and blocking Nick's only way out.

Kate reached the bottom of the thirty-foot pit just as the castle wall collapsed above. Huge stones poured down the shaft, demolishing the well and forcing Kate to take cover in the tunnel. It was about six feet high, four feet wide, and, from what she could see, about a hundred yards long, maybe more. A string of naked lightbulbs and a ventilation pipe ran along the ceiling. It was a straight shot in front of her, and she could see Dragan about forty yards away and running.

She aimed and fired and missed. She adjusted her aim and fired again, hitting him in the leg. He went down to one knee.

"Stay down!" Kate shouted. "I'm an FBI agent. You are under arrest."

"Go to hell," Dragan said, getting to his feet, opening fire on her.

Kate flattened herself against the side of the tunnel and shot back, but he was already on the move, shooting as he limped away.

Her back was soaking wet, and water was dripping on her head. She looked around and saw that the ceiling and walls in this section of the tunnel were seeping water at an ever-increasing rate. The moat was probably right above her head, and the castle was collapsing into it. That couldn't be good news for the structural integrity of the tunnel. She charged forward in a crouch, closing the distance between them. Dragan whirled around to fire off another shot, but she got her shot off first. He cried out in pain and tumbled backward, splashing into the mud at his feet.

Kate got up and approached him warily, her gun out in front of her, feeling big drops of water hitting her head. The lights were beginning to flicker. They'd short out from the water soon.

Dragan was on his back, bleeding from wounds in his right thigh and upper left arm. His foot was twisted at an impossible angle. Probably broken when he slipped in the mud, she thought. Muddy water was raining on him. He wasn't going anywhere on his own and there was no way she could carry him. She picked up his gun, ejected the clip, and tossed the weapon away. She took hold of the foot that wasn't broken and attempted to drag him. She slid in the mud and went down on her back. The floor of the tunnel was too slick to get any kind of traction.

"What's at the end of the tunnel?" she asked him.

"Another dry well," he said, grimacing in pain.

"I'll come back for you with medics and handcuffs. Try to hang on."

· · ·

Nick didn't know where to go. He chose the door to his left and ran down the corridor. Another explosion shook the castle, throwing him off balance and nearly knocking him off his feet. He staggered forward, turned a corner, and found himself in a grand dining room, the chandeliers dropping and crashing onto the table.

He saw a window overlooking the moat. It was his last, best hope. He grabbed a straight chair and was about to toss it through the window, when something caught his eye. Nick looked up at *The Creation of Adam* and was astounded to see Adam with enormous genitalia and Dragan's face. It was so bad that it was mesmerizing.

Another explosion jolted the castle, and a huge crack opened up on the ceiling, cleaving the fresco in half. That got Nick's attention. He heaved the chair through the glass and then took a running leap out the window as the dining room caved in behind him.

He plunged deep into the murky, ice-cold moat, followed by enormous chunks of stone that hit the water like depth charges.

Kate was about ten yards from the shaft at the end of the tunnel, and her eyes were fixed on the ladder bolted into the wall. A stream of water hit her heels and she heard a deep, jagged rumble, the sound rock might make if it were being torn in half.

She looked over her shoulder and saw water gushing out of the ceiling. The moat was collapsing into the tunnel. The tunnel ceiling caved in and an enormous surge of dark water poured in through the opening. The lights went out, plunging the tunnel into total darkness. Dragan screamed, a sound that was immediately drowned out by the powerful flood of water.

Kate ran forward into pitch-darkness, arms outstretched so she wouldn't take a header into the ladder. If she tripped, she was dead.

She hit the wall hard, grabbed hold of the nearest rung, and started climbing. The water slammed into the wall below her and surged up the shaft. She couldn't escape it, and took a last, deep breath. The wave swallowed her completely, yanked her from the ladder, and propelled her upward. She banged against a cover that splintered on impact, and she bobbed to the surface sputtering and splashing, reaching out for something solid. She found the stone wall of the well, heaved herself over it, and flopped onto the ground. Water continued to surge out of the well and swirl around her. She got to her hands and knees, breathing hard. She stood and took a minute to steady herself. The water was no longer gushing over the rim of the well and was gently lapping at the interior wall. The rotted piece of plywood that had capped the well had been tossed onto the mud and grass a couple feet from her.

"Holy crap," she said. "Holy cow. Holy moly."

The well looked like it hadn't been used in a hundred years. It was positioned a short distance from what might have at one time been a caretaker's cottage. The cottage itself was in a patch of woods. There were no roads leading out so she walked toward the smell of smoke and the sound of activity. It didn't take long to break out of the woods into the open field that surrounded the castle.

Kate stopped and stared at the ruins, pushing her wet hair out of her eyes, leaving a smear of mud across her face. The castle was a pile of smoking rubble, an occasional tongue of flame licking out over the moat, which was half as deep as it was before.

Oh man, Kate thought, this wasn't going to look good on form GS205.

Jake and Willie had military-style rifles trained on a clump of men who were sitting on the grass, their arms zip-tied behind them. There weren't any U.S. soldiers in sight and the Apache was gone. Kate's heart skipped a beat when she realized Nick wasn't there.

She slogged across the field and saw Jake smile with relief when he saw her. Her boots squished water, and her clothes were plastered to her and clogged with mud. She was shivering from cold and adrenaline withdrawal.

"You look like you went swimming in a frog pond," Jake said.

"T-t-tunnel leads to a w-w-well," Kate said. "Dragan is still in the tunnel." She looked around. "Where is everyone?"

"You just missed the strike team. They wanted to get back to the military base before dinner. It's steak night."

"Where's Nick?"

Jake tipped his head toward the parking lot. "He borrowed one of the Range Rovers. He didn't want to be around when the police got here."

"Good thinking," Kate said. "We shouldn't be here either."

"We're just hanging out waiting for our ride to show up," Jake said.

Kate heard the familiar *wup, wup, wup* of a chopper, and a six-seater Bell rose out of the woods and landed a short distance away.

"Thank you for being here for me," Kate said to Jake and Willie.

"Well, I wouldn't be much of a father if I didn't occasionally blow up a castle for you."

"And I fired off my first rocket," Willie said. "It was life changing."

Jake looked toward the chopper. "Are you coming with us? Or are you going to stay behind to try to explain this to the authorities?"

"I'm coming with you," Kate said. "No one is left who actually knows who I am. And there's no good way of explaining this. Better to just chalk it up to terrorists. Plus, I need to call Jessup and give him a fast debrief so he doesn't fall off the wagon and start drinking again."

"Good idea not to hang around," Willie said. "You wouldn't want someone taking a mug shot of you right now. Your hair is like . . . *yikes.*"

After weeks in Europe, digging a hole in a sewer, and nearly drowning in a flooded tunnel, Kate was eager to go back to her one-bedroom apartment in Tarzana, and sleep in her own bed.

She flew into Los Angeles on a red-eye and walked in her door at nine in the morning. She followed a trail of Toblerones into the kitchen where Nick was waiting.

"Originally I was thinking of leaving a trail of rose petals, but that didn't feel right," Nick said.

"Toblerones are good," Kate said, peeling the wrapper off one and eating it. "What are you doing here?"

"I thought you'd be hungry so I stopped around

to make you breakfast. I have Frosted Cinnamon Roll Pop-Tarts, Cocoa Krispies, and Cap'n Crunch's Crunch Berries, Eggo waffles, and Jimmy Dean sausages."

"No champagne?"

"I went with Coke and Folgers crystals."

"My kind of guy," Kate said.

"Go figure."

He was wearing a loose-fitting T-shirt, khaki shorts, and flip-flops. She gave him a head-to-toe appraisal and wondered how fast she could get him out of his clothes. Probably pretty fast.

"Is this a con?" she asked him.

He grinned at her. "Does it matter?"

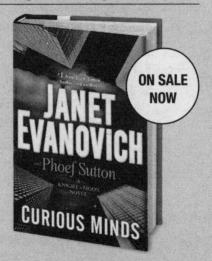

"SUEANNE H[...] INVOLVEMENT IN KILLING"

"ED HOBSON'S TESTIMONY BACKS WIFE'S INNOCENCE"

"FATHER OF SLAIN BOY FILES DIVORCE ACTION AGAINST STEPMOTHER"

"HOBSON WANTS WIFE BACK HOME"

"JURY CONVICTS SUEANNE HOBSON"

These are the media headlines from a case that stunned a peaceful Midwestern town—a case of twisted love, family secrets, and a child's brutal death.

Sueanne Hobson seemed the ideal wife: vivacious and attractive, flawlessly organized, the devoted mother of a pretty young daughter from a previous marriage. And she willingly accepted the troubled past of her new husband, Ed Hobson—a past of horrifying, inexplicable tragedy. Then the nightmare erupted that shattered the unity and destroyed the hopes of the Hobson family forever. On a quiet spring evening, Chris Hobson, Sueanne's stepson, was driven to a remote rural area and shot dead while lying inside the grave he had just dug.

Charged with murder were Sueanne's formerly estranged 17-year-old son, James Crumm Jr., and his high school buddy, Paul Sorrentino. Crumm fingered another, especially unlikely accomplice: his mother, Sueanne. Her crime: hiring Crumm and Sorrentino to carry out the shotgun slaying because, she allegedly said, young Chris was causing too much trouble at home. Unsure of her innocence, Sueanne's husband Ed had divorced her. Then, in a change of heart he remarried her, and now he remains devoted to his imprisoned wife—the woman convicted of engineering the killing of his only son.

FAMILY
AFFAIRS

ANDY HOFFMAN

POCKET BOOKS

New York   London   Toronto   Sydney   Tokyo   Singapore

An *Original* Publication of POCKET BOOKS

POCKET BOOKS, a division of Simon & Schuster Inc.
1230 Avenue of the Americas, New York, NY 10020

ISBN: 0-671-72521-1

First Pocket Books printing June 1992

10 9 8 7 6 5 4 3 2 1

POCKET and colophon are registered trademarks of
Simon & Schuster Inc.

Front cover photo courtesy of Overland Park
Police Department

Printed in the U.S.A.

To my wife, Teresa,
for her unwavering love and support

Acknowledgments

During the years I have spent reporting and writing about the life of Sueanne Hobson, I have become indebted to hundreds of people who gave their time and energy to this project. I am eternally grateful to all those who allowed me to intrude upon their lives.

First and foremost, I must thank Loralee Saxon. Her contribution to this book is immeasurable. Her diligent editing and relentless questioning transformed a series of newspaper articles, interviews, and ideas into this book. I could not have completed the book without her support and encourgement.

I would also like to thank Vicki Montgomery, who, in the dark, early stages of this project, introduced me to Harry MacLean. His support cannot be measured.

Several other people have to be thanked: Scott Smith, Randy Attwood, John Sleezer, Steve Porter, Bob Hoffman, and Roger and Shirley Johnson. Each in their own way provided the support I needed to complete this book.

I would also like to thank my editors at Pocket Books, Dana Isaacson and Leslie Wells, whose patience and professionalism guided a small-town daily newspaper reporter through the maze of the book publishing world. Additionally, I would like to thank my agent, Carol Mann.

Finally, I would like to thank my mother, Pat Hoffman, and my grandmother, Helen Schweitzer, who long ago showed me the true meaning of family and motherhood.

1

> All happy families resemble one another; every
> unhappy family is unhappy in its own way.
>
> —TOLSTOY, *ANNA KARENINA*

APRIL 17, 1980   Paul Sorrentino couldn't remember the first time he had thought about killing someone; the desire was instinctual.

Sitting alone in the living room of his father's apartment, the sixteen-year-old high school student excitedly loaded and then ejected a handful of shells from his .20-gauge pump shotgun.

He rehearsed how he would act, what he would say. He lifted the Stevens' brand shotgun to his shoulder, as if pointing it at his intended victim. He aimed, and then gently squeezed the trigger. The quiet clicking of the hammer on the empty cylinder made him smile. It sure as hell won't sound like that, he thought.

His speculations were interrupted by the honking of a car horn outside. He bounded from the apartment with the nervous zeal of a teenager on his first date, boldly displaying the shotgun like a dozen roses.

Inside the car Jimmy Crumm was agitated.

"Let's get it over with," said the seventeen-year-old.

"All right! I'm ready," Paul enthusiastically responded. "What changed your mind?"

Jimmy looked at him with disgust. He leaned over, opened the ashtray and retrieved a half-smoked reefer, ignoring Paul's question. Jimmy's hand shook as he lit the joint, inhaled, and passed it to the other teenager. They had been smoking and drinking all day, but it wasn't the drugs causing Jimmy's hands to tremble. The marijuana—a daily habit since sixth grade—usually relaxed him. However, on this warm, spring evening it injected his mind with rapid-fire ideas, with thoughts he didn't want to be having.

Jimmy didn't want to talk, he didn't want to listen to Paul ramble, and he didn't want to answer any of his questions.

"Let's just do it, and not talk about it," he told Paul as he backed the car from the driveway. "Okay?"

"Sure, whatever you want. You're the man."

Jimmy tightly gripped the steering wheel of his mother's Datsun as he drove west into the late afternoon sun, into a cluster of upper-middle-class town homes. Sweat beaded on his forehead. His pulse quickened when he saw the white Lincoln Continental parked in the driveway of his mother's duplex. She was still at home.

He started to drive past the tree-shaded town house, but stopped the car in the middle of the street.

"Are we going to do it or not?" Paul asked impatiently.

It was more a challenge than a question. Jimmy had heard the tone before. His mother often used it when chastising him about his clothes, his friends, his attitude—anything that irritated her, and it seemed that almost everything about him did.

Without responding to Paul, he turned the car into the driveway, parking next to the Lincoln. At the same moment, his mother appeared at the front door. In her mid-thirties, Sueanne Hobson was tall, slender, and, as usual, meticulously dressed. Her auburn hair was fashionably styled, closely cropped in the back with wavy bangs framing her penetrating brown eyes.

Jimmy got out of the car. Sueanne strode toward him, stopping near the front of the Lincoln. He glanced briefly at her, then continued toward the house without saying a word. The last thing he wanted to do was talk. Especially to her.

"I'm going to meet Ed for a hamburger. Chris is in the kitchen doing his homework and Suzanne is in the shower," Sueanne said, looking disgustedly at Jimmy's flannel shirt, Levis jeans, and black dress shoes.

Jimmy walked into the house without answering. Paul got out of the car and followed.

In the kitchen, thirteen-year-old Chris, Jimmy's stepbrother, heard the front door slam. He was seated at a glass-topped table surrounded by books. A gangly, freckle-faced boy with mild learning disabilities, he was generally ignored by his classmates, who thought him a nerd. Tonight he was working on his seventh-grade science project. Generally a poor student, Chris's grades had recently improved with the help of a tutor. He continued to study because it made his dad proud.

As Jimmy walked through the orderly, immaculate home, he could hear his sister Suzanne taking a shower upstairs. He headed toward the basement stairs, while Paul went into the kitchen where Chris was studying.

Jimmy had moved out of the house a few weeks earlier after repeated arguments with his mother and stepfather over marijuana and stolen credit cards. He walked to a basement closet where he knew the weapons were stored, opened the door and looked at them. For no specific reason, he chose a .12-gauge Australian-made single-shot shotgun owned by his stepfather, Ed Hobson. Holding the gun across one arm, Jimmy bent down and picked up a single shotgun shell that he stuffed into the back pocket of his blue jeans. He closed the closet door and surveyed the room for anything else he might use. Against a wall on the other side of the basement were several garden tools. His hands started to tremble again as he reached for a long-handled shovel.

Walking up the stairs, Jimmy could hear Paul talking to Chris about a scam—some type of drug ripoff. But instead of going into the kitchen, Jimmy turned and walked out the garage door with the shotgun in one hand and the shovel in the other. He made no attempt to conceal the weapon.

His hands still shaking, he opened the hatchback and laid the shovel and shotgun next to Paul's shotgun. He leaned his hands on top of the hatchback and took a deep breath, hesitated a few moments, looking down the street at two young boys playing on bicycles, then slammed the lid down hard with both hands. He turned and walked back into the house.

Paul, a short, cocky youth with black, curly hair, was looking through the refrigerator for food. Chris, eyes bright with anticipation, held his windbreaker under his arm.

"He's going with us," Paul told Jimmy as he continued to rummage through the refrigerator. "I told him we would give him one third if he would help us."

Chris, his blue eyes still trapped in a baby face, was full of excitement, anxious for Jimmy's acceptance. In his eagerness to be included, he didn't even consider the danger of a drug ripoff or what the consequences would be if his father found out he had left the house with Jimmy and Paul. Nor did he question why they had asked him along. He was happy to be included, whatever the reason.

Instead of acknowledging Chris, Jimmy silently turned and walked toward the door. Chris meekly followed, not wanting to give Jimmy a reason to stop him from going.

Outside, Paul motioned for Chris to get into the backseat, then climbed into the driver's seat. In the front passenger seat, Jimmy reached over and cranked up the car's stereo. He glanced back at Chris, who was smiling broadly, then turned toward Paul, who winked.

Jimmy's stomach churned. He felt confused and out of control. He knew Paul was ready. His mind raced, searching desperately for ways to get out of this situation. But he saw no alternative. He had no choice. For a moment he felt relief. Then he turned cold. His palms began to sweat. It felt like a dream.

Chris looked at his watch, it was seven-thirty P.M.

"How long is this going to take?" he asked. "I've got to be in bed by ten o'clock."

"Don't worry about it." Paul laughed. "It won't take that long."

Jimmy lit up another reefer, took a deep drag and looked out the window while Paul drove slowly through the residential streets of Overland Park. They headed southwest on a four-lane highway out of the city lights, into the darkness.

As they drove west on this warm, cloudless April evening, the setting sun transformed the western horizon into orange and purple hues that glared into the boys' eyes. It was still early spring, two or three weeks away from the evenings when clear, blue skies could be transformed with frightening speed into ominous green or sometimes black clouds, rumbling explosively northeastward.

Tonight was clear. The wind was calm and the temperature was in the upper sixties.

Chris, leaning between the two front seats, watched Jimmy and Paul pass the joint between them. He knew Jimmy smoked pot; he had heard the arguments at home when marijuana had been found in Jimmy's room, but he had never tried it and Jimmy had never offered. And Jimmy wasn't offering any now. But it didn't matter to Chris. He was just happy they trusted him enough to smoke it in front of him.

Chris was excited about the adventure. He had been hunting with Jimmy once before, but had never been included in anything this exciting or dangerous.

Hesitantly, he began to ask questions. He wanted to know what was going to happen, who they were going to rip off, where it was going to occur, whether or not it would be dangerous, and what he was supposed to do.

"Just shut the fuck up," Jimmy snarled over the noise of the stereo. "Just sit back there and shut the fuck up."

Chris, startled by the sudden anger in Jimmy's voice, suddenly felt apprehensive. Jimmy rarely said anything, but on a few occasions Chris had triggered his step-brother's temper, which could be explosive and destructive. Now, he didn't want to make Jimmy mad.

Paul slowed the car down as they approached an interchange. Large road signs identified highways and cities. Jimmy motioned for Paul to pull the car over. He turned up the stereo and he and Paul got out, walked to the rear of the Datsun and opened the trunk.

Chris reluctantly remained in the backseat, his eyes constantly searching the darkened area in anticipation. He felt safer, more secure, in the car. Darkness had always frightened him, but he wouldn't let Jimmy and Paul know.

"Why are we doing this?" Jimmy asked Paul, staring down through the hatchback at the two guns and the shovel. "Why don't we just take him to Wichita and put him on a fucking bus?"

"Yeah, that's okay with me," Paul said. He

shrugged his shoulders. "Why not?" The trunk slammed shut.

Jimmy felt relieved. Taking Chris to Wichita would be a hell of a lot better, he thought, as he climbed back into the passenger's seat and shut the door. He leaned back and took a deep breath, picked up the half-smoked joint from the ashtray and lit it. Maybe now he could relax.

As they drove further into the countryside, the growing darkness was punctuated with occasional lights from small towns and isolated farmhouses, quietly replacing the neon city lights of car dealerships, hotels, and restaurants.

They hadn't traveled ten miles when Paul nudged Jimmy and pointed to a road sign indicating Wichita was 150 miles away.

"How long will it take to get there?" Paul asked Jimmy, pitching his voice beneath the music from the rear speakers, which blared in Chris's ears. "I've got school tomorrow."

"I don't know, probably about three or four hours."

"Shit, it's starting to get late. You sure we oughta drive that far? Why don't we just pull off here and do it?" Paul argued, pointing to an exit sign. "We don't have time to get where we're going. Let's just do it here."

Jimmy was confused and angry. Again he found himself losing control of a situation. He had always liked to think of himself as a rebel, a loner who went his own way. But somehow every time he was confronted by a stronger personality, someone more willing to insist and demand, he became passive, giving in to their desires.

"Well?" Paul prodded. Jimmy disgustedly nodded yes, and Paul turned off I-35. He drove up the exit ramp, went over a bridge across the interstate and turned onto a gravel road that disappeared into darkness.

The car aimlessly wandered down gravel roads lined with trees, weeds and the occasional driveway leading to the distant lights of a farmhouse. After several minutes of twists and turns through the darkened countryside, Paul pulled the Datsun to the side of the deserted road.

"Why don't you drive for a while?" Paul told Jimmy.

While the two exchanged places, Paul calmly opened the hatchback and grabbed his shotgun. He climbed into the passenger's seat, placing the shotgun between his legs, with the barrel pointed toward the roof.

Chris, silent since Jimmy's outburst a few minutes earlier, leaned forward and looked at Paul holding the shotgun. It was dark, getting late, and Chris's fear was growing. The gun scared him. For the first time he realized danger was involved. He began to worry about what his father was going to say.

"How long is this going to take?" he asked in a frightened voice.

"Just sit back there and relax," Jimmy replied. "You said you wanted to go with us. We're almost there."

"I've got homework to do," Chris said, without directly asking him to take him home. "You know how mad Dad's going to be if I'm not home when he gets there."

The evening was quickly fading to night, the sky moonless and black. Jimmy, randomly making right and left turns, was lost. He turned back onto a narrow paved road and drove west for two miles until the blacktop ended, where he stopped.

On the southwest corner of the intersection there was a small, cement-block building, formerly a gas station, that had been turned into a residence. A single Skelly gas pump with weeds growing around its base was in front of the building. A second story had been added to the back of the block structure, and lights could be seen through shaded windows. There were no cars near the building and no movement in the house.

"This is it," Paul said, pointing to a gravel road next to the house. "Let's go down here. This is a good place."

Jimmy turned on his bright lights and drove forward slowly and cautiously. Chris leaned forward, resting his elbows on the back of the front seats. The car passed several more houses on the north side of the gravel road. Trees, vines, and weeds lined the south side. Jimmy hadn't driven a hundred yards when the headlights revealed a rusty sign: ROAD CLOSED. Nailed to the same wooden post was another rusty sign: BRIDGE OUT.

Jimmy looked toward Paul, who motioned for him to keep driving. Jimmy turned down the volume on the stereo, replacing the loud thumping music with the quiet sound of gravel being compressed under the tires.

All three were silent as they drove forward about a quarter mile to the crest of a hill. Jimmy stopped the car for a moment, looking to Paul again for directions. Paul nodded. The car crept down the hill. Jimmy's headlights caught the outline of a third road sign, this one yellow and also rusting. In bold letters, it simply said DANGER.

As Jimmy inched the car forward past the last house, the smooth two-lane road became a single lane of tire tracks with weeds growing in the middle and on both sides. Jimmy sat with his back hunched forward and his arms leaning on the steering wheel. He looked at Paul, who was now grasping the shotgun with both hands. In his rearview mirror Jimmy could see Chris's wide, frightened eyes staring at the thick brush and dense trees lining both sides of the road.

When they reached the base of the hill, thick, tall

trees—elm, oak, black walnut, and hackberry—intertwined with gnarled, suffocating wild grapevines, forming a dark canopy over the narrow road, a black tunnel several hundred yards long. No one spoke.

Jimmy pressed forward past the massive trees, his car lights picking out reflecting tape on the barricades a few hundred yards ahead.

"This is it," Paul said. "Let's do it here."

"Okay," Jimmy replied.

All three got out of the car and walked around the barricades to an area where the road ended near a small, nearly dry creek bed. Large cement and stone foundations on either side of the creek were all that remained of the narrow bridge. The creek was in a large, wooded draw at least a quarter mile from the nearest farmhouse.

The Datsun's headlights illuminated a small clearing along the bank on the opposite side of the creek where someone had been cutting trees for firewood.

"That looks like a good place," Paul said, pointing across the creek to the clearing. "Come on, Chris, why don't you help me?"

The two crossed the creek, while Jimmy walked back to the car. The midwestern spring rains hadn't been that plentiful, and the ground, with ankle-high grass, was hard. Paul tore away the first few shovels of grass and dirt, outlining the shape he wanted the hole, then turned and handed the shovel to Chris.

At the car Jimmy, with hands shaking, laid his shotgun against the back of the Datsun. From his vantage point, he could barely see the silhouettes of Paul and Chris, but he could hear their voices clearly. He walked around to the front of the car, reached inside and kicked up the volume on the stereo a few notches. He took another drag on a joint and waited.

He didn't want to join Chris and Paul until he had to. Jimmy watched Paul walking back toward the car while Chris in silhouette, toiled on, digging along the tree line.

"Let's just leave him here," Jimmy said, a pleading note creeping into his voice. "Let's just leave him and get the fuck out of here."

Paul shook his head. Jimmy knew Paul was in charge now. He began to fear for his own life. For a moment Jimmy considered shooting Paul and then shooting himself. But he knew he wouldn't. It was out of his hands. It had been for weeks. It had to be done. Now.

"It's too late," Paul said, walking to the back of the car, where he picked up his shotgun from the hatchback. "Let's just get on with it."

Jimmy looked at Paul and then, silent again, turned and picked up Ed Hobson's .12-gauge shotgun. He reached into his jeans and pulled out the single shotgun shell. He shoved it into the chamber. They both walked back toward Chris.

Chris had been digging for more than an hour, his blue jeans, long-sleeved red shirt, and white tennis shoes caked with dirt. The hole was now about six feet long, four feet wide, and three feet deep. Paul had helped a little, but Chris had done most of the digging. He had long since lost his sense of adventure. Now all he wanted was to go home. He was afraid, hurting. His hands ached. The soft tissue on the insides of his fingers was blistered. He had felt the skin bubble and then tear away as he continued to dig. Now, through tear-filled eyes, he examined his hands in the darkness for blood.

Sweating and out of breath, Chris looked toward the car's bright lights. He could see two silhouettes ford the small creek and walk toward him. He felt a sudden rush of fear. They both carried shotguns. What was going on? Why had he trusted Jimmy? He thought about running, but where to? He futilely searched the horizon for lights. Only the distant sounds of yelping dogs broke the silence. The darkness swallowed him.

Jimmy handed his shotgun to Paul, reached down and grabbed the shovel from Chris, who was frozen in fear.

"These edges need to be squared off," Jimmy said, shoveling dirt from the sides and corner of the hole.

Chris looked at Paul, then at Jimmy, who had finished removing several shovels of loose dirt from the hole.

"Why don't you try it on for size?" Jimmy said, his voice now hard and angry.

"Why?" a tearful Chris asked as water began streaking down his cheeks.

"We need to make sure it's the right size."

"Is this a joke?" Chris whined in a trembling voice. "It's not funny anymore. I'm scared."

"Get in the fucking hole," Jimmy said, pointing his shotgun at his stepbrother.

"No," Chris pleaded. "Please don't make me do it."

Jimmy grabbed Chris by the shirt and shoved him into the hole. Chris rolled over on his back as he scrambled to get up. He looked up and saw the two teenagers pointing their shotguns at him.

For a moment Jimmy froze. He looked silently down at Chris, then turned and looked at Paul standing on the other side of the grave. Jimmy looked back down at Chris, who was paralyzed with fear, his eyes meeting those of his young stepbrother. Nothing seemed real. As if in a dream, he heard himself shout angrily.

"This is for hitting my mother and for hitting my sister and for getting me kicked out of the house," he yelled, looking straight at Chris, who didn't have time to respond.

"One," Jimmy yelled hysterically.

"Two," Paul screamed.

"Three," Jimmy shrieked as Paul fired a single shot into Chris's chest. The blast ripped through Chris's clothes and the side of his chest. The shattering sound was followed by a second shotgun blast from Jimmy's gun. The two shots echoed down the high creek embankments across the fields, into the night.

Jimmy couldn't move. He stared at Chris, who, at the bottom of the hole, was trying to get up. The boy then slumped backward into the grave, his left hand instinctively grabbing the torn flesh in his chest.

"He can feel it! He can feel it! Put him out of his fucking misery," Jimmy screamed at Paul, who fired a third shot into the side of Chris's head.

Chris, bleeding profusely from the open, jagged wounds, now lay motionless on his back.

Paul and Jimmy both fell to their knees, screaming and babbling, frantically using their hands, their feet, the shovel—anything—to push the dirt over Chris's body. Their voices rambled incoherently while they covered the boy's mangled body, wanting to block it from their sight as fast as they could.

Finished, Jimmy grabbed the shovel and his shotgun while Paul looked for the spent shotgun shells in the ankle-high grass surrounding the grave. He found two shells and stuffed them into his pocket. Both teenagers were frantic to leave, but first Paul turned and looked back at the fresh mound of dirt.

Chris's hand was reaching from the grave. Paul ran back and stomped on the hand, pushing it back into the ground with his feet. He then turned and ran as fast as he could through the creek and toward the car. Jimmy ran behind him.

He drove, spinning the car around, cranking up the stereo, speeding recklessly through the illuminated tunnel of trees. Back on the paved road, Jimmy lit up a cigarette. He took one drag, coughed and spit, then tossed the cigarette out the window.

"It tastes like fucking gunpowder," he said. His hands began to shake again.

"It took me a long time, but I finally realized that Sueanne was only in love with one thing—her image."

—A RELATIVE

MAY 24, 1962 The birth of Sueanne's first child, Jimmy, was not a cause for celebration. The nineteen-year-old woman did not want her son.

At the hospital, she angrily dismissed family and friends, demanding that they obey her wishes not to visit. Her parents were allowed access to their first grandchild only because they had a reason Sueanne couldn't refute: they were paying the hospital bills. Their stays were brief and unemotional, overshadowed by despair.

Jimmy's birth was the culmination of months of anger and loneliness for Sueanne. What had initially been seen as an escape from an oppressive mother had been transformed into a darker, deeper prison. Before, there had been times to escape her parents. As the mother of her own child, however, she had nowhere to flee. She was trapped, now more than ever. She was sullen and introspective, displaying little maternal pride or affection toward her newborn son.

Lying alone in the hospital room, her hair uncurled, nails bare, Sueanne felt powerless and vulnerable. She was angry with herself for getting pregnant, angry at her husband for convincing her to marry him, and especially livid with her parents' I-told-you-so attitude.

"I just don't want anybody here," Sueanne told her husband, Jim Crumm, when the proud, excited father asked whether his relatives could see the baby at the hospital.

Sueanne, a slender, dark-skinned beauty, felt old, fat, and ugly. She was ashamed. According to Jim Crumm, she feared someone would discover the truth: that she wasn't a virgin when she got married. To conceal her secret, she insisted that Jimmy was premature. "At least several weeks," she would say.

———

Sueanne was born Aug. 1, 1942, in Kansas City, Missouri, the only child of Don and Ruth Sallee. In 1950, when she was eight years old, her parents moved into a new home in an exclusive neighborhood on the southern edge of an exploding suburban community.

Outwardly, her family seemed to reflect the attitude and affluence of most families crossing the state line from Kansas City, Missouri, to Johnson County, Kansas. Her college-educated father worked for the Marley Corporation, where he remained until his retirement forty-seven years later, systematically rising through the company while his wife remained at home raising Sueanne. Her parents faithfully attended the same Episcopalian church for years and demanded that she do the same.

Sueanne was spoiled in a material sense, showered with toys, clothes, anything she wanted. But the image of the happy family living in a two-story corner house on an oak-lined street was deceptive. Behind the closed doors and drawn curtains—her mother always kept their home in shadows—Sueanne's life was a chaotic mixture of love and abuse. She was victimized throughout her childhood by her mother's frightening, dramatic mood swings.

"I didn't know if I was going to be kissed or slapped when I came home from school," Sueanne said of life with her mother. She learned early in life that showing emotion was a sign of weakness. Like her father, Sueanne became stoic when dealing with her mother's abusive tirades.

When Sueanne entered high school in 1958, the schism between mother and daughter widened. The more the teenager struggled for her freedom, the tighter her mother's grip became. Ruth dominated Sueanne's life, picking out her clothes, choosing her dates, even refusing to allow her a part-time job.

In her senior year the wishes of mother and daughter coalesced: Sueanne would attend the University of Kansas, thirty miles away in Lawrence. While her parents saw it as an opportunity for education and social advancement, Sueanne saw it as an escape from domination. Living on campus, away from the constant scrutiny of her mother, she would be able to do what she wanted with whom she wanted.

It lasted only a few weeks. Ambushed by her newfound independence and a genuine lack of initiative, Sueanne left K.U. at the end of the first semester because of poor grades. She returned to her parents' home a failure.

A few weeks later Sueanne began dating the man she would marry. She met Jim Crumm, a twenty-

year-old construction worker, at Allen's Drive-in, a
local hamburger stand where teenagers throughout
Kansas City gathered. Sueanne felt she had a boyfriend of her own, not her mother's selection.

Jim was overwhelmed by Sueanne.

"My first true love," he would later recall. "Coal-
black hair, dark skin and dark eyes. The most beautiful woman I had ever met."

His infatuation was as swift and predictable as
her parents' reaction: they disliked him and demanded she stop seeing him. He had little money,
no desire for a college education, and no family
history of success. He was a blue-collar kid from a
large family in a poor section of the city. The bottom line, her mother told her, was that Jim's family
was beneath them.

For the first time in her life Sueanne refused to
obey. "It's time I started making my own decisions," she defiantly told Jim.

Their dates became more frequent. Regardless of
whether she loved him—and Jim had concerns that
she was simply using their relationship to infuriate
her parents—he was desperately in love with her.
As the winter of 1960 turned to spring, he began to
talk of marriage. They began to make love. It was
her first experience and not a pleasurable one. He
teased her, calling her Miss Fair Frigidaire.

"She really had no sexual desires," he recalled.
"We weren't like most kids—once you get started, it
becomes a regular thing. We did it four or five
times. I thought maybe that would change once we
got married."

In early September, Sueanne told Jim she might
be pregnant. Abortion was not an option. It was a
moment of decision. Life at home was unbearable
for Sueanne. Haunted by her failure at K.U., burdened by her mother's constant protests about Jim,
worried about her future, she began to consider
marriage as the only practical solution.

But time was short. A few weeks earlier Jim and a buddy had enlisted in the U.S. Marine Reserves on a dare. He was scheduled to leave in October for six months training in California.

Sueanne agreed to marry Jim. Knowing her parents would attempt to prevent the marriage, regardless of her pregnancy, the two decided to elope. They agreed not to tell anyone. After their marriage, Sueanne would continue to live with her parents while Jim was in the Marines. A wedding announcement would be made when he returned.

Sueanne was nervous, afraid. Jim was ecstatic.

Four days later, in a borrowed car, the couple drove south to Miami, Oklahoma, where they were married. The secret lasted less than twenty-four hours. Within ten minutes of returning to her parents' home, Sueanne was confronted by her mother. She admitted her pregnancy and marriage.

After a furious shouting match, including threats to disinherit her, the Sallees provided the couple with enough money to get a motel room. A week later the couple rented a newly redecorated studio apartment in an upscale neighborhood, also at the Sallees' expense.

Five weeks later, when Jim left for the Marines, Sueanne showed little emotion. She seemed lethargic, despondent. She rarely saw her parents and never saw Jim's family.

"It was almost like she was waiting for me to leave," Jim said later.

Midway through boot camp, Jim started to worry. He hadn't heard from Sueanne since he had left. In an emergency call home, he was shocked to learn that she had returned to her parents and refused to talk to him. Mr. Sallee calmly told Jim that Sueanne was in the process of getting the marriage annulled.

Jim was devastated. He felt abandoned by her and trapped by the military. But a few days later

Sueanne called and told him she had changed her mind and had moved back into the couple's apartment. She blamed her parents, saying she had always loved him and never wanted the marriage annulled.

In reality, the annulment plan was shelved after Sueanne learned it could not easily be acquired because she was pregnant.

By the time Jim returned in April, he had forgotten the threats of annulment. He was anxious to find a job, have the baby and make Sueanne happy. The first two would be simple, the third would be impossible.

His hope that the birth of their son Jimmy would bring happiness to Sueanne never materialized. Nor did his desire that Sueanne would develop a sex drive. She was cold and elusive, to both Jim and their newborn son. She was embarrassed that Jimmy had to wear corrective braces on his legs, and often refused to take him out in public.

"I don't think she was ever happy in her entire life, as far as a normal person's concept of what happiness is," Jim recalled. "Her idea of happy was being able to spend money, keep ahead of the neighbors."

Jim first saw that side of Sueanne when she demanded her own car. Not any car, a new car. The couple, living on Jim's salary as a lineman for Kansas City Power & Light, had little extra money. Jim found several cars that they could afford, but none Sueanne wanted. She demanded that he buy her a 1961 Ford station wagon she had seen on a showroom floor. At first Jim said no, but later acquiesced.

"We couldn't afford it," he recalled, "but I loved her so much, and she wanted it so bad, there was nothing I could do to prevent her from having it. Her parents had given her everything she ever wanted, and she expected it from me, too. She couldn't understand that I didn't have the money her parents had. But I found it was a lot easier to give her what she wanted than to try to argue with her."

The purchase of that car was the beginning of a pattern that would eventually destroy the marriage.

By the time their daughter Suzanne was born, in 1966—also an unplanned pregnancy—Jim and Sueanne's marriage was rapidly deteriorating. Jim, still adoringly submissive to his wife, was now working three jobs to pay the couple's bills. He hoped the birth of their daughter would revitalize the marriage. And indeed Sueanne seemed happy with Suzanne. Her affection for her new baby was a stark contrast to the cold, impersonal way she had treated her infant son. It was obvious she was proud of her daughter.

The joy lasted only a few weeks before Sueanne returned to her old ways. The bills continued to escalate, carelessly fueled by Sueanne's three real passions: clothing, furniture, and interior design. With each new house they bought—and they had three in the seven years they had been married— Sueanne demanded that each room be remodeled to fit her specific tastes. Cabinets, bathroom fixtures, everything had to be replaced.

"It had to be perfect," Jim said later. "Every house we ever lived in was like a museum. You couldn't do anything but just sit there."

Norma Hooker, then a close friend of Jim and Sueanne, agreed.

"Her home was immaculate," Norma recalled. "It looked like a magazine. Nothing was out of place—closets, drawers, kitchen cabinets. I called her Mrs. Clean. She was a perfectionist, and she expected everyone around her to be the same way. It was clearly abnormal."

Sueanne's compulsion for order and cleanliness

inevitably increased the friction between her and her young son. Her inability to cope with Jimmy was compounded by the fact he was diagnosed as hyperactive. She constantly scolded him, restricting his play to his room and an occasional foray outside, where she prohibited him from getting dirty. He would cower at the sound of her voice. She was also abusive, breaking his arm when he was in the second grade. She claimed it was an accident, saying he fell down while they were playing together. His father had doubts.

"I didn't believe it," he said later. "Why? Because she never played with the kids. It was undignified."

The older Jimmy got, the more Sueanne ignored him. She had Suzanne now and would concentrate on raising her. Jim could worry about his son.

With the debts mounting and bankruptcy—Sueanne's worst fear—lingering on the horizon, other problems developed. Jim, frustrated by Sueanne's lack of affection, and burdened by the financial problems, began to drink heavily. Their arguments increased, leading from angry plate smashings to physical confrontations between the couple.

"Sueanne was a slapper," Jim said. "She slapped me, the kids . . . She slapped me one time and I hit her back. I'm not proud of it, but it happened."

In 1968 the couple filed for bankruptcy. The three jobs Jim worked were not enough. Sueanne was forced to go to work as a secretary. That, more than anything, ended the marriage. She realized she didn't need her husband to survive financially.

After an aborted attempt at counseling—the counselor told them the marriage was doomed to failure—Jim reluctantly agreed to Sueanne's request for a divorce. Sueanne claimed that Jim was an alcoholic who physically abused her. Jim countered by saying Sueanne refused his sexual advances and was having an affair with a coworker.

Sueanne was awarded custody of both children in 1971, but chose to take only her daughter. She left her nine-year-old son behind.

"You can have him," she coldly told her husband. "He'll be better off with you."

When relationships became too demanding—with friends, parents, relatives—Sueanne found it easiest to leave, severing her ties to the past. She had done it to her parents, rarely seeing them in the ten years she was married to Jim, and now she was doing it again, this time with her son. Although they lived in the same community, she rarely saw Jimmy in the next seven years, never sending him a Christmas present or acknowledging his birthday.

The severing of ties with her husband and son was a new beginning for her. She saw it as an opportunity for her and her daughter to start a new life.

Sueanne blossomed while Jim floundered. Still haunted by the divorce, he lost his job at KCP&L and continued drinking to excess. He lost everything he had worked for in the ten years he had been married to Sueanne, including his children. Sueanne refused to allow him to see Suzanne, and he gave Jimmy to his sister, saying he was unfit to raise him.

For the next seven years Jimmy would be shuttled among his father's relatives, depending on who had room for him in their homes. Occasionally he would move into an apartment with his father, only to be returned shortly to a compassionate relative.

While Jim struggled to find permanent employment, Sueanne established herself in the grain commodities business. In 1972 she went to work for the Louis Dreyfuss corporation, advancing from switchboard operator to executive secretary. Beau-

tiful, efficient and ambitious, Sueanne became a
company favorite.

She frosted her hair and began to date men once
more, including her own boss. He was so intrigued
by the dark-haired beauty that he rented an expensive apartment for Sueanne and her daughter to
live in. He ended the relationship in late 1975, saying he felt it "was an inappropriate employer-
employee relationship." Others who knew the couple said he was becoming concerned by Sueanne's
possessive nature. Regardless of the reason, he still
had strong feelings for her.

"She was full of life," he said later. "She enjoyed
going out dancing, having a good time. She could
be sharp-tongued, but she was also very intelligent
and could be loving and caring at times."

The relationship's end hurt and confused Sueanne. It was the first time she had ever been rejected by a man. Disturbed, frustrated by her life as
a single parent, and haunted by her childhood, she
began to see a psychologist.

Occasionally she took her daughter with her to
the counseling sessions. After one meeting, eight-
year-old Suzanne asked her why she needed counseling. "Because I don't want you to be raised like I
was," Sueanne replied.

Sueanne also grew intrigued with mind control
methods, and astrology, and began to consult a
Kansas City psychic. During one session in 1975,
the psychic told Sueanne she would meet and
marry a blond man raising a son alone. Two years
later she met Ed Hobson.

———

Ed was born on March 16, 1942, in St. Joseph,
Missouri. When he was a small child he moved
with his parents and an older sister to a farm near
King City, Missouri, about two hours north of Kan-

sas City. He grew up in a poor family with few possessions.

Ed's classmates at King City High School characterized him as a "big, goofy guy with blond hair who was kind of wild." The caption next to his picture in the high school annual said: "Another car passed him once—a police car."

People in King City remember the Hobsons as a poor but hardworking family, who relied heavily on a rich aunt living on a large farm nearby. Mr. Hobson farmed and worked odd jobs while his wife headed the knitting department at a St. Joseph's department store twenty-five miles away.

After high school Ed joined the Navy, then migrated to Kansas City, where he met and married a thirty-three-year-old divorcée with two teenage daughters. Ed was twenty-two. He met Shirley Teed, a former dancer, at the Jewel Box, a Kansas City bar known for its female impersonators. Shirley was a waitress. They were married in 1964 in Miami, Oklahoma, at the same chapel as Sueanne Sallee and Jim Crumm.

Few people could understand the attraction Ed felt for Shirley. He was good-looking with blond hair and broad shoulders. Shirley was eleven years his senior, a once beautiful woman now past her prime. Her aging, lined face was framed by dyed red hair with black roots.

Friends and relatives remember their marriage as happy, but also violent. "It was weird," one relative said. "It was nothing at all for the telephone to ring at our house at four A.M., and my parents would have to go over to their house and break up a fight between them. You could go over there any time of the day or night and find them up. Shirley would be sitting in her chair, smoking cigarettes and reading detective magazines. She loved those magazines."

In 1967 Shirley unexpectedly became pregnant.

Like Jim Crumm, Ed was ecstatic at the prospect of becoming a father, even if Shirley was against it. Her youngest daughter, Tani, was thirteen, and Shirley didn't feel like "raising another goddamn family." Ed, however, convinced her to have the child.

Chris's birth ended a rough pregnancy, including forty-eight hours of labor for Shirley, now 36 years old. Instead of shunning the baby, as relatives feared, Shirley became a possessive mother, prohibiting anyone from holding the child unless they were wearing a mask and hospital gown. The overprotection would continue for years.

In the fall of 1971 the death of Ed's mother began a series of tragedies in his life. Five months later, Ed's seemingly healthy father dropped dead of a heart attack in a farm field near his tractor.

In 1973, while attending the University of Missouri, Ed's stepdaughter, Tani, accidentally killed her fiancé in a tragic accident. They had argued on the way home from a bar, and Gary Hollandsworth, Tani's boyfriend, got out of the truck and decided to walk. After walking a short distance, he changed his mind and cut across the interstate to intercept Tani on her route home.

When he tried to flag her down on the darkened frontage road, she accidentally struck and killed him. The last thing she saw was his face against the windshield.

Tani was arrested for manslaughter and drunk driving. However, two days later the police dismissed the case, saying it was clearly an accident. Tani was devastated. Distraught and guilt-ridden, she felt a deep need to be punished for Gary's death.

That afternoon, family and friends returned to Kansas City, leaving Tani alone in her apartment. That night, she shot and killed herself with her boyfriend's shotgun. Her body was found several hours later by Ed and Shirley and Chris, who was six at the time. The family had returned to Columbia, worried after several unsuccessful attempts to reach her by telephone. Chris was the first to reach the body.

The night before her funeral, Tani's body was defiled in the funeral home. Who did this and why remains a mystery.

"She was a mess," Ed told reporters at the time. "Her blouse was pulled out, her rosary was clear out of her hand, her rose was gone, her hair was all messed up, she was lying over the back of the casket, her skirt was all loose and wrinkled."

Police never discovered who committed the crime, but from the moment of her death, Ed had insisted that Tani's death was not a suicide. The incident at the funeral home deepened his belief that Tani had been murdered and was the victim of an unexplainable plot. Despite overwhelming evidence—police found a lengthy suicide note next to her body—Ed spent all the money he had inherited from his parents to pursue his theories. His constant badgering of authorities in Columbia and Kansas City caused detectives to reopen the case.

"He was so damn insistent that she was murdered that we reopened the case simply to look at him as a suspect," a detective said. "There was absolutely no doubt it was a suicide. That child was definitely distraught."

The tragedies would continue.

Shirley died four years later of cancer.

Ed, shattered by his wife's death, continued to maintain Tani's death was murder. It was the first time Ed would chose to battle police despite overwhelming facts to the contrary. But it wouldn't be the last time.

Shirley's death was also difficult for her son Chris. He watched his mother die slowly, painfully, her mind diluted by painkillers and her body ravaged by the cancer. Shirley spent the last months of

her life in a violent, bedridden stupor. She struck
out at everyone, especially Chris.

A few weeks after her death, Ed and Chris moved
into a new Johnson County apartment. Ed, buoyed
by a new job as a millwright at Ralston Purina in
Kansas City, spoiled his son. He rarely dated, devot-
ing much of the next eighteen months to raising
Chris. He desperately tried to bring some joy back
into his young son's life. They hunted, fished,
skied—anything Chris wanted to do. And anything
Chris wanted, Ed gave him. The only thing missing
from Chris's life was the one thing Ed couldn't provide—a mother. Ed vowed to change even that.

One of Chris's favorite activities was roller skating. At the rink where Ed and Chris went on Friday
nights, Ed met the woman who would become
Chris's new mother, Sueanne. Faced with mounting
financial problems, Sueanne had been forced to
take the part-time job running the roller rink snack
bar in early 1977. At one time the job would have
been beneath her, an admission of defeat, but years
of trying to raise a child alone had hardened
Sueanne to the realities of life. The once naive waif
had matured into a strong-willed, sophisticated
woman determined to get what she wanted.

"There is no question she changed," Norma
Hooker said of the 1977 version of Sueanne. "She
was proud to a fault, but she was also realistic."

It wasn't love at first sight, at least not for
Sueanne. In fact, she found Ed distasteful. He
wasn't her type. He was an unsophisticated, unedu-
cated, blue-collar guy with a loud laugh, bad manners, and atrocious taste in clothes.

Like most men who had encountered Sueanne,
Ed was infatuated. Unlike his first wife, Sueanne
was a lady, the perfect mother for his son. He found
her charming, sophisticated, and classy.

Despite Sueanne's initial rejections, Ed would
hang around the snack bar trying to endear himself

to her. He would tell stupid jokes, run errands for her. Anything she wanted, he was ready to do. Finally, after a month of begging, she reluctantly agreed to go on a date. It didn't work. At two A.M. Sueanne wanted to go home, but Ed didn't want to end the date. It was a mistake that Ed would never make again. Sueanne had asked him to do something for her, and he had refused. She had no reason to go out with him again.

Still infatuated, Ed waited several months before asking Sueanne for another date. When he called, Sueanne mistook him for another man she had been dating and agreed to meet him for lunch. When she arrived at the restaurant, she was surprised to see Ed. After a few minutes of confusion, she hesitantly agreed to stay.

The dates became more frequent as the weeks passed, and in the early fall of 1978, Ed asked Sueanne to marry him. She agreed, but with a stipulation: Ed had to agree that both parents and children would attend premarital counseling sessions. Ed had told her of Chris's emotional problems related to his mother's death, and Sueanne wanted to make sure the four could live together.

"We were going to put four people into one place at the same time and try to make everybody happy," Sueanne said later. "With four distinct personalities, we needed to have some kind of basis to start a good family. We were all four very different people, and we were all very strong-willed people. We liked different things and were used to different things. I wanted harmony and unity."

Several of Sueanne's friends were surprised at her decision to marry Ed. Sueanne's hatred of her first husband was so intense that friends found it ironic that she would marry again, especially to a man so like her first husband.

"It was spooky," her daughter, Suzanne, said. "They were so much alike, especially their mannerisms, the way they smoked, drank coffee, talked."

In a way, Jim Crumm and Ed Hobson were kindred spirits, united by age, poverty, and a devotion to Sueanne that would eventually end in tragedy for both men.

"I didn't think Sueanne wanted to get married, especially to a man like Ed," one friend recalled. "Sueanne didn't give the impression she wanted or needed a man."

But other friends were not surprised. Shortly before their engagement, Sueanne learned that Ed was to inherit approximately $160,000 from his aunt's estate. "It was something that Sueanne always wanted—money. Besides, he was driving a brand new Lincoln Continental," a friend later remarked.

Sueanne quit her job at Louis Dreyfuss and the skating rink, once again returning to the domestic life of books, shopping, and soap operas. The couple bought a duplex in an upscale neighborhood in Overland Park, in the suburban outskirts of Johnson County. Sueanne was busy planning extensive remodeling. The two families moved into the residence a couple of weeks before the December 2, 1978, wedding.

At the same time, another dramatic change occurred in Sueanne's life. After seven years, Sueanne began seeing Jimmy, who was now sixteen. It wasn't Sueanne's idea. The reunion occurred because of twelve-year-old Suzanne's desire to see her brother, whom she hadn't seen since she was five years old.

Ironically, Sueanne asked Jimmy to "give her away" at the wedding. Jimmy was ecstatic.

At first Jimmy only visited Sueanne and Ed at their home on weekends. Then, about four months after the wedding, Ed and Sueanne thought it would be a good idea to invite Jimmy to live with them.

"I felt sorry for him," Ed explained. "He was living like an animal. He had very little. We were starting a whole new family, and it seemed like the right thing to do."

Despite his father's protests, Jimmy moved in with Sueanne and Ed in April 1979. Motivated by hopes that his mother finally wanted and loved him, and lured by promises of clothes, a car, and a swimming pool, Jimmy ignored Jim Crumm's advice to stay away from Sueanne.

"She's different, Dad," the sixteen-year-old Jimmy told his father. "She's been in counseling."

Their hopes for a happy family were short-lived. By the fall of 1979 the problems were becoming intolerable. Sueanne once again found herself confronted by overwhelming domestic conflicts. The entire family was in turmoil.

Initially the problems seemed solvable. Suzanne and Chris would fight, then run to their respective parents for support. When Sueanne would attempt to discipline Chris—and it happened almost hourly—he would seek his father's protection. Suzanne did the same thing when Ed attempted to discipline her.

However, the problem escalated when Ed and Sueanne discovered drugs in Jimmy's room. Whether Chris was responsible for the discovery or not, Jimmy blamed him for tattling. Jimmy also blamed Chris several weeks later, when Sueanne found stolen clothing in Jimmy's room.

Beset by emotional and legal problems, Jimmy dropped out of high school and moved into a friend's apartment.

The problems were becoming so bad that Norma Hooker broke off the relationship with Sueanne until things were resolved.

"It was getting totally out of hand," Norma Hooker said. "All Sueanne did was complain every time I saw her. Everyone was unhappy, especially Sueanne. She couldn't control Chris. He wouldn't

mind her. Every time she disciplined him about his
cleanliness, clothes, or manners he would run to his
dad, who always took up for him."

The last time Norma saw her, Sueanne was in
tears. Sueanne once again felt trapped in a relationship.

"I don't know what to do," Sueanne desperately
told her. "Chris is driving me crazy. He reminds me
of my mother."

3

"I know my son did not run away. There was just no place for him to run. He had no reason to run. He was happy."

—ED HOBSON

Ed Hobson walked rapidly through the quiet, oak-lined residential neighborhood, stopping occasionally in front of the manicured town houses, condominiums, and duplexes to cup his large, thick hands around his mouth.

"Chris," he yelled at each interval, attempting to summon his son from the darkness of some backyard game. Hobson's voice, normally booming and self-assured, was now a threatening mixture of anger and anxiety. He stopped to listen for children's voices. There were none. The streets were quiet.

Ed was angry. He was also worried.

It was nine-thirty on a school night, and Chris knew the rules: showered and ready for bed by ten P.M. or risk being grounded. On this night the gangly seventh-grader's science project was spread across the kitchen table, his room was a mess, and he was nowhere to be found.

Ed walked back into the house and upstairs to Chris's bedroom. His baseball glove and bats were lying on the floor, amid several pieces of dirty clothing. It was a typical Johnson County teenager's room: telephone, stereo, television, desk, bed, and bookcase—all in various stages of disarray. Hobson scanned the room for a third time, but found nothing missing.

"When was the last time you saw Chris?" Ed asked Sueanne, who was standing in the doorway to their bedroom, brushing her hair.

"I saw him about six or six-thirty," she said unconcernedly, turning and walking back into the bedroom. "I haven't seen him since. He's probably out playing with his friends. Maybe he's down at the park."

"Has Suzanne seen him?" Hobson asked of his thirteen-year-old stepdaughter, who was watching television in her room with the door closed.

"I don't think she has," Sueanne answered. "I'll ask her, though."

Already dressed for bed in an oversized T-shirt, Sueanne wasn't going outside to look for Chris. Ed knew that.

"He's all right," she added matter-of-factly, as Ed started back down the stairs. "He just forgot what time it is."

Ed wanted to believe her. But he couldn't. She didn't know his son. He instinctively knew something was wrong. He had to keep looking. He couldn't sit and wait. Ed walked through the kitchen, past the table with Chris's books, and out to the garage. Chris's bicycle leaned against the wall. That bothered him, too. Chris went everywhere on his bicycle.

With growing anxiety, Ed walked two blocks south on Nall Avenue to the park, a seventy-five-acre tribute to progressive leaders and a large tax base. The well-manicured soccer fields, playgrounds, and trails were now empty. Except for an occasional bicyclist, the park was deserted.

Ed stopped for a moment, yelled Chris's name several more times, then continued down a paved path that paralleled Indian Creek, a heavily wooded stream that meandered through the park. The underbrush along the creek was a deep, lush green. He searched along the banks for Chris, but the moonless sky and thick brush made it impossible for him to see. The fresh, spring air had turned cold.

Ed stopped at the end of the path, turned and yelled Chris's name one last time. His voice echoed across the fields. No response. He hurried home to call the police.

———

Officer John Briley, a few minutes from ending his evening shift, was dispatched at ten-fifty P.M., after Ed's call. Briley turned the patrol car onto 103rd Terrace. Ed was standing alone in the driveway when Briley arrived.

Ed's initial anger had given way to fear, bordering on panic. Not only was Chris missing, but Ed had discovered something else while waiting for the police to arrive. A shotgun was also missing.

"My son's gone," Ed said, walking quickly toward Briley as the policeman climbed from his car, "and a shotgun is missing. His mother says a couple pairs of tennis shoes are gone."

"Just calm down, sir. My name is Officer Briley. And you are?" Briley asked officially.

"Ed Hobson. My son, Chris, he's missing."

"May we go inside, Mr. Hobson?" Briley asked, motioning toward the door.

Sueanne, now dressed in a pair of blue jeans and a blouse, was in the kitchen making coffee when the two men entered. She said nothing. Standing in the living room, Briley opened his pad and turned to Ed. "Could you tell me what you know? When was the last time you saw your son?"

Ed didn't know much. The only thing he knew for certain was the gut feeling he had, telling him that something had happened to Chris. He explained that he had attended a two-hour union meeting at the Labor Relations Board in Kansas City after work. Then he met his wife for a hamburger, and they had arrived home about eight-thirty P.M. He said he had read some labor relations papers and watched television with his wife in their bedroom. When Chris hadn't come in by nine P.M., he started looking for him.

"My son did not run away," Hobson insisted. "He had no reason to leave!"

Sueanne was polite, but provided little information. Suzanne came out of her room once, to get a Coke, and lingered on the staircase for a few minutes, trying to listen to the discussion, but scampered back to her bedroom at the flick of her mother's eyes.

"Have you checked with any of his friends?" Briley asked.

"No. Damn!" Ed said, angry with himself that he hadn't thought of something so basic. "He only has one friend, Bobby Flack, and I haven't asked him."

For a moment he felt relieved, but his relief was short-lived. A telephone call informed him that Bobby hadn't seen Chris all day and didn't know where he was. Briley explained police procedure to Ed, telling him the case would be classified as a runaway.

"But my son did not run away," Ed insisted. "He didn't. I know that."

The statement wasn't a challenge. It was a plea for understanding from a distraught parent.

———

The following day Sueanne showed two very different reactions to Chris's disappearance. At Ed's insistence, she agreed to go talk to Chris's teachers while Ed continued his frantic search.

At eight-thirty A.M. she walked into the principal's office at Indian Creek Junior High School and demanded to see Mrs. Lee Shank, Chris's counselor.

Shank would never forget Sueanne Hobson. A short, graying middle-aged woman, Shank had first met Sueanne four months earlier at a parent-teacher conference. At that meeting, required by law to discuss Chris's progress in his special education classes, Sueanne had left several impressions on Mrs. Shank, none favorable.

Shank had instinctively disliked Sueanne. Maybe it was Sueanne's arrogance. Maybe it was her jewelry, especially the ruby-and-diamond wedding ring Sueanne flaunted.

Summoned to the principal's office, Shank expected to see Sueanne in all her intimidating glory: styled hair, designer clothes and dazzling jewelry. Instead, Sueanne stood disheveled and nervous at the front counter, clad in fuzzy, fleece-lined house slippers. Her clothes, hidden by a long coat kept wrapped tightly around her, were wrinkled. Her auburn hair was uncombed. She appeared anxious and upset, her arrogance replaced by urgency. But she hadn't forgotten to don her jewelry. She still wore several gold chain necklaces and the flashy ruby-and-diamond wedding ring.

"My son has run away and I don't know why. I want to know why," Sueanne said in a shrill, demanding voice. "Why would my son run away?"

"I don't know why," Mrs. Shank calmly told Sueanne, motioning her into an adjacent office. "He's been doing real well in school lately. And he seems happy."

"I know that," Sueanne said, fidgeting with the buttons on her coat. "I just don't know what to do. I don't know what to think."

Shank, an experienced counselor and teacher in the Shawnee Mission School District, often dealt with troubled teenagers and their parents. It was not unusual for a child to get mad and leave home. To most teachers, it was no cause for alarm. Years of experience had taught her that they almost always came back home, usually within one or two days.

But Shank had an uneasy feeling about Chris and his stepmother. She didn't know why, other than to remember the January meeting in which Sueanne had talked freely about the problems Chris had created at home between her husband and herself. Shank thought it odd then that Sueanne, having never met her before, would discuss the problems she was having in her marriage. She also found it odd that Chris's father had not attended the meeting.

Now, sitting across from Sueanne, Shank felt worried, concerned about Chris.

"We will ask the children if they know anything," she said politely, "and if we find out anything, we will call you."

"Please do," Sueanne said, rising from her chair. "I'm so worried."

Sueanne's dramatic appearance at the school perplexed those who knew her. It wasn't the Sueanne they were used to seeing. Shank, later recalling Sueanne's interest in Chris's disappearance, felt the same way: "We couldn't exactly put our finger on it, but we were all skeptical."

If Sueanne's concerns over Chris's disappearance were real, they were rapidly conquered. Shortly before noon, Sueanne telephoned Margie Hunt Fugate.

"Chris is gone, he's run away," Sueanne gleefully told her. "What are you doing this afternoon? Let's celebrate."

Margie, a bartender and banquet hostess at Brookridge Country Club, was Sueanne's best friend. They had met in 1976 when they both worked for Dreyfuss Grain. They had something in common: both were single women raising children alone. Margie had two young boys of her own. She and Sueanne remained friends after Sueanne's marriage to Ed. They spent several hours a week together, sitting at Sueanne's kitchen table, talking and drinking coffee.

However, on this day, Sueanne didn't want to stay home. She was ready to go out.

"I'll pick you up and we'll have a drink," she said.

Within an hour Sueanne was at Margie's apartment in full regalia. Although Margie was aware of the minor problems Chris had been causing at home, she found Sueanne's excited reaction puzzling. Her happiness was more convincing than her appearance as a distraught parent earlier that day.

Steve Moore was one of two detectives assigned to the juvenile division of the Overland Park Police Department. The other was Darrell Urban. Working together was about the only thing the two men had in common.

A tall, thin, twenty-seven-year-old with an eager-to-please approach to life, Moore looked more like a juvenile than a detective in the juvenile division.

Moore would always listen to the fifty-six-year-old Urban. There were more sophisticated detectives in the department, but none with as much street sense. Moore understood and appreciated Urban's "good-old boy," common sense approach to police work. As inexperienced as Moore was, he needed Urban's fatherly advice.

"I know every kid and every thing about every kid in this town," Urban would lecture Moore. "And every kid in this town knows me. And by God, they better be afraid of me."

Moore heard Urban's voice down at the end of the hall, kidding the secretary about her weekend plans. Moore hurried down the hall to talk to him about his new assignment.

"Have you seen this report?" Moore said, handing it to Urban.

"Yep," Urban said, showing little interest.

"Do you know them?"

"Yep," Urban said. "Mama's a little highfalutin lady. Kinda thinks she's a little bit better than everybody else. Ed seems all right, but Mama runs the show. Ed's kind of a wimp around her."

"How do you know them?"

"I've had a couple dealings with Jimmy. Busted him on some credit cards a few months ago. First time I met him was about a year ago. Bad home life. Mama brought Jimmy in here, she was dragging him by the ear. She'd found some pot in his room. Wanted me to talk to him. She called me out to the house a few weeks later. Found some more pot. That's when I met Ed and Chris. Chris was a little conniver. He sure had fun pointing out where Jimmy hid his pot. He couldn't wait to tell me. I got the impression he didn't like sharing Daddy with the new family."

"Did you arrest Jimmy on the marijuana?"

"Nope, it wasn't that big of a deal," Urban said. "A pinch of the worst brown pot I'd ever seen—all stems and seeds. All she wanted me to do was talk to him. Take her off the hook."

"What do you think of Chris running away?"

"Doesn't surprise me at all. He probably wants a little more attention from Daddy," Urban said as he cleared the remaining reports from his desk.

———

At nine-thirty A.M. the following day, Moore met the Hobson family for the first time. Sueanne answered the door. She smiled quietly when he introduced himself. Then she invited him into the kitchen, where Ed and Suzanne were seated at the table. Ed's eyes were red from lack of sleep. His blond hair was rumpled.

Entering the home, the first thing Moore noticed was its eerie, unlived-in quality. It was immaculate. Every knickknack, magazine, and plant had its place. There were no dirty dishes. Moore thought Ed, a blue collar, dirt-under-the-fingernails man, looked out of place. In fact, Ed and Sueanne didn't look like husband and wife.

Ed was a mixture of emotions. Angry one minute, distraught, almost whimpering the next, he begged for Moore's help, then lambasted him for his lack of cooperation. Moore wondered why Urban had called him a wimp.

Urban's description of Sueanne didn't fit, either. With Moore, Sueanne showed no emotion at all. She answered his questions in a polite but impersonal way, as if she were responding to a survey at the local mall. Moore thought she really didn't act concerned about Chris's disappearance.

Moore spent about two hours at the Hobson home, discussing Chris and attempting to calm Ed. Sueanne and Suzanne excused themselves to go shopping. Neither seemed upset that Chris was gone. Ed was almost oblivious to their departure, intent on persuading Moore that his son would not run away.

"He is my only blood relative," he told Moore. "He's all I have. You've got to find him for me."

Chris had been gone almost a week and there was still no sign of him. Not a telephone call to a friend or relative; nothing. With each passing day, Ed became more volatile and the detectives more perplexed.

The next morning, six days after his disappearance, Moore received another message from Ed. Moore dialed the Ralston-Purina telephone number in Kansas City, Missouri, a set of digits he now knew by memory. Within seconds Ed was on the line. He urgently relayed the news that Chris's billfold had been discovered in some shrubbery at a nearby shopping mall.

Moore hung up the telephone after arranging to pick up the billfold and meet Ed to identify it.

"They found Chris's billfold at Metcalf South," he told Urban. "I'm going down to pick it up."

Moore was only gone twenty minutes. When he returned to the station, Captain Ron Jackson and Urban were waiting for him in Jackson's office.

Urban opened the billfold. Inside was an Indian Creek Junior High School identification card with Chris's picture on it, a Social Security card, and a photograph of Ed and Sueanne.

"This isn't copacetic," Urban drawled between puffs on his cigarette. "Something ain't right."

"Finding the billfold bothered Urban; it signaled a turn in the case. He knew runaways didn't usually throw away their billfolds. Whatever had happened to the boy, finding the billfold meant at least one thing: someone else probably was involved.

"What's Daddy been saying about the boy?" Urban asked.

"He says everything has been going great," Moore responded. "He tells me Chris has been adjusting to his new family and his schoolwork has improved in the past few weeks."

"I just don't believe everything was all right in that house," Urban said. "What's Mama been saying?"

"Not much. She's been acting like she's not really involved, that it's Ed's kid. She acts supportive. She says all the right things, but—"

"I don't know," Urban said, interrupting Moore. "I could tell things weren't going very smooth when I was over there a few months ago. It wasn't one big happy family like Ed's telling you."

"What should I do?" Moore asked.

"You better start rolling the wheels," Urban said.

"You better start shaking some kids and getting some answers instead of going down there to that school like a jolly good boy. You better go down there and put the fear of God into them. Somebody knows something about where this kid is and you better find out who and what. Six days is a long time. I don't know what has happened, but this isn't normal. Somebody put that billfold at Metcalf South for a reason, and you better find out who did it and why. Maybe then you can find out where that kid is."

Urban had been a policeman long enough to know that most thirteen-year-old runaways will contact somebody—a friend, relative or teacher—within a few days.

"And I think it might be a good idea to search all of that wooded area around the park," Urban said. "That boy could be lying down there at that park, dead."

The detectives discussed several scenarios with Jackson, including the possibility Chris may have killed himself. That could explain the missing shotgun. Unlikely, but possible, they agreed. The idea of murder was immediately dismissed.

"People don't kill thirteen-year-old boys over a few family squabbles," Urban said. "It just don't happen. Suicide? Maybe. Murder? Nope."

———

At eleven-thirty A.M. the next morning, a police helicopter hovered against the bright blue sky, occasionally dipping close to the ground, then spinning away. The helicopter combed the area for about ninety minutes before abandoning the search. Then twenty-eight officers on the ground, some armed with shotguns, began a concentrated search of the thick, rough wooded area along Indian Creek from Metcalf Avenue to State Line Road.

It was by far the largest search Overland Park police had ever conducted for a runaway.

Ed had to work that day. His bosses told him he had already taken too many days off searching for his son. When he got home from work about four P.M., Moore was waiting outside his house, along with a handful of television and newspaper reporters who were curious about the massive search.

The two men went inside, where Sueanne and Suzanne had spent the day.

Moore explained that Chris had not been found, but some clothing had been discovered. About five P.M. Moore returned to the Hobson home with two pair of blue jeans and two shirts found by officers. Strangely, neither Ed nor Sueanne were sure the clothes belonged to Chris.

Shortly afterward, Moore held an impromptu press conference in Ed's driveway. He told reporters police had conducted the search because several aspects of the case didn't fit the pattern of most runaways.

"It appears he had no reason to run away," Moore said. "We have talked to his teachers and they say his grades were good. His friends tell us he was happy."

Ed agreed. "Chris and I have been through a lot together," he said, as Sueanne and Suzanne quietly looked on. "He's a good kid and he's doing real well in school. This really has thrown me."

4

"How would Ed know what a normal family was? What he considered normal, probably wouldn't be to anyone else."

—A RELATIVE

In the days following Chris's disappearance, Ed spent most of his time trying to put together the pieces, to find the answers to the myriad questions surrounding Chris's vanishing. His inability to understand his son's disappearance led to enormous guilt.

Was he to blame? And if so, what had he done wrong? What could he have done differently? Was he so in love with Sueanne that he had downplayed his son's problems? Had he ignored Chris to the point that his son felt unwanted?

Ed questioned every aspect of his eighteen-month marriage to Sueanne, but always returned to the same conclusion: there had been problems, but nothing that would force Chris to run away.

Ed refused to believe that his son's disappearance was related to any of the family's problems. All he had ever wanted to do was protect Chris and give him the things he needed: a home, love, and the mother Chris had wanted so desperately. If Chris's disappearance was related to problems at home, Ed thought, then he was a failure.

For years Ed had been trying to make up to Chris for the tragic horrors of his young life, the nightmares and insecurities that followed his half sister's suicide and his mother's lingering death.

Despite Ed's efforts, the two years following his wife's death in March 1976 had been difficult for both him and Chris. A single parent trying to raise a young boy, Ed found it almost impossible to reconcile his own needs as a man with those of his son. He felt guilty every time he went out on a date, leaving his son with a babysitter.

Emotionally, Chris had been devastated by his mother's death. His longing for her, coupled with the normal stresses of adolescence and moving to a new apartment, school and friends, left Chris weak, meek, and insecure.

"He was the most woebegone little boy I had ever seen," Norma Hooker recalled of her first encounter with Ed and Chris in 1977 at the Overland Park skating rink she operated with her husband. "It was obvious he needed love. Lots of it."

Two images remained vividly clear to Hooker about that initial encounter: the frail, frightened child and the big-hearted, overprotective father who accompanied him.

But those days of anguish and despair seemed to be over for both of them on December 2, 1978, the day Ed and Sueanne were married. Ed described it as the happiest day of his life. The wedding in the small, festively decorated chapel at the Country Club Christian Church was a new beginning for Ed and Chris.

Sueanne appeared to be the perfect person to raise his son. She was intelligent, organized, and well-mannered, all the things that Ed wasn't, and all the things he wanted Chris to be. Unfortunately, those specific traits became the core of problems that initially threatened to destroy the marriage and Ed's hopes for a family.

In discussing Chris's disappearance with Moore, Ed identified three problem areas in the family, starting with Chris's difficulty in adjusting to Sueanne's demanding ways. Her obsession with cleanliness, obedience, and regimen were in direct contrast to the lifestyles that Chris and Ed had been living. Rather than demand that Chris eat properly, keep his room clean and maintain his school grades, Ed had allowed Chris to do what he wanted, when he wanted.

"He had just been through a horrible experience with his mom dying," Ed said later. "Instead of getting down on him every time some piddly little thing went wrong, I let him slide. I told him how great he was."

Compassion was not one of Sueanne's strengths. Regardless of what had happened in the past, Chris was now living in her home and he would do as she said. She required strict obedience from her daughter. And, by God, she expected it from Chris.

During family counseling sessions, which Sueanne required Ed and Chris to attend as a prerequisite for marriage, the discussion always reverted back to her inability to control Chris.

Sueanne's obsession with perfection, coupled with Chris's lackadaisical attitude about everything, strained their relationship from its inception. She was frustrated by her inability to make Chris obey. He often refused to do any chores that she assigned. And when she tried to discipline him, he would run to his father for protection.

Dr. Robert Craft, a psychologist, and also the minister who married Ed and Sueanne, reportedly saw the problems between Sueanne and Chris as troublesome but not overwhelming. It was all a part of bringing together two separate households with distinctly different approaches to life, he apparently thought.

"She was definitely concerned with his discipline," Craft, to whom the Hobsons came for individual and family counseling, later told investigators. "Chris had things to learn, just the basic social habits, eating, cleanliness. But considering that Ed and Chris had lived together so long, basically as bachelors, those were the normal kinds of things that needed to be straightened out."

Ed accepted the initial problems between Chris and Sueanne. He knew about Chris's shortcomings from counselors and teachers at school.

"He was not socially able to get along with people because he didn't know how," recalled counselor Lee Shank, "He was very immature in many ways. He really had no exposure to living with people in a normal house—normal situation."

But Sueanne's constant demands for improvement eventually caused friction between her and Ed, including threats by each to divorce the other. Ed wasn't upset with what Sueanne wanted from Chris, it was how she went about accomplishing it that irritated him.

Chris, and occasionally Sueanne's daughter, Suzanne, were banished from the dinner table if they failed at even the most mundane table manners. Talking with your mouth full or eating with the wrong fork were especially irritating to Sueanne.

Even when Chris tried to please her, it was never accomplished quickly enough or well enough. On one occasion Chris's duties included emptying the dishwasher and putting the dishes away. Sueanne went into a tirade when she found the dishes randomly placed in the cabinet, instead of in the proper order.

"Why does it have to be that way?" Chris shouted at his dad.

"Because she does ninety percent of the housework and that's the way she wants it," Ed lectured him.

In March 1979, Sueanne and Ed decided to cross-adopt each other's children, hoping that would ease the family's second area of confrontation, the bickering between Chris and Suzanne. But instead of easing the problems, it magnified them.

Suzanne, a grade higher than Chris, was angered that she had to take him to the movies, out for a hamburger, everywhere she went. And even when they didn't go out, he was still bothersome. Suzanne repeatedly complained to her mother that every time she had her girlfriends over to the house, Chris wouldn't leave them alone.

"He's just always hanging around acting goofy and doing stupid things," she would complain to her mother. "Why does he always have to go where I go? Can't I have a life of my own?"

They fought over everything—albums, chores, and clothes. Inevitably their fights would require intervention by one or both parents, causing accusations of favoritism.

However, the siblings' battles exploded when Suzanne accused Chris of spreading rumors among their friends that she had taken her clothes off at the skating rink.

Chris denied it, and neither Ed nor Sueanne was able to determine if it had actually happened. Regardless of its veracity, the damage had been done. Sueanne believed her daughter.

"He's a pathological liar," Sueanne angrily told Ed. "You'd better straighten him out."

Again Ed downplayed the seriousness of the problem. It was two children fighting between themselves, he told Sueanne.

Ironically, the constant battles between Chris and Suzanne seemed to subside after that, in part because Suzanne had decided she would never speak to Chris again.

Midway through their first summer together things seemed to be improving. Ed and Sueanne agreed to end the group therapy, although Chris continued with individual counseling at Sueanne's urging.

Craft reportedly saw nothing unusual about their decision to end the counseling.

"They had gotten over some humps in putting these two families together," he later told investigators. "When they decided to discontinue counseling, I was for that because it showed independence on their part."

Although the counseling ended, the problems never did. By the fall of 1979 the family was headed for more turmoil. The third problem Ed had spoken of to Moore was Jimmy.

Encouraged by the small successes Ed thought the family had accomplished in its first eight months together, Sueanne and Ed asked Jimmy to live with them in the summer of 1979. Although Ed didn't adopt Jimmy, he did allow the teenager to use his last name when he enrolled at Shawnee Mission South High School for the fall term.

"I just felt that if we were really going to be a family, Sueanne's son ought to be living with us," Ed said later.

It was a horrendous mistake.

Biologically, Sueanne and Jimmy were mother and son. Emotionally, they were strangers. It took them several weeks before they felt comfortable touching each other.

Initially, Jimmy and his mother got along, although Jimmy later admitted it was difficult.

"It was a new beginning," he said. "I wanted to do everything right. I wanted her to be proud of me. I cut off the drugs. I started playing soccer. I didn't have anything holding me back. I didn't have a bad reputation. It was a new start."

While Jimmy was trying to accommodate his mother, he could already see the signs of trouble brewing in his future. It didn't take long for him to see what was happening between Sueanne and Chris.

"At first, it looked picture perfect," Jimmy said later. "But it became obvious that my mother hated Chris. She told me he was a psychotic, a pathological liar, and a troublemaker. My sister hated him, too. But I think that was only because my mom forced her to."

Interestingly, Jimmy also observed something else. Sueanne treated Chris differently when Ed was at home.

"I kind of felt sorry for Ed," Jimmy recalled. "He just couldn't see what was going on."

Ed, who was working five days a week and attending a technical school two evenings a week, tried to be the peacemaker when he was at home. In Ed's mind it was Jimmy's problems that seemed to overshadow the other difficulties disrupting the family.

These problems came to a head midway through the fall term. When Jimmy had initially enrolled at South for his senior year, the counselors told him he didn't have enough credits to graduate in the spring. Sueanne was appalled. She arranged for him to take his full class schedule in the daytime and enrolled him in classes at another high school two nights a week.

"You will graduate on time," she told him. "Especially after I have brought you over here and given you this nice home."

The pressure was too much. Jimmy tried to make the grade, to do as his mother wished, but nothing was good enough. If he made a B, it should have been an A. Even his teachers at South were confused and angered by Sueanne's domination. One of Jimmy's teachers, Gerald Colwell, called Sueanne's expectations unrealistic.

"I told her to back off," he recalled of one conference. "She wanted him to be an excellent student, instantaneously. The trouble was, he couldn't be, no matter how hard he tried. He was a senior reading at the ninth grade level, and she wanted him to make straight A's. Outwardly, she was a nice-looking, well-dressed person. But she came across so strong, so harsh. She just was so hardened."

Jimmy felt helpless. Once again he had failed to live up to his mother's expectations. He went back to an old friend: drugs. He sought out a classmate who he thought could find what he needed.

"You know where I can get any liquid LSD?" Jimmy asked Paul Sorrentino.

"Probably," Paul said with a cocky smile. "I'll check."

By January of 1980 Jimmy had given up all hope of continuing in school, and his troubles were mounting at home. Ed and Sueanne had found drugs in his room on several occasions. He was also convicted in juvenile court of using a stolen credit card. Despite his legal problems, Jimmy was using drugs daily. Instead of going to class, he would go to an older friend's apartment where they would get stoned on anything they could find. In early February 1980 he quit school and moved out of the Hobson residence.

"I had to," he later said, and laughed. "My mom grounded me for life."

Jimmy left the Hobson home, once again pathetically willing but unable to please his mother. Meanwhile, Chris was a growing thorn in Sueanne's side and she encouraged Jimmy to feel likewise. She told him that Chris was the one who had snitched on him about the drugs, and that Chris had struck her and Suzanne on several occasions. Neither of these statements was true.

Whether Ed was unaware, or simply chose to ignore it, the stage was being set for tragedy. Ed might have been more fearful and less confused about Chris's disappearance if he had known of the lethal nature of Jimmy's friendship with Paul Sorrentino.

5

"Chris was a real jerk. If there was three gallons
of milk in the refrigerator, he would drink two
and three-quarters of it and leave the rest."

——PAUL SORRENTINO

Leila Anderson, over-
weight, eighteen, and a high school dropout, had
had minor brushes with the law since junior high,
mainly due to her desire for jewelry and her use of
stolen checkbooks.

A bleached blonde with an easy smile, Leila was
eager for people to like her. Her moral lapses re-
sulted from weakness, not malice. She had a habit
of taking other social outcasts under her wing.

Now she couldn't shake the nervous, painful ache
in her stomach. Ever since she had heard the
rumors circulating among friends that Paul had
killed the missing Hobson boy, she couldn't eat or
sleep. She didn't want to believe it. But maybe now
she would get the truth.

Paul had called and asked her for a ride. It was
late in the afternoon on April 30 when she pulled
her car to a stop in front of the condominium that
Paul shared with his father and brother. Paul's
mother had returned to her family on the East

Coast several years before, leaving her husband to raise two sons and a daughter.

Paul bounded out of the house with an air of excitement. Short, with wavy black hair, he had a broad, cocky smile that the high school girls loved.

"Hi, Leila, thanks for the ride," Paul said, walking around to the driver's window. "Can I drive?"

"Why not?" she replied, sliding over to the passenger's side. She liked Paul. There was an air of excitement surrounding him. And he was good-looking. In fact, she'd had a crush on him for several months.

Most women liked Paul, whether they were classmates, teachers or employers. Abandoned by his mother when he was nine, Paul made women want to protect him, nurture and love him. Leila was no different, and that's why she wanted to know the truth. She couldn't and wouldn't believe the rumors unless she heard him admit it himself.

"Where are we going?" she asked.

"I have to go over to Jim's house," she said, spinning the tires as he pulled away from the curb.

Leila shrugged. She didn't want to visit anyone, much less Jimmy. He frightened her.

"I've seen him around, but I've never met him," she said, displaying a calm demeanor. "What's he like?"

"He's a good guy. He's cool," Paul assured her. "We won't be long. I just have to talk to him a couple of minutes."

Leila wanted to talk but she decided to wait and see what happened at Jimmy's apartment. During the fifteen-minute drive, Paul kept up a steady, rambling monologue on everything that passed before his eyes. Nervous chatter, Leila thought.

Jimmy was home alone. He tried to be friendly when Paul introduced Leila, but she sensed something was wrong. The apartment's bare walls and sparse furnishings befitted a seventeen-year-old high school dropout trying to make it on his own.

After a few minutes conversation, Paul asked Jimmy about Chris's disappearance.

"Did you see it on television?" Paul asked. "All those cops carrying shotguns around . . ."

"Yeah," Jimmy mumbled.

It was obvious Jimmy didn't want to talk about it, especially in front of Leila. He flashed Paul a stern look, mumbled something about how Chris was crazy to run away, then changed the subject. They discussed an upcoming party until Paul decided it was time to leave. Leila was relieved. She felt uncomfortable and intrusive. She was beginning to believe the rumors.

Back in the car, Leila didn't wait long to confront Paul. He hadn't even pulled out of the parking lot when she turned to him.

"Paul, I don't know what's going on between you and Jim, but I've heard the story about his little brother," she said as Paul drove east down 95th Street, past the Oak Park Mall.

"Where did you hear it from?" he asked, acting surprised.

"Jerry Boring told me."

"Well, not very many people know the whole story," he said, smiling. "I'll tell you about it if you want to know."

"Did you really kill the kid?" she asked, hoping Paul would admit that the rumor was just another one of his attempts to impress people and gain attention.

"Yes, I did," he said calmly, almost proudly.

"Why?"

"Because Jim's mom asked him to get rid of the kid, and I owed Jimmy a favor. She didn't like him, either."

Leila didn't grasp the reason at first, only the confirmation of her fears. Then the thought collapsed on her.

"Jim's mom asked you?"

"Well, I never talked to her directly, but Jim said she told him she would pay to have my motorcycle fixed if I would help him."

"So you killed him? I just don't understand why," she said angrily.

"Well, if you knew the kid, you'd know that he was a real jerk and you'd do the same thing."

Leila's stomach began to churn and she thought she was going to throw up. Her head ached. Her sense of outrage mixed with cold fear as she realized she was alone in a car with a self-confessed murderer. She kept quiet while Paul drove randomly through the quiet residential streets. But she couldn't remain silent.

"I just don't understand why you would kill a thirteen-year-old boy. I just can't understand it and I don't want to believe it," she said after several minutes of silence.

"Well, I tell you, he was a real jerk," Paul said again. "If they had three gallons of milk in the refrigerator, he would drink two and three-quarters of it and leave a quarter for the rest of the family for the rest of the week."

Leila had no response to this.

Paul continued to talk, driven by a need to tell someone everything. He told her how they made Chris dig his own grave, how they made him lie down in it before they shot him. Paul was the first to fire, striking Chris in the head. When Chris attempted to get up, Jimmy "took a shot." Then Paul shot him in the "heart and face to make sure he was dead."

Leila sat in the passenger seat numb, speechless, motionless, while Paul kept repeating how stupid Chris was, what a jerk he was for getting himself into that situation.

"Now, you know, if we took you out there and we were sitting there playing with guns while you dug a hole, would you lay down in it?" he asked, his voice rising in disgust. "That's how stupid he was."

"But Paul," Leila answered, her voice pleading for understanding, "he probably trusted his step-brother and had no reason to think that you all were going to kill him. If you asked me to do the same thing, I would do it for you because I would trust you. Just like that boy trusted his step-brother."

The words caught in her throat. She couldn't believe what she was saying. She couldn't believe what Paul was saying. She wanted to cry.

"I don't want to hear any more," she said.

"Do you want to know—I can even tell you the exact time the kid was dead," he said teasingly. "Nine thirty-seven P.M. We covered him up and we were out of there by 9:42. After I did that I just went into a frenzy."

"I just don't understand how you could do that."

"Well, we went out and got really messed up before we did it," Paul said. "That's the only way I could have done it."

Leila couldn't feel the fresh, spring air brushing against her face as Paul drove back to his house. It was late in the afternoon and she watched several children walking home from school. They were probably about Chris's age, she thought numbly. She didn't know what to do, or how she was supposed to feel. Never before had she felt this sad or helpless.

"Paul, how many people have you told? You have to realize that for every person you've told, at least two more people know about it. If you want to get away with something, first of all, you don't go out and tell everybody about it."

Paul thought for a few seconds, then confidently told Leila, "I've only told a couple of people and they won't say anything. And I know you won't say anything." He looked her in the eyes. "If I can do it once, I can do it again," he said.

She looked back at him and shook her head. "At least twenty or twenty-five people know about it, including Jerry and John Boring's parents," she said. "There are rumors all over school and people are talking about it at Metcalf South and Oak Park Mall."

Paul shrugged as he pulled into his driveway.

"Do you want to come in?"

"No, I'd better be going."

She drove away slowly, wondering what to do.

———

At noon the following day Leila called the Overland Park Police Department.

"I have some information about the missing Hobson boy," she said. "I think he's dead."

John Douglass, twenty-nine, was the only detective available when her call was put through to the detective division. He was aware of the missing youth, but hadn't been directly involved.

Leila had only spoken for a few minutes when Douglass stopped her in mid-sentence. Whether her story was true or not, Douglass was convinced that at least Leila believed it was true.

"This is very important. Would you be willing to come by the police station today?" he asked.

She agreed.

Douglass hung up the telephone and thought for a few moments. He didn't believe Chris Hobson had been murdered. It was probably a case of some kid trying to gain attention from his friends.

When Leila arrived, Douglass was waiting in Captain Jackson's office with a tape recorder in place. Although Moore was the detective assigned to investigate Chris's disappearance, the importance of the case had changed rapidly—from a runaway to a murder in the span of one telephone call—and Jackson wanted Douglass, his top investigator, involved.

Moore joined Douglass in the interview room,

but from the beginning it was Douglass's interview. He sat expressionless behind the desk in the windowless, second-floor office. Leila sat across the desk from him and Moore sat next to her. Douglass was straightforward. Moore gave her a boyish smile.

"Leila, why don't you tell us what you know about what has happened? Why don't you start from the very beginning?" Douglass said, his voice serious and official.

"Okay, day before yesterday, Jerry Boring came to me and said, 'I need to talk to you.' He told me that somebody I knew was paid off to kill the little kid that was missing. He told me my friend had helped kill the kid. And he told me the missing kid's step-brother and mother were involved. He said the mother paid her son to kill his stepbrother, and my friend helped him."

Moore was overwhelmed.

"Who is your friend?" Douglass asked.

"Paul Sorrentino."

Douglass and Moore both knew Paul as a local high school punk with a reputation for trouble.

"So Paul and who else?"

"Jim."

"What's Jim's last name?" Douglass asked Leila.

"Hobson," Moore interjected, explaining that when Jimmy had moved in with Ed and Sueanne, he had taken Ed's last name. Douglass glared at him. Moore was eager and inexperienced. Douglass was beginning to wish Moore wasn't even there. Let her tell it, Douglass thought to himself.

"Was it Hobson?" Douglass asked Lelia.

"Yes."

"Okay," Douglass said. "Go ahead."

"Jerry just told me Paul told him they were paid to kill this kid. Jerry didn't tell me any more about it because he didn't really know about it. So yesterday I went over to Paul's house and I acted like, you know, like I didn't know anything.

"I said, 'Look, Paul, Jerry told me all about it.'"

For the next ten minutes, as Moore and Douglass listened, Leila recounted her conversation with Paul.

While she talked, Douglass was thinking. At first, about how incredibly stupid Paul was. And then he realized it wasn't just stupidity, it was youth. At sixteen years old, Paul was young to be involved in a brutal murder. Douglass hadn't even begun to grasp the idea that Sueanne Hobson had hired her son to commit the murder. In fact, he was having difficulty believing the story at all.

"Did he tell you why they did this?" Douglass asked.

"He said—his excuse for it was that everybody in the family hated Chris but his dad, the father. And he was the kind of kid—this is exactly as he put it to me—that if they had three gallons of milk in the refrigerator, this little kid would drink two and three-quarters of it and leave a fourth of a gallon for the rest of the family for the rest of the week.

"And that's another thing that got me stirred up," she said, "because that's no reason to kill somebody."

Moore, his boyish face now a sullen ash white, nodded his head in agreement.

"Did he describe this area to you?" Douglass continued.

"No, he just said it was out in the country and he mentioned 248th Street. I can probably find out the cross street if you make sure he doesn't know I came up here and talked to you."

"How can you find that out?" Douglass questioned.

"I can ask Paul or I can ask Jerry Boring," she said. "Everybody has overheard it. Jerry's dad, Mr. Boring, has overheard the whole thing, and he was in tears thinking that Jerry was involved. And nobody knows what to do because they are afraid of Paul and Jim. I mean, if his mother can pay him off to get rid of the boy, why can't she pay him off to get rid of anybody else who is going to turn them in? So everybody is pretty paranoid about what they're going to do."

It was the first time Douglass had shown any emotion. He shook his head in disgust. Douglass could understand how a teenager might be frightened. But how could an adult—even if his son might be involved—have information about the murder of a child and not notify the police?

"Would any of these people talk to us?"

"I don't think so."

Douglass, growing anxious, tried to calm down. It was obvious Leila was frightened, but somehow he had to keep her talking.

"Did Paul tell you what he shot him in the head with?" Douglass asked.

"A rifle, I guess. It wasn't the little kid that took the rifle from the house, it was Jim who got it the night they killed him."

"Did they tell you what they did with it?"

"No, but I can . . . All I know is what I told you. But I can find out more."

"How soon?"

"Tonight or tomorrow. I'm sure I could go up and talk to him and have him tell me more. If they don't know I've been up here."

"I don't want you getting into any trouble," Moore said, genuinely concerned about her safety.

"How old are you?" Douglass asked. He was concerned about her safety, but he also wanted information to convict those responsible for the murder.

"Eighteen. I just don't want them knowing, because I don't want them to hurt me. If it came down to it, I would testify against Paul. I would do the whole thing if I knew for a fact that I could be protected."

"Let me tell you about Paul, okay?" Douglass said angrily. "Paul is a penny-ante little crook. Without a doubt he is not a big-timer. He's not a big any-thing. He is a penny-ante little crook. Now there is every possibility in the world that he told you this because he is trying to take advantage of the situation . . ."

"I know he did it," Leila said firmly. "I know he did it."

"If he did do it and you have to testify against him, we are not going to let him hurt you," Douglass said.

"What if he gets out?"

"He's not going to get out," Douglass said, nervously sensing that her fear of Paul could end the interview at any time.

"He's not going to get out, not for cold-blooded murder," Moore added encouragingly, almost naively.

"I told him that," Leila said, regaining her composure. "I said, 'Do you realize what you've done? That's premeditated murder. Do you realize what is going to happen to you?' And he just goes, 'Leila, the only way I can live with it myself is just to blow it off.' Now I'm scared. If he can do that . . ."

"Did he tell you what he did with the money, or how much he got?" Douglass asked, trying to get specifics.

"He hasn't gotten it yet. He made an arrangement that all he wanted was somebody to pay off the motorcycle for him and give him like three or four hundred cash for spending money. Okay? Like it was no big deal to him. He goes, 'If you knew the kid, you'd do the same thing.' And I thought that was kind of humorous because while he was driving my car there was a bird in the road. He stopped and honked the horn for the bird to fly off so he wouldn't hit it. I turned to him and I go, 'You can murder a kid, but you can't run over a bird.' The guy is sick and he needs help. I don't know, maybe it wasn't my place to come in here."

Leila was getting tired, and Douglass needed facts. He knew they couldn't do anything until the body was located.

"When they were talking about going out, did he say that they were very far from the road? Did they walk back in the woods?"

"He said they covered him up. He said, 'I can tell you the exact time he was dead . . . It was 9:37 P.M. We were back in the car by 9:42.' So it can't be very far from the road."

"Okay, Leila," Douglass said. "If you get any more information from these people about where the boy is, where the guns are, what they did, if they did get any money, we certainly want to know. Did Paul tell you any more about how this was set up? Did the stepmother set this up with Jim ahead of time?"

"It was obviously set up," she said. "Paul said they were going to do this a long time ago. Paul said he owed Jim a favor."

"Are they running around telling everybody about this?" Douglass asked in disbelief.

"Well, you see, Jerry Boring really has a big mouth. When he gets the news, he goes and tells his friends. Paul and I used to be pretty close, well, not real close friends, but I knew him well enough and I trusted the guy, you know? So, I went up to him myself and asked him to tell me the whole deal."

"Did he act surprised that you wanted to know?"

"He asked me who I heard it from. He said, 'Listen to me, if this gets out and around, we're going to get caught for it.' I told him that I wouldn't say anything. But I just couldn't . . . that's not me."

"Are you going to be able to maintain your composure around him?" Moore asked. "I just want to make sure you can do it."

"Oh, yeah, I'm pretty good at acting. I can put on a pretty mean front."

Leila's voice trailed off as she looked at the floor. For a moment her attention turned inward. Amid the silence, she looked up at the two detectives.

"I knew I'd come," she said, trying to convince herself she was doing the right thing. "After I heard it, I was sick to my stomach all day yesterday. It didn't really bug me that much until I heard it from him."

"How old is Paul?" Douglass asked.

"Sixteen. Paul doesn't have any conscience at all."

Douglass looked at Leila. She was probably right, he thought.

"Do you think you can find out from Paul where the grave is?" Moore asked Leila.

"The grave, God, he was laughing at the fact that the kid dug his own grave," she said, shaking her head in angry amazement.

"We have to know where on 248th Street," Douglass said.

"When he told me, I had so many questions that I just didn't know where to start," she said, disappointed because she didn't know the answers to many of Douglass's questions. "I was just kind of numb and then I realized what he had told me and I got scared, because if it came down to it and if I didn't say anything, then maybe I am an accessory in some way."

"You're okay now," Moore said, putting his hand on her shoulder.

"That's about all the questions I can think of," Douglass said. "Thank you."

Moore escorted her out of the room. He handed her a card with his home telephone number on it.

"If you need anything, or find out anything, you can call me at this number," he said. "Okay?"

"Thanks."

As soon as Leila left, Urban and several other detectives entered the office. Douglass relayed the information from the interview.

For the next twenty minutes, while they listened to the tape, the detectives sat in stunned silence, occasionally shaking their heads in anger and disbelief as the grisly, almost unbelievable tale unfolded in Leila's young voice.

"I just can't believe it," Moore said.

"It's starting to make sense," Urban told the group. "I never did think Mama was shooting us straight. I never thought murder, but I had a feeling she wasn't telling us everything she knew. All her answers were too polite. Too trite. I sure as hell never considered murder, but think about it. We all know everything wasn't as nice as Ed has been telling us. We all know Chris was a little conniver, that he ratted on Jimmy about the marijuana."

"Remember how Jimmy was shaking when we went over there to question him about Chris last week?" Moore asked Urban. "Damn, I bet he thought we'd come over to arrest him."

Jackson still wasn't convinced.

"You think a mother would really use her son like that?" he asked speculatively.

"I believe Leila," Douglass said. "At least I believe that she believes it's true. There are just too many specifics. Too many things match what we already know. Right, Steve?"

"Yes. It seems to fit."

"One thing, though, Paul said he never directly talked to Sueanne about this," Douglass added. "Could Jimmy just have been using that to convince Paul to help him?"

No one had an answer. Even as experienced cops, they found themselves stunned at the thought of a suburban housewife masterminding the murder of a thirteen-year-old boy.

"We need to find a body," Douglass said. "That's the first thing we need to do."

"What about the boys?" Moore asked. "Should we talk to them?"

"No need to do that right now," Urban said. "They're kids, they ain't goin' anywhere."

"All we've got is hearsay and circumstantial evidence right now," Douglass added. "Let's concentrate on trying to find Chris's body."

"It's late and it's starting to get dark, no reason to try to find the body tonight," Jackson said. "Let's meet here at eight A.M."

Moore had one last question: "What do I tell Ed? He calls or comes by the station every night."

For two reasons, they all agreed Moore would tell Ed nothing. They were not positive Leila was telling the truth, and if Ed thought Sueanne was involved, he might become violent.

"Just tell him we are continuing to look for his son," Jackson told Moore. "That's the truth."

Moore arrived at the police station the next morning with interesting news. Leila had called him three times the night before with information. Nothing concrete about where the body was located, he told the detectives gathered in Jackson's office, but she did agree to return to the station that morning.

When she arrived at noon, Douglass and Moore reinterviewed her for two hours, trying to gain specific information. She tried to help, but didn't have any more information. Douglass finally asked her to call Paul. Leila agreed. She was eager to please the two detectives.

Douglass was excited. If she could get Paul to talk about it, he not only might find out where the body was, but he would also have Paul on tape, evidence that could be used in court. In all but a few, specialized circumstances, tape recorded statements were admissable as evidence in court even when the parties were unaware a tape was being made.

About three-twenty P.M. Leila made the call. Douglass sat in the room with her.

"Just relax," he said. "I'll be listening. If I have

any questions, I'll write them on this tablet and pass it to you. Okay?"

"Okay," she said, dialing Paul's number.

Douglass smiled and nodded reassurance. He might look calm, he thought, but his stomach was churning.

"Hi, Paul, this is Leila," she said, her voice calm and friendly. "I've been thinking that maybe we should go out and make sure the kid is buried."

"No," Paul said forcefully. "Don't even fuck with it. No one knows. Just shut up. Everything is cool. There's been no problems. Don't go back to the scene of a crime. God damn."

"Listen to me, okay?" she said.

"No, you listen to me," Paul said, his voice growing angrier and more menacing. "Don't do it. Leave it alone."

"No, listen to me for a second, would ya?" Leila pleaded as she looked across the desk at Douglass.

"What?" Paul said disgustedly.

"The last time it rained was the seventeenth."

"So?"

"Okay, if you guys put wet dirt over him . . ."

"Yeah, it was dry dirt when we put it on him."

"It was dry?"

"I think so, yeah, it was . . ."

"You think or you know?" she asked.

"It was moist."

"It was moist?" she asked, her voice speculative. "Okay, when it dries up, it is going to go down."

"No, it hardens when it dries."

"Yeah, but it's also going to sink," she said.

"Maybe a little bit, but we made it pretty even. As a matter of fact, we piled it up a little bit."

"All right, but even you told me when you looked back that his hand was sticking out," Leila said. Douglass grimaced with disgust.

"But I buried that already. I put dirt on top of it and stomped on his fingers and put more dirt on top of it."

"Oh, God, you stomped on his fingers?"

"Yeah, I pushed his hand further down and put dirt on it."

"All right, fine, I'll tell you a dog can smell that," Leila said, shaking her head with repulsion.

"Well, that's cool."

"They're going to smell it and dig it up."

"They're not even going to begin looking out there," Paul said. "A dog smells a lot of things. A dog even smells a snake hole. It's just a goddamn field where farmers grow corn and wheat. I'm not going to worry about it. There's no problems. But if you feel like there's a problem, you can cruise out there."

"Okay," Leila said, nodding her head at Douglass. "I need to know how to get there."

"I don't know and neither does Jim," Paul said. "We had to stop to get directions on our way back to find Antioch."

"To find Antioch?" Leila asked.

Urban quietly opened the door, handed Douglass a note and then silently left the room.

Urban wrote: Antioch dead-ends about 175th Street, outside the city limits a few miles. The kids go out there to smoke dope and drink beer. It dead-ends because the bridge is out.

Douglass looked at the note, then showed it to Leila. She nodded yes. She was familiar with the area.

"You went clear down Antioch, down to the dead end by those fields?"

"I don't know where it is," Paul said. "Don't even . . . I don't know."

"So, if I took Antioch all the way down, then I'd find it?"

"Hopefully, I told you—I really don't know. If you smell something, you know you're there."

"That's disgusting."

"Well, you probably will," he said, laughing.

"He's been there two or three weeks. His body has maggots all over him."

"Oh, God. If that's the case, then a dog has dug him up."

"Maybe, but, hey, a dog doesn't just dig up bodies."

Douglass needed more information. He scribbled a question on a note pad and slid it in front of Leila. She read it and nodded her head.

"Okay, is it down by the dead end where there are no cross streets?"

"There's one cross street."

"What is it?"

"I don't know," he said angrily. "I wish I could tell you, but I really don't know how to get out there."

"All right, I'm going to check it out. I just want to make sure because my butt's in this, too," she said, looking at Douglass for instructions. "And I don't want my ass in a sling."

"Nobody knows. So just keep quiet."

"I'll keep quiet, but I don't want my ass in a sling for what you did. I'll give you a call in a little while. What are you doing tonight?"

"I'm going to try and find a way to Brian's party," he said.

"I can take you," Leila said.

"All right," Paul said. "We'll see you later."

"Bye-bye," Leila said, smiling as she hung up the telephone.

Douglass had mixed emotions. He had gotten Paul on tape, but he still didn't have a very good idea where the body was buried. Douglass thanked Leila, told her to be careful and not tell anyone about the telephone conversation. He also cautioned her about going anywhere with Paul.

"I'll be okay," she said, smiling. "I can put up a pretty good front."

Douglass shook his head. "It's up to you."

While Moore escorted Leila out of the room, Douglass remained at his desk. When Jackson and

Urban entered the room moments later, their faces were charged with excitement.

"Let's get to work," Jackson said. "This guy doesn't belong on the street."

"Did it help us?" Douglass asked. He hadn't been able to hear Paul's comments, which the others had listened to on an extension in another room.

"He admitted it," Jackson said. "But he says he doesn't know where it happened."

"I need to hear the tape," Douglass said.

Paul had given the detectives one thing they wanted. They had him on tape talking about the murder, and that would be invaluable evidence in court. But they were still left dangling on another important aspect of the case. They needed the body, and Paul had given only sketchy information on its location. The detectives couldn't decide whether Paul was telling the truth or decoying Leila. Either way, they still had more work to do.

After listening to the tape a third time, the detectives agreed that until they had more specific information, it would be useless to organize a massive search. They also agreed no arrests would be made until the body was found. And the new developments were to be shared with no one, especially not Ed Hobson.

"Hopefully, we can get a break," Moore said to no one in particular. "We're going to need some luck finding this kid. A lot of luck."

6

"The boys were doing what teenagers should be doing on a Saturday afternoon: fishing."
—A MIAMI COUNTY SHERIFF'S DEPUTY

Less than twenty-four hours later police got the break they needed. Once again two teenage boys drove to the site of the murder, this time to do some fishing.

Barry Carpenter and Mark Burger were anxious to get outside and explore the fields and small streams in the rolling Miami County countryside near their homes, about thirty-five miles southwest of Overland Park.

Within the next few months the area would be covered by a 4500-acre man-made lake. The U.S. Army Corps of Engineers had decided to build the lake to prevent flooding in the Marais des Cygnes River valley and to provide water to the small communities of Spring Hill, Gardner, Edgerton, and Paola.

The lake had been in the planning stages since 1954 and the project was nearing completion. Many farmhouses had been abandoned, the roads closed and bridges removed.

May 3 was a warm, sunny Saturday, and the boys

decided to go fishing along a narrow stretch of the Big Bull near a dead-end gravel road. After thirty minutes without a bite, their interest waned.

"Let's go searching," Burger, blond and seventeen, said to his friend, who was three years his junior. "This ain't any fun."

"Searching for what?"

"I don't know. Anything. Let's walk up there," he said, pointing to an area upstream.

The two boys left their fishing poles on the east side of the creek, where Burger's car was parked. They used rocks as stepping-stones to ford the creek, the water not more than shin deep where they decided to cross. They walked past a large stack of cement blocks and steel that used to be part of the bridge and into a clearing where a farmer had removed a row of hedge trees to increase his acreage.

"Hey, look," Burger said, rummaging around a small area of tree stumps where firewood had been cut, "I found some baby mice. Let's get something to put them in. I want to take them home."

Barry searched the area for a container while Mark cornered the mice with his hands. About twenty feet away Barry found an empty mason jar near a pile of discarded trash. The two boys coaxed the four mice into the jar and smiled with boyish delight at their find. It was about four P.M. They decided their day had been a success. They started home.

Clutching the mason jar, the boys walked along the edge of the creek, looking for a place to cross.

"What's that?" Barry asked, pointing to a mound of fresh dirt in short grass near the creek bed. They walked over to investigate.

Except for a piece of blue jean sticking from one side and a torn shred of red cloth a few feet above it, brown dirt covered an area about ten inches high, six feet long, and four feet wide.

Barry grabbed a stick and poked at the cloth, using it to scrape dirt away from the material. He tried to move the material. A rotten, decaying smell swept across them.

Simultaneously they came to the same conclusion.

"It's a body," they cried in unison.

Mark dropped the jar, shattering the glass and freeing the baby mice.

The two boys stared at the grave for few moments. Then Barry used the stick to remove a few more chunks of dirt, exposing what appeared to be a knee.

"We better go tell my mom," he said, frightened. The boys bolted across the creek to the car, heedless of the water splashing their clothes. When leaving, Mark spun the tires recklessly, spraying gravel and dirt in the air as they raced through the canopy of trees to daylight.

———

Dr. James Bridgens, an area pathologist, arrived just as Miami County sheriffs were starting to remove the dirt from the upper part of the body. Bridgens, an expert in forensic pathology, thought it necessary to go to the crime scene. "The body talks to you," he would tell people.

The autopsy facilities in Miami County were limited, and Bridgens suggested the body be taken to Shawnee Mission Medical Center in Merriam, where he was director of laboratories.

As soon as he looked at the body underneath the autopsy room lights, he was sure he knew who it was.

He called the dispatcher at the Overland Park Police Department and asked for the height, weight and age of the missing Hobson youth. When he heard the description, he told the dispatcher to notify the department's detectives.

"I've got your boy on an autopsy table at Shawnee Mission Medical Center," he said. "I'm getting ready to do the autopsy. Send them over."

Within minutes Urban, Moore, and Douglass were on their way. By the time they arrived at the hospital, Bridgens was already proceeding with the autopsy.

The temperature inside the autopsy room was about sixty degrees. A blackboard, with an eraser and chalk for listing weights of the organs, was positioned near the head of the table. The stench from the body was almost unbearable. Ceiling fans circulating fresh air provided little relief.

Bridgens was oblivious to the stench. His lit cigarette nearby, he opened the black bag he carried to all autopsies. Inside were his tools: a pair of pliers, a hooked carpet knife, a couple of butcher knives, a small scapel, a pair of scissors, and a fully automatic .35 millimeter camera. He tied a plastic apron over his street clothes. No gloves. No mask.

The cursory examination revealed three shotgun wounds: one to the left side of the face; a second to the right side of the chest; and the third to the back of the head.

Bridgens then X-rayed the decomposed body, which seemed to be moving on the table because of the massive amount of maggots that crawled from it. The X-rays revealed dozens of metallic pellets imbedded in the face and chest. Scattered pellets also were identified in the skull and left hand. Shotgun wounds, he told the detectives.

The Overland Park detectives had seen enough. The body, although the face was indistinguishable, matched Chris's description: blond hair, blue eyes. Positive identification would only come through dental records. That would take a few hours; time they didn't have to spare.

7

"We didn't know what to expect. Sure they were teenagers, but we also knew they had cold bloodedly killed a thirteen-year-old boy."
—OVERLAND PARK DETECTIVE JOHN DOUGLASS

In the crowded training room on the second floor of the Overland Park police station, excitement and anticipation were high. Detectives and patrolmen mingled in small groups, discussing their ideas on what should be done. It was an incongruous gathering for the station. Miami County sheriff Chuck Light wore a pair of bib overalls. Steve Moore was still wearing his square dancing outfit: plaid shirt, blue jeans, and cowboy boots. Urban, who had been at home celebrating his wife's birthday, was wearing a suit and tie.

The mood was serious but upbeat. There was planning ahead, as well as politics to overcome. Several questions remained unanswered. What department was going to handle the investigation? Who was going to interview whom?

At this point three separate agencies were involved. The body had been found in Miami County, and, most agreed, the murder probably had occurred there, too. That meant the Miami County

Sheriff's Department had jurisdiction. But they had already called in the Kansas Bureau of Investigation for assistance. Should the KBI conduct the interviews? The kidnapping had occurred in Johnson County, and Overland Park detectives had been investigating the case for two weeks. They knew the suspects. They had Paul's taped statement. Should they be allowed to take the lead?

Jackson, Light, and Douglass met privately in Jackson's office for a few minutes. Light was briefed about the case, including Paul's taped statement.

"Hey, I've got a small sheriff's office," Light told them. "You guys have done all the background work on this thing. You've got the sources. You've got the tape. You know the personalities. Why don't you do it, and we will assist you in any way we can?"

The only thing Light requested was a little time. His two detectives, Kenny Niesz and Ron Orton, were still at the autopsy, along with the KBI agents Malson and Wood.

Douglass was anxious to move right then.

The men walked across the hall to the training room, which had been turned into a temporary command center. Jackson was the chief of detectives, but Douglass was running the investigation. Driving from the medical center to the police station, Douglass had already started planning how the investigation would proceed. He told Jackson what he thought needed to be done and who should do it. Jackson agreed. Douglass's suggestions: three teams of two detectives, accompanied by at least two uniformed patrolmen, would go simultaneously to each of the three suspects' residences. Light and Jim Hight, an Overland Park detective, would go to Paul's home. Urban would take another detective and go to Jimmy's apartment. Douglass and Moore would contact Ed and Sueanne at their home.

No one knew what to expect. Several considerations remained: How would Ed react? Would the two boys resist? The detectives discussed the layouts of the residences and how they would proceed. Precautions needed to be taken; all three situations could be volatile. Hight called downstairs to ask the dispatcher to send additional patrol cars into the area.

About ten minutes later, as the teams were preparing to leave, the telephone rang in the training room and Douglass answered it.

"You aren't going to believe this," he said, after hanging up the telephone. "Paul just called. He's having a party at his house and he's locked himself into a pair of handcuffs. He wants to know if we can send somebody over there to help him out of the cuffs. He asked that we be a little quiet because he doesn't want to scare the people at the party."

The room exploded with laughter.

"We sure can," Jackson said with a smile.

"Why don't I go over there with them," Urban said. "I might know somebody at the party who will sing me a little song. Hell, Jimmy might be at that party."

At eleven-twenty P.M. Hight, Urban, and Light pulled up to the front of Paul's apartment complex in an unmarked car. Two patrolmen in marked units followed closely behind. Paul was standing outside the apartment near the street, his hands cuffed in front of him, a mischievous grin on his face.

The men got out of the cars.

"Sorry about this," Paul said, walking toward them.

"Mr. Sorrentino, my name is Detective Hight," the officer said as he began removing the handcuffs from Paul. "We would like for you to voluntarily come down to the police station. We need to talk to you."

"About what?" Paul said cockily. "All I did was get myself locked in a pair of handcuffs."

"We want to talk to you about the disappearance of Chris Hobson," Hight said. "His body was found today in Miami County."

The color drained from Paul's face. He began to shake. He looked at Hight, then at Urban.

"I'll go inside and break up the little party," Urban told Hight. "Is Jimmy inside?"

"Who?" Paul asked.

"Jimmy Hobson."

"No," Paul said, attempting to regain his composure. Then he started babbling about the disappearance. "Sure, I'll tell you everything I've heard. What do you want to know? I've heard a lot."

"This is not the proper setting," Hight told him. "I think this matter would best be discussed at the police station."

During the ride back to the station, Paul was full of questions. Hight knew what he was doing. He was trying to find out how much the police actually knew.

Hight and Light escorted Paul past several detectives and patrolmen who were still gathered in the training room. Everyone wanted to be involved in the case. Paul was placed in a small interview room with a glass window that faced across the hall to other small cubicles.

———

Urban and two uniformed police arrived at Jimmy's apartment at 11:35 P.M.

"One of you go around back in case he tries to run," Urban said. "I'll knock on the door."

Urban and the other officer walked to the ground-floor apartment and knocked on the door. They could hear music being played inside.

"Yeah," Jimmy said when he opened the door. "What's up?"

"It's time to go to the police station," Urban said.

"What for?"

"I can't tell you about it here. We just need to go to the police station."

"Well, can't you at least tell me what it's about?" Jimmy asked nervously.

"No, I can't tell you here," Urban said. "I am asking you to go with me voluntarily. If you don't go voluntarily, I am authorized to arrest you."

Jimmy could see a change in Urban. In all his past dealings with the detective, Urban had been friendly and casual. There was nothing friendly or casual about him now.

"I'll go with you," Jimmy said. "You don't need to arrest me."

Jimmy rode silently in the front seat, his hands folded in his lap, as Urban drove back to the police station. Urban walked him upstairs to a small, windowless interview room on the juvenile side of the detective division. Jimmy did not know Paul was down the hall being questioned by detectives.

———

Moore and Douglass, along with three uniformed patrolmen, were already on their way to Sueanne and Ed's house. Both men were nervous, anxious. Not only did they have to tell Ed that his son had been murdered, but they also had to tell him that his wife and her son were probably involved.

Ed, sitting at the kitchen table drinking coffee with Sueanne and her best friend, Margie, was startled into action when the doorbell rang at the stroke of midnight. Ed knew someone calling at this hour could mean only one thing: the police had found Chris.

He opened the door to see Moore standing there with another man Ed didn't recognize.

"What is it?" Ed asked urgently.

"We have some information about Chris," Moore

said. "We need you and your wife to come to the police station with us."

"What is it? What's happened?" Sueanne asked.

"We think it would be better to discuss this at the police station," Douglass said.

"Ed, this is John Douglass, a detective," Moore said, introducing the two men.

"Is Chris okay?" Sueanne asked, her voice rising. "Is something wrong with my son?"

"We need to go to the police station," Douglass said.

Sueanne turned and walked to the stairs, holding the banister to steady herself. "Something's happened to my Chris," she said, stopping halfway up the stairs. "Tell me what's happened. Is he all right?"

"I can't tell you right now. You all need to come down to the station and talk to us," Moore said.

Ed stood motionless, his eyes fixed on Moore. He submissively waited for the detective to tell him what to do.

Douglass looked at Suzanne, who was standing at the top of the stairs, a blank expression on her face.

"Does Suzanne have to go?" Sueanne asked, walking back downstairs from her bedroom.

"No," Moore said.

Douglass and Moore escorted Ed and Sueanne to their unmarked vehicles parked in the driveway. Ed rode with Moore and Sueanne went with Douglass. The drive to the police station was swift and silent.

Moore took Ed to the station officer's office on the first floor, while Douglass escorted Sueanne to a second-floor interview room.

"Ed, earlier today some young boys found a body, and we are trying to figure out right now if it is Chris," Moore said, doing his best to maintain his composure. "And some people have been brought to the police station for questioning. That's all I can tell you right now."

Ed clutched Moore's hand and squeezed it tightly. Speechless, his face crumpled and his deep blue eyes filled with tears that began to stream down his cheeks as he kept Moore's hand in a tight grip.

"Ed, I have to go back upstairs to do some additional work," Moore said, fighting to hold back his own emotions. "This is Officer Turner. He will stay with you. If you need anything, he can help you. I'll be back down in a few minutes."

Ed wouldn't let go of Moore's hand. He squeezed it tightly as he began sobbing.

"I'm sorry," Moore said, using both hands to grip Ed's hand in his. "I'm very sorry."

8

"Do you know what it is like to have a seventeen-year-old son that you love desperately and that you want to help?"

—SUEANNE HOBSON

Douglass solemnly led Sueanne upstairs, past the curious crowd of lawmen gathered in the detective division, into a small-windowless, gray-walled room.

"Have a seat," he said. "I'll be right back."

Sueanne maintained her composure. She sat with her back straight, elbows resting on the table. Her eyes, dark and inquisitive, followed Douglass's every move. The meeting at Sueanne's duplex a few minutes earlier had been the first time the two had ever met. She looked him over cautiously.

Douglass, without acknowledging Sueanne's stares, left the room to talk with Jackson. The atmosphere in the division was electric.

A few feet down the hall, Hight and Light were interviewing Paul. Across the hall, Urban and Dave Wood, a KBI agent, were beginning to interview Jimmy. None of the suspects knew the others were being questioned.

Inside the small room, Paul's cocky smile had vanished almost immediately. He was agitated and nervous. He wanted to know what they knew and what was going to happen next.

Hight sat for a few moments at the small, metal table, ignoring Paul's questions as he reviewed the police department's rights waiver form. Light sat passively in a chair next to him. Paul, on the other side of the table, faced the men uncertainly. His back was to the lone window that looked out across the numerous cubicles in the detective division.

Hight, a senior detective in the department, wanted to take special precautions because of Paul's age. He systematically reviewed the rights waiver with him, indicating that he could have his parents or an attorney present during questioning.

Although Hight had never met Paul before, he was confident the sixteen-year-old would crumble when faced with the evidence against him. He was wrong. The youth would be as difficult as any adult Hight had ever interviewed.

"Do you understand your rights?"

"Yes."

"And do you want to waive those rights?"

"Yes," Paul said anxiously. "I want to find out what the hell this is all about."

Hight looked at the olive-skinned youth seated across the table from him, his arms folded against his stomach. His breathing was rapid, heavy.

"Mr. Sorrentino," Hight said, looking up from the waiver form. "As I told you earlier, Chris Hobson's body was found today in Miami County. We believe you are a prime suspect in his murder. We have information that you have been telling people specific things about this case that only Chris's killer would know."

"Like what?" Paul interrupted. "Just tell me what you've heard, what you have."

Hight looked at Paul for a moment, letting the wave of fear sink into the teenager's mind. Hight didn't want to tell Paul of the taped statement until later. He wanted to keep that as his final piece of evidence—his hammer.

"The information we have is that you have told several people that you killed Chris Hobson," Hight said. "That you told them of the method of death and the location of the body."

Paul paused for a few moments, considering his options.

"Sure, I said some things," he said feigning cooperation. It was a con Paul had used to perfection before with teachers, counselors, and cops. "I heard about him running away on television. Everybody was talking about it. I made up some stuff. I was lying. I was just trying to impress my friends."

Hight shook his head in disagreement. He told Paul there were too many similarities in what he had said for him to have made it up. Hight was forceful, serious. Paul's smile faded.

"I'm telling you the truth," Paul said defensively, antagonistically. "You're lying. Who told you this? I didn't do anything. Why are you guys always hassling me?"

"Well, if you're not involved, we want to do everything we can to prove your innocence," Hight said. "Would you be willing to take a polygraph test?"

"No way," Paul said angrily, looking away from the two men as he shoved himself away from the table. "I don't have to prove anything to you. Why should I help you? I'd rather see you guys work your butts off anyway."

"If you're innocent, we want to help you prove it," Hight offered.

"Fuck you," Paul responded.

Hight, without mentioning the taped conversation between Paul and Leila, continued to probe for answers. But the boy had quickly regained his composure. It was now obvious to Hight that Paul wasn't about to admit anything voluntarily.

Angered and frustrated, Hight left the room. He returned a few minutes later with Larry McClain, an assistant Johnson County District Attorney.

"Mr. Sorrentino, I want to formally advise you that you are under arrest for first-degree murder in the killing of Chris Hobson," Hight said as McClain plugged a tape recorder into a wall socket.

"We are not playing games here," Hight said. "We believe we have enough evidence to not only arrest you, but to convict you of the murder of Chris Hobson."

Paul looked at the three men, then turned away. He showed no emotion. Hight knew it was a bluff. No one, especially a sixteen-year-old boy, could really be that calm when faced with pending murder charges.

"Mr. Sorrentino, we have something we want you to hear," Hight said, hoping the tape would break Paul's stonewalling. "You might find this interesting."

"Hi, Paul, this is Leila . . ." the tape began. "I think maybe we should go out and make sure the kid is buried."

Paul appeared stunned as he listened to his own voice. His mouth opened, but words did not materialize. He moved forward in his chair. He glanced at the three men, then shifted his eyes to the floor. He listened to the tape for a few more moments, then looked up.

"That's not my voice," he said, responding to the men's stares. "Who's that girl?"

"Just listen to the tape," Hight cautioned him. "You'll have plenty of time to talk when it is completed."

Paul continued to shake his head as the tape played on. By the time it ended, Paul had regained a semblance of composure, but the impact of the tape was apparent.

"Well?" Hight asked.

"I want to see an attorney," Paul said. "I'm done talking to you."

———————

In contrast to Paul, Jimmy seemed almost relieved at the chance to talk about Chris's death. The burden seemed too great for him to bear. Within minutes he had admitted everything to Urban and Wood. He was remorseful, composed, and almost cooperative. He wasn't the tough teenager that Urban had interviewed about the stolen credit cards. There was something sad about this boy.

Jimmy's head drooped as Wood read him his constitutional rights with the same patience Hight had shown Paul.

"Do you understand your rights?" Wood asked.

"Yes."

"And you know that you have the right to have either or both of your parents here? Or anyone else of your choosing?"

"Yes, but I don't want either one of my parents here," Jimmy said. "I'll talk to you, but I don't want them here."

Urban moved toward the tape recorder at the edge of the desk.

"We need to get this down on tape, Jimmy," Urban said.

"I don't want it tape-recorded," Jimmy said. "I don't want anybody to hear my voice. I don't want my mother to hear this."

"Okay, fine," Urban said as he pulled a piece of white typing paper from his notebook and dated it twelve-fifteen A.M., May 4. "What we'll do is write down what you say and then you can initial it, okay?"

Jimmy nodded his head as Urban slid his chair around the table so there was nothing between the two of them. He looked at the teenager, whose head remained lowered.

"Jimmy," Urban said. "Jimmy, look at me. I think it would make you feel a lot better if you would just tell us what happened. Who pulled the trigger?"

"Paul. He shot him."

"Why was he killed?"

"Because my mother asked me to do it."

In a slow, deliberate voice Jimmy recounted how the murder had occurred, who was responsible, and why.

"I couldn't shoot him," he told the detectives. "Paul shot him."

"Why was he killed?" Urban asked.

"My mom wanted me to get rid of him for her," Jimmy said, his eyes searching the floor. "I knew I couldn't do it myself, so I called Paul Sorrentino and asked if we could get together. I explained the situation to him and told him he would be paid well. Paul, you know, he always talked like he was some mafia big shot."

"So what happened then?" Wood asked.

"About a week went by and I talked to my mother again. She said something had to be done immediately. She had been trying that week to do it herself and she couldn't. She asked if it would be done that week. I talked to Paul and he said yes."

"What were you going to get out of this?" Urban asked.

"My mother was going to pay Paul's repair bill on his motorcycle for doing this job," Jimmy said, raising his head to look at the two detectives. "She was going to buy me a new car."

Jimmy described how they took Chris from his home, drove to a wooded area and made him dig his own grave. Twenty minutes later the men had a four-page signed statement from Jimmy, implicating his mother and Paul.

At that, Urban and Wood looked at each other in repugnant disbelief. Wood got up and walked out of the room, leaving Urban alone with the boy.

"It's hell to be involved in someone else's death, isn't it?" Urban said, looking down at Jimmy as tears welled in the boy's eyes.

"Have you ever heard a dying man gurgle?" Jimmy said, staring into space. His mind drifted back to the moment of Chris's death.

"No, Jimmy, I've never heard a dying man gurgle," Urban said, disgusted with the boy. "Tell me what it's like."

"You don't want to know," Jimmy said, heavy sobs breaking his words. "You . . . don't want to know . . . just . . . just take me to jail."

Urban looked at Jimmy. His anger subsided. For the first time he felt sympathy, almost compassion for the boy. And he hated Sueanne.

"Can I stay here by myself for a few minutes?" Jimmy asked, wiping his tears with the palms of his hands.

"Sure," Urban said. "I'll be back in a little while."

Urban checked to see whether Jimmy had a belt or shoestrings—anything he might use to kill himself. He didn't. Jimmy was wearing black dress shoes and blue jeans with no belt. Urban walked to the door, looked back at Jimmy for a moment, then closed the door, leaving the boy alone.

Jimmy pulled three metal chairs together and lay down on them. He turned on his side, curled up in the chairs and tried to sleep.

———

Jimmy and Paul were teenagers, street punks at best. Sueanne, on the other hand, was intelligent, independent, and iron-willed. She would prove to be a formidable challenge.

When Douglass, accompanied by Moore, returned to the room fifteen minutes later, Sueanne was still sitting in the same position. Wearing a red-and-white polka dot blouse and black slacks,

Sueanne appeared feminine, intelligent, and demure. Her hands were adorned with her ruby and diamond rings, and Krugerrand necklaces were draped around her neck.

Douglass had never interviewed a female murder suspect. He was nervous. He had been reared in a traditional family where women were treated with deference. It was clear Sueanne expected be treated that way.

"What's this all about?" she asked coolly. "Could you tell me what's going on? You come to my house at midnight, take me away from my husband and bring me to the police station."

Douglass had a gut feeling that Sueanne was guilty. Paul's taped statement had been damaging and, although Douglass didn't know exactly what Jimmy was saying to Urban, initial indications from Jackson were that Jimmy had implicated her in the murder. Douglass had two goals: to get Sueanne to confess, and to understand why Chris was killed. From Sueanne's initial demeanor, he suspected neither goal would be easily accomplished.

"Mrs. Hobson, your stepson's body was found today in Miami County," Douglass said.

"What?" she gasped. "Oh my God."

"We believe your son Jimmy, Paul Sorrentino, and maybe yourself are involved in his death."

"Involved in his death? What do you mean?"

Instead of responding, Douglass read Sueanne her rights, enunciating each word, precisely, almost angrily.

"I just can't believe this is happening," Sueanne said indignantly.

"I can understand that," Douglass continued, "and at this point in time, we are just trying to find out exactly what has happened. The information we have indicates that your son and Mr. Sorrentino took Chris out to a field, used a shovel from your garage, shot him . . ."

"What?" she interrupted, looking surprised but not horrified.

". . . and buried him. They did this because they were paid by you to do so. Do you know anything about this?"

"I wasn't at home the night Chris disappeared. I was with my husband," she said.

"That's correct. But that doesn't mitigate any possible responsibility in the conspiracy," Douglass said, refusing to be sidetracked. "Did you know that it was going to happen ahead of time?"

"No, sir."

"Did you ask anyone to do this for you?"

"No, sir."

"Did you talk to your son about purchasing a motorcycle or a car in the last few days?"

"Uh-huh."

"How about Mr. Sorrentino?"

"No, not Mr. Sorrentino," Sueanne said, still sitting quietly, her hands motionless in her lap. "But the car deal with Jimmy is for back child support. I am suing my ex-husband for back child support . . . we were divorced seven and a half years ago, and he never paid me child support. I told Jimmy I would buy him a car based on what we got from the child support settlement because I feel like the money is just as much Jimmy's as it is mine."

Sueanne was calm and collected. Just as Douglass was about to tell her of Paul's taped statement, Moore interrupted.

"Mrs. Hobson, the information we have is that you hired these boys to go out and kill Chris because you hated his guts," an excited and inexperienced Moore said. "We have a telephone conversation—"

"A taped telephone conversation," Douglass interrupted, trying to regain control of the interview, "between Sorrentino and another individual, in which he discusses the murder. He talked about your involvement. Were you involved?"

"No."

"Why would he say that if it's not true?" Douglass asked.

"I don't know."

After sparring with Sueanne for several minutes, Douglass was summoned from the room by Jackson. He returned a few minutes later armed with new evidence he felt would shock Sueanne into a confession.

"Mrs. Hobson, your son has just told the detectives exactly what happened," Douglass said, standing over Sueanne. "And he has implicated you in the murder of Chris Hobson. Now, before you say anything, I want you to understand that in my opinion your statement is not going to be necessary to arrest or convict you."

"I don't understand," she said timidly. "My son what?"

"Do you still maintain you don't know anything about Chris's death?" Douglass asked. "Did you know about it after it happened, Mrs. Hobson?"

Sueanne sat silently, considering. She studied Douglass across the table.

Then she began, "Do you know what it's like to have a seventeen-year-old son that you love desperately and that you want to help?"

She leaned forward in her chair. Her voice was composed; she sounded sure of her ability to convince them.

"You try to keep him out of trouble, and you want him to make something of himself. And you want him to forget the hurt and the pain . . . Jimmy told me some terrible things that happened to him when he lived with his father. We tried to get him help . . ."

"Get who help, ma'am?" Douglass said, interrupting the flow before Sueanne could get any further afield.

"Jimmy. We tried to get him psychiatric help."

"Did Jimmy tell you what he did to Chris?" Douglass asked.

"If I answer any more questions without an attorney, is that going to hurt my son?" she asked, sounding naive.

"Is this going to hurt your son?" Douglass repeated, outraged.

"I don't want to hurt him by answering . . . I don't know what to do," she said.

Douglass wasn't confused by Sueanne's attempts at sympathy. He believed she was guilty. Paul's original statement and now Jimmy's confession were given independently of each other. Why would they lie? Especially Paul, Douglass thought. He believed that Sueanne was the mastermind behind the murder. He was determined to get her confession. But faced with her ability to parry questions, he wasn't sure how he should proceed.

"Your indication to me is that he's already told you something, or you wouldn't ask me that question," Douglass said. "I can't tell you whether that will hurt him or not. He's in there right now telling the other detectives what happened. I don't think you're going to be able to hurt him any more than he's hurting himself.

"But what we are trying to find out is if you're involved in any way, shape, or form. Him telling you is one thing, and you conspiring with him is another. Did you know he did it? Did he tell you he did it? Did he tell you after he did it?"

"Yes," Sueanne said in a whisper, admitting for the first time that she knew of Jimmy's involvement in Chris's death.

"Did he tell you that night?"

"I didn't see him that night."

"When did he tell you?"

"I honestly don't remember."

"Why would your son tell the detectives that you paid him to do this?" Moore asked.

"I don't know," Sueanne said, still poised. "When Jimmy came to live with us over a year ago, Ed and I told him we would get him a car. He expected a brand new car, but instead we let him drive one of ours. He told his sister that all hell was going to break loose if he didn't get a new car. I told Ed about it and Ed talked to him and said, 'I didn't promise you a brand new car.' "

"Do you feel, then, that he is saying these things about you to get back at you?" Douglass asked.

"I don't know," Sueanne said, shaking her head. "I know that he feels like I abandoned him when I took Suzanne and left after I divorced his father. And I know Jimmy hates me. And I know he loves me."

Douglass looked at Sueanne with increasing frustration and repugnance. Clearly, Sueanne was not worried about Jimmy. She had readily implicated her son in the killing. She was only worried about herself.

"Let me ask you this," he said. "Did Jimmy tell you why it happened?"

"He said he did it because Chris narked on him about using the credit cards and taking drugs," she said.

"What did he say to you? Did he just say, 'Mom, I've killed Chris,' or, 'I know Chris is dead.' How did he put it to you? How did you learn?" Douglass asked sarcastically.

"I can't think right now," she said. "I don't remember."

"Why would Paul Sorrentino say the same thing?"

"I don't know."

"It can't be an illusion that both of them share," Douglass added. "As far as I know, Paul has no ax to grind with you. Let me be perfectly honest with you. I think you are being less than truthful with us. I think if it happened the way you've said, you should have much more information. You should know when he told you, you should know what he told you, and, as Chris's stepmother, even if you didn't care for him, you would have asked some details about what happened. I think it's time for you to be honest with us."

"I have been, as best as I can recollect at this point," Sueanne said, her arms folded in front of her, looking Douglass straight in the eye.

"Would you take a polygraph?" Douglass asked.

"If I have to, I guess so," she said. "I don't know anything about polygraph tests. I've only heard that they are not a hundred percent accurate."

"Okay, wait, wait, wait," Douglass said, raising his hands as he got up from his chair. "Let's stop right here for a minute. Let's quit skirting around and dancing with the issue. I've worked a great many homicide cases, and the same thing I saw in them I'm seeing in you right now. Every time we ask you to do something to prove your innocence, you back up."

"No, I want to take the polygraph," Sueanne said firmly. "I want to."

"Then let's do it," Douglass said. "I'll get it set up."

———

While Douglass and Moore waited for the polygraph test to be conducted, Jackson decided someone should talk to Ed, who had remained downstairs, unaware of the additional pain he was about to suffer.

"Somebody needs to go downstairs and talk to Ed," Jackson said. "He's been down there for almost two hours and he's been asking questions. He wants to know what's going on." He added, "Dr. Bridgens has the dental records and they match. It's Chris."

The two detectives walked down to the first floor,

where Ed had been waiting in the watch commander's office. Douglass had delivered death messages before. He had placed people under arrest for murder and informed people their relatives had committed murder. But never had he been faced with a situation such as this. He had to tell Ed that his son had been murdered and that the woman he loved had probably masterminded the crime.

Moore took a deep breath before opening the door, allowing Douglass into the room first. Ed jumped to his feet, his eyes red and swollen, his expression hopeless.

"Mr. Hobson, I wish I could tell you something else," Douglass said, "but the body we found was Chris."

Ed slumped back into the chair and began trembling.

"I'm sorry, Ed," Moore said.

Ed looked at the two detectives, then across the small room to where Turner sat. He didn't speak, he just sat there trembling.

"Mr. Hobson," Douglass said, sitting down next to him, "there is something else, something I wish to God I didn't have to tell you. From our investigation, it appears that Jimmy and another boy, Paul Sorrentino, are the ones who killed your son."

Ed didn't look up. His hands, clasped together in front of him, shook against his legs. He started to cry.

"And Mr. Hobson, we also believe that your wife might be involved in your son's death," Douglass said, looking at Ed, who remained silent. "She is in the process of taking a polygraph test right now."

The four men sat in silence. Douglass waited patiently for a few minutes to allow Ed time to gather his thoughts.

"Mr. Hobson, Detective Moore and I have to go back upstairs, but Officer Turner will remain with you tonight," Douglass said. "If you have any questions or if there is anyone you would like to contact, he will be able to help you."

The strength and the explosive temper that Ed had displayed during the two-week search for his son were gone. He had neither the strength nor the desire to react.

"Jesus, that was tough," Moore told Douglass as the two men walked back upstairs. "God, I feel sorry for that guy."

"I'm not sure it even sunk in that Sueanne was involved," Douglass said.

"What an incredible bitch," Moore said.

"Yeah, really," Douglass said, even more intent on getting a confession from Sueanne. "Let's get back to work."

———

The polygraph examination took about ninety minutes. Douglass and Moore had little doubt that Sueanne would fail the test.

"It's funny," Douglass told Jackson. "She never became flustered once during the interview. At first I thought she might give it up, especially when we told her that Jimmy had fingered her, but she didn't. She just kept talking and asking questions, talking and asking questions. She's as tough as any man I've ever interviewed."

About 4:15 A.M. the polygraph examiner entered the training room.

"She's lying about almost everything," he said. Douglass and Moore nodded their heads in agreement.

———

The interview resumed at four-thirty A.M. Sueanne was sitting at the table, calmly smoking a cigarette, when the two detectives returned to the room with the polygraph results. Douglass didn't know what to expect from her, but he did intend to get a confession.

For the next twenty minutes Douglass and Moore hammered at Sueanne's story. She wouldn't budge. She would only admit to covering up after the murder. She said her only crime was trying to protect her son.

"I feel guilty because I feel if I had said something to Ed or somebody else the first time Jimmy made a threat about Chris, then this would not have happened," she said, shaking her head. "I don't want to admit that this happened."

"Why did you lie to us?" Douglass asked.

"Because Jimmy is my son," she said emphatically. "Don't you understand that?"

Interviewing Sueanne was like trying to corner a mole, Douglass thought. Every time he thought he had gained an advantage, he found Sueanne tunneling off in a new direction. For every new piece of evidence he uncovered, she had a new story. For every lie he caught her in, she had a cunning—and believable—explanation. In fact, her story might have been credible if she hadn't adjusted it so many times when confronted with new evidence.

"Now wait a second, Mrs. Hobson," Douglass said. "Let's go back and talk about the truth. We already know you had a deal worked out with Jimmy to buy him a car because you told the polygraph operator that you had arranged to get your son a car."

"I told Jimmy I would get him a car, depending on how much money I got out of the child support settlement when we went to court on May seventh," Sueanne said, sounding sulky. She appeared to be exasperated by Douglass's continued questions. "But I haven't paid anybody anything."

"No, Mrs. Hobson, you haven't paid them. They told us that," Douglass said angrily, feeling almost like a parent dealing with a recalcitrant child. But this was no child. This was a woman suspected of masterminding a brutal murder. "But you certainly sent them out to do that."

"No, I did not. But you are going to continue to say I did and I am going to say I didn't. Are you going to win or am I? What's going to happen?"

"I think one thing's going to happen. I think you're going to have a very difficult time convincing twelve persons that you didn't do it," Douglass said. "Especially when you keep giving us stories that any four-year-old could recognize as not being true.

"What you've told us is not consistent. It's not logical. It doesn't make sense. At least give us a story that makes sense."

"I don't feel logical," she said. "I just feel like I'm at loose ends. This is my son we're talking about."

"No, Mrs. Hobson, we're talking about you," Moore reminded her. "The billfold is at Metcalf South; we know that for a fact. How did it get there?"

"I put it there," Sueanne said, "because I wanted it found and I didn't want Jimmy to be blamed. I didn't want him to be caught. I wanted everything back the way it was."

"When did you put it there?" Moore asked.

"The next day. I took it out of his room the next day."

"When did Jimmy tell you about the murder?" Douglass asked.

"The next day," she admitted. "The day after Chris disappeared. He told me what had happened. I just don't want to admit that Jimmy did this. I don't want to admit that this even happened. This . . . this is my child, my little boy. I don't want to believe that he did it . . ."

Douglass, frustrated by Sueanne's stonewalling, decided to switch gears.

"Let me ask you this," he said. "When did your daughter know about it?"

"Right after it happened."

"Who told her about Chris's death?"

"I did. I told her what Jimmy had told me. She worships Jimmy. I thought she ought to know."

Douglass wasn't startled by Sueanne's admission that her daughter also knew of the murder. He was amazed by Sueanne's total self-absorption. By attempting to cover her own tracks, Sueanne had inadvertently given Douglass another avenue to pursue. Depending on what Suzanne had to say, Sueanne might have just given up her other child in order to protect herself.

He was anxious to interview Suzanne. According to Jimmy, Suzanne had been present the day Sueanne had talked to him about Chris—the same day Chris had disappeared.

Douglass and Moore left Sueanne alone in the interview room. It was five-thirty A.M. and Douglass wanted to question the girl as soon as possible. He convinced Jackson and McClain to allow him to bring the girl to the police station immediately. As a courtesy, and to avoid any appearance of impropriety, McClain told Douglass to ask Sueanne's permission.

"If she doesn't give it, we'll go get her anyway," McClain said.

Surprisingly, Sueanne was cooperative when Douglass asked whether he could talk with her daughter. She only asked that she be allowed to accompany the officer home.

On the way, Sueanne tried to talk to Douglass. He expected it. Sueanne had spent most of the early morning hours desperately trying to convince him of her innocence. But Douglass didn't want to listen. He was tired. He needed a break from the continuing battle of wits with Sueanne.

"Mrs. Hobson, I think it would be better if we didn't discuss anything right now," he said firmly. "I'll give you the opportunity to say anything you want when we return to the station."

Douglass also refused to talk for another reason. During the interview, he had learned that Sueanne talked constantly in an attempt to control the situation. By refusing to talk now, he was in control, something Sueanne found very uncomfortable.

"I just wish you'd believe me," she said, looking at Douglass. "I didn't make a deal with those boys to kill my son."

Douglass didn't answer. He looked straight ahead, glancing occasionally in his rearview mirror at Moore, who was following in his own car.

It was still dark when Douglass pulled into the driveway of the darkened house at about six A.M. It was an eerie moment. Douglass, sitting in the front seat of his car, wondered what could have happened inside that house to unleash such savagery and hate.

"Are we going in?" Sueanne asked, shaking Douglass from his thoughts.

Inside the house, Sueanne opened the door to her daughter's bedroom and turned on the light.

"Honey," she said, walking to the side of the bed. She sat down and began to gently shake Suzanne awake. "Suzanne, wake up. Chris is dead and these men here want to talk to you about it."

Suzanne rolled over on her back, her hand shielding her eyes from the light.

"These are detectives and they want to talk to you," Sueanne said quietly. "It's okay to talk to them."

Sueanne got up and walked past the detectives, who were standing at the end of the bed. When she got to the door, she turned and looked back at her daughter.

"Just tell them the truth," she said. "That's all you have to do."

She closed the door and walked into the hall, where a patrolman was standing. Sueanne's friend Margie, awakened by the noise, came out of the master bedroom, where she had been sleeping.

"What's wrong?" she asked Sueanne.

"Chris is dead," Sueanne said, starting to cry for the first time. "Chris is dead. Jimmy killed him and they think I'm involved."

"Chris is dead?" Margie shrieked. "Oh my God. Chris is dead? Jimmy killed him? Oh, I can't believe it. No, no, no."

The women tearfully embraced for a few minutes, then walked downstairs to the kitchen followed closely by the patrolman. In less than five minutes Douglass and Moore came back downstairs.

"We need to take your daughter to the police station," Douglass told her. "You can ride back with me, and Suzanne can go with Detective Moore."

"Can Margie go with her?" Sueanne asked.

"That would be fine," Douglass said. "Let's go."

Back at the station, Douglass met with Jackson and McClain. Jimmy and Paul had both been arrested on first-degree murder charges and transported to the juvenile facility in nearby Olathe, the county seat. The detectives had agreed that because the murder had occurred in Miami County, the boys would be transferred to the Miami County jail within a few hours.

"What did the girl say?" McClain asked Douglass.

"She knows a lot," Douglass said. "The main thing she said was she heard Sueanne tell Jimmy to 'get rid of Chris.'"

"What?" McClain asked in disbelief. "Sueanne said that in front of her daughter?"

"That's what she said," Douglass answered. "As soon as I heard that, I decided we needed to get her back down to the station and tape-record it. I've got a feeling this is a one-time shot."

He and Moore walked back into the room where Suzanne and Margie waited. Douglass was amazed at Suzanne. She didn't look nervous or worried.

She sat passively next to Margie. She looked chillingly like her mother, composed and defiant.

"Suzanne," Douglass started, simultaneously starting the tape recorder, "we want to go over in some detail the things we talked about at your house about fifteen minutes ago. You gave us some information that we want to clarify."

Suzanne, who had a cold, sniffled and sneezed as Douglass reviewed the information they had talked about briefly in her bedroom.

"You told us that about a month ago there began to be some serious problems between you and your mother, your brother and Chris," Douglass said. "Could you tell me what kind of problems those were?"

"Yes," Suzanne said in a calm, soft voice. "Chris was causing problems between Ed and Mom. I don't exactly remember what kind of problems they were, but my mom and Ed got in fights all the time over Chris."

"How do you know this?"

"Because I could hear them talking or yelling all the time about Chris."

"About a month ago, about two weeks before Chris disappeared, were they having problems then?"

"Serious problems. They weren't getting along."

Moore looked at Margie, who was listening intently to Suzanne.

"Did your mom ever talk about doing anything about the problems?" Douglass asked.

"Not then," Suzanne said. "But she did about a week later with Jimmy."

"What did she say to Jimmy?"

"Uh . . ." Suzanne hesitated, looking scared for the first time.

"I know we are at a difficult part, but what did she say?"

"She told him that something had to be done

because Chris was causing too many problems."

"Did she ever say what that something was?"

"No."

"Did your mother talk to Jimmy about Chris the day he disappeared?"

"Yeah, we went over to his house the day Chris disappeared."

"Where did your mother talk to Jimmy?"

"Out in the parking lot."

"When we were over at your house, you told us you overheard part of that conversation," Douglass said. "What did you overhear?"

"That Jimmy and whoever were going to take Chris out wherever and get rid of him."

"What did they mean, 'get rid of him'?"

"That's what they said. She told Jimmy that something had to be done. And he said, 'We'll go out and get rid of him.' "

"What did your mom say then?"

"She didn't say anything."

"Did she say anything about Ed being gone that evening?"

"Uh-huh."

"What did she say?"

"She said that she was going to get Ed out of the house."

"Was that so Jimmy could take Chris out of the house?"

"Yes."

Douglass glanced at Margie, whose eyes were wet with unshed tears. She was clutching Suzanne's hand.

"Did your mom ever tell you before that something was going to happen to Chris?" Douglass asked.

"Yeah, she said that something had to be done about Chris. She didn't say what."

"Did your mom ever say what happened to Chris?"

"She said that Jimmy went out and took care of him. But I wasn't sure what she meant."

"The day that Chris disappeared, did your brother tell your mother who was going out with him that evening?"

"No. I thought someone was, maybe not. They were talking about somebody. I don't know who."

"Have you ever heard the name Paul Sorrentino?"

"Yes."

"Did you hear Jimmy talking about Paul?"

"Yes. I heard Jimmy talk about taking Paul or something. I don't know. They were out in the parking lot and Jimmy said that he was going to take Paul, or something like that."

"When your mom told you that Jimmy took care of Chris, what did you think she meant?"

"I didn't know what to think. I didn't know if they just beat him up or what."

"When he didn't come home, what did you think?"

"I figured that he had killed him."

Douglass looked at Moore, who in turn was watching Margie. Large tears had formed in her eyes and were now streaming down her cheeks. She grasped Suzanne's hand in hers. Margie, realizing what Suzanne had been a part of, couldn't look at Douglass or Moore. Suzanne remained stoic.

"When Jimmy and your mom were having the discussion in the parking lot, what did you think?"

"I knew that something was going to happen that night."

"But you didn't know what?"

"Not exactly. They didn't say a whole lot."

"The day they were out there in the parking lot, did your mother ever talk to Jimmy about killing Chris?"

"They never said that word for word. They were just going to get rid of him. That's all they said.

They didn't say that they were going to kill him."

"Did your mom ever tell you what you were supposed to do that night?"

"Yeah, I was supposed to stay upstairs. She told me to be in the shower when Jimmy came over."

"Do you know anything about Chris's wallet? How it got to Metcalf South?"

"My mom told me she threw it up there that night. It was in Chris's room."

Douglass looked at Suzanne, who showed no emotion. Margie, on the other hand, was trying to get a grip on herself.

"I think that's enough right now," Douglass said, looking at Margie and Suzanne. "You two can stay in here for a while."

Douglass and Moore left the room, leaving Margie with Suzanne.

"You poor baby," Margie said, patting Suzanne's hand. "You poor, poor child."

Jackson and McClain were waiting outside the interview room, but Douglass wasn't in the mood to talk. He had a few things he wanted to discuss with Sueanne.

"The girl's a little clone," he said about Suzanne.

"What did she say?" Jackson asked.

"We've got Sueanne," Douglass said. "I just want a couple of minutes with her."

———

Douglass was prepared to arrest Sueanne on the murder charges right then, but based on their earlier conversations, he knew Sueanne still wanted to talk. He didn't see why he should stop her. Douglass believed Sueanne thought she was clever enough to convince him of her innocence. But Douglass also prided himself on his abilities. He badly wanted Sueanne to confess. As much as he hated to admit it, he was in a battle of wits and he was determined to win. Armed with Suzanne's incriminating statements, Douglass confronted Sueanne one last time.

"Mrs. Hobson, we want to ask you a few more questions," he said briskly. "I realize we've been asking you questions for several hours now. You don't have to answer any more questions."

As a precaution, Douglas again read Sueanne her constitutional rights. He was indignant; she was solemn. She looked worried and restless, but still maintained some semblance of poise and control. Her confidence irritated him more than anything he had ever experienced during an interview.

"Okay, I'm going to put it to you very bluntly," he said, leaning across the table. "We talked to your daughter and she told us that on the day of the disappearance, you went over to Jimmy's apartment and discussed Chris's disappearance."

He repeated what Suzanne had told him. Then he paused, waiting for Sueanne to respond. She didn't.

"The things she said were true, weren't they?" Douglass asked. "Did the word 'killing' ever come up when you talked to Jimmy?"

"No."

"Did the words 'get rid of him' ever come up?"

"Probably, but not in that context," she said.

"Well, Mrs. Hobson, what other context is there? How does a seventeen-year-old boy get rid of a thirteen-year-old boy besides taking him out in the boondocks and blowing his head off?"

"You just scare him so that he doesn't threaten Suzanne again," she said. "That's all I wanted."

"So when it all boils down, you did know that Jimmy and some boy were going to take Chris out somewhere that night and—"

"Scare him," Sueanne said, finishing Douglass's sentence.

"And scare him," Douglass said sarcastically. "Why didn't you tell us that an hour ago? Why do you wait until we have talked to Suzanne, who was supposed to prove you innocent? Why do you wait until now to tell us that?"

"Because I am scared to death," she said. "I didn't think Jimmy would go that far. And after it happened, I couldn't do anything about it. I was scared to tell my husband. You have to understand, I've never been involved with anything like this before. And I was scared after I found out. I didn't know what to do about it. He's my son."

"Well, Mrs. Hobson," Douglass said, "how far did you think it would go?"

"Jimmy was just going to scare him," she said. "He was going to threaten him that if he hurt Suzanne again he was going to beat him up. That's all."

"Your daughter had the impression at that meeting with Jimmy that you knew and Jimmy knew that 'get rid of him' meant that Chris was not coming back," Douglass reminded her.

"That's not what she said to me," Sueanne said.

"That's what she said to us," Douglass said with finality as he stood up from the table. "She had the feeling that Chris was not coming back."

"No, no," Sueanne said. "No, it was just to scare him."

"And it went too far, right?" Douglass said, turning his back on Sueanne to prevent his emotions from exploding.

Moore looked at Douglass, whose back remained turned. Then Moore looked at Sueanne, who, for the first time, looked tired and drained.

"It was just to scare him, that's all," she said, still trying to convince the detectives of her innocence.

This woman must have nerves of steel and a will to match, Douglass thought, amazed at Sueanne's ability and desire to keep battling.

"I think that about wraps it up," Moore said, turning off the tape recorder.

"What's going to happen now?" she asked.

Douglass whirled and looked angrily at her.

"What's going to happen now Mrs. Hobson is that

you are under arrest for first-degree murder in the killing of your thirteen-year-old stepson," he said.

"But I didn't kill him," she pleaded. "I want you to believe me. I didn't want this to happen."

"But it went too far, didn't it?" Douglass said wearily, finally realizing he was not going to get his confession. "I'm finished."

When Douglass and Moore left the room, Sueanne began to cry, slowly and without sound. The controlled face with the set jaw and penetrating eyes melted. She slumped forward, holding her face in her hands, and cried slowly, giving in to the nervous tension she had stubbornly held back during the interview. She wrung her hands, twisting the ruby-encrusted diamond ring she had worn so proudly. She was scared, horrified. Not for Jimmy, but for herself.

———

Moore returned a few minutes later and took Sueanne downstairs to the booking room, where a uniformed officer prepared to photograph and fingerprint her.

"Mrs. Hobson, you are going to have to remove your jewelry," Moore said. "You can't take it with you to the jail."

"What is going to happen to it?" she asked, hesitantly removing the Krugerrand and gold chains from her neck. "Even my wedding ring?"

"Yes," he said. "I can put it in the police safe, or you can give it to Margie to take home."

"I'll give it to Margie," she said, handing the jewelry to Moore, who put it in a manila envelope that he placed on a table.

He walked to a room adjacent to the booking area, where Margie and Suzanne waited. Margie was still crying. Suzanne's eyes were dry and apathetic.

"Margie, would you come with me, please?" he

said. "Suzanne, you can wait here for a few more minutes."

Moore took Margie into the booking area, where the officer was completing the fingerprinting. Sueanne looked old, tired, Margie thought.

"Will you take my jewelry?" Sueanne asked Margie.

"Yes," she agreed curtly.

"And will you take Suzanne home with you?"

"Of course," Margie said.

Moore told Sueanne to place her hands in front of her, and handcuffed her.

"What's going to happen now?" she asked plaintively.

"You will be transported to the Johnson County jail in Olathe," he said. "There will probably be a hearing on bond Monday."

"May I see my daughter before I go?" she asked.

Moore led Sueanne across the hall to the small room where her daughter waited. He left the mother and daughter alone.

Suzanne was shocked. The veneer of sophistication and invincibility that her mother usually wore as boldly as she did her jewelry was gone. Sueanne's reddened eyes were a mixture of anger, fear and pain. Suzanne stared at the handcuffs. She, too, was afraid, not for her mother, but for herself. Her life seemed to be crashing around her. She didn't want to stay alone with Ed.

"What did you tell them?" Sueanne demanded.

"The truth," Suzanne said defensively.

"Are you sure you really know what the truth is?" Sueanne said in a tough, exacting voice. For a moment Sueanne was back in control, demanding her daughter's attention and obedience.

"I don't know," Suzanne said, realizing for the first time that maybe she didn't know what the truth really was. Thoughts and questions swirled through the teenager's mind. She looked at her mother. "What's going to happen now?"

"You're going to stay with Margie," Sueanne said, avoiding the larger issues.

The mother and daughter, similar in so many ways, stood apart. Suzanne didn't feel like touching her mother. At that moment she felt like her mother was a stranger.

Moore returned to the room with Margie. He had arranged for a police officer to take Suzanne and Margie back to the Hobson home so Suzanne could get some clothes.

"Bye, Suzanne," Sueanne said as an officer escorted her from the room. Suzanne stared blankly at her mother.

The trip home was quiet. No one spoke. Suzanne sat in the backseat staring out the window at the early Sunday morning traffic.

When she got home, she began stuffing her clothes angrily into two trash bags. She didn't have a suitcase. She looked across her room at several framed pictures of her mother, her mother and Jimmy, and one of Jimmy alone. She tore Jimmy's picture from the frame and began to rip it into shreds. She started to cry as she tore it into smaller and smaller pieces.

"I hate you Jimmy," she screamed. "I hate you."

9

"Ed could get real mad and do some crazy
things. He could get angry and threatening, but I
would always think of what Tani liked to call him
behind his back, 'Little Casper Milktoast.'"

—A FRIEND OF TANI

If Johnson County District Attorney Dennis Moore had known about Ed Hobson's past, he might have been better prepared for what would occur in the weeks and months following Sueanne's arrest.

Ed, who had spent the past thirty-six hours in a haze of booze, anger, and confusion, was searching for answers when he appeared at Moore's sixth-floor office Monday a few minutes before Sueanne was to make her first appearance in court. Detectives had warned Moore of Ed's potential for violence. At times during the investigation he had been gruff and belligerent. But he was eerily calm during his fifteen-minute meeting with Moore. He was a wrinkled, battered man, numbed by booze and the tragic loss of his son.

"I really don't want to see her. I don't know what I would do to her," Ed told Moore. "But I do want to know what is going to happen to her."

Moore, who had started the first victim/witness program in the state, patiently and compassionately explained to Ed that Sueanne would initially be charged with conspiracy to commit murder, but that he expected to file additional charges of first-degree murder as the investigation progressed. He also told Ed he was working closely with Miami County authorities to determine what charges would be filed against Jimmy and Paul and whether they would be tried as adults.

However, Moore refused Ed's request for specific details of the case, including what Sueanne had said to police the night of her arrest. Moore did tell Ed that, because the crime involved several family members, he would ask the court to prohibit Sueanne from contacting him or returning to their family home. Ed passively agreed.

After the meeting, Moore told detectives and assistant prosecutors involved in the case that he was satisfied Ed would be cooperative. But what he didn't know was that Ed was already beginning to waver over Sueanne's involvement in his son's death. Earlier that morning Ed had contacted his own lawyer, asking him to appear with Sueanne at her first court appearance.

"I didn't know what to do," Ed later told friends. "I hated her and I loved her, all at the same time. I knew she was in trouble and needed help."

That was only the beginning.

10

"My mother is the only person I have ever known
and loved. How could the detectives expect me to
believe what they were saying?"

—SUZANNE HOBSON

MAY 5, 1980   Ed continued to drown
his grief in alcohol. He sat at his kitchen table,
smoking cigarettes and sipping whiskey from a
brandy snifter, a loaded pistol nearby. His son, his
only living relative, was dead. The woman he loved
and had brought into his home to raise his son was
responsible for the murder. At least that's what the
police said.

It was one thing to have a child die violently—Ed
still regularly felt the pain of Tani's death—but it
was incomprehensible for him to think that the
woman he loved and adored had orchestrated his
son's murder.

Dr. Robert Craft, the minister who had married
the couple, tried to console him. The friends who
brought food and sympathy were as confused as he
was. No one understood what had happened or how
it could have occurred. Most of the people in his
house were friends of both Ed and Sueanne. They
didn't know what to say to him. Most privately
refused to believe that Sueanne could be guilty.

Since his son's disappearance, Ed had invited the media to share in his private tragedy. Even in his worst moments he had continued to be available. He allowed reporters into his home that Monday afternoon to talk about Chris and Sueanne.

"One thing about it, there ain't a hell of a lot left," he told reporters. "I just don't understand it. I didn't know there was anything wrong. Chris and Sueanne had their ups and downs the past year and a half, but I didn't see anything abnormal."

Ed remembered the happy times he had spent hunting and fishing with Chris at the family's farm in King City, Missouri. He talked of plans for Chris to go to college, to be a computer programmer. But the words were often suffocated by sobs, and many of his sentences trailed off. At times, he appeared to be in a trance, staring blankly at the walls. Everywhere he looked reminded him of Sueanne. Her friends were his friends. It was her house. She had picked out the paint, the wallpaper, and the furniture.

His voice cracking, Ed again told reporters how he had been convinced from the moment Chris disappeared that he had not run away.

"Chris did not like darkness," he said, crying. "As long as I was with him, it didn't bother him."

Ed shook his head, wiping tears from his eyes with the palms of his hands.

"One thing I had taught him all his life was that he couldn't run away from his problems. If he had done something wrong, he had to face it. And now I wish to God I had told him to run."

———

Across town, Sueanne was trying to regroup. Shortly after she was formally charged in Johnson County District Court with conspiracy to commit murder, Sueanne posted a $50,000 bond and went to Margie's residence, where Suzanne waited. At

Ed's request, the judge told Sueanne she was not allowed to return home or to contact Ed. The order did not apply to Suzanne.

Suzanne was sitting in the living room with Margie's two young sons when Sueanne walked in, looking tired, beaten. Suzanne didn't get up. They said hello to each other, but neither was in the mood to talk. Margie was polite but distant. Suzanne was silent, sullen. Sueanne wanted to bathe and change clothes. She looked helpless, skittish. The thirty-six hours spent in the county jail had aged her dramatically, Suzanne thought. Her mother looked frightened, even more afraid than when she had been in handcuffs at the Overland Park police station.

A shower and a change of clothes seemed to help Sueanne. She wasn't cheerful, by any stretch of the imagination, but she did seem more in control.

"Why don't we go for a walk?" she asked Suzanne. "It might ease my nerves."

The mother and daughter walked slowly, silently, around the complex, finally stopping to sit on a bench.

"Suzanne, I think you need to go back home and stay with Ed," her mother said.

"I don't want to," Suzanne answered angrily. "I don't want to. Do I have to?"

"Yes," Sueanne said sternly. "He's going to need you. You can stay here with me at Margie's tonight, but you must go back sometime. Probably tomorrow."

Suzanne had learned at an early age that her mother always won the arguments. There was no reason to talk back. She knew she had to go home.

"What are you going to do?" she asked.

"I don't know. The judge says I can't talk to Ed and I can't go home. I guess I'll just stay here with Margie for a while."

The two sat for a few minutes in the bright afternoon sun, watching the traffic pass along Wornall Street. Suzanne wanted to ask her mother a million questions. She wanted her mother to tell her it wasn't her fault that Sueanne had been arrested. She wanted to ask her mother about Jimmy, to find out what was going to happen to him. But she sat silently, waiting for her mother to speak.

"Suzanne, I don't think you understand what is happening," Sueanne finally said, looking at her. "I didn't ask Jimmy to kill Chris, I just wanted him to scare him so he would leave you alone. Do you think I would ask my own son to kill Ed's son? Jimmy was just supposed to take him out and scare him. I didn't know anything about the killing until after it happened. Jimmy told me Paul was going to kill all of us if I said anything. I know it was wrong for me to not tell Ed, but what was I supposed to do?"

Suzanne looked at her mother. She wondered if she remembered it all wrong. Maybe she didn't understand what had happened. Maybe Jimmy misunderstood.

"I'm confused," Suzanne said, shaking her head. "I don't know anymore. I don't know what happened."

"Why did you tell them that I dropped the billfold off Thursday night?" Sueanne asked. "It was Friday night, after Jimmy had told me Paul killed him."

"It was Thursday night."

"No it wasn't," Suzanne said angrily. "It was Friday night. Remember, I dropped you off at the skating rink right after that. Why don't you remember?"

"I don't know."

Suzanne was now more confused than before. She tried to think back to the two weeks before. She had gone skating that Friday night.

They talked for several more minutes about what

Suzanne had said to the police and about what had happened between Jimmy and Sueanne the day Chris disappeared. The more they talked, the more confused the thirteen-year-old became. Her mother seemed so sure of what had actually happened. She seemed so convinced of her own innocence.

"I'm trying to remember, Mother," Suzanne said, standing up and walking back to the apartment. "I'm trying."

———

Wednesday afternoon, May 9, was warm and bright. The sunshine glistened on the hoods of cars lining the one-lane chat roads that wandered through the Johnson County Memorial Gardens Cemetery.

Margie sat between Ed and Suzanne under a green canopy on a hill overlooking the rapidly expanding city of Overland Park. Relatives and friends of the Hobson family, along with dozens of Chris's junior high classmates, gathered around the gravesite.

Suzanne didn't want to sit next to Ed. She squeezed herself into a folding chair between Margie and Chris's grandmother in the front row. Ed sat on Margie's left, clutching her hand in his.

Listening to the minister talk of heaven and love and understanding, Suzanne could not cry. She felt guilty. Chris's death hadn't seemed real until she saw the casket and the flowers. She thought of all the times she had run to her mother, complaining about Chris. She wanted to feel more sorrow and grief, but she couldn't. She felt more anger than sorrow. She was angry at everything and everybody. She stared at the television cameramen and newspaper photographers who circled the gravesite like vultures. She looked at her classmates, many of whom had never spoken to Chris. They're only here because it gets them out of school, she thought. But what angered her the most was seeing two Overland Park detectives acting as pallbearers. Ed, still in a daze, had forgotten to enlist enough pallbearers for the service. At the last moment he had asked the Overland Park detectives to assist.

Suzanne was already beginning to hate them. During the two days since her release from jail, Sueanne had told her daughter how unfairly the detectives had treated her, how they had refused to listen to her side of the story.

Suzanne was also angry with her mother because Sueanne had told her she was to return home with Ed after the funeral.

"You're going to the funeral with Ed, you are going home with Ed, and you are going to stay with Ed," Sueanne had said repeatedly, despite Suzanne's angry protests. "That's final."

The graveside services lasted only thirty minutes, but it seemed like hours to Suzanne. After the services, Margie drove Suzanne back to Ed's, where several people were gathered.

Suzanne reluctantly went inside the house. It was crowded, but she recognized very few of the people. She knew the minister; he had been the family counselor. Some friends of Ed's and Sueanne's were also there. Food was stacked everywhere in the kitchen. Suzanne went straight upstairs to her room, where she closed the door and turned on her stereo, lay down on her bed and began to cry.

Margie came upstairs about an hour later.

"I've got to leave," she said. "Will you be okay?"

"Do I have to stay here?" Suzanne asked.

"Yes. Your mother wants you to stay. Don't worry, I'll come back tomorrow. Maybe you can come and stay with me then."

The two hugged each other. Suzanne loved Margie and she thought Margie cared about her.

About an hour later Suzanne decided to go downstairs. She really didn't want to talk to anybody, but she was getting hungry. The house was still full of people. She walked into the kitchen where Ed sat at the table, talking. He looked tired, old. He had been crying.

Suzanne looked angrily around the room. Ed and several others were drinking as if they were at a party. Some people were even laughing. She felt alone, frightened and confused. She looked in the refrigerator, grabbed a beer and took a big swallow. To her surprise, no one stopped her.

After several beers Suzanne went upstairs and passed out. When she awoke, she found her world turned upside down again. A friend of her mother's told her Margie and Sueanne had had a fight and Sueanne was moving to another friend's house. Suzanne knew what that meant. She would never get to see Margie again. Distraught, she ran and called Margie.

"Why did you do it?" she cried. "I want to know why you kicked her out."

"Because I think you deserve better," Margie answered obscurely.

"What do you mean?" Suzanne screamed. "What are you saying?" she began to cry hysterically. "Why? Why?" she screamed.

The telephone dangled in Suzanne's hand as she continued to cry uncontrollably. Regardless of what Margie and her mother had argued about, she knew she would never see Margie again. Sueanne wouldn't allow it. Sueanne would hold a grudge. She couldn't forgive.

———

It didn't get any better for Suzanne. Early the next morning she was awakened from an alcohol-induced sleep by the incessant ringing of the doorbell. It was Steve Moore and John Douglass with instructions to take her to the courthouse for questioning by the District Attorney's office.

After a frantic telephone call to her mother, Suzanne defiantly told the detectives she wouldn't leave until Ed returned home. Within minutes Ed arrived and the group left.

At the courthouse Suzanne was taken to a jury room for questioning while Ed waited in the District Attorney's office. Present with Suzanne were Assistant District Attorney Steve Tatum, Judge Buford Shankel, Shankel's court reporter, Douglass, and John Gerstle.

Gerstle, who was at the courthouse on unrelated matters, had been asked to the meeting by Shankel to aid Suzanne in understanding the proceedings and to make certain the District Attorney's office didn't overstep its authority in questioning her.

"State your name, please," Shankel said to Suzanne.

"Suzanne Hobson."

"And, for the record, your age?"

"Thirteen."

"Are you a student?"

"Yes. I go to Indian Creek Junior High School," Suzanne said hesitantly. She could feel pressure building inside her. She wanted to do the right thing for her mother. Looking around the small room, she felt detached and isolated.

"You understand you are under oath?" Shankel asked. "You know what being under oath is, don't you?"

"Yeah."

"And naturally, at thirteen, you understand the difference between the truth and a lie?"

"Yeah," she said, sounding defiant. Often, when challenged by authority or confronted by the unknown, Suzanne would react by remaining silent. But it was already clear that she would have to talk to these people.

Douglass began slowly, trying his best not to be intimidating. He felt sorry for Suzanne, but he also had a job to do. At a meeting earlier in the day, the prosecutor's office had already told him how important Suzanne's statements could be to prosecuting Sueanne.

"Suzanne, I want to ask you some questions concerning things that you observed around your house in the last six weeks," Douglass said. "It will be on the order of the questions we asked you the other night. Okay? Six months ago, how many people lived at your house?"

"I don't know," she said. "I don't remember when my brother moved out."

"Wouldn't it be safe to say that within the last few weeks, you lived at home with your father, Ed Hobson; your mother, Sueanne Hobson; and your stepbrother, Chris Hobson. Right?"

"Yeah."

"To your knowledge, has there been any difficulty between your mother and your father concerning your brother Chris in the last several weeks?"

"Not serious ones, no."

"What kind of problems were there?"

"I don't know," Suzanne said stubbornly. "I don't ask."

Scared and confused, Suzanne was afraid she was going to get her mother in more trouble.

"Have you heard them arguing?"

"Yeah, but I don't know what about," she said.

"Last Sunday morning, when we discussed these problems, you said you could hear them arguing and yelling. Could you tell me anything more about what you heard or what you observed between your mother and Ed, concerning your brother Chris?"

"No," she said, dismissing Douglass's question.

"Why is it today you describe them as not being serious?"

"I don't know. I just didn't think they were that serious. They were serious, but not that serious."

"Did your mother ever mention anything to you about these problems?"

"Not really."

"When your brother, Jimmy, left home, was your mother upset over this?"

"Yes," she said, continuing the pattern of short, noncommittal answers.

"Did she blame your father for this?"

"No."

"Did she blame Chris?"

"No."

Douglass could see this was a different Suzanne. She hadn't been friendly during the first interview, but at least she had tried to answer his questions. Today it was clear she had no intention of cooperating.

His worst fear was coming true: Sueanne had gotten to her daughter before the detectives could get a sworn statement.

"Last Sunday, when we asked you if your mother had discussed this with you, you mentioned that she had, on numerous occasions."

"Discussed what?"

Douglass's sympathy for Suzanne was rapidly dissipating. This wasn't the pitiful child caught in the middle of a murderous plot that Douglass had interviewed early Sunday. Today, Suzanne reminded him of her mother. She was acting like Sueanne: alternately defiant and cagey.

"Suzanne, I am talking about the problems between Ed and your mother involving Chris," Douglass said.

"Yeah, I guess she said she had problems."

"Did she tell you what kind of problems?"

"No, just that Chris had been causing problems."

"Did you have any problems with Chris?"

"Not really, we fought, but you know . . ."

"Did he ever threaten you? Did he ever harm you?"

"No. But he did tell me he'd get me out of the house, exactly the way he got Jimmy out."

"Did he tell you that?"

"To my face," Suzanne said, looking straight at Douglass.

"Did he tell your mother that, too?"

"She was standing in the room when he said it."

"When did that take place?"

"A couple of weeks before his disappearance, I guess."

"What did your mother have to say about that?"

"What could she say?" Suzanne said, using the same tactic her mother had used many times during her interview: answering a question with a question.

Tatum leaned forward to hear her answers, intently scribbling notes on a yellow legal pad. He had a troubled look on his face. He could already see problems developing with the case. They would need Suzanne's statement to successfully prosecute Sueanne, but the girl was already backtracking.

Douglass was walking a thin line. He was frustrated by Suzanne's answers and wanted to bear down on her, but he didn't dare. The last thing he wanted was for Shankel or Gerstle to think he was harassing the girl. Just keep calm, he thought, and keep asking her questions patiently.

"Once again, Suzanne," Douglass said, "when Chris said that to your mother, what did she say?"

"Not much," Suzanne said, shrugging her shoulders. "She asked him how he planned to do that. And he said, 'I'm not sure yet. I haven't thought of it.'"

Douglass didn't believe her. He suspected she was deliberately misleading him. He was sure her mother had already told her what to say. Sitting across from her, Douglass thought how cold and hard she looked. She was a miniature Sueanne, but unsophisticated in the art of lying.

Suzanne sat silently, staring at Douglass. She hadn't formed an opinion about Douglass during her initial interview early Sunday, but she was beginning to believe now what her mother had told her about him: he could be an asshole.

Douglass was starting to ask another question when the door to the jury room opened and Ed walked in.

"Who are you?" Shankel asked.

"This is Ed Hobson," Tatum told him. "He is the adoptive father of Suzanne, is that correct?"

"Yes," Ed said, sitting down at the end of the table. Suzanne looked up at him, then turned her eyes downward.

Shankel stopped for a moment, but when no one opposed Ed being in the room, Shankel allowed the questioning of Suzanne to continue.

Great, Suzanne thought, that's just what I need. It was bad enough to be talking about this in front of people she didn't know, but to have Ed in the room increased her uncertainty and fear of the situation. She didn't know how he would react to her.

"Suzanne, I want to talk to you about the disappearance of your brother," Douglass began again. "On April seventeenth, the date of your brother's disappearance . . . do you remember that day?"

"Yeah."

"Did you accompany your mother anywhere on that day?"

"Yeah."

"Where to?"

"Jimmy's house."

"Why did you go over there?"

"To talk to Jimmy. They were talking out in the parking lot."

"Were you with them?"

"No. I was in the car."

"Could you hear what they were saying?"

"Vaguely."

"Do you remember telling us that you overheard your mother make the comment that 'something had to be done about Chris?'"

"Yeah. But she didn't mean to kill him. All she

wanted to do was have Jimmy talk to him."

"How do you know?"

"How do I know what?"

"That all she wanted was to have somebody talk to him?"

"Because she told me she was going to have Jimmy talk to Chris."

"Okay, okay, Suzanne," Douglass said, visibly frustrated. "Last Sunday you made a statement, which is recorded here. I asked you a question: 'What did you overhear?' And your response was that Jimmy and whoever were going to take Chris out wherever and get rid of him. Do you remember making that statement?"

"Kind of," Suzanne said. "But I didn't mean it that way."

"Then how did you mean it?" Douglass asked sarcastically. He looked toward Tatum for guidance.

"All they were supposed to do was talk to him."

"Did your mother say that?"

"Yeah."

"Could I ask you then why, last Sunday, you told us that they were going to take him out and get rid of him, rather than what you are saying now?"

"Because I was upset. It was six in the morning. I didn't know what you were saying. You were booking my mom for conspiracy to commit murder. My brother was sitting in jail for murder."

Ed listened intently. He leaned forward, resting his crossed arms on the table. He had never heard any of this. He stared at Suzanne.

"Would you like a glass of water?" Douglass asked Suzanne.

"No," she said, her face showing the stress of the interview. Her eyes watered and she fumbled with pieces of paper on the table in front of her. She stared at the floor.

"I understand you are upset," Douglass said, looking at Tatum to see whether he wanted him to continue the interrogation. The Assistant District Attorney gave no sign he was to quit.

"Really, Suzanne, all we want is the truth," Douglass said, his voice compassionate, "and it's very important that you tell us exactly what was said."

"That's exactly what was said," Suzanne retorted.

"Then why did you make it sound worse Sunday than you are now?"

"I don't know," she said, finally looking at Douglass. "I was upset. I didn't know what I was saying."

That's for sure, Douglass thought.

"Do you remember me asking you about Chris's billfold?" Douglass said, moving on to another important area of questioning.

"Yeah," she said reluctantly. This was an area Suzanne clearly didn't want to talk about.

"Did your mother take Chris's billfold?"

"Yeah."

"What did she do with it?"

"She put it up at Metcalf South."

"Why did she do that?"

"Don't ask me, she didn't tell me."

"When did she do it?"

"I guess that night."

"The night Chris disappeared?"

"Yeah."

At least her story was consistent on the billfold, Douglass thought.

"Did your mother ever say anything to you that day about being upstairs when Jimmy came over to see Chris?" Douglass asked.

"Well, she wanted me upstairs so they could talk, or go out and talk, I don't know," Suzanne said, trying to avoid looking directly at anyone. "She just said to go upstairs and leave them alone. Yeah, to leave them alone so they could talk."

"Did your mother ever tell you what happened to Chris?" Douglass asked.

"She didn't, she—" Suzanne stopped in mid-sentence, trying to think of what to say. "No."

"Did she ever tell you that Chris wasn't coming back?"

"No."

"Do you remember telling us last Sunday that she did?"

"No."

"Do you remember telling us that she also mentioned to you not to tell Ed?" Douglass asked, pointing to Ed, who leaned forward to hear Suzanne's answer.

"Well, she didn't know what Jimmy had done with him," Suzanne said without looking at Ed.

"If I told you that your mother told me that she did know what Jimmy had done, and that she did tell—"

"I don't think she did know," Suzanne interrupted.

"Have you talked to your mother since we last talked?" Douglass asked.

"Yeah."

"Has she discussed this with you?"

"No."

"Did you talk with your mother this morning?"

"Yeah."

"Why?"

"Why?" Suzanne asked incredulously. "Because she's my mother."

"Did she discuss with you what happened with Jimmy and Chris?"

"No."

"Has she discussed this with you at all since we last talked?"

"No," Suzanne said, looking down at the table as she shook her head from side to side.

Douglass paused. He picked up Suzanne's taped statement from Sunday morning. Those in the room remained quiet, anticipating. Ed, sitting at the far end of the table, stared at Suzanne, then at Douglass.

"I want to direct your attention back to last Sunday and our conversation," Doulgass said. "When I asked you about taking care of Chris, we were talking about the fact that your mother had mentioned to you that Jimmy had taken care of Chris. I asked you, or Detective Moore asked you, 'When your mom told you that Jimmy had taken care of Chris, what did you think that meant?' And you answered, 'I didn't know what to think. I didn't know if they just beat him up, just enough to put him in the hospital or not.'"

"I didn't know if . . ." Suzanne said before Douglass could make his point or ask a question. "I didn't know what they were going to do. When he didn't come back, I didn't know what Jimmy had done."

Douglass continued: "And Detective Moore asked you the question: 'When he didn't come home, what did you think?' And your reply was, 'I figured that he killed him.'"

Douglass looked up from the transcript. He waited for Suzanne's response, but none came. She stared at him, eerily focusing her brown eyes on him like her mother had done three days before.

"Do you remember any of that conversation?" Doulgass asked in an irritated but controlled tone of voice. "Any of it?"

"Yeah, some of it," Suzanne said calmly. "But I didn't—"

"Suzanne, can I ask you an honest question, straightforward?" Douglass said, his raised voice commanding her attention. "It seems now that after we've talked on many, many important things, that you seem to be changing your mind, and going in an entirely different direction from the stuff you told us Sunday. Is there a reason why you are telling us a different story now?"

"Why, do you think I'm lying?" Suzanne asked, taking the offensive, as her mother had done often during her interview with Douglass.

"No, I am not saying that you are lying," Douglass said, although there was little doubt in his mind that she was. "I'm simply asking you for the truth. Why did you tell us that then and why are you telling us something completely different now?"

"Because I didn't know what I was saying then," she said.

Douglass smiled. Suzanne had finally told the truth, he thought. If Suzanne had been an adult, Douglass would have pounced on her like a tiger. But she was only a child, trying desperately to protect her mother. Douglass was surprised at himself. His anger with Suzanne was gone, directed instead at Sueanne. He hated Sueanne. For Suzanne he felt only pity, just as he had for Jimmy several days before.

"Is there anything else you want to tell us?" he asked politely.

"No," Suzanne said, looking away.

"I understand."

11

"I know my wife did not want Chris killed. I know that because I've got somebody way bigger than us here on Earth guiding me."

—ED HOBSON

The Sueanne Hobson murder case was growing difficult for the team of prosecutors and detectives working on it. Not only were they worried about the legal issues involved, but there was increasing concern about key witnesses in the case. To no one's surprise, Suzanne had already recanted the damaging evidence against her mother. Now Ed was showing signs of wavering.

While Johnson and Miami county prosecutors worked on the legal matters, Douglass continued probing for answers.

Douglass had no doubts about Sueanne. She was a ruthless, cold-hearted, and manipulative woman with absolutely no conscience. In his opinion she would stop at nothing—even sacrificing her own children—to achieve her goals. He was convinced of her guilt and wanted to see her punished.

On the other hand, Douglass was perplexed about Ed. Those involved in the investigation had expressed concern about Ed's temper and inability to control his emotions. Douglass himself had heard Ed threaten to kill anyone involved in his son's death, including Sueanne. Still, Douglass wasn't convinced Ed could really do it. Ed talked about vengeance, but so did a lot of other people who rarely carried out their threats.

In two meetings with Ed since Sueanne's arrest, Douglass had seen him vacillate between anger, confusion, and helplessness. One day Ed was totally convinced of Sueanne's guilt. The next day he wavered. He filed for divorce one day, then told friends he couldn't live without her. It was hard to tell what he actually believed. And, more important to Douglass, why.

In the first interview, conducted a few days after Sueanne's arrest, Douglass had seen a man grasping for answers. Douglass was also struck by something else. Ed was either the most naive man he had ever interviewed or knew a lot more about the situation than he was revealing.

During the interview, Ed had discussed two areas that shocked Douglass but elicited little concern from Ed. In the two-week period between Chris's disappearance and the discovery of his body, Sueanne had unexpectedly sold her Datsun and given away all of the furniture in Chris's room, Ed told Douglass.

Douglass was aware of the car sale—Jimmy had told investigators that his mother had sold the car he used to carry out the murder—but Douglass was astonished to learn about the furniture.

Ed had explanations for both.

"My wife sold it," he said of the Datsun. "I guess she sold it, we don't have it anymore. I really don't know. She said she sold it. I believe she sold it. Her and Margie took it over to Missouri about a week after Chris disappeared.

"She said she was going to put some money on some charge accounts we have. And put some money in savings. She wasn't working and she felt uncomfortable with her charge accounts being as high as they were and me the only one making any money."

The issue of the furniture had been raised accidentally during the interview when Douglass innocently asked one of his standard, interview-ending questions.

"Since Chris's disappearance, has your wife said or done anything unusual?"

"Well, I guess it is unusual now that I think about it," Ed said. "Sueanne suggested we get rid of all of the furniture in Chris's room."

Douglass tried to maintain his composure, but Ed's answer and the serenity with which he said it had floored him. Ed's response was calm, almost timid. He showed no anger or any outward awareness of the ramifications of Sueanne's actions.

Ed told Douglass he had given Chris's box spring and mattress to a man at work. He said Sueanne had given most of the other pieces of furniture and some of Chris's clothing to Margie.

"Did she tell you why she wanted to do this, especially at this particular time?"

"Well, we had been redoing the house room by room," Ed said. "And Sueanne thought this would be a good time to redo Chris's room."

"Did you think that unusual?"

"Well, she was very conservative on spending money," Ed said. "Then, all of a sudden we are going to spend a thousand dollars on furniture for his room . . . she wanted to make it a den instead of a bedroom."

Douglass was astonished. But it would only get worse in the second interview.

Several days later Douglass received a telephone call from Dennis Moore, informing him that Ed had talked with Sueanne and he was concerned that police might not know the entire story.

Moore, his voice a combination of anger and disgust, told Douglass "to talk to him and go over the evidence with him to make sure he knows what we have."

When Ed arrived at the Overland Park police station a few hours later, he was accompanied by John Adams, a minister he knew before he met Sueanne. After a few minutes it was clear Ed was still confused. But his attitude had changed. He told Douglass that he had recently talked with Sueanne and that he now believed she might not be directly involved in Chris's death.

"She told me Jimmy was trying to get back at her," he said. "And I believe her. I know what kind of boy Jimmy is. He's a liar and a thief and a drugger."

Ed spent several minutes going over the details of the battles he had had with Jimmy over the stolen credit cards, drugs, and the teenager's repeated lying.

Douglass looked at Ed, puzzled that he had ignored the court order—given at Ed's request—prohibiting Sueanne from contacting him. Douglass felt sorry for Ed. It was obvious that he was no match for Sueanne. She was proving to be a more formidable opponent than Douglass had expected.

Douglass listened as Ed defended Sueanne's actions.

"She only wanted Jimmy to talk to Chris," Ed said. "Jimmy had done it a few times in the past and it seemed to help."

"You've told us before that you didn't think your son and your wife were having problems," Douglass asked. "Did she tell you that she was having a problem with Chris and that she wanted Jimmy to talk to him about it?"

"Well, the problem Sueanne and Chris were having was that Sueanne had never raised a boy and didn't understand a lot of it," Ed said, appearing sincere. "The little childish pranks that boys pull off, Sueanne couldn't deal with.

"She was an only child all her life, and then for the last several years it's just been her and Suzanne. She didn't understand how to deal with other people or their children. She didn't know what to do. You don't know her like I do."

Ed talked at length. He became Sueanne's advocate. During the previous interview, Ed had seemed to be genuinely confused, angry and heartbroken. But not now. For whatever reasons, Ed seemed convinced of Sueanne's innocence.

Douglass studied him closely, trying to place himself in Ed's shoes. Knowing Sueanne's manipulative abilities, Douglass realized it was not only possible but probable that Sueanne had simply talked her way back into Ed's life. His lack of intelligence and sophistication would make him easy prey for a beguiling woman like Sueanne.

But there were other possibilities that Douglass was required to investigate. Although there was absolutely no evidence that Ed was involved in his son's death, Douglass couldn't completely rule out that possibility. Maybe Ed knew Sueanne was responsible, but decided that since his son was gone, the only thing he had left in life was Sueanne. And he was going to fight to keep her. That was more disturbing to Douglass than any other possibility. He needed to find out.

Ed told Douglass that Sueanne had explained that the boys had taken Chris "out in the woods, and once they got out there, Paul went berserk and killed Chris." The next day Jimmy came over to the house and threatened Sueanne, Ed said.

"He told her, 'If you say anything to anybody, I'll kill Ed or I'll have him killed.' That's when she took the billfold up to Metcalf South."

Douglass smiled. He had to give Sueanne credit. It was obvious Ed loved her, and what better way to make him believe her story than to use his love for her as a way to convince him of her innocence.

"So she threw the billfold at Metcalf South to

cover for Jimmy and to protect you?" Douglass asked, trying to mask his sarcasm.

"Yes," Ed said convincingly. "I don't know if you understand Sueanne. She is a grown woman and also a very small child. She has never been around criminals. She's never been around arguing and fighting."

Ed leaned forward and spoke urgently. He desperately wanted Douglass to believe him.

"There are so many things about my wife that you don't know," he said. "There were times in the past when I would look at her and think, 'I'm dealing with a thirteen-year-old girl, instead of a grown woman.' She hasn't had the worldly knocks and bruises that the rest of us have. She doesn't know how to do a lot of things. I mean, it was to a point where she was scared to death to go down to the license bureau and get a license on the car because she didn't know how to do it."

"She led a sheltered life?" Douglass said dryly.

"Very sheltered." Ed nodded, hoping Douglass was beginning to understand his wife.

Douglass listened while Ed rambled, detailing incidents that he believed showed Jimmy was capable of lying to police. And, more important, a motive for the murder and his subsequent implication of Sueanne.

"Jimmy wanted to get back at her because he thought she had left him," Ed said.

Douglass listened patiently, then decided to take the offensive.

"The night your son disappeared, your wife knew that Jimmy took him out to talk to him," Douglass said. "While you were looking all over the neighborhood for him, why didn't your wife tell you where he was?"

"Because she didn't know what had happened," Ed said. Like Suzanne, Ed had been schooled well by Sueanne. She had apparently anticipated every question and provided Ed with the answers.

Again Douglass tried to place himself in Ed's shoes. What would he do if the woman he loved were accused of killing his son? Douglass realized that he pitied Ed, just as he had the other two people under Sueanne's domination, Jimmy and Suzanne.

Although he realized it was probably a waste of time, Douglass felt he owed Ed an explanation as to why the police believed Sueanne was guilty.

"Ed, if the only evidence we had against your wife was the word of Jimmy, it would be very different," Douglass said. "I want to give you some of the other information that we have gathered and let you respond. Some of it is going to be painful, but I don't know any other way I can tell you."

"That's all right," Ed said understandingly. "Maybe I can explain some of it."

"We've spent a great deal of time trying to find out about Sueanne," Douglass said. "Her personality is erratic. She treats one person one way and another person another way. You mentioned the fact that she had a very childlike personality. You're not the first person who's told me that.

"We've talked to many people who know Sueanne, including officers from the juvenile court. Their opinion is that she often responds in a childlike fashion."

Ed sat quietly, smiling occasionally, as Douglass continued to discuss the evidence he had against Sueanne. Douglass talked about Jimmy's statement and about Suzanne's two statements. Douglass told him he thought Suzanne had been telling the truth during the first interview, but had changed her story after talking with her mother. Douglass hoped Ed would see the similarities between Suzanne and himself, but he didn't.

"I want you to understand that Suzanne is in a very difficult position," Douglass said. "First of all, she's a young girl and, at thirteen years old, no matter what your mother says or does, she is right."

"I understand that," Ed said.

Douglass read Suzanne's two statements to Ed, pointing out the differences between the two interviews. He also compared Suzanne's first statement with Jimmy's statement, pointing out the similarities. He laid the printed statements on the desk, waiting for Ed to respond.

"I am not sitting here saying that you don't have probable cause," Ed said. "I'm not sitting here saying she didn't do some things that look bad, but you've got to understand my wife. That's what I am asking you to do. Before you convict her, please try to understand her."

Douglass tried to decide how to proceed, whether there even was a reason to proceed.

"Ed, my personal opinion is that Sueanne is a very sick lady and needs some help. I don't think she realizes the consequences of her actions," Douglass said, watching closely for Ed's reaction. "I'm not giving you this evidence hoping you will say, 'Yeah, she's a really rotten person and I hate her.' I don't want that to happen."

"Nope," Ed said. "It won't."

"I've given you this evidence because I want you to understand why the state will pursue its prosecution and allow a jury to decide whether Sueanne is involved or not."

"Oh, I understand that," Ed said. "I came down here today after talking to Sueanne last night. I don't doubt in my mind that she is a very mixed-up lady. At the same time, I know that she did not want Chris killed, as well as I knew my son never ran away. I know that because I've got somebody way bigger than us here on Earth guiding me."

Dennis Moore had been told of Ed's comments, so he wasn't surprised when he was summoned to Judge Shankel's courtroom on May 13 to hear a request from defense attorneys for a modification of Sueanne's bond.

Sueanne's life had been a roller coaster of emotions since her arrest. Living with friends while trying to reconcile with Ed and Suzanne were difficult, but Sueanne also had other problems. She didn't have any money. Ed had frozen her accounts and she was left with nothing but the charity of a few friends. But that was all about to change. For the first time in days, Sueanne could smile. Dennis Moore saw it when he walked into the courtroom.

Sueanne was already seated at the defense table with defense attorney David Gilman when Moore entered the courtroom. Ed sat in the front row. Even though Sueanne's bond had clearly prohibited her from having any contact with Ed, it was obvious to the spectators that the two had been communicating.

Although it was an unscheduled hearing, word had spread rapidly through the courthouse that Sueanne was going to appear in court and that Ed was going to be with her.

The news of Chris's death and the arrests of Sueanne and the two boys had swept through the community with a gruesome mixture of curiosity and disbelief. Murder in Kansas City's low-crime suburbs always garnered attention throughout the city, but the involvement of a mother and son in a murder plot was especially intriguing.

From the moment of her arrest Sueanne had become an enigma few in the city would be able to ignore. People who knew Sueanne were confused. They, too, were faced with the dilemma detectives had encountered when confronted with evidence that Sueanne was involved: the inability to believe a mother would employ her own child to kill another child. It was a hurdle everyone involved in the case eventually had to overcome.

Now there was a second, even bigger, hurdle to

clear: that the dead boy's father was defending his wife's innocence.

Most people in the courtroom were shocked by the couple's behavior, unaware of what Ed Hobson had already told Moore and the Overland Park detectives. To most, including the newspaper and television reporters who had rapidly assembled for the hearing, Ed was a threat to Sueanne's safety. During the past few days Ed had told anyone who would listen, especially reporters, that if he got the opportunity, he would seek revenge from everyone involved in his son's death. And to most people, that threat included Sueanne.

But now he sat smiling at Sueanne.

Gilman began the hearing by providing the court with a standard request for a bond modification. Gilman explained to the court that Ed was now prepared to accept his wife's return to their home.

Shankel ordered Ed to the witness stand.

"Mr. Hobson, you are the husband of Sueanne Hobson, the defendant in this case, aren't you?" Gilman asked.

"Yes."

"And at the time she was first charged, she appeared before a magistrate. When bond was set, a condition of her bond was that she was not to return to your home, is that correct?"

"Yes."

"And yesterday you came to my office with her and requested me to make arrangements to amend that condition so she could return to your home?"

"Yes, I did."

Each of Ed's answers were delivered firmly and succinctly. He showed no emotion, instead concentrating on the questions Gilman asked. Sueanne was quiet and seemed self-assured.

In the courtroom some spectators whispered disbelievingly.

Gilman walked back to the defense table and sat

down next to Sueanne, telling Shankel he had no more questions. Shankel motioned for Moore to proceed.

"Mr. Hobson," Moore asked, "you had a conversation with Larry McClain of the District Attorney's office last week, didn't you? And you asked for the condition that your wife be kept away from you, didn't you?"

"Yes, I did."

"Are you changing that request now?"

"That's correct," Ed said firmly.

"You had a conversation yesterday with Detectives Douglass and Moore from the Overland Park Police Department," Moore said. "And they went over some of the evidence in this case, is that correct?"

"That's correct."

"Even in spite of the evidence they presented to you yesterday, you wish to ask that this condition of bond be lifted?"

"Yes, I do."

"Mr. Hobson, I understand that your attorney, Mr. Sheldon Crossette, recently filed a petition of divorce on your behalf?"

"Yes, I think he did."

"Is that still on file?"

"I don't know," Hobson said, shaking his head.

"But you haven't contacted him and asked him to withdraw the petition?"

"No, I haven't really," Ed said. "I didn't think about it until right now."

"Mr. Hobson, where is Sueanne staying right now?"

"With friends of ours."

Moore turned his back, shaking his head as he walked back to his seat. "I have no further questions," Moore said disgustedly.

Shankel asked Ed if he intended to instruct his attorney to dismiss the divorce petition.

"Yes, Your Honor."

"All right," Shankel said. "You may step down, Mr. Hobson. Is there anything else?"

"Your Honor, this condition of bond was made at the specific request of Mr. Hobson," Moore said with resignation, turning the palms of his hands upward. "I guess if Mr. Hobson feels the way he says he does, we can't really say much about it. I'm kind of at a loss to understand it, but he's stated his feelings here today."

After several minutes, Shankel agreed with Gilman's request, freeing Sueanne to return to her home.

Sueanne stood up, turned and smiled at Ed, who had returned to his seat in the front row. As Gilman escorted her through the swinging wooden gate separating the court from the spectator's area, Sueanne reached out and grabbed Ed's hand. With their heads held high, the two walked proudly down the aisle past several people who stood motionless in their rows, staring at them in disbelief. Declining to answer reporters' questions, the couple walked down the courthouse steps hand in hand, got into Ed's car and drove away.

12

"I think Sueanne Hobson really believes that she is in control of the situation and will never be convicted."

—DISTRICT ATTORNEY DENNIS MOORE

Dennis Moore, a tall, articulate first-term prosecutor, had spent the past thirty minutes looking out the window of his sixth-floor office contemplating his next move in the Hobson murder case. Although the case was only seven weeks old, Moore was already feeling the pressure. Reports from his staff had indicated the state's case against Sueanne had problems.

The issues complicating the case didn't involve the police's investigation; Moore knew the detectives had done a good job. The problems stemmed from something Moore had no control over: the availability of key witnesses to testify against Sueanne. Specifically, the testimony of Jimmy Crumm and Paul Sorrentino, who were refusing to testify.

Sitting alone in his office, Moore considered his options. Should he continue to pursue his case against Sueanne and risk losing it because the boys were unavailable to testify? Or should he dismiss the charges, weather the public outcry, and hope that he could secure the boys' testimony against her?

Moore was worried not only about the public's reaction to the dismissal of charges, but also about the reaction of the detectives on the case.

Like most murder cases where arrests have been made, the detectives involved in this case were more confident than the prosecutors.

The Overland Park detectives who had arrested Sueanne had been surprised and angered during a recent meeting with Moore when he had informed them there was a possibility he might have to dismiss the charges against her. They had pushed Moore to proceed with the prosecution.

"I think her statements to us are very damaging," Douglass had said. "I believe we've got enough to convince a jury of her guilt."

Dennis Moore wasn't as sure. He argued that it was one thing to believe someone had committed a crime, but another thing to convince a jury beyond a reasonable doubt.

Moore needed the testimony of the two boys. Even though Jimmy had implicated his mother in the murder, and Overland Park police had Sorrentino on tape discussing Sueanne's involvement, it was unlikely that either boy's testimony would be available to Moore within the next few months, if ever.

The boys had a right to protect themselves against self-incrimination, Moore had explained. Under Kansas law, he couldn't simply subpoena them to appear at Sueanne's trial and expect them to answer any questions he asked. If he did that, the boys' attorneys would invoke their clients' rights against self-incrimination. The trial court would have no choice but to prohibit Moore from questioning them, in essence ruining his case against Sueanne.

Moore told the detectives that the boys' lawyers, Edward Byrne and Richard Roe, were focusing their attention on trying to prevent prosecutors from having the youths tried as adults. "They aren't interested in making any deals," Moore said.

The hearing on whether the youths were to be tried as adults had already been continued until August to allow the boys to undergo psychological testing. Until that issue was resolved, Byrne and Roe had no intention of discussing any plea negotiations with the Johnson County District Attorney's office.

The boys were being held in the Miami County jail in lieu of bond. From Moore's discussions with Miami County prosecutors, even if they were to be tried as adults, it would take at least six months to complete their cases. And that presented another problem for Moore.

Sueanne's attorney, Dave Gilman, was aware of Moore's dilemma and was eagerly pushing Sueanne's conspiracy case forward in Johnson County District Court. Gilman knew that without at least one boy's cooperation, Moore couldn't prove the conspiracy case against Sueanne. Under Kansas' speedy trial law, Sueanne had to be tried within 180 days of her arraignment. The quicker Gilman got her to arraignment, the less chance Moore had of convicting her.

Although the boys' availability was the major problem, Moore was faced with other potential pitfalls. Ed was now clearly on Sueanne's side. The last thing Moore needed was the dead boy's father testifying before a jury that he believed his wife was innocent. As a prosecutor, Moore had always relied on the jury's compassion for the victim's family.

Moore also suspected he would have difficulty using Suzanne's initial statement against her mother. Gilman had already implied that he would try to block the admission of that statement, indicating the true version of what had occurred was contained in Suzanne's sworn statement taken several days later. Moore was confident he would be allowed to use Suzanne's initial statement at trial, but he had learned early in his career never to take anything for granted. He felt Suzanne's statement was critical, and fully expected lengthy hearings on the issue of its admissibility. Considering all those facts, Moore turned from the window and summoned his top four assistants to his office to discuss the legal and political consequences of dismissing the charges against Sueanne. He was leaning toward dismissal, but wanted input from others in the office.

Under Kansas law there were no time constraints for charging a person with first-degree murder. Moore could dismiss the charges against Sueanne and wait until after the boys had been prosecuted in Miami County to refile the charges against her. Moore was primarily concerned about the legal problems, but he was also concerned how the public would perceive the decision.

Moore, the first Democrat to be elected District Attorney in Johnson County in eighteen years, was running for reelection. He knew the public was outraged by Chris's death, and anything short of life in prison for those responsible could become an issue in his reelection campaign in four months.

After a one-hour meeting, it was the general consensus among his assistants that he had only one choice: dismiss the charges and hope that sometime in the next few months he could make a deal with at least one of the boys for his testimony. With some misgivings, Moore agreed.

On July 11 Moore issued a three-paragraph statement announcing his dismissal of the charges. In the statement he said, "In order to prosecute Sueanne Hobson we need to present the testimony of witnesses who are not presently available."

Moore declined to identify the witnesses and refused to discuss the decision with reporters.

"The investigation is continuing," he said tersely. "Hopefully, someday we will be able to refile the charges."

13

"Ed is confused, to say the least."
—JOHN ADAMS, ED HOBSON'S MINISTER

The idyllic picture of Ed and Sueanne walking hand in hand out of the Johnson County Courthouse was deceptive. The family was in turmoil. The fact that Dennis Moore had dismissed murder charges against Sueanne did little to relieve the household tension. Her attorneys told her the dismissal was simply a delay, indicating that the refiling of charges was inevitable.

Sueanne was consumed by the specter of prison, and Ed was a bundle of unresolved emotions. Depending upon his level of sobriety, his opinions of Sueanne's involvement in Chris's death ran the gamut from her complete innocence to knowledge after the fact to masterminding the murder. The couple attended counseling and sought comfort in prayer.

John Adams was as close to the couple as anyone. A few weeks after the murder, following one of the couple's numerous screaming matches, Adams discussed the problems with Detective Steve Moore. The detective, who had heard about continuing problems between the couple, contacted Adams out of concern for thirteen-year-old Suzanne.

"They were arguing about Chris's death," Adams told Moore. "Ed believes that Sueanne is not responsible for Chris's death, but he's upset with the way she's acting. Ed thinks that Sueanne is only worried about what's going to happen to her, while Ed is only concerned about the loss of his son."

Adams told Moore that Ed was seeking sympathy and understanding from Sueanne and she was unable to give it. She, in turn, was seeking the same comfort from Ed, and he couldn't give it.

"I don't think they can live together until they get that straightened out," Adams said.

Suzanne was trapped in the middle. Unlike her brother Jimmy, freed from his mother's influence in jail, Suzanne had nowhere to turn. She had to listen to the fights, to the constant rehashing of the evidence and the statements—especially hers. Every day was shadowed by the presence of Chris. Everywhere she turned, she felt him near.

"In a way, it was over for Jimmy," Suzanne remembered. "Once he had admitted it, he could go on. He didn't have to live at home. I did. Jesus, I had to walk by Chris's room every day."

For Suzanne, the specter of her dead brother was unbearable. She felt guilty, and responsible for his death. She couldn't talk to her friends. They either shunned her or wanted all the grisly details. She thought about running away, but she had nowhere to go. Sueanne had been her entire life. Her natural father, James Crumm Sr., was a stranger to her.

The one person she unknowingly had on her side was a person she hated: Steve Moore. He was concerned about Suzanne's welfare, but unfortunately, her problems were emotional, not physical. She showed no outward signs of abuse. There simply wasn't enough evidence for the state to legally remove her from the home.

With the approval of his superiors, Moore had an informal discussion with a district judge in Olathe about placing Suzanne in a foster home. But the issue wasn't resolved. Moore dropped the idea after talking to Adams. The minister was opposed to placing Suzanne in a temporary shelter, saying it would have a worse effect on Suzanne than leaving her with her mother. He said Sueanne needed Suzanne with her and might have a nervous breakdown if Suzanne were taken from her. Adams told Moore that Sueanne, Ed, and Suzanne were going to begin counseling.

The counseling didn't work. By late July, with the arguments escalating, the marriage seemed destined to end in divorce. Ed contacted his attorney, Sheldon Crossette. It wasn't only the issues of guilt or innocence that continued to tear at him. He also was facing financial difficulties. Sueanne already owed $10,000 in lawyer and bondsman fees. If charges were refiled, the legal costs would soar. Ed could lose everything defending the woman accused of killing his son. He wrestled with the issue for days, then reluctantly decided on the divorce.

"The emotional ties were obviously still there," Crossette recalled, "but there were other matters involved."

The night before the divorce was to be filed, Ed talked to Suzanne, his adopted daughter.

"I'm divorcing you mother," he told her. "I still love her, but every time I look at her, I see Chris's face. I need some time alone to figure this out."

He told her that she would live with her mother, but that he loved her and would support her. He also promised to pay for her college education when she graduated from high school. Suzanne was relieved. She wanted out of the house and away from Chris's memory.

Sueanne agreed to an emergency divorce, but

didn't attend the hearing. The divorce was granted on grounds of incompatibility.

Sueanne and Suzanne moved to an apartment in Grandview, Missouri, just across the state line. Suzanne began using the name Sallee and started her freshman year of high school cloaked in the security of anonymity, free from the constant scrutiny of her classmates. School was her only escape. Life at home was still intense. There were fewer arguments, but Sueanne's life was still consumed by the uncertainty of her future. She sought comfort and support from many friends who continued to believe her innocence. They helped her financially and emotionally.

After a few weeks, Ed began to call and then visit Sueanne. They had long talks. They prayed. The issues that separated them still existed, but Ed seemed to mellow each time he talked to her. Although she was still preoccupied with her troubles, he found her more understanding of his pain and suffering. He tried to stay away from her, but couldn't. Again and again he found himself driving to Grandview to see her.

By mid-November the couple was considering remarriage. Ed's doubts were fading. On December 7, Pearl Harbor Day, Ed and Sueanne were remarried in a simple ceremony. Sueanne and Suzanne returned to the family home that night. The following day Sueanne began work at an area apartment complex, using the money to help defray her legal expenses. Ed was ready to fight for the woman he loved, regardless of what anyone else would say. He was once again Sueanne's husband.

"I just couldn't think clearly because of the depression over the loss of my son," Ed said, describing why he had initially divorced her. "It's different now. I remarried her because I love her and I know she's innocent. If she wasn't totally innocent, I would have killed her and we wouldn't be here today talking about it."

14

"Jimmy and Paul were as different as night and day. Jimmy was the sad one. Paul was the likable one."

—JUDY JOLLEY, A DEPUTY SHERIFF

While Sueanne and Ed continued to wrestle with their marital problems, Jimmy and Paul sat day after day in the small confines of the Miami County jail, where guards who came to know the boys had difficulty remembering they were charged with murder.

It was no surprise to those who knew Paul that he was in trouble, but the gravity of his problems was another matter.

To most people, Paul was a rascal, not a killer. He was a teenager with an abundance of energy, but little guidance or motivation. He had been suspended from high school many times and placed in an alternative program in junior high school because of disciplinary problems. But he had no juvenile police record and rarely displayed any propensity for violence.

Paul was a likable, proud youth with an easy smile and a desire to be known as a ladies' man. He also was very lonely. Like Jimmy, Paul's mother had abandoned him at a very early age. After years of

152

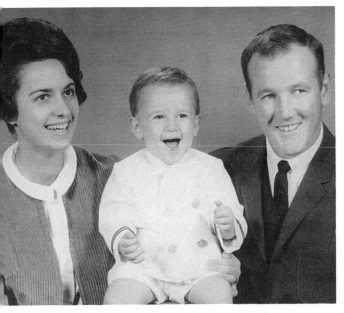

A deceptively happy picture of a young family—one-year-old Jimmy Crumm and his parents, Sueanne and James Crumm, Senior.

Suzanne and Sueanne a few weeks before Chris Hobson's murder.

After Sueanne married Ed Hobson, she moved to this home, where she was determined to live out her suburban dream.

The devotion Ed Hobson felt for his wife was apparent in his face—even after she'd been charged with the murder of his son. *(Jan Housewerth, THE KANSAS CITY STAR)*

One of the few photos of Chris Hobson.

Paul Sorrentino, a handsome and popular high school student, in 1979.

Local boys out fishing discovered a knee emerging from Chris Hobson's crude burial place in rural Miami County. *(Miami County Sheriff's Department photo)*

Sueanne minutes after she had been charged with the murder of her stepson. *(John Sleezer, OLATHE DAILY NEWS)*

Ed and Sueanne returning to the Johnson County Courtroom to hear the verdict in her trial. *(John Sleezer, OLATHE DAILY NEWS)*

The Miami County Courtroom in Paola, the scene of Jimmy's trial. *(Scott Smith, OLATHE DAILY NEWS)*

Jimmy being escorted back to the Miami County jail shortly after his conviction on first-degree murder charges. *(Larry Funk)*

Jimmy in prison, 1990.

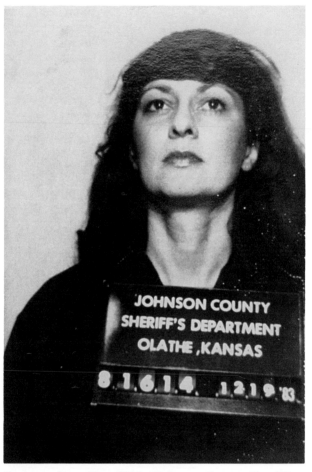

Sueanne, December 1983. *(Johnson County Sheriff's Department photo)*

marital strife, Paul's mother had returned to her family home in New England when Paul was six, leaving her husband Pat to raise Paul and their two older children in Kansas. The constant bickering between his parents had left Paul a psychological mess.

"When Mr. and Mrs. Sorrentino were living together, they got along very badly," said Dr. Paul Laybourne, a psychiatrist who examined Paul after his arrest. "There was a lot of quarreling and physical fighting . . . When she returned to New England, the children were left alone a lot. Paul's father was gone a lot because of his work and wasn't very effective in helping Paul get control of himself. In some ways he excused Paul. If Paul didn't do his laundry, his father would buy him three times as many clothes as he needed. Paul never really had an opportunity to get the kind of training, direction, structure, and guidance that he should have."

It was clear to everyone—counselors, teachers, and police—that Paul had the intellectual and social skills to succeed. He just didn't have the desire or the parental discipline.

Priding himself on being Italian, Paul bragged about a relative who he thought was a "hit man" for the mafia. He confessed to causing trouble because he was bored or just "felt like it." But in more vulnerable moments, he openly longed for his mother.

By the time Paul reached high school, disciplinary problems consumed most of his time. His grades plummeted. He had never been a good student, but he received D's and F's in all classes his sophomore and junior years, except physical education and driver's education. For Paul, school was social, not educational. When things didn't go right, he would leave, often going to a friend's house to do drugs or drink.

"Paul has a long history of not adjusting well in school, going clear back to Massachusetts," Laybourne said. "He didn't have a very high motivation toward learning, he had emotional problems, difficulty with authority, mouthing off to teachers, things of that sort."

Midway through his junior year he was placed on probation for excessive absences. Three weeks before classes were scheduled to end, and about two weeks after Chris had been killed, Paul was called to the assistant principal's office at Shawnee Mission South High School.

There, he was told he was suspended. If he wished to continue at school, he would have to attend a hearing before the suspension committee. Paul shrugged his shoulders. "I'm quitting school, you can't suspend me," he said, and walked out the door.

———

Jimmy and Paul met in the summer of 1979. Jimmy had just moved to Overland Park to live with Sueanne and Ed. Sueanne got him a part-time job working for Norma Hooker at Skateland. Paul was also working there.

The two boys became friends. Jimmy knew no one and Paul knew everyone. They became pals, running buddies. They spent a lot of time together, drinking, doing drugs, and chasing women. Jimmy was the tall stranger from across town. And Paul was his mischievous sidekick.

"Jimmy and Paul were very, very close," Ed said later. "Paul was at my house weeks on end. He ate at my table all the time."

When school started in the fall of 1979, Jimmy and Paul remained friends, but spent less time together. They played soccer and still hung out, but Jimmy was beginning to have troubles at home and with the law. But when Jimmy contemplated killing Chris, he remembered his buddy Paul.

"He just seemed like the kind of guy who would do it," Jimmy later told investigators. "He needed some money. He was kind of desperate to get his motorcycle fixed. And I said, 'What do you think about killing somebody?' And he said, 'What for?' and I said for money. He said he would do it. All he wanted was three hundred dollars to fix his motorcycle."

The striking differences between the two boys was evident in their reactions after the murder. Jimmy lost several pounds during the two weeks between the murder and the discovery of the body. He couldn't eat and he couldn't sleep unless he drank, took drugs, and exercised, sometimes doing five hundred push-ups a night just to get tired enough to lie down.

Paul reacted differently. He bragged about it.

While the police were frantically looking for Chris, more and more teenagers were discovering the truth. Jimmy, who had heard the rumors about Paul's bragging, knew it was just a matter of time before the police found out.

Ironically, when the two boys were arrested, their behavior changed dramatically. The talkative Paul clammed up, refused to say anything, and Jimmy became the sieve, talking to Overland Park detectives the night he was arrested and continuing to talk to Miami County deputies most of the next day. It seemed he wanted to share every detail about the murder with detectives. It was a pattern that would continue for most of the next year.

———

There is no harder jail time than a year in a county lockup, especially for a teenager. No exercise, no stereo, a little television, few books and even fewer visitors to break the monotony. Jimmy and Paul's days in the fifteen-cell jail consisted of hours of boredom, interrupted by occasional small chores the two were allowed to do around the jail.

Their lives were full of despair. They sometimes talked to each other, but never about the murder or why it happened. Except for their fathers, an occasional friend, and the attorneys representing them, the boys had few visitors. They celebrated two Christmases and their birthdays in the Miami County Jail, alone and apprehensive.

Neither boy had any real hope of being acquitted of the crime and released from custody. Jimmy had confessed to the murder and, although Paul had refused to talk to detectives, he had talked to enough other people prior to his arrest to make his conviction a certainty. Bond for each boy had been set at $250,000.

Except for the few days that they were given psychological evaluations at area hospitals, their hours were spent waiting for their next court appearance and their eventual trips to prison.

Their only hope was to be tried as juveniles instead of adults. Jimmy was seventeen and Paul sixteen at the time of the murder. If convicted as juveniles, they could only be kept in custody until their twenty-first birthdays. If tried as adults, they could spend the rest of their lives in prison. But even that sliver of hope was short-lived. In the fall of 1980, a few months after the murder, a Miami County district judge ruled both boys would be tried as adults. Preliminary hearings were held in early spring of 1981 and both boys were ordered to stand trial on charges of first-degree murder.

"It was sad," said Judy Jolley, a Miami County deputy who worked nights at the jail. "They were so lonely. It was hard for us, after knowing them for a while, to really believe they were charged with murder. They were really a couple of kids you could feel sorry for, even though you knew what they had done.

"Jimmy was the saddest person I have ever met. He was tight-lipped, standoffish. He had the saddest eyes. You could just see the pain. Paul was different. He was outgoing, funny. If Paul liked you and he thought you needed his help, he would go to the ends of the earth for you. It was important to Paul that you liked him. It wasn't to Jimmy. It seemed like Jimmy had given up trying a long time ago."

The only time Jolley ever saw Jimmy show any emotion occurred while he was watching a television news broadcast of the case in the spring of 1981.

"I'll never forget it," Jolley said. "Jimmy saw his mother on television saying that she couldn't understand why her son was saying those things about her. And he just started screaming and yelling 'you bitch, you lying, dirty bitch.' It was the only time I heard him raise his voice or lose his temper in the year that I knew him."

15

"Insanity is not *a* defense in this case, it's the *only* defense."

—ATTORNEY ED BYRNE

APRIL 27, 1981   Steve Tatum sat alone at the counter of Asher's Drug on the town square in Paola, quietly munching on doughnuts as the regulars straggled in for their morning coffee. For weeks, most residents of Miami County had anticipated the beginning of the biggest murder trial in decades, the trial of young Jimmy Crumm. The coffee drinkers, indifferent to Tatum seated at the counter, talked earnestly about the trial. What Tatum heard made him nervous.

Those gathered for their morning coffee were talking more about Sueanne than Jimmy. Although few expressed sympathy for Jimmy, there seemed to be an inordinate amount of hatred for Sueanne. Tatum had worried about that for weeks. He had to keep the jury focused on Jimmy's guilt, not Sueanne's role in the murder. He knew Ed Byrne, Jimmy's lawyer, would try to paint Sueanne black, deflecting the jury's attention from Jimmy. There was no doubt that Jimmy had a horrible childhood; Tatum knew that. But he also believed Jimmy was guilty of murder. He had to convince the jury that the teenager must be held accountable for killing Chris.

Tatum also was worried about Byrne's use of the insanity defense. In accordance with Kansas law, Byrne had notified prosecutors several weeks before the trial that he intended to rely on the insanity defense. That allowed prosecutors enough time to have their own doctors examine Jimmy. Although Tatum had prosecuted several murder cases, it was his first trial involving the insanity defense. He had spent several days studying other cases, reaching a disturbing conclusion: they have their experts, you have your experts. The jury has to decide which experts to believe.

There were other concerns. Though Tatum had been brought up in a small town, he was unfamiliar with the county and its people. In fact, he had spent all of his career prosecuting cases in large, metropolitan counties. He knew what to expect from those juries, and what they expected from him. He didn't have that in Miami County.

David Belling, the Miami County attorney, presented another problem. A former sports writer turned lawyer, Belling had won election by default several months before. He was the only candidate for county attorney, and that was as a write-in candidate. It was not only his first murder trial, it was his first trial ever. While he had asked for Tatum's help, he also wanted to appear competent in front of his constituents. He informed Tatum he wanted to be an active participant, not just an observer. Tatum understood. He allowed Belling to question several witnesses, most of them from Miami County. That gave Belling a visible role in the trial and still allowed Tatum to have the responsibility of examining all of the key witnesses, including the psychiatrists and psychologists.

Tatum finished his coffee and doughnuts and walked to the courthouse a block away. He was surprised by the amount of activity. He had to weave his way through a crowd at the door. Inside the courtroom, Byrne was already seated at the defense table. He had been there for over an hour. Like Tatum, Byrne was faced with his own set of unnerving questions and doubts.

It was his first murder trial. And he was only two years out of law school. Furthermore, with Jimmy, Byrne was presented with a dilemma every criminal attorney eventually encounters: whether to plead his client guilty to a lesser charge, greatly reducing prison time, or proceed to trial, hoping for an acquittal.

Byrne had wrestled with the question for months. He believed the psychological reports, especially those from the Menninger Foundation in Topeka, made an insanity defense a realistic option. Besides, he had nothing else.

"Jimmy's confessed and it's legal," Byrne told associates a few days before the trial was to begin. "We definitely can't try it on the merits or facts. The insanity defense is not *a* defense in this case, it's the *only* defense."

Byrne, fully expecting to be rebuffed, gave prosecutors his one and only plea offer two weeks before the trial. The offer: Jimmy would agree to testify against Sueanne and Paul if prosecutors reduced his charges from first-degree murder to involuntary manslaughter. The reduction would allow Jimmy to become eligible for parole with 180 days, instead of the fifteen years required of first-degree murder.

Prosecutors countered, offering to allow Jimmy to plead guilty to first-degree murder as an aider and abettor, in exchange for his testimony against Sueanne and Paul. Prosecutors said Jimmy would be eligible for parole within five months if convicted as an aider and abettor. Byrne, aware of the Kansas parole system, agreed that Jimmy would be eligible in a few months if convicted as an aider and abettor, but eligibility didn't always mean parole. Byrne believed it highly unlikely the parole board would grant early release to a man convicted of first-degree murder, even if he were convicted as an aider and abettor. He rejected the offer and the negotiations ceased.

———

The first day of Jimmy's trial was anticlimactic, an uneventful prelude to the drama about to unfold. A jury would be selected from a panel of farmers, housewives, railroaders and businessmen. They were cooperative, but anxious. Many of the candidates immediately looked for ways to be excused from consideration.

Judge Leighton Fossey sternly gave the group a civic lesson. He acknowledged the personal and financial hardships often felt by those called to serve. But he forcefully encouraged them to do their duty.

Within five hours the attorneys had agreed on a six-man, six-woman jury. Two alternates were also selected for the week-long trial.

———

On the second day of the trial the atmosphere in the courtroom was electric. Jimmy sat at the defense table, flanked by Byrne, Kathy Dillon—an attorney in Bryne's office—and Gary Compton, a private investigator hired by Jimmy's family.

Tatum, dressed in the same blue polyester suit he had worn for the first day of trial, stood at the podium in the center of the turn-of-the-century courtroom. Rays of light filtered through the stained-glass windows high above the courtroom, illuminating the large, curious crowd. Tatum looked about the room, at the high ceilings, hand-carved oak benches, tables and railings. All of it, even the flags and pictures of former judges, seemed to evoke a sense of firm serenity. At the back of the courtroom were wood-and-wrought-iron chairs, fastened to the floor in rows of seven. They were all occupied, and even more people stood two deep in the back of the courtroom. Curious spectators had begun lining up by eight A.M., hoping to capture one of the one hundred seats.

Tatum's anxious anticipation was overcome by the courtoom's soothing silence. He felt this was where he belonged; in a courtroom protecting the community. The thirty-nine-year-old Tatum, son of an Assembly of God minister, was raised in a small, rural town in northeast Kansas. Although he taught high school for three years after graduating from college, he had always wanted to be a prosecutor. Not just an attorney, but a prosecutor. His background seemed to fit a prosecutor's life. He combined his father's ability to preach with his teaching experience.

He smiled as the jury was escorted to their seats, trying to make eye contact with each juror. His first goal was to make them feel comfortable with him, to make them believe he was a credible prosecutor who would present the facts honestly and fairly.

"You may open for the state," Fossey said.

Tatum took a deep breath. In a deliberate, fatherly tone, he outlined the state's case, identifying each witness, what he believed they would say, and how their information was important to the case.

"As the evidence is presented, it will show the complicit involvement of Paul Sorrentino and Sueanne Hobson," he said, mentioning their names for the first time. "You may feel strongly about their involvement, as you well should. However, the purpose of this trial is to determine the ultimate guilt of Jim Crumm."

He described how Chris had been taken from his home and made to dig his own grave, and was then shot dead within it. He told them who found the body and the fact that Chris was buried in a remote area that was soon to become part of Hillsdale Lake.

Tatum described the two statements Jimmy had given police as self-serving. He pointed out the inconsistencies between those statements and the evidence, including Jimmy's refusal to admit he actually shot Chris. He also began educating the jury on the insanity defense.

"I can tell you that the state's evidence will clearly and unequivocally demonstrate that the defendant knew the difference between right and wrong . . . I am confident that at the close of the case, we will have shown clear, convincing proof that Jimmy Crumm is guilty of premeditated murder with a shotgun; that he planned, organized and participated in the killing of his stepbrother; that he made his stepbrother dig his own grave; and that he shot him with the shotgun as he lay in the grave.

"The evidence will show that Jimmy was not legally insane, that he committed the cold-blooded, chilling act, fully aware of the difference between right and wrong. At the close of the evidence I will ask you to return a verdict of guilty of first-degree murder. Thank you."

As soon as Tatum was finished, Byrne rose from his seat at the defense table.

"Judge, I would like to reserve my opening statement," Byrne said. "But I do want to offer a stipulation. We do at this time admit that Christian Hobson, age thirteen, did disappear from his home in Overland Park on April seventeen, 1980. He was shot to death by the defendant, James Crumm, Junior, who was armed with a shotgun . . . In particular, we would agree with Mr. Tatum that this murder was carried out at the behest of the defendant's own mother, Sueanne Hobson."

By stipulating, or admitting, to the charges, Byrne was attempting to prevent the state from putting on its witnesses. The only real issue Byrne wanted the jury to consider was insanity. He didn't want the jury to see the pictures of the crime scene, hear Jimmy's confession, or listen to law enforcement officials. That would only enrage the jury against Jimmy. To win the case, Byrne knew he had to make the jury sympathetic to Jimmy's plight.

"The sole issue is insanity; we do admit the ultimate act," Byrne told the court.

Tatum quickly rejected Byrne's stipulation. He wanted the jury exposed to the brutality of the crime. He wanted the jury to listen to the people who were at the scene, who removed the body from the grave, who questioned those responsible for the murder. He didn't want the trial to simply become a sanitized debate between psychiatrists.

Fossey accepted the state's request to present its case to the jury.

"You may call your first witness," he said.

Ed Hobson walked determinedly to the witness stand. As he was sworn in, he turned and stared at Jimmy seated a few feet away. Jimmy did not look up. Several deputies stood attentively around the courtroom. Ed had made so many threats in the past year, court officials were concerned about his reaction in this first encounter with Jimmy.

Tatum, partly because he knew Ed Hobson's dislike for him, allowed Belling to question him.

Ed's voice was solemn, authoritative. He tightened and relaxed his fists as he answered Belling's questions. He described his marriage to Sueanne, the fact that they had crossed-adopted their children. He described the night Chris disappeared, and told of searching the neighborhood for his son, and of finding a shotgun missing from the residence.

At one point Belling asked about Chris's billfold. Ed seemed to stiffen, his eyes growing moist and red. He slowly reached into his coat pocket and removed the wallet. He told how it had been found at Metcalf South a few days after Chris's disappearance. He said it was returned to him by Detective Steve Moore.

"How do you know that is your son's billfold?" Belling asked.

"It had his school identification in it; it had my wife's and my picture in it; it had his Social Security card in it; and on top of that, I bought the billfold," he said, staring at the inside of the wallet.

Belling's examination was brief, offering the jury very little except to see the dead boy's father. Belling carefully avoided asking Ed about Sueanne's possible participation in the murder. Tatum believed the less said about Sueanne, the better.

While Belling's examination was hesitant, Byrne's cross-examination was quick and purposeful.

"Mr. Hobson, am I correct in understanding that you are of this date married to and living with the mother of the defendant?" Byrne immediately asked.

"Yes."

"Did you ever find out who put the wallet at Metcalf South?" Byrne asked, moving toward the witness stand.

"I believe my wife did; but I don't know for sure," Ed answered.

"Thank you," Byrne said, ending his examination as abruptly as he had begun.

For the next three hours Tatum sat patiently as Belling plodded through the dull mechanics of a murder investigation. Belling called one of the two boys who had discovered the body. He called the clerk who had found Chris's billfold. Belling presented the testimony of several law enforcement officers, who systematically detailed the crime scene, evidence they recovered from the grave, and the results of the autopsy. Large, color photographs illustrating the grave and body also were presented to the jury for examination.

That afternoon, Tatum took over the questioning of the state's key witnesses. He quietly moved the podium to the center of the courtroom, where he waited until the jurors were seated. They looked eager, interested. The eight witnesses that Belling had called earlier in the day had left little doubt as to how Chris was murdered. Now everyone in the courtroom was anxious to know why.

Tatum called Overland Park detective Darrell Urban, who had arrested Jimmy the night Chris's body was found. Speaking in a low, almost hillbilly drawl, the balding Urban told the jury of Jimmy's arrest and subsequent statement to detectives. He told how Jimmy immediately confessed to the killing and then implicated his mother and Paul. As he talked, the jury was provided a copy of Jimmy's five-page statement.

Tatum didn't spend long questioning Urban. The written statement spoke for itself. Tatum questioned Urban about Jimmy's actions the night he was arrested. Knowing Byrne intended to rely on insanity, Tatum thought it important to illustrate at every opportunity the fact that Jimmy did know right from wrong, that he wasn't hallucinating or suffering from any mind-debilitating diseases.

Knowing what Tatum expected, Urban answered directly and with a sense of purpose. He testified that Jimmy was sober, he did understand the questions and, yes, he did appear nervous, though aware of what was going on around him.

Byrne's questioning was even less intrusive. He

simply wanted to know why Urban had failed to notify Jimmy's natural father of his arrest prior to questioning him.

"He told us he didn't want either one of his parents present," Urban said.

As Urban left the stand, several jurors continued to read Jimmy's five-page confession, jumping back and forth between the pages. Those in the back of the courtroom looked anxiously on. Because Jimmy had refused to allow Urban to tape-record the interview, most of those in the courtroom were not privy to what Jimmy had said about the killing. All that was going to change.

The mood in the courtroom seemed to surge when Tatum announced that his next witness would be playing a tape-recorded statement Jimmy gave to Miami County deputies the day after his arrest.

The witness, Miami County deputy Ron Orton, was nervous. It was his first big case. It seemed as if every pair of eyes in the courtroom was staring at him.

Orton, leaning forward in his chair, told the jury that Jimmy had wanted to talk to him and Kenny Niesz, the Miami County undersheriff, the day after his arrest.

At that point Tatum asked Orton to play the tape for the jury.

Sitting on the witness stand listening to the tape, Orton's thoughts drifted back to that May afternoon. He had felt sorry for Jimmy. He could still see him sitting in the small office at the Miami County sheriff's office, wearing a drab, jail-issued jumpsuit. Then, as now, Orton thought Jimmy looked unlikely as a murder suspect. He was young, cleancut, and polite.

The tape was an odd mixture of innocence, pathos, and unbridled brutality. The jury was enthralled. It was the first time they had heard Jimmy's voice. Some jurors listened intently to the tape, rarely looking at the transcripts Tatum had provided. Other's eyes never left the transcript, reading every word. Most of the spectators, including Jimmy's family, who were in the front row, leaned forward trying to hear every nuance of the scratchy tape.

Seated at the defense table between Byrne and Compton, Jimmy showed no emotion. He absently scribbled on yellow legal paper as he listened to his own voice recount the gruesome details of Chris's murder.

At one point during the interview, Orton asked Jimmy who had killed Chris.

"Tell us the truth, Jimmy," Orton said. "Who actually did the shooting?"

"Will this tape be heard by other people?" Jimmy asked.

"I have to say I don't think we can honestly answer that," Niesz said. "It may be heard by the jury if it goes to trial."

"Only the jury, though?" Jimmy asked, showing the same concerns he'd had when he talked to Urban. He asked whether his mother would hear it, or Sorrentino.

"I don't think we can answer that," Niesz told him. "I don't know what's going to happen down the road."

"All we want you to do, Jimmy, is be completely honest with us," Orton said. "We are giving you this chance to tell us the truth, that's all."

"Paul shot him," Jimmy said with some hesitation. "Paul did the whole thing. I fired over him. I'm not good with guns."

Jimmy was then asked whose idea it was to kill Chris.

"My mother's."

"What were you supposed to receive out of this?"

"My sister's security and a car."

"Who was going to buy the car?"

"My mother."

"What was Paul supposed to get?"

"He was going to get his motorcycle fixed."

"And your mother was going to pay for that also?"

"Yes."

Byrne smiled. It was what he had wanted the jury to hear. Jimmy's statement could only help his defense. He sounded like a child, calmly telling detectives how his mother had promised him a new car in return for killing his stepbrother. Byrne thought Jimmy's story was too bizarre not to be believed. He expected the jury to agree.

At one point during the interview the detectives asked Jimmy how long he and Paul remained at the murder scene.

"A long time."

"Why?"

"The hole had to be dug, and I just kept telling Paul, 'Let's just leave him here and just go back.' And Paul said, 'No, we couldn't, not now, it's too late.'"

"Did he [Chris] know why he was digging this hole?" Niesz asked.

"Well, we told him some sort of story about a truck."

"Where was he when he was first shot?"

"Laying in the hole . . . He was told to try it on for size."

"Was anything said before the shooting took place?" Niesz asked.

"One, two, three," Jimmy responded. "I just said 'one,' Paul said 'two,' I said 'three,' and I stopped and then I heard him fire. I fired the second shot, but I raised up and shot into some trees."

The jury sat in silence, occasionally glancing toward Jimmy. His voice seemed so clear, so unemotional, that it was hard to believe he had just described the shotgun killing of his stepbrother. Orton leaned forward. At that moment he no longer felt sorry for Jimmy. Like everyone else in the courtroom, his thoughts shifted to Chris, to the last horrifying moments of his life.

"Did he try to get up out of the hole after Paul shot him?" Niesz asked.

"He fell back, and I heard him whimper after I fired, and I said, 'Put him out of his misery.'"

Jimmy described how he and Paul had fallen to their knees and hurriedly scraped the fresh dirt over Chris's body. "I was a babbling idiot for about the next hour and a half."

By chance the detectives drifted into another, less brutal line of questioning. The courtroom seemed to breathe a collective sigh of relief as the questions again turned to the mechanics of murder: the type of weapons used; the location of the weapons; possible fingerprints; and the car that was used to transport Chris to the murder scene.

"It was my mom's car. It was a Datsun with 'Spirit' on the license tag," Jimmy said, explaining that Sueanne had sold the car a few days after Chris disappeared.

"What happened to the billfold?"

"I didn't do anything with the billfold," he said adamantly. "You see, Paul and I were supposed to pick him up after school, and I chickened out. Then Paul goes, 'Yeah, that's fine, let's not do it.' Then my mom called me at my apartment and wanted to know what happened. And I said, 'We decided not to do it.' She said, 'It's too late, I've already got rid of his billfold and some other stuff. If Ed comes home and Chris tells him some of his stuff is missing, I'm dead.' And it was true, she would have been."

"Why was that?"

"Because Ed believed everything Chris said, and he lied a lot."

"Was there hatred between you and Chris?"

"Yeah . . . for hitting my mother, for hitting my

sister, for getting me busted. Yeah, there was hatred, but I found out there still wasn't enough hatred to pull the trigger."

There were a few moments of silence on the tape. It allowed jurors a brief respite. Some looked at Jimmy, while others continued to thumb through the transcripts. As the tape continued, the detectives moved into other specifics about the case: what time Chris had been killed; what had happened to the clothes Jimmy was wearing; what roads the boys took to Bull Creek. Jimmy answered dutifully, but added few details beyond the specific answers. The detectives continued that line of questioning for several minutes, then switched abruptly.

Orton asked whether Jimmy had discussed the murder with his mother.

"She said something like, 'How did it go last night?' or 'What happened last night?' And I just told her it was over. That's all that was said."

"Do you love your mother?" Orton asked.

"Yes. I know I shouldn't, but I do," Jimmy said.

"Would you do anything in the world to protect her?"

"I would do anything in the world to protect my little sister. I'd give up my life for her."

"Would you do anything to protect your mother?"

"Close to it. I wouldn't lie for her."

"Are you lying now?"

"No."

"Did you ever think you were going to get caught?"

"Yeah, every night and every day," Jimmy said. "I knew I would, with my luck. That's the reason I didn't want to do it."

"Do you have a lot of bad luck?" Orton asked.

"I've had it all my life."

The courtroom sat in stunned silence as the tape

ended. Jimmy's words seemed to echo throughout
the room, leaving each person with his own feelings: sorrow, anger, or pity. But Jimmy showed no
emotion. He sat silently until everyone had left the
courtroom for the day. He was then escorted back
to his cell to await the next day's fateful meeting
with his mother.

16

"I haven't been a very good father. In a sense, I dumped my son."

—JAMES CRUMM, SR.

The soft clicks of Ed Byrne's cowboy boots against the second-floor wooden stairs were the only sounds in the empty Miami County Courthouse. It was seven A.M. on the third day of Jimmy's trial.

He walked to the defense table, took a thermos from his briefcase and poured thick, black coffee into a paper cup. Sipping his breakfast, he thought about his first witness, his key witness, Sueanne. It was important to Byrne that he maintain control over her testimony. And the evidence presented by all the other defense witnesses—psychiatrists, psychologists, and Jimmy's relatives—would revolve around her. Willingly or not, she was the foundation of his case.

Byrne had wondered for weeks whether she would appear. She had ignored his subpoenas and the judge's orders on other occasions. And if she did honor this subpoena, what type of woman would the jury see when she took the witness stand: a mother or a murderer?

Byrne had met Sueanne only once, when she had

testified at Jimmy's preliminary hearing three
months earlier. That fifteen-minute encounter was
all Byrne needed to solidify his pity for Jimmy and
his intense dislike of Sueanne.

Although Byrne had accomplished next to
nothing at that hearing—"We both just sniffed
around at each other, like a couple of dogs," he
commented later—her demeanor alone had convinced him of her involvement in the murder.
Byrne was convinced Jimmy would not have killed
the boy without Sueanne's manipulation, or as one
psychologist described it, brainwashing.

The night before, while watching the late news,
Byrne had seen Ed Hobson being interviewed by
reporters.

Blond, muscular, and wearing a gray pinstriped
suit, Ed had looked more like an attorney than a
grieving father. His look was forceful and focused as
he stared into the television cameras.

"I think it's a bunch of crap," Ed had said about
the insanity defense. "Jimmy isn't insane. I don't
know how they are going on the insanity plea. I
know he knows right from wrong. I lived with him
for about a year, and he never gave me any indication of it."

Byrne's emotions ranged from anger to disgust
and ultimately to amazement when he realized the
implications of Ed's comments.

"I thought it was the damnedest, most stupid
thing for that man to be saying," Byrne recalled
later. "It would have been greatly to Sueanne's advantage for Jimmy to be acquitted on insanity. Not
only would he go free, in a manner of speaking, but
if she were ever prosecuted, she could say: 'Look,
my sole accuser has been determined to be insane.'
It was a terrible thing for Ed to be saying."

By eight-thirty A.M. the jurors were in their seats
and anxiously awaiting Byrne's opening statement.
The attorneys, seated at their respective tables,
quietly reviewed notes and transcripts. When the

jury had been seated, Jimmy was escorted to the defense table by deputies. He sat silently at the table, his eyes trained on the floor.

"I am prepared to proceed with defense opening," Byrne told Fossey without hesitation.

Byrne placed the three-ring notebook containing his opening statement on the podium facing Fossey. Grabbing each side of the podium, he dragged it to the center of the room, where he turned to face the jury. As he did, he was startled at a glimpse of the packed courtroom. Lawyers are used to working with their backs to the gallery, and Byrne was now keenly aware that all eyes were upon him. Regaining his concentration, he looked back at the jurors. Most had their arms folded and legs crossed. They appeared guarded and skeptical.

He took a deep breath, adjusted his wire-rimmed glasses, turned toward the jury and began his opening statement.

"You have already heard the state's case, and my stipulation, so I don't have to deal with all of those factual matters that we admitted to at the outset of this trial.

"What I intend to do during the course of our defense is paint for you a portrait of the defendant. Who he is. Where he has been. And who he is now.

"During the course of our case, you will be hearing from a number of witnesses who will tell you about this young man. By the time you have heard from all the witnesses, you will have all the pieces of the puzzle, and you will see the portrait."

Byrne's voice was calm and authoritative. He had worked hard at his delivery, perfecting it in minor criminal cases where his only audience had been a few court officials and a handful of the defendant's family. But now, speaking before the largest audience of his professional life, his voice did not crack and his mouth was not dry. He confidently informed the jury about his medical witnesses, their qualifications and reasons for testifying.

"Now, from these medical witnesses, and from the family members that will testify, you are going to see certain patterns emerge," Byrne said as he walked from the podium to where Jimmy was sitting. Facing the jury, Byrne laid both hands on Jimmy's shoulders.

"The first and most critical pattern, and the one that you will hear over and over again, is the pattern of a child abandoned. You will learn that in 1971, when Jim was approximately eight years old, just shortly before his ninth birthday, his parents were divorced . . . You will learn from the testimony and evidence that his mother, his natural mother, whom you have heard so much about, Sueanne Hobson, received legal custody of Jimmy, as well as his younger sister, Suzanne.

"You will learn that for eight years, from 1971 to late 1978 or early 1979, she did not have a single contact with her son. I want you to understand right up front that it wasn't because anything prohibited her from having that contact. Jimmy was living in Kansas City. You will learn that Sueanne was here, and you will learn that there was no contact whatsoever. I mean not a Christmas card, a birthday present, a telephone call, anything.

"The doctors will tell you that if you wanted to take one simple idea to explain this young man . . . he is a picture of a boy searching for his mother.

"Jimmy went from one household to another. His mother abandoned him and his father was stuck with him. You will be hearing from Jimmy's natural father today or tomorrow. I will tell you right now, the father will admit to you that by no means was he an ideal father. In a sense, he dropped the ball, too."

Byrne, catching his breath, looked at the jury. They were listening. At least two were pushed forward in their seats, waiting for his next words. He scanned the two rows of jurors, purposely making eye contact with the two who were leaning forward in their chairs. Since the beginning of his statement, the courtroom had been deadly still. But for the whirring of two ceiling fans, Byrne's voice was the only sound.

"Before you hear from any of the other witnesses, the doctors and family members, you will hear from Jimmy's mother, Sueanne Hobson. She will be here in a few minutes, and she will be the first witness to testify.

"Let me tell you right now, she is not on my side, and I don't know what she is going to say. But you have got to see her, because she is the key that unlocks the door to understanding what was going on in Jimmy's mind when he killed his thirteen-year-old stepbrother. That is why I am a little bit scared about it. If you don't understand this woman, and if I can't make you understand over the next couple of days what impact she had on him, the psychiatric testimony isn't going to help you too much. So please watch her carefully.

"This witness tells you as much or more in her eyes and on her face as her words ever could. Watch her and listen to her, but especially watch her. When you have heard from Sueanne, and when you have heard all of the medical evidence, I am confident that you are going to be able to put the picture together. You are going to learn from Sueanne and from the doctors that this boy who was searching for a mother for eight years finally and unfortunately found his mother in 1979, because out of the blue, out of eight years of absence, Sueanne surfaced in his life. I mean she literally just popped up. She didn't come in from out of town; she had been here all along, but she suddenly and unexpectedly contacted him and said, 'Jimmy, I am your mom, and I want you to move in with me now.'

"Jimmy did move in with her because he was still

searching. He was happy when he heard from her. This is the person he had been looking for all that time, and maybe now everything would be okay. You will learn that when he moved in with her, for weeks and for months, she showered him with every kind of material thing, expensive clothes, coats, jewelry, spending money, the promise of an automobile, every kind of material thing which he hadn't had. You will learn that most of the time during those eight years, he was lucky if he had had clothes and food.

"From the time he was eight years old, when his mother left him, until he was seventeen, when she suddenly popped back up, he had thirteen different jobs. I mean jobs where he went out and paid his own way.

"Sueanne lured him into her home. She had just married Ed Hobson and was starting out a new life. She lured him into her home with the promise and reality of all those material things he never had."

Tatum, sitting behind Byrne, moved uncomfortably in his chair. He could see the look on the jurors' faces. They were interested. Byrne could see it, too.

"I think you will learn from the evidence that there was a reason why she contacted him after eight years," Byrne continued. "I am confident the evidence will show you that it wasn't because all of a sudden she had some normal parental interest in her son.

"Chris Hobson, the victim in this case, was living at home, too. At some point, for some reason, Sueanne Hobson decided that little Chris, her stepson, the natural son of her new husband, Ed Hobson, had to go."

With that statement, Tatum had had enough. He jumped to his feet.

"Judge, I am going to object to this because it doesn't go to the insanity defense," Tatum said as he nervously walked to the center of the courtroom.

"And I don't believe this is evidence that he will be able to present."

"Your Honor," Byrne said while still focusing his eyes on the jury. "It is evidence that I will be able to present. It is very, very critical evidence in the final diagnoses that were made by the doctors."

"Overruled," Fossey said without emotion or emphasis.

Byrne, returning to the podium, looked across the courtroom at the defense table where Jimmy was sitting. He hadn't moved. His eyes were still on the floor, his hands folded in front of him.

"I can't tell you why she wanted him dead," Byrne continued. "I don't know why that happened, why she decided Chris had to go.

"Neither does he," Byrne said, pointing toward the table where Jimmy was seated. "But Sueanne decided that Jimmy, her own son, whom she managed to get back into her house, would be the instrument. Sueanne would be the brains, she would come up with the idea, the method, the process—"

Tatum was again on his feet.

"Judge, I'm sorry to interrupt, and I want him to have his opening statement, but I object to him going into the mental state of Sueanne Hobson. I assume he is telling us what the psychologist and psychiatrist will tell us that Jimmy told them, but I wish it would be couched in those terms."

Byrne didn't argue Tatum's objection. He had already gone farther in his opening statement than he thought Fossey would allow. And he could tell by looking at the jury that he had planted an idea in at least a couple of jurors' minds.

Byrne went on: "Jimmy continued to live in the Hobson residence for a period of one year, from March of 1979 until just a few weeks before Chris was killed. Over this period of time, weeks or months, Jimmy was regularly and continuously subjected to the demand that Chris must be killed.

"At some point in March 1980, Jimmy moved out. Even after he moved out, his mother's demands continued. The doctors will be able to explain to you in much more comprehensive, detailed fashion than I can how these demands for Chris's murder affected Jimmy, and how they propelled him to carry through with this act.

"We know what happened on the evening of April seventeenth. I am confident when you have seen and heard all of the evidence, you will appreciate fully that Jimmy Crumm was there at the scene on April seventeenth, physically, and his hands held the shotgun, and his arms raised the shotgun, and his finger pulled the trigger, but in every sense of the word, he was not mentally responsible for the act that occurred.

"I just ask you to listen to the evidence very carefully as we are moving into the critical stage of the trial. Listen to our case, and when you have heard it all, you really will know the rest of the story."

As Byrne walked back to the defense table, the courtroom remained cloaked in silence. Many of those on the jury panel and in the audience looked toward Jimmy, who, as always, remained passive.

"At this time I believe we will take our morning recess rather than going into the first witness; that will occupy some time," Fossey said. "I will again admonish the jury during this recess that you will not discuss the case among yourselves, nor allow anyone to discuss it with you, or in your presence. If anyone attempts to do so, please advise the court."

Luckily, the judge's warning didn't apply to those in the audience. As soon as the jury had been escorted to the jury room and Fossey had left the bench, the courtroom exploded into numerous conversations. Most focused on the next witness, Sueanne.

"I can't wait to see what Sueanne looks like," one

woman said to another as they shuffled out of the
courtroom into the crowded corridors on the second floor. "What can she say?"

Everyone called Sueanne by her first name. Prosecutors, judges, defense lawyers, friends or en-
emies. Even those who didn't know her, had never
met her and didn't want to meet her, referred to her
by her first name when discussing the murder. To
almost everyone, it was simply Sueanne.

———

Jimmy and Sueanne hadn't spoken to each other
for more than a year. Now they were ten feet apart
in a room not much bigger than a walk-in closet,
and they still weren't speaking. But it wasn't exactly a face-to-face meeting.

Sueanne stood in one corner of Judge Fossey's
chambers, shielded from her son's view by her attorney, Hugh Kreamer. At Ed's urging, Sueanne had
retained Kreamer, an attorney who was a member
of the law firm Ed had used previously. Jimmy,
handcuffed and seated in a wooden chair in front of
the judge's desk, looked at the floor. His view of
Sueanne was blocked by Byrne, who sat next to
him, and a deputy who stood at his left shoulder.

Sueanne and Jimmy both were attractive, with
deep-set brown eyes, long narrow faces, pointed
chins, and sharp jawlines. It was obvious they were
related. But mother and son were now separated,
not by ten feet, but by years of estrangement.

Sueanne's attorney was the first to speak.

"Judge, my name, of course, is Hugh Kreamer. I
am here representing my client, Sueanne Hobson.
She has been subpoenaed to testify in this case and,
in fact, was put under a bond which I assume will
be lifted after her testimony.

"For the record, my client was previously
charged as a conspirator in this same case in
Johnson County. The charges were later dismissed,

apparently because there was no evidence to substantiate the charge, other than the testimony of her son.

"I told Mr. Byrne, knowing the statute of limitations on murder in the first degree continues to run forever in Kansas, that if we are going to testify in this case, it is going to have to be with certain limitations. And if we aren't going to do it with limitations, then we are going to invoke our Fifth Amendment rights against self-incrimination . . . and won't answer the questions."

Byrne, tired of listening to Kreamer's speech, looked disgustedly at Fossey.

"Could I get on the record, Judge? The parameters of my interrogation will be this: first of all, everything or anything which Sueanne may know about Jimmy in his developmental years, from the time he was born up until the time she was divorced from Jim Crumm Senior.

"The second general area: I wish to interrogate the witness on any matters which she conceded, admitted or discussed during her tape-recorded interview with police officers at the time of her arrest last year."

"No way will I ever agree to that," Kreamer said emphatically, staring at Byrne.

"We also have several objections to that," Tatum added, thumbing through a statute book.

While the lawyers argued angrily, the crowd inside the highly charged courtroom waited impatiently for a glimpse of Sueanne. The spectators' attention was focused not on the empty tables and jury box, but toward the single door leading to Judge Fossey's chambers.

Behind that closed door, the lawyers strenuously argued points and counterpoints. Fifteen minutes later Fossey had heard enough.

"Mr. Byrne, you are in a unique position with the insanity defense as far as the burden of proof is concerned," Fossey said sternly. "And I don't think it is proper to require this witness to testify to matters which may tend to show any participation or any influence on her part in the actual commission of the crime. I am limiting your interrogation to matters that bear on the defense of insanity."

Fossey's ruling elicited mixed emotions. Kreamer was satisfied. His client's rights would not be violated. Tatum viewed Sueanne as a wild card. He was still worried about what she might say. Byrne was furious.

"May I sit in the courtroom?" Kreamer asked Fossey politely. "I'll try not to participate if I can avoid it."

"You may sit in the courtroom. If you try to participate, I will take appropriate steps," a smiling Fossey said as he stood and pulled his black robe over his gray suit. "Let's proceed."

The clamor of dozens of isolated conversations ended abruptly when the door to Fossey's chambers opened. Jimmy was the first to appear, followed closely by a deputy, then Byrne and Tatum.

Jimmy kept his head down, his eyes staring forever at the floor. His hands, clasped together in front of him, were trembling. Byrne, arms folded, scanned several pages of questions he had organized in a three-ring binder. He unconsciously reached over and patted Jimmy's shoulder when Fossey banged his gavel.

"Mr. Byrne, will you call your first witness?" Fossey said.

"The defense calls Sueanne Hobson to testify."

Kreamer, his hand cupped under Sueanne's arm, guided her slowly to the witness stand. She put one hand on the bible and clutched a white, linen handkerchief in the other hand. She stood alone and erect while Fossey administered the oath.

Byrne thought Sueanne appeared calmer and more in control than she had in chambers just moments before. Like a chameleon, she had assumed a new face, a new manner. Byrne knew there would be no guilty confession from this woman. Tatum noticed the transformation as well.

He knew she had to be nervous, but it didn't show. Her gaze was straightforward. It was apparent she wasn't going to show any emotion.

Dressed in a white skirt, blouse, and jacket, Sueanne settled into the witness chair. A blue purse hung from her shoulder. She sat erect and looked at Byrne, who continued to shuffle through reports.

Tatum's brow furrowed as he nervously stroked his chin. He was uneasy. He didn't like the unknown, especially in court.

Byrne positioned the podium in the middle of the courtroom, directly between Jimmy and Sueanne. He looked at the jury to his right, then turned and looked at Sueanne.

"Would you state your full name?"

"Sueanne Hobson," she responded softly.

"Where do you live?"

"In Overland Park."

"Do you see your son in this room?"

"Yes."

"Would you point him out?"

She glanced briefly at the defense table, then quickly back to Byrne, who remained at the podium.

"He is sitting at the table by the woman in the red suit," she said matter-of-factly, pointing in the direction of the defense table her eyes still on Byrne. Jimmy didn't look up. He pretended to read something he had just written on a yellow legal pad.

"Mrs. Hobson, before today, when you walked into this courtroom, when was the last time you saw Jimmy?"

"At the preliminary."

"The preliminary hearing in February—is that right?"

"Uh-huh," Sueanne said, her voice barely audible to those in the courtroom.

"When was the last time before that that you saw him?"

"I don't know."

"Do you know what year it was?"

"In 1980."

"Was it before or after he was arrested?"

"Before."

"Do you understand that your son is sitting here charged with first-degree murder?" Byrne asked, raising his voice for emphasis.

"Yes," she said quietly.

Byrne stopped and looked down at his notes. Sueanne was flat. No emotion. That was all right, he thought. The only thing he expected the jury to get from Sueanne were her feelings, emotions, and reactions, or her lack of them.

Byrne moved to the side of the podium. He started to ask his next question when he noticed her slowly, almost imperceptibly, rock back and forth in her seat. There's no emotion on the outside, but there's a hell of a lot going on inside, Byrne thought.

"Can you tell me when it was that you first became aware that your son had been arrested and charged with first-degree murder?"

"Sometime after it happened," she said, inaudible to most of those in the courtroom, including Fossey.

"Would you pull the mike up and talk into it?" Byrne demanded.

"I can't hear you very well, either," she said, her voice rising momentarily. She seemed detached, mechanical, even indifferent.

"When did you first become aware that your son had been arrested and charged with first-degree murder?" Byrne repeated.

"Sometime last year."

"How did you become aware of it?"

"I believe a police officer told me."

"That your son had been arrested?"

"Uh-huh."

"At any time after your son was arrested in May of last year, to date, have you visited with your son in the Miami County jail?"

"No."

"Do you understand that he has been sitting down here for over a year?"

"Yes."

"Have you had any telephone contact with him?"

"No."

"Have you exchanged letters with him?"

"No. I was told I couldn't have any contact with him."

"Who told you that?"

"My mother told my daughter, who told me that his father was the only one that could visit him."

"Did you make any inquiry on your own to see if you could see or talk to him?"

"I talked to Mr. Kreamer about it."

"He advised you not to have any contact with your son?"

"I don't remember whether he advised me one way or the other."

"You never tried on your own to see him, though?"

"No."

The rocking had stopped. Sueanne was back in control. Byrne hoped the jury would understand Sueanne as he did. Her lack of feeling or emotion was extremely important in itself, he thought. After all, she was testifying at her own son's trial for murder.

An artist hired by a television station sat on the front row sketching Sueanne in chalk. The artist's busy hands were the only visible movement in the audience while Byrne continued his interrogation.

Asking questions from a prepared list, Byrne

focused on Jimmy's early life, including Sueanne's divorce from James Crumm Sr. and her decision not to take custody of Jimmy after the divorce.

"When you got your divorce, how old was Jimmy?"

"Nine."

"You specifically requested custody of Jimmy, didn't you? And that is what the court ordered?"

"Yes."

"You took Suzanne, who was five, with you, didn't you?"

"Yes."

"Did you take Jimmy with you?"

"No," she said matter-of-factly.

"Why not?"

"Because his father wanted him."

"Did you want Jimmy with you?"

"Yes."

"Did you fight your former husband over Jimmy?"

"No. But I tried to get him back several times."

"How did you do that?"

"Daddy and I tried to get him back several times," she said, her voice slightly raised for emphasis. "My parents hired private detectives to find him."

"And they couldn't find him?" Byrne asked, irritated by Sueanne's reference to her parents. He knew Sueanne hadn't spoken to her parents for several years, and was now trying to make it seem they were a close-knit family.

"Did you remain in the Kansas City area after the divorce?"

"Yes."

"And you never saw Jimmy after the divorce? You didn't see him for eight years?"

"I saw him for the first couple of years after the divorce."

"How often did you see him?"

"I don't remember," she said, sounding irritated by Byrne's persistence.

"Was it once a week, once a month, once a year?"

"I don't remember that," she snapped, her control slipping a little.

"You can't recall that at all?"

"No. The only time that I can remember right now is Suzanne's birthday and Jimmy's birthday," she said, her voice still irritated.

"So, in the first year or two after your divorce, you can think of only two occasions when you saw Jimmy?"

"Specifically, yes."

"Was it during that time or after that time that these detectives told your father they didn't know where Jimmy was?" Byrne asked sarcastically.

"After that," Sueanne responded calmly, regaining control.

"Did you ever go to your former husband and say, 'Look, I have custody; he is going to stay with me.'"

"No."

"Why not?"

"I don't know. I just didn't . . ."

"You said you wanted him, didn't you?" Byrne questioned, walking toward the witness stand.

"After I lost track of him I . . ." Sueanne trailed off. She started to rock back and forth in her seat again.

Sensing his client was in trouble, Kreamer jumped to his feet.

"Your Honor," Kreamer said, intentionally trying to disrupt Byrne's line of questioning, "this is way out of the parameters of what we agreed he could ask her."

"Judge, I think it goes very much to her feelings toward her son," Byrne argued.

"I really feel you have inquired into the subject sufficiently, Mr. Byrne," Fossey said sternly. "Proceed."

Byrne walked back to the podium and looked at his notes. He reviewed several questions he had already asked. He was still angered by Sueanne's reference to hiring detectives to look for her son. He didn't believe it was true, but he also knew he couldn't prove that to the jury.

Byrne looked up from his notes to Sueanne, posing quietly and erect in the witness chair. Her eyes never left Byrne's face. She still had not looked directly at her son. Byrne decided to go back to the issue of the detectives.

"So it was at the end of 1972 that you lost track of him; is that right?"

"Uh-huh," Sueanne said quietly.

"When was the next time that you gained track of him or knew where he was?"

"In August 1978."

"Six years later?"

"Uh-huh."

"Did you or your daddy have these detectives out searching for Jimmy for six years?"

"No."

"When did you stop having detectives search for your son?"

"I don't know how long they looked."

"During that six-year period that you didn't see your son, did you think he just vanished off the face of the earth? Or did you think he was right here in Kansas City? What was going on in your mind?"

"I didn't know where he was."

"Did you care?"

"Yes. My parents and I talked about it. I don't know how much contact they had with detectives. And I don't remember for how long they looked."

"You didn't know that Jimmy was living with his aunt and uncle in Prairie Village?" Byrne asked, emphasizing Prairie Village, a suburb of Kansas City.

"No."

"Your parents didn't know that?"

"I don't know whether they knew that or not."

Byrne walked to the side of the podium. His right hand caressed his chin as he pondered his next question.

"Who are your parents?"

"Mr. and Mrs. Sallee."

"Were you in regular touch with them during this six-year period of time?"

"Not during the entire period of time, no," Sueanne said. "I was not in touch with them between 'seventy-four and 'seventy-eight."

"At any time, before 1974 or after 1978, did they tell you they were seeing Jimmy regularly and knew where he was living?"

"No."

"But, apparently, you now know that he was seeing them . . ." Byrne said as Tatum rose from his chair.

"I object to Mr. Byrne's statements unless he wants to testify."

"Sustained," Fossey ruled before Byrne could argue. Tatum's objection broke the tension. It gave everyone in the courtroom, including Sueanne, a chance to catch their breaths, to momentarily relax before Byrne's next assault.

Byrne walked to the defense table, where he picked up a few sheets of yellow legal paper full of notes. Jimmy, alternately scribbling on a tablet and looking at the floor during his mother's testimony, did not look up when Byrne approached the table. After the first few hearings, Byrne had learned not to expect much emotion from Jimmy. He laughed as rarely as he cried. Byrne always had the feeling that Jimmy was there in body only.

Byrne turned and walked back to the podium, again concentrating on Sueanne.

"How was it that Jimmy resurfaced in your life in 1978?" Byrne asked.

"My daughter, Suzanne, found out where he was."

"How?"

"I don't remember. I think she called him."

"How old was your daughter when she did that?" Byrne asked, feigning amazement at Suzanne's ability to find her brother.

"At that time, I think she was twelve," Sueanne said, ignoring Byrne's facial expressions.

"Do you remember whether that was by some accidental or coincidental occurrence, or did she just open a telephone book and find his name there?"

"I don't know how she found him."

Despite Byrne's attempt to anger her, Sueanne showed no emotion, no sensitivity to the tragedy her family was involved in. Her answers were systematic, mechanical, devoid of parental instincts. Byrne was depressed. How could a mother sit there, so matter-of-factly, and witness the ruination of her son's life? he wondered.

"You invited your son to your house after Suzanne located him?"

"Yes. He started spending weekends with us."

"How old was he when he resurfaced?" Byrne asked.

"Sixteen."

"You probably didn't know how old he was when he showed up, did you?" Byrne asked, in an angry, condescending tone.

"Yes," Sueanne responded defensively.

"After that absence of seven years, were you able to develop a relationship of some sort with your sixteen-year-old son?"

"Yes."

"Can you describe for me what kind of things you did to patch up that long absence, what kinds of things you would do together, what kind of relationship you had?"

"As a family?"

"No, you and Jimmy, as mother and son."

"We talked and we went places together. I answered every question he asked."

"Did he have a lot of questions about the fact that you two had not seen each other or had any contact for seven years? Did that seem to be a big problem for him?"

"Uh-huh. Yes."

While Byrne paused to adjust his glasses, Sueanne looked toward the audience where her minister, John Adams, was sitting. Adams, a pastor at the Leawood Baptist Church, had driven Sueanne to the hearing because Ed had had to work. Sueanne smiled when Adams gave her a thumbs-up sign.

Byrne glanced at the jury. Several jurors were sitting forward in their seats, striving to hear every word Sueanne said. Other jurors seemed relaxed, as if they were being entertained.

"When Jimmy moved into your home with you and Ed in early 1979, how was he situated, materially speaking? Did he have any possessions, clothes, shoes, sporting equipment, whatever?"

"He had very little clothing," Sueanne said, her voice again fading to almost a whisper. "It was old, ratty-looking. And he didn't have a lot of possessions.

"The first thing Ed and I discussed was the fact that he didn't have any clothing. We went out right away and started buying him—he didn't even have any underwear—clothes."

"Were there any problems between the children after Jimmy moved in?" Byrne asked, setting up his next line of questioning.

"I think jealousy was always there. I think all children are jealous of one another," said Sueanne, an only child.

"When you and Ed went out and bought him

things and acquired material possessions for him, were you in a sense trying to make up for your absence all those years?"

"Probably."

"You thought you would make up with these material things?"

"Jimmy had told us that he got very little, and that anything he did have, his grandparents bought him, and neither Ed nor I could stand to see him the way it was."

Byrne continued to quiz her about the year Jimmy had lived with the family in Overland Park and why he had eventually moved into an apartment.

"He got into some trouble over some stolen credit cards," she told Byrne. "That is when he left the house."

"Did you kick him out?"

"No. He just left on his own."

"Do you know that Chris Hobson disappeared on April seventeenth?"

"Yes."

"How many times did you see Jimmy between March 1980, when he moved out of your home, and April seventeenth, when Chris disappeared?"

"Oh, at least a couple of times a week . . . He would come over to our home. Or I would go over to his apartment."

"Did you have an occasion to see your son after April seventeenth and before Chris's body was found on May fourth?"

"I don't know whether I did or not."

Byrne stopped and looked at Sueanne, then turned and walked around the defense table to where Jimmy was sitting. Resting his hands on Jimmy's shoulders, Byrne was startled when he looked down at the yellow legal pad Jimmy had been scribbling on. Amidst the doodling, Jimmy had scrawled: "Oh God, please open up the floor and let me out of here."

Byrne looked back at Sueanne. He was unconsciously rubbing Jimmy's shoulders.

"Mrs. Hobson, before I release you from the subpoena today, let me ask you, do you love your son?"

"Yes," Sueanne said firmly, but without passion.

"Before you get off the witness stand, is there anything you want to say to the court and jury in his behalf?"

Tatum was on his feet before Sueanne could answer.

"I am going to object to that as improper questioning, hearsay and leading."

"Sustain," Fossey said firmly.

Byrne continued to rub Jimmy's neck. He stared at Sueanne. He couldn't believe her composure. When he had asked the question, Sueanne had looked through Jimmy to Byrne without the slightest expression—like she was looking at a side of beef, Byrne thought.

He walked back to the podium and collected his notes.

"That is all I have, Your Honor," he said, turning his back on Sueanne.

Byrne sat down at the defense table and sighed. He wasn't satisfied with her testimony, but he had accomplished what he wanted. He hoped the jury saw Sueanne as he did: self-possessed, and so controlled she failed to convey any compassion for her son.

"You may cross-examine," Fossey told Tatum as the tall, bearded prosecutor walked to the podium. Tatum was relieved. He didn't think Sueanne had helped or hurt Byrne. He'd had no control when Byrne was asking the questions, but he did now.

Sueanne sighed and braced herself for Tatum's cross-examination. She had met him once before, when she was charged with conspiracy to commit murder in Johnson County.

Tatum centered his questions on testimony that

would help him attempt to prove that Jimmy was legally sane when Chris was killed.

Sueanne testified that Jimmy had always dressed neatly, had not changed his behavior drastically, seemed lucid and was cooperative in the days and weeks before Chris's murder.

"When he was living with you, did you detect a serious drinking or drug use problem during that time?" Tatum asked.

"He had a drug problem," Sueanne responded disgustedly. "We found drugs in his room on several occasions."

"During this time, did he have any duties or responsibilities around the house?"

"Oh, yes," she said as she nodded. "He had to keep his room clean, he had to clean his bathroom, he had to help clear the table, and sometimes he had to set the table for dinner."

"Thank you," Tatum said politely. "I have no further questions."

Kreamer walked to the front of the courtroom, where he talked briefly with Fossey, then turned and motioned to Sueanne.

"Step down, Sueanne, it's over," Kreamer said, reaching for Sueanne's hand. She stood up, straightened her coat and placed the handkerchief in her purse. She remained stoic as she left the courtroom through a side door.

Jimmy glanced briefly at his mother when she left the courtroom, then shifted his eyes back to his scribblings. Those in the courtroom were drained. They had waited anxiously during the forty-five minute testimony for Sueanne to do something dramatic or make a startling revelation. Instead they had seen a woman devoid of any outward emotion.

The spectators sat together wearily waiting for the next witness.

Then, without warning, the silence of the courtroom was rocked by bloodcurdling screams, the shrieks of a hysterical woman. There was no doubt in the courtroom who the woman was. Moments after leaving the courtroom, Sueanne had broken down. She was on the stairs stomping her feet and screaming angrily, hysterically. Sueanne had finally given them what they wanted, what they expected.

Byrne smiled.

———

Jimmy's father was the next witness. Unlike Sueanne, James Crumm Sr. carried his emotions on his sleeve. A gruff, rugged man, Crumm often choked back tears as he described his ten-year marriage to Sueanne and their subsequent divorce. He explained how the courts had awarded custody of their two children, nine-year-old Jimmy and five-year-old Suzanne, to Sueanne.

"What happened to the children after you were divorced?" Byrne asked.

"Suzanne went with her and Jimmy stayed with me. She didn't want Jimmy. She told me before the divorce that she didn't want him, that he was to stay with me. But she did want legal custody of him."

Crumm said his drinking had increased and Jimmy was passed among relatives for several years. Choking back tears, Crumm said he had left Jimmy with relatives because he didn't think he was fit to be raising a child. Unlike Sueanne, who tried to avoid showing any emotion, Crumm was open and honest on the witness stand, trying desperately to answer the questions. He offered no alibis for the way he had treated his son, only remorse.

"I was having a hard time dealing with the divorce and I was drinking too much—I just couldn't handle it," he said, looking sorrowfully at Jimmy, who also had tears in his eyes.

He said Jimmy was shuffled between aunts and uncles for several years. Occasionally Crumm would allow Jimmy to live with him, only to return him to relatives when Crumm's drinking or financial problems became too great. Crumm admitted that the lifestyle was horribly confusing to a young boy. He said Jimmy often appeared hurt by the constant upheaval, but never complained.

Crumm said Jimmy rarely, if ever, saw his mother from 1971 to 1979. Nor did Crumm see his daughter, Suzanne. Crumm said Jimmy re-established contact with his mother after Suzanne called him on the telephone. He said the meeting a few weeks later between the four—Sueanne, Crumm, and their two children—was sad.

"It was like four strangers meeting for the first time," he said. "Nobody knew anybody, really."

Crumm said Suzanne's telephone call started a string of events that eventually led to Jimmy moving to Overland Park to live with his mother and her new husband, Ed. Crumm testified that he warned his son not to move. He told him she was the same woman who had abandoned him years before.

As Crumm testified, Jimmy began to weep. At first his sobs were silent, apparent only by a sudden surging of his shoulders. But as his father continued to detail Jimmy's young life, the boy became visibly shaken. For the first time in the trial, Jimmy began to weep openly, laying his head on the table to muffle the sounds.

"I haven't been a very good father," he voluntarily admitted. "In a sense, I dumped my son."

When he left the witness stand, Crumm walked to the defense table where he and Jimmy embraced.

"I love you, son," he whispered.

After a few minutes' recess, Byrne called Jimmy's aunt, Dorothy Reffitt. A large, matronly woman with several children of her own, it was imme-

17

"To Jimmy, Sueanne was an extremely powerful, omnipotent woman who controlled everything and everyone."

—A PSYCHOLOGIST WHO EXAMINED JIMMY

During the next three days, the jury heard eight hours of testimony from the five expert witnesses. Their testimony was tedious and conflicting. Byrne and Tatum each tried to fight their way through the contradictory testimony. All five experts did agree that Jimmy was a confused boy who was driven to murder by a mother he loved and feared at the same time, and a woman he thought was the most powerful person in the world.

Byrne's first witness was Dr. Alan Felthous, a staff psychiatrist at the Menninger Foundation in Topeka. During four hours on the witness stand Wednesday afternoon, the articulate but understated Felthous detailed the history of Jimmy's life as it was related to him by Jimmy and his father. Felthous said he had examined Jimmy during a five-day stay at Menninger's approximately three months after the killing.

In a narrative form, only occasionally interrupted by a Byrne question or a Tatum objection,

Felthous described three specifics of Jimmy's troubled life: his life with Sueanne from birth to nine years old; being shuttled among relatives until he was 17; and his return to his mother's home and dominance during his senior year of high school.

Felthouse said Jimmy was born prematurely and was required to use legs casts, then braces, and finally corrective shoes in his early years. He also had speech difficulties. The problems, both physical and mental, caused Jimmy to have nightmares and to talk in his sleep, and to feel, at a very early age, like an outcast.

"He told me his mother was ashamed to take him out in public because of his deformities," Felthous explained.

Jimmy was also diagnosed as a hyperactive child and given the drug Ritalin to slow him down. Other problems also developed. Sueanne was beginning to physically abuse him. He became terrified of his mother.

"Jim recalls that she was a very emotional, angry, and powerful woman," Felthous said. "He said nobody ever defied his mother; that she always won every argument by intimidation . . . He recalled that she frequently screamed at him and slapped him. On one occasion she struck and kicked him, and in the process of trying to get away from her, his left elbow was broken. That was when he was in the second grade."

Although Sueanne was abusive, Jimmy felt tied to her, Felthous said. It was the beginning of a love/hate relationship for him.

As an example of Jimmy's mixed emotions about his mother, Felthous explained how Jimmy described his parents' divorce. "He recalls his mother saying, 'Do you want to live with me or your father?' And he said, 'I would rather live with my father.' And she took her daughter and left."

Felthous said Jimmy was then shuffled among

several relatives and was unable to develop a sense of consistency or continuity in his life.

Despite the shuffling—at least four different families in eight years—Jimmy was developing some good traits along with the bad ones, he told the court.

"He did some very constructive things," Felthous said. "He was involved in Little League baseball, Boy Scouts, even aspiring for the Eagle rank. He liked photography. But there were also signs of turmoil. He drank excessively. His drinking spanned his adolescent years. He developed signs of tolerance. Jimmy estimated that he consumed between a six-pack and/or a fifth of scotch daily."

At the same time Jimmy was drinking heavily, he was also working feverishly. He had several jobs, including assistant manager at a local gas station for about two years. But the more he tried to straighten his life out, the more confused he became, Felthous explained. He said Jimmy felt directionless, powerless, and unloved.

Then, when Jimmy was seventeen, Suzanne, his thirteen-year-old sister, called him. They talked and he was eventually reunited with his mother, the woman who virtually had abandoned him.

"According to Jimmy, his mother invited him to live with her and offered him some material inducements," Felthous explained. "Jimmy felt he would be living on a higher standard. He would have a nice home, nice clothes, perhaps a sports car, a swimming pool—the good life by material standards. He attached a lot of importance to material things. My impression is that he also felt [that by moving into her home] he would at last gain the acceptance of his mother."

Felthous said Jimmy also believed that his mother had changed.

"He understood that his mother had undergone considerable psychotherapy herself, and he believed that she was probably more stable emotionally and that their relationship would have a better chance of success."

The happiness and positive attitude that guided Jimmy into that relationship lasted only a few weeks. Sueanne grew domineering and abusive. At first her anger was directed only at Jimmy. Then, Felthous said, Jimmy saw his mother's ire slowly turn from him toward Chris.

"Apparently, Chris was something of a scapegoat for the family," Felthous explained. "From what Jimmy said, his mother had a very strong negative emotional reaction to Chris.

"Jim said his mother complained to him that Chris was spreading scandalous rumors about Suzanne at school, that Chris had struck Sueanne, although Jimmy wasn't sure it occurred . . . and that Chris was spreading scandals about her. His mother also told him that Chris was telling people she was having men in the house, and that Chris told his stepfather about this."

"Let me just stop you there," Byrne interrupted. "Did Jimmy tell you he believed those things were happening?"

"Sueanne was complaining to him that these things were happening," Felthous said. "But Jimmy said he was not aware of these kinds of problems. He said Chris may have stopped up the bathroom sink and caused some minor flooding, but other than that, he didn't really know Chris was actually causing any of these problems."

"How did Jim report his own personal relationship with Chris?" Byrne asked.

"From what he said, it sounds like they had virtually no relationship whatsoever. Even though they lived under the same roof, they had virtually no contact. My impression of Jimmy is that he seemed pretty indifferent to Chris."

Felthous said that although Jimmy didn't express any anger toward Chris, he believed there was some hostility between Jimmy and Chris because Jimmy thought that Chris had "narked" on him about the stolen credit cards.

Problems continued to increase in the Hobson home, Felthous explained, especially between Chris and Sueanne. Felthous said that Jimmy told him that as time passed, he saw his mother grow more impatient with Chris. She talked of sending him to a military school. She fed him at different times than the rest of the family.

"Jimmy said his mother attempted to poison Chris on a couple of occasions. Once she put six Quaaludes in his ice cream, and once she put cocaine on a stick of gum."

As time passed, Jimmy said Sueanne spent more and more time alone.

"Sueanne would lock her bedroom door as though she was trying to keep herself safely away from Chris."

Felthous said that Jimmy told him things started to unravel in late 1979 and early 1980. For a variety of reasons, he moved out of the family home and into an apartment. However, he continued to see his mother.

"He said she visited him at his apartment every other day. Whenever she visited, she asked him to do something about Chris, and by that, he understood that she was asking him to kill Chris. He said his mother began carrying a torque tool for protection from Chris.

"Jim thought his mother was paranoid about Chris, but said he couldn't tell her or his stepfather because Sueanne was so powerful she would win any argument."

Felthous said Jimmy told him his mother's visits increased, along with her overriding desire to be rid of Chris.

"At one point she told him: 'After all the things I

have done for you, you can't do this one thing for me?'"

"Meaning what?" Byrne asked.

"Jimmy thought it meant killing Chris. He told me she offered to buy him a sports car if he would do it. She also threatened him, telling him she would turn him in to authorities for breaking probation by moving out of the family's residence. He had been charged with using stolen credit cards and he was on probation."

Felthous said Jimmy told him Sueanne continued to apply daily pressure, often visiting him at his apartment to discuss Chris.

"Under this pressure, he felt like he had to do something," Felthous added. "He said he tried to put her off, but eventually it got to the point where he felt he couldn't put her off any longer. He said that the most important thing was getting her off his back, even more important than the inducement of a sports car. So eventually he approached a friend named Paul, whom he identified as a kind of rough fellow who might be capable of doing something like killing his stepbrother."

Felthous told the jury of Jimmy's description of Chris's murder, including the fact that Jimmy told him he didn't actually shoot him.

"He told me he shot away, into the woods."

Felthous said psychological testing had shown that Jimmy was in touch with reality, showing no signs of psychosis. He said Jimmy's IQ was in the bright-normal range, between 117 and 118.

"What we found on some of the tests was that Jimmy has a very passive, impressionistic way of thinking," Felthous explained. "He does not think about things critically and creatively. He does not have a good sense of who he is, where he is going in life, or what he wants to become. He does not have a good sense of values. His sense of himself is very fragmented.

Throughout the interviews and testing, Felthous said, Jimmy showed a preoccupation with wealth and power.

"He put a lot of emphasis on that," he said. "In other words, if he saw a person who he thought was powerful and wealthy, he admired that, and wanted to curry favor with that person. But at the same time, he was easily threatened by it.

"He doesn't have a good sense of himself as a man, either. He doesn't really see himself as very male or female, but more of a weird misfit."

Felthous said Jimmy knew the killing was wrong, but didn't have the mental capacity to fully appreciate the consequences of his acts. Although Felthous refused to say whether he believed Jimmy was legally insane at the time of the killing, he did say the boy was suffering from mental disorders relating to his childhood.

During cross-examination Tatum again questioned Felthous on the legal issue of insanity. Again Felthous refused to be specific.

"I want to be as helpful as I can," Felthous replied. "But I don't want to give a yes or no answer to that question, which has legal and moral implications. The ultimate decision as to whether or not he knew right from wrong, I will leave to the jury."

Byrne's next witness, Dr. Charles Welsh, a psychologist and Presbyterian minister, was as adamant in his belief as Felthous was noncommittal.

Welsh told the jury that Jimmy was criminally insane at the time of the killing. He said the boy was suffering from major depression with psychotic overtones and had been "drifting in and out of reality right here in the courtroom."

During the trial, Jimmy scribbled incessantly on a legal tablet, rarely looking up during testimony, or showing any emotion. Welsh said the scribblings, which had been introduced as evidence, clearly indicated "personality disintegration right here on the spot."

During his two hours on the witness stand, he testified that Jimmy had been brainwashed by Sueanne into believing Chris should be killed. He said Jimmy was coerced into the killing and was not in control at the time the murder occurred.

"When I first met Jimmy, the question in my mind was not who loaded and fired the gun killing Chris," he said. "But who loaded and fired Jimmy Crumm."

Welsh said the answer clearly was his mother, Sueanne. He said she would lavish gifts on him, such as buying him sixty pairs of slacks when he first moved in with them, and then, without warning, she would turn on him. "The giving and withdrawing of affection, the tension, the material goods, those kinds of things were a way of developing and maintaining control over him."

Welsh said that as Sueanne continued to pressure Jimmy into killing Chris, the boy became more confused, unable to distinguish right from wrong. Welsh said Jimmy didn't want to go through with the crime, but eventually did so because of his desire to please his mother.

"Jimmy is not a leader," he said. "He is not a plotter and a schemer. He is a follower, and is much more likely to be the kind of person who could only successfully carry something off at the direction of and in participation with someone else."

During cross-examination by Tatum, Welsh said Jimmy may have appeared normal before, during, and after the killing, but that was not an indication that he knew right from wrong, or that he was legally sane at the time of the killing.

"He knew what he believed was right," Welsh said. "Not what we know is right. In that sense, he did not know right from wrong."

Byrne's third and final witness, Dr. Jan Roosa, a

clinical psychologist for almost thirty years, also agreed that Jimmy was unable to determine right from wrong at the time of the killing. "Jimmy is a rather disorganized young man, a man very fearful of what other people might think, extremely self-critical.

"He blames himself for his mother's rejection. If something hadn't been wrong with him, or if he had been a better person, she would have stayed around."

Roosa said when he returned to live with her "she continued to talk to him [about killing Chris]. It was constant. Not only did he believe he had to do it, he also believed he owed it to her. He wanted to please her. He was hoping that by doing this for her, he could somehow gain her acceptance, that she would become the mother he really wanted. It became the predominant thing on his mind."

Byrne was satisfied. He had achieved what he had hoped. Although not all three of his witnesses agreed that Jimmy was legally insane, they did provide the jury with a portrait of a hopeless child, longing for the love and acceptance of a mother who had abandoned him years before.

Now it was Tatum's turn. Throughout the cross-examination of Byrne's witnesses, Tatum had continually asserted that Jimmy was sane. He pointed to Jimmy's burying the body, dismantling the gun, losing thirty-five pounds because of anxiety over the killing, and lying to police as examples of a person who knew it was wrong to kill.

The two witnesses that Tatum called, Dr. Gerald Vandenberg, a psychologist, and Dr. Charles Glazzard, a psychiatrist, both agreed that those actions were indications that Jimmy wasn't psychotic and knew right from wrong. Although they both agreed that Jimmy was the victim of a horrific childhood, they discounted Welsh's theories that Jimmy was out of touch with reality.

"At the time of the crime, he was definitely able to understand the nature and quality of the act," Dr. Vandenberg said. "I absolutely do not agree with [Dr. Welsh's theories]. There is depression, but it is not of psychotic proportions. Jimmy does not lose contact with reality. Mr. Crumm is not, nor has he ever been, psychotic. He is depressed."

As Tatum had expected, Dr. Glazzard agreed.

"I think the words right and wrong mean several things," he explained. "There are moral meanings and legal meanings. In both of these meanings, I think Mr. Crumm did understand the difference between right and wrong.

"For example, when talking about his mother allegedly encouraging him to kill his brother, he said, 'I continued to put her off. I thought she was not right. I have got to leave her to get her off my ass.' He also said, 'I never was convinced I would do it. I backed out a thousand times. I told Paul it was obvious I could not do it. I knew it was wrong when I went down to kill my brother.'

"Following the murder, he immediately threw down the gun, proceeded to cover the body so it could not be found. And, on the night of his arrest, he felt relieved. He said he was sorry that he did it."

———

The jurors' faces were solemn as they walked back into the hot, overcrowded courtroom Friday afternoon to hear closing arguments. It was the fifth and final day of the trial. The smiles, pleasantries, and other courtesies they had extended to each other during the first few days of the trial were gone. The gravity of their duties now weighed heavily, almost overwhelmingly, on them. Each juror sat in stony silence, waiting for instructions from Judge Fossey.

Jimmy appeared weary and uninterested. He sat slumped forward in his chair, his elbows resting on the table. The past few days his life had been retold through the eyes of family, friends, and experts. He had heard his own voice on tape detailing the killing. Moments before walking into the courtroom for final arguments, Jimmy had only one request. "Let's just get this over with," he told Byrne. "Whatever happens, happens. I just want out of here."

As Fossey began to read the instructions that would guide the jury in its deliberations, members of Jimmy's family in the first two rows behind the railing began to cry. Jimmy's father sat in the front row, clutching his sister's hand. Others, not related to Jimmy or his family, could also be seen dabbing handkerchiefs against their eyes. The scene wasn't lost on Tatum. It was obvious that sympathy for Jimmy was running high. Tatum felt it was his responsibility to make the jury understand that their sympathy for Jimmy or hatred for Sueanne should not color their judgment. Under the law, Jimmy was responsible for Chris's death and must be held accountable.

Tatum also noticed something else that made him sad. Unlike other murder cases he had prosecuted, there were few relatives of the victim there. Ed was not there nor, of course, was Sueanne.

Each side had agreed to forty-minute closings. Belling would speak for twenty minutes—the first half of the state's allotment—followed by Byrne's forty minutes, then Tatum would give the remaining twenty minutes of the state's time.

Belling rose from his seat, his hands visibly shaking as he carried his handwritten statement to the podium. It was obviously his first closing argument. His voice cracked. He lost his place in his prepared speech and he repeatedly stumbled over words and phrases. But he got the job done. At Tatum's request, Belling spent most of his twenty minutes reviewing the testimony and what importance should be given to that testimony. At the end of Belling's twenty minutes, Tatum quietly sighed. The state's case was still intact.

As soon as Belling had finished, Byrne jumped from his seat and walked briskly to the podium. He had worked on his closing the night before, and unlike Belling, his speech would be spontaneous, from the heart. Jimmy's life had consumed him for months. Byrne was as confident as Belling had been nervous.

"It strikes me as kind of ironical that Jimmy is right now where he has been all his life," Byrne told the jury. "This is judgment day, and you twelve jurors are strangers to him. And in a very real sense, that is the way he has spent most of his life: alone in the presence of strangers."

Byrne was intense, emotional, as he strode around the courtroom, stopping behind Jimmy for effect, then moving back to the podium to make another point. He was articulate, animated, compassionate.

"The ultimate question that you have to decide is whether Jimmy was insane at the time Chris Hobson was killed," he said. "The prosecutors say, 'Nobody stood behind him and pointed a gun at him and forced him to do this.' How true that is. Nobody did. The prosecutor wants you to look at this as a black-and-white issue. But it's not that simple. If it was, we wouldn't be here.

"You heard one doctor ask the question: 'Who loaded and fired Jimmy Crumm?' I hope you know the answer now. It was Sueanne Hobson. In a very real sense, Sueanne Hobson destroyed three lives that night.

"This is the obvious one," Byrne said, pointing to a picture of Chris. "But no matter what your verdict is, she destroyed the life of that boy right there"—pointing toward Jimmy—"and she destroyed the life of another seventeen-year-old boy [Paul Sorrentino] who has been sitting over in that jail awaiting his trial. What has happened to Jimmy is, in a sense, worse than what happened to Chris Hobson."

Byrne was emotional. He stopped for a moment at the podium, trying to regain his thoughts. The courtroom was silent. Those squeezed into every corner seemed to be breathing in unison, taking deep breaths only when Byrne paused. Outside the courtroom, people jammed their ears to the glass doors, yearning to hear what was being said.

Byrne stood behind Jimmy, resting his hands on his shoulders.

"Before you walk out of this courtroom, take a good hard look at this boy," he told the jury. "A prosecutor told you when this trial began Monday that he would show you a bloodthirsty killing and a brutal criminal. Before you begin your deliberations, you ask yourself if this kid is a brutal killer.

"Do something for him that nobody else has ever done, not his mother, not his father, not anybody in his family. Give him an identity. Give him a starting point. Give him a chance to become something and somebody someday."

Byrne stood, looking at the jury. His eyes were moist. He continued to clutch Jimmy's shoulders, trying to maintain his composure. "Thank you," he finally said.

If they had taken a vote then, the verdict probably would have been not guilty. There were few dry eyes. But the case wasn't over. It was now Tatum's turn.

He walked quietly, solemnly to the podium. He was dignified, stern. The son of a minister, he was full of compassion, but also indignation that Chris had been killed. He summoned his years of experience as a prosecutor. Like Byrne, this was the biggest case of his life, too.

While Byrne was emotional, Tatum was methodical and level-headed. His statement was a subtle combination of preaching and teaching. He had to peel away the sympathy for Jimmy, focusing the jury on the brutal fact that Chris had been killed. The case, at least for the last three days, had centered almost completely on Jimmy and Sueanne. Chris had been forgotten. Tatum's goal was to bring that boy back to life in the eyes of the jury. But first he attacked the defense's case.

"This whole insanity defense can really be summed up as two things: First, it is a sympathy defense for Jimmy Crumm," he said. Byrne jumped to his feet.

"I object, Your Honor," Byrne said angrily. "An insanity defense is a defense which is recognized in this state, and I move to strike that comment."

"So ordered," Fossey said without additional comment.

"Ladies and gentleman, you evaluate the comments made by Ed Byrne and see if they go to insanity or sympathy," Tatum said without missing a beat.

"The second phase of his defense is that he has tried Sueanne Hobson in front of you. I really don't object to that, but we are here to try Jim Crumm."

Tatum explained that it might be difficult for the jury to understand why Sueanne Hobson could "walk into this courtroom and walk back out" a free person, while Jimmy was being tried for the murder. He told them each case must be "considered at the proper time," asking them to believe that justice would be served.

Then he stopped, took a deep breath and changed directions. He walked over to the table where the exhibits were stacked. He picked up Chris's picture, looking at it for a few moments. Then he turned to the jury.

"We have talked so much about Jim Crumm that we have almost forgotten Chris Hobson," Tatum said, holding Chris's wallet in one hand and his picture in the other. "This is all that is left of Chris Hobson and his life. It's been just over a year since he was killed. We have been thinking all week about Jimmy, his problems and his hard life. Maybe we ought to think about Chris.

"Imagine him out there on this lonely, deserted spot, digging his own grave and seeing them get those guns, seeing Jimmy load that gun. And then being told to lie down in that grave.

"Sometime, right in there, the cold realization of what was going to happen to him must have broken over him like a wave of panic. Then James Crumm shot him, tearing into his jaw, chest, and head. James said he heard him whimpering, that he tried to sit up."

Tatum turned and stared at Jimmy, who still hadn't looked up from the floor.

"You know, I have got to believe that when that dirt settled around Chris's body and the warmth started going out of his body, James Crumm and Paul Sorrentino had no idea they would ever get caught. But an incredible quirk of fate occurred two weeks and two days later when two boys discovered the decomposed body out in that deserted countryside. James Crumm should pay for his participation.

"I have seen tears shed for James Crumm in this courtroom all week. I have seen him cry. But Chris Hobson will never laugh or cry again or do all those things that a boy does growing up. There is no noise of doctors' voices coming around to tell you he had a hard life and he didn't know what he was doing. All I hear is the sound of his casket being lowered into the ground. Who is going to cry for Chris Hobson?"

Tatum, still holding Chris's picture in front of the jury, paused for a moment, caught in his own thoughts.

"I ask you to convict James Crumm of first-degree murder. Thank you."

Tatum walked quietly back to his seat as Byrne leaned over and hugged Jimmy.

"It's over now," Byrne said. "All we can do now is wait."

———

Everyone expected lengthy deliberations. They were wrong. Just as they were settling in for the long wait, the buzzer rang from the jury room. They had a verdict. It had been less than two hours. Word spread rapidly, and within minutes the courtroom was again bulging at its two doors.

Jimmy, wearing blue jeans, sneakers, and a pullover shirt, stood next to Byrne as the foreman, Darrell Williamson, announced the verdict.

"Guilty of first-degree murder," was the simple declaration.

The courtroom exploded into a combination of shrieks and sobs. Everyone looked to Jimmy for his reaction. There was none. He shook Byrne's hand, then turned and embraced his father while two deputies looked on. He was taken back to the Miami County jail to await sentencing the next month. At Byrne's request, he was placed under a twenty-four-hour suicide watch.

Byrne left the courtroom immediately. He was angry the jury had not taken more time to deliberate. During questioning by reporters on the courthouse steps, an angry, defiant Byrne said it was unlikely Jimmy would ever testify against his mother.

"And they can't convict her without his testimony," he declared.

Byrne seemed confused by the jury's quick verdict, telling reporters the jury "couldn't have given fair consideration to all the facts. There was too much evidence to consider in such a brief time."

Williamson, the jury foreman, disagreed. As he hastily left the courthouse, he told reporters that all the evidence had been considered and that two votes were taken.

"There were two votes taken because there was a question of sympathy," he said. "Most of the jurors felt sorry for the boy being an instrument of his mother. I imagine most of the jurors would rather have seen his mother on trial. But we believed that he was guilty of murder under our law."

Another juror agreed.

"It's a shame to say, but I don't think he would have done it if his mother hadn't told him to," he said. "His mother was the ringleader. If she isn't charged, someone is wacky."

Across the courtyard, James Crumm Sr. was collapsed against the side of the county jail, openly weeping.

"I have failed him," he kept sobbing.

18

"Prosecutors had a chance to do something for Jimmy, but they failed him, just like everyone else in his life had failed him."

—ED BYRNE

Dennis Moore could feel the heat. The publicity generated by Jimmy's trial in Paola, specifically the jurors' public comments that Sueanne was the ringleader and should be charged with the murder, had created an enormous interest in Sueanne's fate. Moore was inundated with angry letters and telephone calls demanding that Sueanne be brought to justice. The public wanted to know when Sueanne would be arrested.

As the pressure mounted, Moore considered every possible alternative. However, little had changed in the year since he had decided to dismiss the murder charges against Sueanne. He still had a strong circumstantial case against her. He had her initial statement to police, with all its inconsistencies, and he had Suzanne's statements. But they still needed at least one of the boys to testify against her. Unfortunately, neither was available. Although Jimmy had been convicted of the murder, he was not willing to testify.

"He still feels a loyalty to his mother," Byrne explained. "It is a difficult, love-hate relationship."

Paul was another matter. His trial was still a few weeks away. Although Paul's attorneys were publicly preparing for trial—they had requested and received a change of venue from Paola to Fort Scott, miles away—Moore believed there was still a chance for a plea. Even with a change of venue, prosecutors believed Paul had little chance of acquittal. Police had him on tape, discussing the murder with Leila Anderson, and the tape's admissibility in court was not in question.

Unlike Jimmy, Paul had no insanity defense. Psychiatrists had testified that Paul was not suffering any significant mental diseases that would have impaired his ability to understand right from wrong. Yes, he had psychological problems, but none that reached a level that would allow defense attorneys to mount a successful insanity defense. He was not psychotic. His problems were impulse control, immaturity, and anti-authoritarian behavior.

"At some point we are going to have to go ahead and charge Sueanne," Moore told his staff. "But not right now. Let's wait and see what happens with Paul."

———

Across town, Ed Byrne's anger was dissipating. The indignation he had felt after Jimmy's conviction still simmered, but it was tempered by a strong desire to help Jimmy and to see Sueanne brought to justice. He suggested a deal in which Jimmy would testify against his mother in exchange for intensive psychiatric counseling while serving his prison sentence. Otherwise, Jimmy would be placed in a prison, with little chance for counseling.

Although reluctant to testify, Jimmy gave Byrne

permission to approach prosecutors with the offer. Two weeks after the trial, Byrne contacted Moore and Tatum with the proposal: Jimmy would agree to testify against Sueanne if prosecutors would ask Judge Fossey to sentence Jimmy as an aider and abettor; request state officials to provide psychiatric counseling instead of simply warehousing Jimmy in a prison; and grant Jimmy immunity against prosecution in Johnson County for conspiracy. Although Jimmy had been convicted of first-degree murder, Byrne believed Fossey had the authority to sentence him as an aider and abettor, thus making him eligible for parole in seven and one-half years instead of fifteen years.

It was a deal prosecutors could accept. Moore, anxious for Jimmy's cooperation, traveled with Tatum and Byrne to Paola a few days later to meet with Belling and Judge Fossey. Without Fossey's approval, the deal could not be made. Byrne's argument for a deal was simple: Jimmy had been directly involved in Chris's murder, but of the three people involved, Jimmy was the least morally culpable.

"Let Jimmy get counseling and get on with his life," Byrne suggested to Fossey. "Even if he is sentenced as an aider and abettor, he will still have to serve at least seven and one-half years, probably more."

Fossey listened intently, but gave no assurance that he would accept the deal.

"I'll have to think about it," he said. The attorneys, especially Byrne, left the Miami County Courthouse confident they could reach an agreement. They were wrong.

Two weeks later, as Tatum, Belling, and Byrne prepared to argue post-trial motions, Fossey summoned them to his chambers. Byrne was surprised when Fossey told him that if the motion for a new trial was not granted, he intended to sentence Jimmy immediately.

Byrne reminded Fossey of the earlier meeting, indicating he hadn't had time to finalize the plea agreement with prosecutors. Fossey said it didn't matter. He had reviewed the case and the proposed agreement and had determined that he could not, in good conscience, sentence Jimmy as an aider and abettor because the evidence wouldn't support it.

"He was one of the two men who pulled the trigger," Fossey told the men.

Byrne looked to Tatum for support. But Tatum remained silent. Since the judge had made it clear he did not intend to follow the proposed agreement, Tatum decided not to speak. Byrne was furious.

"What about a presentence report?" Byrne asked Fossey, trying to delay Jimmy's sentencing for a few days.

"There's no need for it," the judge responded. "There is only one sentence I can impose for a man convicted of first-degree murder and that is life in prison. Besides, I heard the psychological testimony at trial. I really don't need a presentence report."

Byrne angrily left Fossey's chambers and returned to the courtroom where Jimmy sat passively next to a deputy. Once again Byrne felt betrayed by the state. If Tatum had said something, maybe they could have convinced Fossey to change his mind. But Tatum didn't.

"There's no deal," Byrne told Jimmy. "The judge won't do it."

Jimmy didn't show any emotion. Byrne didn't expect him to. There was no hope in Jimmy's eyes, and there hadn't been for months. In a way, Jimmy didn't think he deserved a deal. Regardless of his life, he had killed Chris. He was going to prison where he belonged.

Byrne's motion for a new trial was heard and quickly denied.

"Let's proceed with sentencing," Fossey said.

Byrne motioned for Jimmy to stand. Dressed in blue jeans, a blue shirt, and tennis shoes, Jimmy nervously clenched his hands into fists.

"Do you have anything to say before sentencing is imposed," Fossey asked.

"No."

Fossey then sentenced Jimmy to life in prison.

As Jimmy was led from the courtroom, Byrne stared at Tatum, who left through a side door.

A few minutes later Byrne appeared on the courthouse steps. He was furious.

"I was satisfied that if the state came forward and made some concessions to Jimmy's benefit that I might have convinced him to testify. It was within their power to jointly request with us that Jimmy be committed to a hospital instead of a prison, but they didn't do it.

"There is no way to ever convict Sueanne Hobson without Jimmy's live testimony on the witness stand, saying 'That's my mother and she told me to kill him.' And he will not do it. Ever."

———

Three days before Paul was to stand trial, Moore got the break he needed. Paul's attorney, Richard Roe, contacted prosecutors in Miami and Johnson counties and told them they would accept the same deal Jimmy had been offered initially. The deal was simple: in exchange for his testimony, prosecutors would allow Paul to plead guilty to the charge of aiding and abetting first-degree murder. Under that plea, Paul would be eligible for parole in seven and one-half years instead of fifteen.

The agreement was reached, and a few weeks later Paul, dressed in a suit and tie, appeared in Miami County District Court to be sentenced.

It was the old Paul.

"You want my profile?" he cockily asked a news

photographer who was stationed near the court-room door. He smiled brightly as the deputy led him into the courtroom where his father and brother waited. He walked to them, shook their hands, and then playfully straightened his father's tie. He appeared relaxed and confident.

The hearing, before a handful of deputies, report-ers, and courthouse employees, was quick and to the point. In exchange for his testimony against Sueanne, he would be sentenced to prison as an aider and abettor.

Unlike Fossey, District Judge Stephen Hill read-ily accepted the plea agreement. Prosecutors had told Hill they needed Paul's cooperation. Based upon Byrne's statement a few days earlier, they believed Jimmy would never testify against his mother.

Tatum told Hill he didn't want to make a deal with Paul, but felt he had to under the circum-stances.

"The picture that emerged from Jimmy's trial was that Sueanne was the one truly responsible for Chris's death," Tatum later explained. "When that became apparent, we had to ask ourselves, 'What do we have to do to make sure that she is brought to justice?' It really came down to the fact that we needed one of the boys to come forward, take the stand and testify against her."

Sueanne's worst nightmare for more than a year became reality when she was formally charged with first-degree murder and conspiracy to commit murder on June 22, 1981.

Shortly afterward, Sueanne and Ed granted a lengthy interview to the Kansas City *Star*. It was a mistake that would haunt her forever.

In the article, Sueanne lambasted Jimmy, de-scribing her son as a lying, drug-taking thief who couldn't be trusted. She said Chris's murder was simply the result of sibling rivalries.

"Jimmy lived in a fantasy world," she said.

Ed agreed.

"I think he is very emotionally disturbed, but he's not crazy," he said.

It was more than Byrne could take. Even though he felt betrayed by prosecutors in both Miami and Johnson counties, he wanted justice served. He doubted Sueanne could be convicted without Jimmy's testimony. He called Jimmy's father to discuss the newspaper article and the need for Jimmy to testify. Byrne was concerned that Paul's testimony wouldn't convict Sueanne. Paul had never talked directly with Sueanne about Chris's murder, and everything Paul knew about Sueanne's involvement in the murder was through Jimmy.

"The truth needs to come out," Byrne told James Crumm. "Even though it won't help Jimmy legally, he needs to testify."

Crumm agreed. The two men discussed it with Jimmy, who was afraid of having to confront Sueanne again. He wanted to put the case behind him and get on with serving his sentence. But after several hours of discussion, Jimmy reluctantly agreed. The next day, Byrne sent Moore a letter.

In recent days, I must state candidly that I have been quite troubled over the prospect of something less than the full truth being presented at Mrs. Hobson's trial. It bothers me to think that justice might be evaded in this case if Jim fails to come forward and tell the whole truth about what really happened.

I have visited with Jimmy in an effort to convince him to testify . . . He knows there is no legal benefit for him to do it, but after considerable discussion, he has agreed to testify. It was not an easy decision for him to make, and I highly respect and commend him for having the courage to come forward and tell the truth. You are advised that my client is ready and available to testify against Mrs. Hobson.

Three days after the agreement with Paul, Moore filed murder and conspiracy charges against Sueanne. At her preliminary hearing a few weeks later, Sueanne remained stoic as her husband, son, and daughter testified. It was a day of contrasting emotions.

Ed, as he had been at Jimmy's trial, was forthright. It was difficult not to feel sorry for him as he described the night his son had disappeared, the emptiness he had felt upon learning that Chris had been killed and that the woman he loved had been implicated in the murder.

But the courtroom onlooker's sympathy turned to disbelief when he explained how he had divorced Sueanne, then remarried her a few months later when he had finally determined that she was not involved in the murder.

Ed's portrait of Sueanne was that of a caring woman who was the victim of her son's evil, drug-induced deeds. In Ed's eyes, she was a naive woman striving to bring two families together, to make all their lives happier.

It was not the woman Jimmy described when he took the stand. It was the first time Jimmy had publicly discussed the murder. Showing no emotion, he tapped his finger absently as Moore questioned him about his life with Sueanne and Ed. Throughout his testimony, Sueanne stared at him. Ed, because of a rule prohibiting witnesses from remaining in the courtroom, stood outside, staring at Jimmy through the glass windows. Because of threats Ed had made toward Jimmy and Paul in the past, security at the hearing was extremely tight.

Speaking in a soft, indifferent tone, Jimmy detailed the events leading to Chris's death. Without emotion, he squarely put the responsibility for the murder at his mother's feet. He described Sueanne as two-faced.

"She would be real nice and motherly toward Chris when Ed was around," Jimmy said. "When

Ed wasn't around, she acted like Chris wasn't even there."

While Ed and Jimmy were each sorrowful in their own way, it was Suzanne's testimony that generated the widest range of emotions. It was obvious on the witness stand that she felt trapped, confused, and scared.

In the days leading up to her mother's preliminary hearing, Suzanne couldn't eat or sleep. She was afraid, not only of what might happen to her in the courtroom, but also of facing Jimmy for the first time in a year. In her eyes, he was responsible for everything that had happened. Like her mother, she had grown to hate him.

On the morning of the preliminary hearing she became physically ill. She threw up continuously. Nothing could calm her.

"I can't do this," she told her mother as they were preparing to leave their Overland Park home for the courthouse in Olathe. "Please, don't make me do this."

"You have to," her mother said. "You have no choice. Dennis Moore is making you do this, not me."

On the witness stand Suzanne was evasive, quick-tempered and defiant. When asked about the statements she had made to police the night her mother was arrested, Suzanne repreatedly said she couldn't remember or hadn't said that. Often she acted as though she didn't know what Moore was talking about.

"She was a little bitch," Moore said. "Just like her mother."

The hearing lasted most of the day. Moore quizzed witnesses about when Sueanne had dropped the billfold at Metcalf South. He laid the groundwork through Jimmy's testimony of Sueanne's obsessive desire to "get rid of Chris," and characterized Suzanne as a reluctant witness who initially told the truth to police, then recanted four days later at her mother's request.

"You've got to understand, Judge, that this little girl is still living with this family and she's under a lot of pressure not to say anything against Sueanne Hobson," he said.

On the other hand, Sueanne's attorneys, Hugh and Scott Kreamer, targeted Jimmy as the key to undermining the state's case. Hugh suggested prosecutors had made a secret deal with Jimmy in exchange for his testimony. He accused Jimmy of being a pathological liar. He questioned him about his use of the insanity defense at his trial in Paola.

"These things we have heard from Jimmy come as no surprise to us because they come from the mouth of a known liar," Hugh told Judge Jones in arguing for the charges to be dismissed. "He's told so many different stories to so many different people that it's hard to believe anything he says."

Hugh attempted to downplay Suzanne's statements by accusing detectives of badgering Suzanne into making a statement that was "basically their words, not hers."

Throughout the testimony, Sueanne sat placidly in her chair. Wearing a white lace dress, she listened intently, but showed no emotion. She wanted to testify, to tell her side of the story, but the Kreamers said no.

"This is a preliminary hearing. There's no reason to take the stand today," Hugh Kreamer told her. "You'll get your chance at trial."

———

Sueanne was frustrated. For the past year she had been forced to remain silent, unable to challenge the lies she said Jimmy and Dennis Moore were spreading about her. She felt the media's coverage of Jimmy's trial and her preliminary hearing had been brutal, full of lies and innuendo. She was still angry that she hadn't been allowed to testify at the preliminary hearing.

If she could publicly explain her side of the story, then everyone would know she was the victim of a vengeful son and a politically motivated District Attorney, and not the wicked mother that was being portrayed. She had convinced her husband of her innocence, and almost all of her friends "who knew the truth" believed her.

Several days after her preliminary hearing, she and Ed began to contact reporters. Despite warnings from her attorneys not to get into a public battle with Dennis Moore, Sueanne and Ed blanketed the community with their side of the story. They granted numerous print interviews and appeared on television.

"I am not an evil person," she told reporters. "I was raised in a nice family, a happy family."

At the core of her campaign were two simple premises: Jimmy is a troubled, resentful boy, and Dennis Moore is a political opportunist who made a deal with two killers to further his own career.

In each interview Ed was by her side. They held hands, often wore matching shirts, and gazed into each other's eyes. Sueanne was charming, intelligent, and convincing. Ed was violent, forceful, and demanding. They made an interesting couple: a mother betrayed by a vindictive, maniacal son, and a father grieving for his murdered child. It was high drama.

On several occasions Ed wore a T-shirt that read: *They promised me justice. I promise them revenge.*

His anger was directed squarely at Moore.

"Last year Dennis Moore promised justice," Ed would say repeatedly. "He said they were going to go for first-degree murder on both of those boys and wouldn't stop until they got it. Dennis Moore told me he wasn't going to plea bargain, but he has. He has lied to me.

"I think everyone has forgotten about Chris. I think they have forgotten about what justice is, too. I think they made deals with killers simply to hang my wife."

Ed claimed that a quirk in the law would allow Paul to be eligible for parole within a year, a charge that Moore denied.

As Ed's anger would rise, Sueanne would calmly pat his hand, reassuring him that she was by his side. He in turn would dutifully tell the world of her innocence.

"If she was guilty, I would have killed her and we wouldn't be here today talking about it," he would say.

She would nod her head in agreement.

"He's a strong man," she would offer. "You don't tell him what to do, and you can't change his mind."

It was a striking contrast. She was the genteel wife, raised in an upper-class family devoid of scandal. He was the hardworking husband striving to be free of the tragedies that had plagued his family for years.

Now they were in a battle for their lives. They had already spent more than $100,000 on Sueanne's defense. They had sold their cars and a boat, and the bank was attempting to foreclose on their home, which now had four mortgages. Ed was so intent on aiding his wife's defense that he had failed to pay an $800 fee to the mortuary that had buried Chris. They were willing to risk everything to prove her innocence, they told reporters.

"We have to for Suzanne's sake," Sueanne would explain.

The only thing that kept them going was their love for each other and for Suzanne, and their belief in God.

"We have the facts and honesty and God on our side," Sueanne would say. "That will see us through."

19

"My mother wasn't a religious person until Chris died. Then she made me start going to church twice on Sundays. I think it had more to do with appearance than religion."

—SUZANNE HOBSON

The description of the happy home that Ed and Sueanne presented to the media was not the life Suzanne was leading. The family was under siege. There were always arguments, accusations, and subtle threats. The pressure was immense.

Suzanne often wished she had been Chris. It would have been much simpler. She would not have had to suffer the doubt, guilt, and confusion that consumed her life. She frequently considered suicide, an easy end to an unbearable life, she thought.

She had always believed in her mother, trusted her, worshiped her. In Suzanne's eyes, Sueanne had always been a hardworking single mother, trying to raise a child alone, a beautiful woman with many friends. Then Chris was killed and the disorder that followed left Suzanne full of doubts. Questions about her mother's involvement in the murder were jumbled with doubts about her own sanity.

Not once since Chris's murder had her mother

ever told her to change her story. The subtle implication, however, was that Suzanne was too young to understand what had really happened. The more Suzanne relived the events prior to Chris's death, the more confused she became.

Suzanne wanted to believe in her mother's innocence. Her mother had been the only person she had ever really loved, the only person who had loved her. She remembered how proud she had always been of her mother, especially when Sueanne came to visit her at school. Her friends would tell her how beautiful and sophisticated Sueanne was.

Unlike her mother, Suzanne's father was a distant, unwanted relative, his memory marred by Sueanne's accusations that he had abandoned Suzanne. For years he had never called or visited. She often told friends she didn't have a father. She believed it was easier than telling them he had abandoned her.

Booze was truly her only escape. Although only fourteen, accessibility to alcohol was not a problem for Suzanne. Sueanne rarely drank, but Ed often did. Suzanne became adept at hiding her drinking from her parents, and her desire for it became greater as the trial inched closer. When she was drunk, which happened at least once a week, she could forget her problems. It was the only time she could forget about Chris and Jimmy and her mom. She had few real friends and no boyfriends. People did not want their children associating with her or her family.

"If a stranger had killed Chris, it would have been different. I would have probably gone back to Indian Creek," Suzanne later recalled. "But my brother and mother were accused of his murder. I couldn't go back. It was too embarrassing, too painful to face all of them."

Suzanne never completed a year at the same

school again. Although she started each year, she always dropped out, finishing the year in Homebound programs, free from the scrutiny of cruel, insensitive classmates, but never far from the constant pressures of her mother. When she would walk into a classroom, or up to a group of students in the halls, the conversations would stop. She always thought they were talking about her, making fun of her.

There were times, during arguments with her mother over different aspects of the case, that she longed for the simple cruelty of fellow students. She could deal with that. It was impossible to silence her mother.

Once, a few weeks before her mother's trial, when she returned home from school with a bad report card, her mother berated her for not applying herself.

"What's wrong with you? Tell me why you can't make better grades," Sueanne demanded.

"It's just a little difficult, Mother," Suzanne said sarcastically.

"What do you mean?" Sueanne asked angrily.

"I can't concentrate. I'm worried, scared."

"About what?"

It was the opening Suzanne had wanted. "I just don't remember things exactly the same way you do."

Sueanne stared at her daughter. They were standing alone in the kitchen. "What?"

"Well, the billfold, for one thing. I remember it was Thursday and you say it was Friday."

"It was Friday, because I dropped you off at the skating rink."

"No, it was Thursday because you brought me out those coconut tingalings from Russell Stover's and then we went home and you saw Chris's bicycle. And you got mad and called Jimmy."

Sueanne looked at Suzanne with an icy stare. It

was the only time they had confronted each other over the billfold.

"Do you want me dead? Do you want me to go to prison?" Sueanne asked coldly. "Because if you do, keep saying those things and that's what will happen to me. Suzanne, I don't want to go to prison for the rest of my life because you can't remember what actually happened. It was Friday. Why can't you remember that?"

The issue was settled; at least, in Sueanne's mind. It was never mentioned again. Sueanne had said it with such conviction that Suzanne began to believe that she truly had confused the events. She was worried that her statement would convict her mother. She began to believe that she was the bad person, not her mother.

***

"You just never talked back to her, ever," Suzanne said in an interview later. "It made her furious, and I knew it."

On one occasion, when Suzanne was about ten years old, Sueanne got upset because Suzanne had left fingernail marks on a bar of soap in the shower. It was something Sueanne had warned her about in the past. A shouting match ensued, and when Suzanne talked back, her mother flew into a blind rage.

"She tried to hit me in the mouth and missed," Suzanne recalled. "She hit me in the eye and gave me a black eye. Before I went to school the next day she put makeup on it so my teachers couldn't see it."

Another time, on Christmas Eve, Suzanne sassed her mother. At first the argument was a minor squabble over table manners, but it escalated into a screaming match. Sueanne banished Suzanne to her room, threatening to return all her Christmas presents. For two days the presents sat unopened under the Christmas tree. Then, as if nothing had ever happened, Sueanne called Suzanne into the room and told her she could open her presents.

Sueanne would give love and then withdraw it.

"She could be the best mother a person could ever want," Suzanne later recalled. "Then she would get mad at me and go for days without talking to me. The silence was worse than the spankings."

To Sueanne, grades, manners, and appearance were the important elements to a successful life. When Suzanne failed to abide by the simplest rules, she would be punished, often with spankings with a wooden spoon.

Suzanne grew up thinking her mother was infallible. She believed everything Sueanne did to her was reasonable, acceptable punishment.

"I always thought that everything she screamed at me about was my fault," Suzanne later recalled. "I fully accepted my mother's behavior because that was all I knew. I felt I should be punished because I wasn't perfect like her."

————

In February, two weeks before the trial, the anxiety over her mother's involvement in Chris's death and her testimony at the trial was replaced by another, deeper despair. Suzanne believed her mother had cancer. A sudden painful illness in her stomach had forced Sueanne to the doctor. She was diagnosed as having a pelvic tumor and had to undergo surgery.

"I thought she was going to die, and I think she thought she was going to die," Suzanne said later. "I remember sitting in the hospital during my mother's operation. I didn't care about the trial, about Jimmy, about myself. All I wanted was for my mother to live, for me and my mom to be happy again."

Sueanne's tumor, which was benign, delayed the trial for six more weeks. When she returned home, the vigor with which she had battled Moore seemed to wane. Because of a court-implemented gag order, the public tirades had ceased. But even if Sueanne had been allowed to continue her public tirades against Moore, she wouldn't have. Suzanne would come home to find her mother standing in the shower, crying. It frightened Suzanne. Her mother never cried. Sueanne also spent increasing time in bed alone. She read, watched soap operas, and waited for her eventual day in court. When she wasn't sleeping, she was going berserk, flying off into rages of uncontrolled anger, screaming at Ed and Suzanne, berating anyone and everyone over matters as simple as changing the cat's litter box.

The Friday before the trial, Sueanne picked Suzanne up after school. Suzanne knew immediately that something was wrong.

"I don't care anymore," Sueanne screamed at her daughter. "I don't care about anything."

Sueanne, the careful, calculating ice princess, was losing control. Her nerves were frayed. She didn't clean the house, rarely put on her nice clothes, and hardly ever left the house. When she did, she often covered her head with a scarf and wore sunglasses.

"We couldn't go anywhere," Suzanne recalled. "If we did go out, everyone would recognize her and would point at her. In public, she acted like it didn't bother her, but she would go home and cry. She couldn't stand them talking about her."

The night before the trial, Sueanne ordered Suzanne to go with Ed to a movie. Suzanne argued that she had a paper due in school the next day, but uncharacteristically, Sueanne ordered her to the movie.

Suzanne was upset. She knew her mother was going to do something, but she didn't know what.

As soon as she and Ed got home, Suzanne bounded into the house and up the stairs to her mother's room to make sure she was all right.

She wasn't. When Suzanne tried to wake her mother, she couldn't. An empty bottle of pills was on the nightstand, Sueanne's breathing was shallow, almost imperceptible. Her skin was pale and clammy.

"Come up here, come up here," Suzanne screamed at Ed, who was downstairs in the kitchen. "I can't wake her up. She won't wake up."

Ed ran upstairs, where he saw Sueanne in her nightclothes, lying limply across the bed. He grabbed her and began to violently shake her, repeatedly, desperately calling her name. She would not respond.

"We've got to get her to a hospital," he said, his eyes showing the fear of a man who has seen death before. "Hurry, go open the garage door."

Clutching Sueanne in his arms, he ran downstairs, where he placed her in the backseat. Suzanne climbed in next to her mother, crying hysterically as she shook her in anger and fear.

Ed carried Sueanne into the emergency room at Shawnee Mission Medical Center a few miles away. Sueanne was placed on a bed behind a screen, blocking Suzanne's view.

For the second time in weeks, Suzanne was overwhelmed by the thought of her mother dying, this time by her own hand. At the hospital she tried to stop crying, but she couldn't. She didn't know if her mother's overdose was accidental, suicidal, or simply an attempt to delay the trial one more time, but she didn't care. The only thing she wanted was for things to be the way they used to be when she and her mother lived alone.

20

"The case against Sueanne Hobson relies on the testimony of two high school punks who say she did it. She says she didn't. That's what the case comes down to."

—SCOTT KREAMER

APRIL 27, 1982 Hugh Kreamer was not in the mood to hear that Sueanne had been hospitalized because of a drug overdose. The trial already had been postponed four times, and Hugh, who was taking chemotherapy for cancer, didn't know how much time he had left. The fifty-six-year-old defense attorney desperately wanted to finish Sueanne's case with his son, Scott, before the disease became too debilitating.

The pair immersed themselves in the case. They both found it ironic that a father and son who loved each other so much would be defending a woman who appeared to be devoid of family instincts.

Whether Sueanne was innocent or not didn't matter to either of them. In fact, they never discussed it.

"Our approach was simple," Scott recalled. "We asked Sueanne to tell us the facts, and then we tried to figure out what we had to do to get her off."

The Kreamers had listened for months to

Sueanne's story. They believed there were enough unanswered questions to convince a jury of a reasonable doubt about her involvement.

"There just wasn't enough incentive or reward for Sueanne to do this," Scott said later. "When you have a doubtful motive and little reward, there's always a chance of acquittal."

Their theory of defense was set. The murder had been committed by Jimmy, with Paul's help, in revenge for Chris tattling on Jimmy about stolen credit cards and drugs. When confronted by police, Jimmy had tried to implicate his mother—the mother he had hated for abandoning him at an early age.

The damaging evidence against Sueanne would be contained in the testimony of four witnesses: Jimmy, Paul, Suzanne, and Margie, Sueanne's former best friend. Although worried about Sueanne's original statements to police, they thought Sueanne would be able to explain her own incriminating statements when she took the witness stand.

But the defense team hoped to show each of the witnesses against Sueanne was either lying or confused.

Jimmy and Paul, Sueanne's two main accusers, both had motives for lying about Sueanne's involvement. Jimmy was a vengeful son who had made a secret deal with the District Attorney's office. His motive was revenge for a mother he believed had abandoned him as a child. Paul's motive was more obvious. He was guilty of the murder and had simply made a deal to reduce his prison sentence.

Margie's motivation was greed. The night Sueanne was arrested, she had given Margie $40,000 worth of jewelry that the Hobsons said she failed to return.

Suzanne's statement incriminating her mother could be explained. She was a small child who had been victimized by overly aggressive detectives trying to make a murder case. They had awakened her in the middle of the night and talked to her alone in her bedroom, during which time they led her into making incriminating statements. Then they took her to the police station, where they recorded her statement.

The Kreamers' ace in the hole was Ed. The fact that the murdered boy's own father believed in Sueanne's innocence was a powerful statement in her defense. Surely the man closest to the situation and to the murder victim would know whether Sueanne was telling the truth.

Hugh Kreamer, self-assured, savvy, well-known as one of the ablest defense attorneys in Johnson County, fully expected to undercut the key prosecution witnesses in cross-examination and expose their weaknesses to the jury.

Sueanne, after several months of public diatribes against Jimmy and Dennis Moore, was ready to meet them head-on and convince the jury of her innocence.

Both had miscalculated. Although no one on the defense team—Ed, Sueanne, Scott, or Hugh—realized it, they were about to meet their match in the seven-man, five-woman jury of Johnson County citizens.

The first jolt to Sueanne's confidence came on Tuesday, the first day of her trial. After sitting through eight hours of jury selection, she was informed by Judge Robert Jones that she would subsequently be confined to the Johnson County jail at night.

"We can't take a chance that she'll do something again," Jones told the Kreamers. He was still angry that the case had to be continued for one day because of Sueanne's overdose.

Sueanne went to pieces.

"What about my hair?" she pleaded. "How will I get my clothes?"

In desperation, she offered to go home with Moore.

"I don't mean to be facetious, but I would be willing to be under your jurisdiction, and I don't mean that sarcastically . . . I just don't want to go back to jail."

The suggestion, which stunned both prosecuting and defense attorneys, was so bizarre it was ignored.

Sueanne still attempted to thwart the judge's decision.

"The main thing I am worried about, Judge, is my daughter has one month of school left," she said. "She's had three years where she has never been able to finish school . . ."

Jones told Sueanne his decision was final.

———

Sueanne appeared no worse for wear when she threaded her way through the crowd outside the courtroom Wednesday morning, the first day of actual testimony.

Dressed in a brown tweed suit, she calmly took her place at the defense table as Dennis Moore prepared to give his opening statement.

By eight-thirty A.M. the courtroom was jammed. The first two rows were reserved for media. Outside the courtroom several dozen people stood in line awaiting their chance to enter. Some would stand all day in vain.

At one point Sueanne turned and smiled at several people, friends from her Silva mind-control group. They were there to give her moral support. She had asked the Kreamers for permission to allow them to attend the trial.

"Yeah, they can attend, just like anyone else who wants to stand in line," Scott told her. "But I don't want anybody to know they're there, especially the media."

Scott was nervous enough about the trial without having to worry about the jury's reaction to a mind-control group sitting in the courtroom. His job was to prove Sueanne couldn't have manipulated her son into committing the crime. The knowledge that she belonged to a mind-control group, however goofy he thought it was, would only make his job harder.

Moore stood at the podium, nervously fidgeting with a yellow legal pad that contained a handwritten outline of his opening statement. Now, after all of Sueanne and Ed's accusations, innuendo, and threats of retribution, Moore was ready to present his case to the jury.

His opening statement was routine. He detailed the witnesses he would call and the evidence that would lead them to an inevitable, horrifying conclusion: Sueanne Hobson had coldly calculated the murder of her stepson and orchestrated that murder by using her own son.

"The real mystery is why," Moore told the jury. "The essence of Sueanne Hobson's complaints about Chris? He messed up in school, he didn't do things right around the house, he intentionally tried to irritate her, his table manners were bad and he ate like a pig. He caused problems between Sueanne and Ed. He manipulated Ed and she was tired of it, and last, but not least, she simply didn't like him."

———

Ed Hobson was the first witness. He walked boldly into the courtroom, a small, gold cross hanging around his neck. During his three hours on the witness stand, it was obvious he had spent hours rehearsing what he would say, how he would say it. To Moore, he was intimidating.

Scott thought Ed's testimony would be as important as anybody else's, including Sueanne's. He was the dead boy's father, and he was willing to come into court and defend the woman accused of Chris's murder. And defend was the right word. Ed's devotion to Sueanne was clear from the outset.

On the other hand, Moore hoped Ed's bizarre devotion to Sueanne would exemplify to the jury her ability to manipulate and control other people.

When Moore asked Ed to point out Sueanne to the jury, Ed smiled and pointed toward the defense table.

"She's that lovely lady sitting right there," he said, holding her gaze for a few moments, then turning back to Moore.

Moore asked Ed to explain his decision to divorce, then remarry Sueanne.

"After all this had happened and everything, between the advice of my attorney and my own emotional state, Sueanne and I got divorced," Ed said. "Within a very short time I realized the mistake I had made. I love this lady. She's a nice, wonderful woman, and I married her back."

Ed's loyalty to Sueanne was confusing when placed against the backdrop of his son's death. It was apparent he grieved for his son, yet he refused to acknowledge any aspect of his wife's involvement.

He was a proud father. Looking straight at the jury, Ed told them of his son's accomplishments, his son's love of fishing and hunting and the fact that he missed him very much. He explained how Chris's first mother had died of cancer, and told about the difficult time Chris had in accepting her death.

"He was a good son," Ed said, choking back tears. "He was mischievous, very intelligent. My son was an asset and a companion to me for many years. He was a good boy and he was learning to be well-mannered. Like I said, he was ornery. Him and his sister fought off and on. One minute they were fighting, the next minute they would be out playing football together."

Ed admitted there were minor problems between Chris and Sueanne, but indicated things had been improving. He said most of their problems revolved around Sueanne's demand for discipline.

"After we got married, Sueanne and I sat down and discussed the discipline of the children, what they were supposed to do."

Ed said Sueanne was a stickler for order and discipline and demanded that the children have specific duties and specific times for their homework.

"You mentioned some chores that Chris and the other children had to do," Moore said. "What chores specifically did Chris have to do?"

"He had to clean his room and clean his bathroom every other day. Chris and Suzanne shared a bathroom. He had his turn doing the dishes or putting the dishes in the dishwasher. Just household duties that Sueanne wanted him to do.

"And if Sueanne asked him to do something, he was supposed to do it without any hassle or anything like that. My wife is an immaculate housekeeper. The dishes in the cupboard have to be put in there just so-so, the glasses have to be lined up like little soldiers. When you open her cupboard, everything has to be in proper perspective. The whole house is that way."

Ed said Sueanne would become angry at Chris when he "didn't line the dishes up" properly or failed to do his chores and homework within the guidelines she had established.

"These little piddly things would upset her to a great extent," he added. "But it was nothing I saw as a big problem. We were making progress."

While he did admit to some "small adjustment problems" between Chris and Sueanne, he said he wasn't aware of any problems between Chris and Jimmy.

Moore also asked Ed if he had ever allowed Chris to go hunting with Jimmy.

"I didn't, but Sueanne did," Ed explained.

A few months before Chris disappeared, he said, Sueanne allowed Chris to skip school one day and go hunting with Jimmy. When Ed came home from work that night, Chris told him about the incident.

"He says, 'Jimmy and I went hunting together today. Mom let me skip school.' He says, 'I'm not supposed to tell you.'"

"Did you talk to Sueanne about it?"

"No, I didn't because in my own mind I could see what she was trying to do. I know my wife as well as I know my own son."

He told the jury it was his belief that Sueanne was simply trying to develop trust and understanding, and by letting him skip school, she was trying to show Chris that she liked him.

Ed said when Chris disappeared, he frantically searched most of that night and the next day for his son.

"I walked the neighborhood. I searched his room and found his billfold with his school identification."

"When did you find the billfold?"

"The next morning."

Moore walked toward Ed, holding Chris's billfold in his hand. Moore knew the billfold would be a key piece of evidence if Sueanne were to be convicted. It was important for two reasons. Although Suzanne had recanted most of her original statement to police, she had remained firm on the billfold—her mother had placed it at Metcalf South the night Chris disappeared. Second, prosecutors believed that the placing of the billfold at Metcalf South by Sueanne was her first attempt to deceive.

During questioning the night of her arrest, Sueanne had first denied knowing anything about

Chris's billfold. Then, after failing a polygraph examination, she had told detectives she dropped it off at Metcalf South the day after Chris disappeared.

According to both Jimmy's and Suzanne's statements, the billfold had set the murder in motion. Once Sueanne had dropped the billfold at Metcalf South, there was no turning back.

"Can you identify this?" Moore asked.

"Yes, that's my son's billfold," Ed said, tears appearing in his eyes.

"When did you see it last?"

"The eighteenth, the morning after he disappeared. It was in his desk."

Moore let the issue slide. Other witnesses would be able to shed more light on it. Anyway, it was clear Ed was convinced he saw the billfold in Chris's room the day after the murder.

"During the days that Chris was missing, did you have any conversations with Sueanne or did she suggest to you what might have happened to Chris?" Moore asked.

"She said Chris probably ran away. But I said, 'No, he didn't run away.'"

"Did she seem satisfied with that?"

"Yes. She was very upset during this time. It was a very emotional, trying time for all of us."

Moore asked Ed whether Sueanne had done anything with Chris's belongings after Chris had disappeared, but before his body had been found.

"We got rid of his furniture," Ed said.

He explained that Sueanne had suggested they redecorate Chris's room. Ed said he gave some of Chris's furniture to Margie Hunt Fugate, along with some of Chris's clothing. Other pieces of furniture he gave to a coworker. He and Sueanne had given away Chris's dresser, table, lamp, bed frame, and mattress.

"Sueanne wanted to redecorate the room," Ed said. "We had already discussed it with him.

Sueanne and him had talked on several occasions, and it ended up that Sueanne was going to make his room into a den for him. He thought that would be a big deal and he really wanted that."

Moore, satisfied he had made a point on the bizarre nature of Sueanne's actions, moved forward to the week Sueanne was arrested.

Ed said he had refused to see Sueanne after the discovery of Chris's body because he was unsure how he would act. He said the police had told him she was involved in the murder, and he was afraid he might harm her. A few days later, however, Ed said he had a burning desire to meet with Sueanne, to ask her to tell him the truth. That meeting, at their home, was attended by their minister.

"Sueanne said Jimmy had told her that Chris had been killed, and if she said anything to anyone, that Jimmy would kill the rest of us," Ed said. "She also knew that if she told me, I would have found Jimmy and Paul and I would have killed them. Later she also told me that she didn't tell anyone because she was also trying to protect her son."

Moore returned to the subject of the billfold.

"Did you have any conversation with Sueanne about the billfold?" Moore asked. Ed said Sueanne later explained how the billfold got to Metcalf South.

"My wife took it up there Friday evening, the day after Chris disappeared, so they would think Chris was a runaway, to keep the police looking for him and to protect her son."

Moore was happy. He believed he had achieved what he wanted. He had laid the groundwork for the testimony of several other witnesses.

As Scott rose from his seat to begin his cross-examination, Ed relaxed. He had been on the defensive during questioning by Moore. Now Scott would give him the opportunity to explain his belief in Sueanne's innocence.

Scott's questions were designed to elicit sympathy for Ed. They discussed the string of tragedies that had followed Ed throughout his life: the death of his parents, his stepdaughter, and his first wife. Ed told the jury how he longed for a happy home life for himself and his son.

But his mood changed when Scott inquired about Jimmy. Ed told the jury how he had approached Sueanne and suggested Jimmy move in with them.

"I felt very sorry for Jimmy," Ed said, explaining that Jimmy was living in horrible conditions with relatives of Sueanne's first husband. "He told me he had to work and couldn't go to school. He didn't have any clothing."

Ed said he remodeled the basement, building Jimmy a bedroom and dark room. At first things appeared to be going fine, but the situation degenerated. Ed described Jimmy as a liar, a thief, and a drug user, a thug who carried a buck knife strapped to his belt. Ed said he and Sueanne repeatedly suggested Jimmy attend counselling with the rest of the family, but he refused.

"If everything was going Jimmy's way, everything was great," Ed said. "If everything wasn't, it was hell to pay."

A few months before Chris's death, Jimmy moved out of the house, Ed said. It was a welcome relief.

Scott asked Ed to describe the relationship between Chris and Sueanne during the months just prior to Chris's disappearance.

"Chris would kiss her every morning before he went to school. He called her Mom even before we were married. They would put their arms around each other. They would do things together. They were planning to take a cooking class together. They were getting closer. There was a lot less tension around the house. The only one we were having any problems with was Jimmy."

At the end of Scott's ninety-minute examination, it was clear that Ed believed everything Sueanne had told him about her involvement in Chris's death.

"She was frightened for her son and the rest of the family," he said. "I could understand her completely."

Ed's testimony was the highlight of the first day. The remainder of the day was spent going through the gruesome specifics of the crime. Moore called the boys who found Chris's body, the man who discovered the billfold at Metcalf South. Miami County sheriff's detectives testified about the recovery of the body. Dr. Bridgens explained how the boy died. Kansas Bureau of Investigation experts testified about the ballistics, how they matched the weapon found at Paul Sorrentino's home. Steve Moore relayed Ed's anxious search for Chris and the unrelenting pressure he placed on detectives to find his son.

All the while, Sueanne sat complacently at her desk, appearing oblivious to the gruesome descriptions of the murder scene. Ed wandered the halls, smoking cigarette after cigarette, occasionally peering through the glass windows on the doors leading into the courtroom. As a witness, he was prohibited from being in the courtroom, except when he was testifying.

As would be the case for the entire trial, the testimony was often interrupted by lengthy legal discussions at the bench. Moore and Scott Kreamer handled most of the questioning. Tatum, the key prosecutor at Jimmy's trial in Paola, had been relegated to the status of legal expert in Sueanne's trial. Hugh had spent most of the day sitting next to Sueanne, making notes and offering suggestions to his son. He was saving his strength for later in the trial when his cross-examination of Jimmy and Paul would be critical.

When the trial was recessed, Sueanne returned to the county jail to spend another night alone, desperately worrying about her fate.

21

"I've never been close to death, but my fear of
testifying is far greater than my fear of death."

—SUZANNE HOBSON

APRIL 29, 1982 The day had finally arrived, and Suzanne couldn't face it. The past week
had been almost unbearable. She rarely slept, and
when she did, the nightmares were terrifying. She
would bolt upright in bed, sweat pouring from her
face. She could barely breathe. The image of her
mother, lying unconscious on her bed, was inter-
woven with frightening thoughts of testifying before a packed courtroom of strangers. When she
was awake, she vomited constantly.

She hadn't realized until her mother's preliminary hearing how important her testimony would
be, how brutal Moore's questions could be. But she
knew, because Scott had told her, that she had been
a terrible witness at the preliminary hearing. For
days prior to the trial she practiced how she would
walk, what she would say, how she would respond
to Moore's relentless questions.

"You have to look young and innocent," her
mother told her.

"But I don't feel young and I'm definitely not innocent," Suzanne said caustically.

The fear of testifying was magnified by the fact that her mother had not been allowed to spend nights at home. She worried about how her mother was surviving in jail. Suzanne hated being home alone at night with Ed. He was drinking, angry that he couldn't be in the courtroom to hear the testimony. They watched the news of the trial on television at night, wondering what the future would hold.

Ed drove her to the Kreamers' law office early Wednesday, where she met briefly with her mother, Ed, Scott, and Hugh. Her mother simply stared at her. Without being told, Suzanne knew how important her testimony would be. She was petrified of facing her mother if she didn't perform up to her expectations.

Within minutes she was summoned to testify. The courtroom and adjacent halls were again jammed with the curious waiting to get in. Suzanne trembled as she walked past the crowd. She felt like she was the one on trial.

The court reporter looked at her and then moved a trash can closer to the witness stand. Suzanne's complexion was a sickly green.

"You can throw up in the trash can if you get sick," the court reporter told Suzanne as she sat down.

Moore started slowly. He didn't want the jury to hate him for appearing to mistreat an obviously scared girl. He started by asking her to explain the family relationships leading up to the killing of Chris.

She admitted there were problems in the home, but nothing out of the ordinary. She presented a scenario similar to Ed's testimony: two families trying to become one. She admitted fighting with Chris, but said they were normal arguments between two teenagers vying for the love and attention of their parents.

"When you got in fights with each other, what would happen?" Moore asked.

"We'd go tell our parents and they would talk about it."

"Who would you go tell?"

"My mother."

"Who would Chris go tell?"

"Ed."

"What would happen then?"

"Sometimes they'd get in arguments about it, sometimes they wouldn't. I don't really remember."

She admitted that she was angry when Chris spread rumors about her at Skateland, and had begged her mother to make him stop.

"What kind of rumors?"

"That I would take my clothes off up at Skateland."

"And that wasn't true, of course, was it?"

"No."

"Was your mom upset at Chris about that?"

"Very. My mom and Ed had a fight about it. I heard them arguing upstairs."

Moore stopped for a moment and reviewed his notes.

"What kind of relationship did Jimmy and Chris have?"

"Well, it was good sometimes, but mostly Jimmy ignored him. He really didn't spend that much time around him."

"How would you describe the relationship between Chris and your mother?"

"It was the best one in the house. They got along fine."

Moore stopped and looked at Suzanne for a moment. She stared coldly back at him, almost daring him to ask her another question. Her fears were gone, or at least under control. She was like a cat backed into a corner, ready to fight to protect herself and her mother. She kept her arms folded tightly in front of her.

All the things that Sueanne had said about Moore during the past several months flooded into Suzanne's mind. He was mean and cruel and he didn't care about anything or anybody, she thought. She stared at him, oblivious to her surroundings. Her answers became shorter and more specific with each enusing question.

Frustrated by her stonewalling, Dennis Moore returned to the prosecutor's table, where he picked up a transcript of Suzanne's statement to Douglass and Steven Moore the night of her mother's arrest.

"Suzanne, do you recall a conversation you had with Detective John Douglass on May fourth, 1980?"

"Yes, I also talked to Steve Moore," she said sarcastically.

Moore began to question her about her statement, but her answers were riddled with "I can't remember," "I don't know," and "I didn't say that."

Suzanne didn't lose her cool. She had been taught long ago by her mother that you did not show emotions in public and did not let anyone know how you feel. Regardless of the fear that was boiling inside her, she was going to fight Moore to the end.

"Pardon me, I couldn't hear you, Mr. Moore," Suzanne said, her eyes boring through him. She was fifteen going on thirty-five. She was ice.

Instead of responding to her obvious attempt to rile him, Moore bore on. He simply repeated the question.

"Did you tell the detectives on May fourth that your mother said something had to be done with Chris because he was causing too many problems at home?"

"Yes."

"Where did you get that information?"

"From Detectives Moore and Douglass. They told me about that."

"Miss Hobson, did you make the statement to the detectives that Jimmy and whoever were going to take Chris out to wherever and get rid of him?"

"Yes. I heard that something had to be done about Chris, meaning that Jimmy was going to talk to him, not kill him."

"Who said anything about killing him?"

"That's what the cops told me. John Douglass and Steve Moore told me that the morning they came to my house."

"Did you tell the detectives that you heard your mother tell Jimmy that something had to be done and Jimmy, responded, 'We'll go out and get rid of him.'" Moore said as he read from her statement.

"I don't remember that," she said. "All I remember them saying is that something had to be done."

"Would you like to refresh your memory?"

Suzanne looked at the statement, then handed it back to Moore.

"Yeah, it says, 'We'll go out and get rid of him,' but I don't remember saying that to the detectives and I don't ever remember hearing it."

"Well, did you say it, or did you not?"

"I don't remember."

Moore continued to harp on each and every aspect of Suzanne's statement, and she continued to fight back. All the while, her mother sat passively watching the battle, arms folded, listening intently. Almost every question was answered with an "I don't know" or "I don't remember."

"Did you make a statement to the detectives about the billfold?" Moore asked, introducing the most damaging evidence contained in Suzanne's statement.

"Obviously I did," she said, motioning to the statement in Moore's hands. "But I don't remember anything about the billfold. Nothing. I didn't know anything about the billfold until they told me where it was."

"Did you tell the detectives that your mom threw the billfold up at Metcalf South?"

"Yeah, I did, but—"

"That's enough, thank you."

Hugh Kreamer had heard enough. He jumped to his feet. "Let her answer," he angrily told the judge.

"You can have her answer it when you cross-examine her," Moore said, becoming increasingly frustrated with Suzanne's testimony.

"Suzanne, you have lived with your mother since this happened and you are still living with her now, aren't you?" Moore asked.

"Yes," she said defiantly.

"No further questions at this time," Moore said. "However, we may want to recall this witness later."

Suzanne remained seated, nervously biting her lower lip. She felt old, beaten, and abused. She desperately wanted to cry, to relieve all the emotions that had been building inside her for months, but she knew her mother wouldn't allow it. She looked toward the defense table for her mother's sign of approval, acknowledgment of a job well done. There was none. Her mother stared blankly across the courtroom. Suzanne's heart sank.

Scott Kreamer stood up, walking slowly to the podium. Her testimony had been poor. She had created more doubts than answers, and he knew Moore would eventually play her original taped statements, which were even more devastating. He had to find a way to minimize the damage, to convince the jury that Suzanne was the victim of over-zealous cops. He had to persuade the jury that, although it was Suzanne's voice, she was only repeating information the detectives had told her earlier.

He wanted to start slowly, to give Suzanne a

chance to calm down, to relax. He asked her her age, about her early life with Sueanne, and about the problems that occurred when Ed and Sueanne were first married. It had all been asked and answered before. But now her voice was not as bitter and spiteful as it had been earlier. Scott turned his attention to the conversation between Jimmy and her mother at his apartment the evening Chris disappeared.

"Is there anything at all about the conversation between your mother and Jimmy that led you to believe that Chris was going to be killed?" he asked.

"No."

"How long did that conversation take place?"

"Five, ten minutes."

Scott, a tanned, good-looking thirty-two-year-old, smiled at Suzanne, trying to calm her before moving into questioning about her original statement to detectives the morning her mother was arrested.

"Tell me what happened that morning when the detectives came to visit you at four-thirty or five A.M."

Suzanne told the jury how she was awakened by her mother, who was accompanied by the two detectives. She said her mother told her she had to talk to them. She said her mother was ordered from the room, leaving her alone with the detectives for more than an hour. Suzanne said she remembered sitting up in her nightclothes, while the two stood beside her, talking to her.

"And the door was closed?"

"Yes."

"And you were only thirteen?"

"Yes."

Then he asked a series of questions designed to portray the detectives as devious and manipulative. He wanted the jury to believe they had unfairly trapped Suzanne into making incriminating statements about her mother.

Did they allow you to use the restroom? Did they allow you to get a drink of water or orange juice? Did you have anything to eat? Did they allow you to change clothes? Did they have any recording equipment? So, we don't really know what was exactly said in that room and who said it, do we? Scott asked.

Suzanne answered each question with a firm, resounding "No."

He then turned to the taped statement Suzanne gave a few minutes later at the police station. Like Moore, Scott picked only the quotes from the statement that he thought favored his side. Even though the questions were tempered, Suzanne gave the same responses.

"I really don't remember anything from that statement," she said, her voice again taking on a distinctive edge.

"Did you tell them that your mother wanted Jimmy to talk to Chris?"

"Yes."

"She wanted him to talk to Chris because it has worked before, right?"

"Right. I knew Jimmy was going to come over and talk to Chris, that's all."

She admitted using the term "get rid of," but said that was simply because that was the term Douglass and Moore had used when they interviewed her alone in her bedroom.

"That was what they told me Jimmy had told them," she said adamantly. "They probably said it to me fifty times. They kept telling me what Jimmy and Paul said my mother had done."

Scott ended his examination with a simple question.

"Do you know the difference between a lie and the truth?"

"Yes."

"And what you have told this jury today is the truth?"

"Yes."

At the end of Scott's questioning, Moore jumped to his feet. Suzanne's eyes immediately turned dark and defensive.

"You said Jimmy was supposed to just talk to him, right?" Moore asked.

"Right. Because it had worked," Suzanne said defiantly.

"Yes, it worked this time, didn't it Suzanne?" Moore said, intimating that her mother's request was not simply a conversation, but murder.

Moore, trying to control his emotions, stared at Suzanne. She stared back, giving no ground. Moore walked back to the podium, asked a few additional questions, then sat down, his face bright red. He was angered and insulted by her testimony.

Suzanne's three torturous hours on the witness stand ended. She walked defiantly from the courtroom, past the crowds lining the halls and into the elevator, where she began to sob. She knew she had been unable to pull it off. She began to shake. She held her breath, not wanting to throw up. When she reached Hugh's office, she walked into the bathroom and got sick again.

Although Suzanne had left the courtroom, her credibility was about to take another severe blow. Moore's next witness was Detective Douglass, and he carried the ten-minute taped statement. Douglass was a striking contrast to the portrait Scott had tried to present. He was professional, outgoing, and helpful. He was not antagonistic. He appeared to be a detective simply trying to do his job. He explained how he had come to interview Suzanne.

"We, Detective Moore and myself, had interviewed Mrs. Hobson for a lengthy amount of time that night," he explained during questioning by Moore. "At one point I asked her if we could meet with her daughter to see if she had any knowledge of the events surrounding Chris's death. She told us we could."

Douglass said they had gone to the Hobson home and talked to Suzanne for "five or ten minutes." He said it became readily apparent that she had information that would be helpful, and they took her to the police station where they could tape her statement.

Moore asked Douglass to play the statement. Despite several minutes of protests, legal arguments, and harangues, the Kreamers were unable to change Judge Jones's mind. The tape was valid and admissible, and the jury should be allowed to hear it.

The jury sat silently as Suzanne talked on the tape of the day Chris had disappeared. Her taped statements directly contradicted what she had said on the witness stand minutes before.

"Chris was causing problems, serious problems," she told the detectives in a soft, childish voice. "My mother and Ed fought all the time . . . they weren't getting along."

Suzanne said the day Chris disappeared, she had gone with her mother to Jimmy's apartment. She said she waited in the car while Jimmy and her mother talked in the parking lot. She said she overheard her mother tell Jimmy "that Chris was causing problems and that something needed to be done. And Jimmy said, 'We'll go out and get rid of him.' "

Suzanne admitted that when Chris didn't come home, she first thought Jimmy had "just beat him," but several days later her mother told her that "Jimmy went out and took care of him." Suzanne said she wasn't sure what "took care of" meant, but when he didn't come home, "I figured Jimmy had killed him."

Suzanne also said her mother had dropped Chris's wallet at Metcalf South the night he disappeared.

Sueanne didn't move a muscle during the playing of the tape. While Suzanne's voice crackled in the hushed courtroom, Sueanne sat in stony silence. The tape was devastating. She knew it, her attorneys knew it, and by the looks on the jurors' faces, they knew it. Despite everything that Suzanne had tried to say on the witness stand, the tape spoke for itself. Suzanne didn't sound intimidated or scared. It sounded like she was simply following her mother's orders that night: just tell the detectives the truth.

APRIL 30, 1982

Sueanne had sat passively throughout most of the trial. Even during her own daughter's torturous testimony she had seemed unaffected. That would all change.

Margie Hunt Fugate, Sueanne's former best friend, was the first witness called Thursday. She was a tall, attractive blonde in her thirties. From the moment she took the witness stand, it was apparent that she was no longer Sueanne's friend. She looked at her with anger and disdain.

In a strong, forceful voice, Margie told the jury how she had met Sueanne in 1976 and become fast friends with her. She was working at a local country club at night and would spend several hours a day drinking coffee and chatting with Sueanne at the Hobson home. She said she had considered Sueanne a dear friend.

"Her house was beautiful. It was perfect," she said. "It looked like a Hallmark shop. Everything was hers, completely. She decorated every wall, every knickknack shelf. She spent a lot of money and a lot of time on it, except Chris's room. Chris's room was the bare necessities."

Tatum, who was questioning Margie, asked how Sueanne and Chris had gotten along in the months prior to his death.

"She didn't like him. He was causing problems in their home, especially between her and Ed," Margie said. She said Sueanne often said Chris had mental problems and needed to be institutionalized. Sueanne had described him as an "extremely violent primate schizoid," Margie said.

"She refused to go out in public with him," she added. "She said he acted like a three-year-old and was always embarrassing her."

In the early spring of 1980, Margie said, she was shocked when, over coffee, Sueanne casually asked if Margie knew anyone in the mafia.

"She asked me if I had any idea how much it would cost to have somebody done away with, and she asked me if I ever heard the name Sorrentino connected with the mafia."

"How did you find out Chris was gone?" Tatum asked.

"Over the telephone," Margie said. "Sueanne called me about noon the next day. She wanted to know what I had to do that day. She was in a very good mood. She said that Chris was gone, that he had run away. I was surprised that she and Ed weren't out looking for him. She said Ed couldn't take off work. She said, 'Let's go out and celebrate, he's gone.'"

Margie said they had gone out to have a drink, then picked up Suzanne and drove out to Belton, where they had another drink.

A few days later, Margie said, Sueanne offered her some of Chris's clothing and his bedroom furniture.

"The first thing she gave me was the suit Chris wore to their wedding," she said. "I have two boys. They're a little younger than Chris, but Sueanne said they would grow into them. Then she gave me sheets off his bed, some odds and ends, a desk, lamp, and chair that he used in his bedroom, and his dresser. She told me she was going to redo the room as a study."

Tatum asked her how much time she had spent

with Sueanne between Chris's disappearance and when his body was discovered.

"A lot."

He asked whether Margie had ever seen Sueanne and Jimmy together during that time.

"Yes. I went over to his apartment with her a couple of times. She would buy him stuff. She bought him an iron and different household things that a young man starting up his first apartment could use."

"During that time, did she appear frightened or afraid of him?"

"No, not at all."

Tatum also asked Margie about the night Chris's body was discovered. Margie told the jury that she was at Sueanne's home when the police came to the door. She said she stayed with Suzanne and later accompanied her to the police station, where she gave the taped statement to police.

"Was she crying when she gave the statement?"

"Yes. I think Suzanne could feel the effect of everything that she was saying," Margie responded.

"Did you ask Suzanne about it later?"

"Yes. When we were alone I asked her how she could sit by and watch her mother do that. Suzanne just said there was no way of stopping her mother once she had her mind set on something, that she would just get mad."

Margie's direct testimony had been devastating. It was damaging simply because there was no reason for her to be so angry, so adamant in her dislike for Sueanne. By her own admission, they had been good friends. Hugh only had one choice—to attack Margie's credibility. After three days of allowing his son to carry the burden of the trial, Hugh came out swinging.

Sueanne, too, was alert, aggressive. For the first time in the trial she leaned forward, staring at Margie.

In the months prior to the trial, Hugh had at-

tempted to have Moore file felony theft charges
against Margie for allegedly stealing Sueanne's
jewelry. Moore had refused. He thought the request
was a ploy to discredit a key witness. When Moore
didn't comply, Hugh found a little-used law that
allowed individual citizens to file their own com-
plaint in district court when the prosecutor refused. Margie was charged with felony theft, but
few law enforcement officials took the warrant seriously. Margie had left the state soon after the
murder and was living in Connecticut. In addition
to the criminal charge, Hugh had filed a civil suit
against Margie, also involving the jewelry.

Hugh immediately asked Margie about the
jewelry, why she had taken it and then refused to
give it back.

"I gave it back to her," said Margie, a streetwise
woman who wasn't about to take anything from
Hugh. "It was the day after she was released from
jail. We were upstairs in my bedroom."

"Was anybody else there?"

"No."

Hugh continued to badger her, but Margie
wouldn't budge. Sueanne leaned forward and
stared angrily at Margie. The atmosphere in the
courtroom was electric. Sueanne was finally revealing some emotion. Margie's testimony had goaded
Sueanne into showing uncontrolled hostility.

During cross-examination Margie said Sueanne
often had talked to her about putting Chris in an
institution, but that Ed would not allow it.

"She mentioned that to you?" Hugh said.

"Yes. She said she had tried to convince Ed, but
he wouldn't have anything to do with it. He refused
to let Chris leave home."

"Did Chris act like an extremely violent primate
schizoid?" Hugh asked incredulously.

"No, he didn't," she said firmly. "He seemed just
fine to me."

Hugh asked her about the clothing. "How long

had Sueanne been giving you Chris's outgrown clothes?

"That was the first time she ever had."

"That is your testimony?"

"Under oath?" Sueanne suddenly blurted angrily from the defense table, startling everyone in the courtroom, including her own lawyer.

"Yes," Margie said, staring back at Sueanne.

"And they gave you a dresser from the basement, do you remember that?" Hugh said.

"I thought it was out of his room," Margie said sarcastically.

"Bullshit!" Sueanne exclaimed.

She had watched and listened without expression as her daughter and husband had struggled pitifully, painfully, to defend her. The first emotion she had shown wasn't concern or anxiety for her loved ones, but anger over Margie's refusal to knuckle under. Several jurors looked at Sueanne in amazement as Hugh ended his questioning and Margie left the witness stand. If it hadn't been so serious, it would have been comical.

———

The crowded courtroom wrestled to attention when Jimmy was led to the witness stand by deputies. They could see a resemblance between mother and son, but they could have been strangers passing on a city sidewalk. Neither acknowledged the other's presence.

Sueanne had regained her composure and returned to her impassive pose. She occasionally brushed the sleeves of her white dress, appearing impervious to the drama of being accused by her firstborn.

Jimmy was a stark contrast to his sister. He seemed resigned, emotionally unattached to his mother or the task ahead. His skin was the pale, milky color that comes from months in prison. He had now been incarcerated for more than two years and had acquired the demeanor of someone resigned to spending his life in prison. He was still thin, but a rigorous weight program at the state prison in Hutchinson had given his arms and shoulders some definition.

He was not totally indifferent, as he appeared to the crowd. In fact he was embarrassed. He looked to the back of the courtroom where several former classmates sat.

Like Suzanne, Jimmy wanted the task of testifying over with. He wasn't scared, but he wanted to move on and to forget what had happened.

Moore began by asking Jimmy about the events leading to the murder and the reunion with his mother and sister.

Speaking in a soft, indifferent tone, Jimmy tapped his finger absently on the witness stand as he methodically revealed his life. Without remorse or even a trace of bitterness, Jimmy described how he hadn't seen his mother for more than eight years, but was reunited with her in 1979 because his sister wanted to see him again.

"It wasn't my mother, it was my sister," he told the jury. He said he was ecstatic when he was later asked to join the Hobson family in Overland Park. He said initially everything appeared normal. But that didn't last long. He said his mother soon began complaining about Chris and the trouble he was causing. Jimmy said he didn't see the problems, but did see that Chris was being treated differently than the rest of the family.

One day, Jimmy said, Chris approached him while they were alone. "He asked me if I thought my mother liked him," Jimmy said, shaking his head. "I said, 'Well, I think so, yeah, I would imagine so.'"

"Were you telling him the truth?" Moore asked.

"Not really. I didn't want to hurt his feelings. I

didn't think she liked him by the way she had talked about him to me. So, instead of hurting his feelings, I thought I'd just go ahead and tell him that."

Jimmy said by late 1979 Sueanne's comments had changed from simple complaints to suggestions that he find someone to kill Chris.

"At first, she was kind of vague about it," he said. "Then she finally just came right down to the fact that she wanted him dead. She talked about making it look like a suicide or an accident, or possibly a drug overdose."

Moore asked for examples. Jimmy told of a hunting trip Sueanne had arranged on a school day.

"I was supposed to take him out hunting, and once we got out there, I was supposed to shoot him and get rid of the body," he said, matter-of-factly. "I took him hunting, but I didn't shoot him. When we both came home, my mother was very upset because I was not able to do that for her. That's when she told me if I couldn't do it myself, to find somebody who could."

Jimmy said he had tried to ignore her demands, but she increased the pressure. She told him Chris was unstable and she was afraid he was "going to go off the deep end" and hurt her or Suzanne. She said Chris also was spreading lies about Suzanne.

Jimmy said his mother became so desperate that she even tried to kill Chris herself by putting eight Quaaludes in a bowl of ice cream and cocaine on a stick of gum.

"I was with her when she did it," he said, adding that Sueanne made Chris eat the entire bowl of ice cream even though he complained that it tasted funny. "He got real groggy and went upstairs and passed out. He slept for a long, long time. She was disappointed when he woke up."

Jimmy admitted getting in trouble while living at the Hobson home, for drug use and having stolen credit cards. He said his mother told him that Chris was the one that had informed on him about the stolen credit cards.

Finally, Jimmy said, after weeks of her constant badgering, he approached Paul Sorrentino and asked him whether he would be willing to kill somebody. Paul said he would and suggested a $350 fee, the amount it would cost to repair his motorcycle.

"I told my mother what Paul had said, and she said it sounded reasonable."

"Were you supposed to get anything?" Moore asked.

"A new car."

Although Jimmy initially arranged the murder with Paul, he didn't pursue it because he hoped his mother would change her mind. Then, in early April, Sueanne suggested a specific day. She told him that Ed was going to be at a meeting on Thursday, April 17, and that they could pick up Chris at racquetball practice and kill him that night. Jimmy reluctantly agreed.

Acting on her instructions, Jimmy said he picked up Paul and prepared to commit the murder. But after drinking and smoking marijuana for several hours, they decided not to do it. He and Paul went home. It wasn't long before an irate Sueanne contacted him.

"She called my apartment and wanted to know why Chris was at the house and why we had not picked him up," Jimmy said in an expressionless voice. "I told her we had decided not to do it. She was angry. She said it was too late to back out. She said she had already gotten rid of his billfold and clothing . . . and if Ed came home and found the things missing, Ed would kill her."

"What did you tell her?" Moore asked.

"I told her I was sorry. I called Paul and we went over and picked Chris up."

Jimmy said that Chris thought they were going to

do some drug scam, that he was excited about the adventure.

He described Chris's effort to dig the hole, and then his final realization that they intended to kill him. Jimmy said he had ordered Chris to lie down in the hole; he and Paul counted "one, two, three," and then shot him. He said he and Paul returned to his apartment, where they continued to drink and smoke marijuana.

He said his mother called about six A.M. the next day and told him that Ed was out looking for Chris and if there was anything in his apartment that might show what had happened, to get rid of it.

"Did she ask you what happened?" Moore asked.

"Not at that time, but she did later."

"What did you tell her?"

"I just told her that it was over, that it was done."

A few days later Sueanne called and asked him to follow her to a car dealership in Missouri, where she sold the Datsun he had used in killing Chris.

"Did you have any conversations with your mother about Chris at that time?"

"She said it was a lot more peaceful around the house now that he was not there," he said.

Although she had sold the car, Jimmy said she never offered to pay Paul for his part in the murder. Jimmy said Paul continued to badger him about the money, but none was ever paid.

Moore asked whether Paul had ever talked directly to Sueanne about the killing or the lack of payment.

"I don't think he ever talked to her about anything like that."

When they broke for lunch, Sueanne stormed into a nearby witness room where she angrily kicked a trash can against the wall.

"That little bastard is lying about everything," she said to Ed.

———

After lunch, Hugh began his cross-examination of Jimmy. His attack on Jimmy's credibility was swift, direct, and relentless. He accused him of making a secret deal with Moore in exchange for his testimony against Sueanne. He accused him of being a pathological liar, and he questioned his use of the insanity defense at his trial in Paola.

All the while, Sueanne sat at the defense table, impassively watching her son defend himself. She had shown more emotion in two minutes of Margie's testimony than she had during three days of her own family's testimony.

"Now Jimmy, do you still have a mental disease?" Hugh asked, initiating an attack he hoped would destroy Jimmy's credibility.

"I do not know," Jimmy said calmly.

During his examination, Hugh asked whether Jimmy had ever told friends that he hated Chris.

"It is possible, I very well could have."

"Did you ever tell anyone that you wanted to take Chris out and cut him into little pieces?"

"No, sir."

Hugh shuffled through a few stacks of statements. He seemed eager, ready to proceed, but unsure of which direction to go.

"Now, so the jury will understand you," Hugh said, "you have told lies about this case to the police officers on every occasion that you have talked to them up until July fifteenth of this year? Just answer yes or no."

"Yes," Jimmy said passively, again deflating any momentum Hugh hoped to achieve. Whether by design or simply a lack of any real feelings, Jimmy's attitude was flat, devoid of any anger or animosity toward anyone.

"Now, on July fifteenth did a light shine in your window? What caused you to start telling the truth?"

"Well, no light shone in my window," Jimmy said

with a wry smile that quickly disappeared. "I finally realized that it doesn't matter anymore, that it just doesn't matter anymore."

At the end of more than an hour of examination, it was obvious Hugh had not been able to crack Jimmy's central story of his mother's desire to have Chris killed. Jimmy, although apparently victorious in his battle with Hugh, showed no happiness, only resignation. He sat quietly, staring straight ahead.

Jimmy continued to stare ahead as Moore rose from his seat.

"Regarding your use of the insanity defense," Moore said, "did you think you were insane at the time?"

"I'm not sure."

"Did the jury think you were insane?"

"Evidently not."

"Even though you lied to police about shooting Chris, you are admitting it now?"

"We admitted it at my trial. Yes, I admit it."

Moore stood near the jury. He then looked at Jimmy, forcing the boy to turn his face toward the jury.

"You have told the truth today in court, haven't you?"

"Yes, sir," Jimmy said.

"No further questions."

Hugh was quickly back on his feet.

"So you're telling this jury that everything you have told us today is the truth?" Hugh said incredulously.

"Yes, sir."

"No further questions," Hugh said. He smiled ruefully at the jury, then turned and walked back to the defense table.

Jimmy and Sueanne left the courtroom without acknowledging each other. The first week of the trial was over. Ironically, for the first time in years,

Sueanne and Jimmy would be spending the night in the same building—the Johnson County jail. The trial would resume at eight-thirty A.M. Monday with the testimony of the third person involved in the murder: Paul Sorrentino.

———

The trial resumed on Monday, May 3, exactly two years to the day since Chris's body had been found in the shallow grave in Miami County. Paul Sorrentino, the state's sixteenth witness, had been in custody two years. He was now eighteen years old.

Tatum was anxious. The one thing he despised in the courtroom was uncertainty, and he was definitely uncertain about Paul's testimony. Although he had given investigators a lengthy statement following his plea in Miami County, Tatum wasn't sure what Paul would say or what impression he would leave on the jury.

The crowd, which had grown daily, was now large and restless. Many had stood in line for two hours and, once in the courtroom, had been forced to wait for an additional thirty minutes while lawyers argued legal issues in Jones's chambers.

The nervous chatter that buzzed through the large courtroom ended as Sueanne walked through a side door, accompanied by Scott and Hugh. She looked better than she had at any time during the trial. She had even smiled as she and Ed walked hand in hand through the halls to the courtroom earlier that morning. She seemed almost indifferent as Paul took the witness stand.

Unlike Jimmy, Paul was excited. He rubbed his hands together and endlessly squirmed in the witness chair. His eyes darted around the courtroom. Paul had a habit of smiling when he was nervous, and that trait did not endear him to those who had jammed into the back rows of the courtroom. During his testimony several spectators could be heard making disparaging remarks, and at one point Jones admonished the audience to remain silent or risk being removed from the courtroom.

Tatum's questioning was direct and brief. Unsure of how Paul would respond, he decided to stick to the fundamentals. He got what he needed: Paul's admission that he was involved, that he was to be paid for the killing, and that Sueanne was involved. He said that although he had kept his end of the bargain, he had never received the money to fix his motorcycle.

In an attempt to defuse cross-examination by the defense, Tatum ended his questioning by reviewing the plea agreement Paul had made with prosecutors in Miami County.

In contrast to Tatum's concise questioning, Hugh's cross-examination was calculated to emphasize Paul's venal nature. Hugh was argumentative and challenging. He interspersed questions with his own comments. He accused Paul of lying. He insinuated Paul was testifying, not to tell the truth, but to shorten his own lengthy prison term.

"Look at me when I talk to you, Paul," Hugh demanded at one point during the questioning.

Holding Paul's court file in his hand, Hugh stood near the jury box and read aloud the entire plea agreement. He wanted to make sure the jury fully understood what had transpired in Miami County. He had to give the jury a reason to disbelieve Paul's testimony. Paul was straightforward when Hugh questioned him about the plea agreement.

"I didn't want to do fifteen years in prison," Paul said, indicating that his agreement with prosecutors would allow him to be eligible for parole in seven and a half years.

Hugh had set the stage. He then immediately switched to the night of the murder.

"Tell us what happened out there," he said, still holding the plea agreement in his hand.

Paul's comments were sparse, but chilling. He showed no remorse.

"I started digging, but the ground was too hard, so we went over by a creek," he said. "We all took turns digging, and then Chris was instructed to get inside the grave. He had his back to us. And we spontaneously started counting off, 'One, two, three.' I believe I started. I said, 'One,' and Jimmy said 'Two,' and by the time I said 'Three,' Jimmy was walking around to Chris's right and was facing him.

"Jimmy pointed the gun at him and they started to argue. Jimmy was telling Chris what he was going to do and why he was doing it.

"I can't remember exactly what Jimmy said, but it was something like, 'This is for hitting my mother and for hitting my sister and for getting me kicked out of the house.' Then I shot. I was about ten feet away. And then Jimmy shot and Chris fell back. I came around to Chris's left side and Jimmy said, 'Put him out of his misery.' And I shot Chris two more times. Then we threw dirt over him, got in the car and left."

Once again, those in the courtroom had been catapulted back to the reality of why they were there. Paul had retold the last horrifying moments of Chris's life with a casual indifference that seemed to hang in the air. Hugh looked at him with disgust.

"You're the one that fired the first shotgun blast into this poor child, aren't you?" Hugh asked, his voice rising in anger. "And you're the one that all the authorities let plead guilty to something less than first-degree murder?"

Before Paul could answer, Tatum was on his feet to object.

"I can cross-examine your witnesses," Hugh said, looking irritatedly at Tatum. "You're the one that made the deal with him."

"I don't object to your cross-examination. I do

object to you making speeches," Tatum said, trying to divert Hugh's calculated attempt to anger the jury.

"Our client's charged with first-degree murder and she never left home," Hugh said, looking with dismay at the jury.

"I object to that," Tatum said angrily. "I ask that he be admonished to quit making speeches until closing argument."

Jones agreed, prohibiting Hugh's additional comments. Hugh was unfazed by the judge's rebuke. He had made his point to the jury. A wry smile creased his lips as he walked back to the podium and continued his questioning.

Paul's testimony during the next twenty minutes paralleled what Jimmy had said except for a few minor discrepancies. Paul said they had picked up Chris at the racquetball courts, instead of at home. But that difference was minimized when he admitted his memory of the event was hazy because of the amount of drugs he had consumed and the fact that the murder was now more than two years old.

"The years have passed away," he said.

Hugh also questioned Paul about the relationship between Chris and Sueanne.

"Everything you have heard about the disagreement between Sueanne Hobson and Chris came from Jimmy, didn't it?" Hugh asked.

"No. When I was over at their house I got the impression that she never really cared for him," Paul said. "I don't think she wanted him around."

Hugh knew he had made a mistake with that question and tried to minimize the damage. "Did you know that she'd gone to the trouble and expense of adopting this boy as her own?" he asked.

"No."

"All right," Hugh said. "So you didn't know that when all the media for two years has been saying Chris was her stepson, that they were wrong, that Chris was her own loving son?"

The audience, almost in unison, let out a noisy reaction that rejected Hugh's characterization of Chris as Sueanne's loving son. The response startled Hugh and almost everyone else directly involved in the case. Jurors instinctively turned to the audience. If there had been any doubt before, it was clear to everyone now that the majority of those in the courtroom believed Sueanne was guilty.

The response angered Jones because it disrupted the decorum of his courtroom. He quickly gaveled the onlookers back into silence.

"The court will ask the persons in the courtroom to be quiet and not respond to any questions or answers, or this courtroom will be cleared," he said firmly. "The court will also ask counsel to ask questions and not elaborate or make comments disguised as questions."

Hugh shrugged his shoulders. He ended his examination with the one he thought was the most important: Sueanne and Paul had never talked together about the killing.

"Did you ever go to her and say, 'Sueanne, I want my money?' "

"No, sir."

"Because she never told you she was going to give you any, did she?"

"No, sir, she didn't."

"All the information that you got that led up to this murder came to you from Jimmy?"

"Yes, sir."

Although the spectators had been disgusted with Jimmy's testimony on Friday, they hadn't been openly hostile to him, as they were to Paul. When he left the witness stand, many stared angrily while others muttered their disapproval.

22

"I loved Chris and I love my husband. How could
I possibly do this to him?"

—SUEANNE HOBSON

MAY 3, 1982   Sueanne's two-year wait
was over. Now she could tell the world her side of
the story. The state had rested its case after the
noon recess. The focus was now on her, and she
welcomed it. Although the state's case had been
damaging on the surface, she felt confident she
could counter anything Jimmy, Paul, or Margie had
said. Her confidence seemed to grow as Scott
Kreamer outlined to the jury what the defense
would be.

He admitted there were problems combining the
two families and that Sueanne had, at one point,
asked Jimmy to talk to Chris about the problems he
was causing. But she had never intended for Chris
to be killed. The ultimate act, he said, was engi-
neered by a seventeen-year-old son full of hatred
and revenge.

Sueanne stood, straightened her shoulders and
strode to the witness stand. She turned in her chair
so she could look directly at the jury. She was stunning in a cream-colored dress and tight, tailored

tan jacket. Her hair was perfectly styled. She looked more like a professional called to testify in someone else's case, than the woman on trial for killing her son. It was two P.M. She would be on the witness stand for three hours.

Although outwardly she appeared calm, her voice cracked as she began to speak. She tightly gripped a Kleenex in her hand.

"I know you are nervous, Sueanne," Scott said reassuringly. Then he began his gentle questioning about Sueanne's life, marriages, and family.

Sueanne was flawless. She had rehearsed her answers until they were almost automatic. She gave the answers in a quick, almost systematic way. She would look at Scott, listen to his question, then turn to the jury and answer.

She characterized Chris as a loving child who had called her "Mom" from the beginning of her marriage to Ed. She waited patiently for the right moment to explain Jimmy and all the problems he had brought into their happy home.

"Were there problems with any of the children in 1979?" Scott asked.

"Jimmy came to live with us in 1979," she said, seizing her first opportunity. "Yes, there were problems. Jimmy got caught stealing and we found drugs in his room. We punished him and took the Lincoln away from him. He also ditched school a lot."

Sueanne said she had been afraid of Jimmy because he carried a knife in his belt and one in his boot.

Contrasting her relationship with the two boys, Scott asked Sueanne about her relationship with Chris.

"We did things together," she said, again looking toward the jury. "We liked to read. I was trying to teach him to cook. He wanted me to teach him how to iron, but I wouldn't. I wouldn't even teach

Suzanne how to iron. It's one of those nerve-wracking things for me. Ed went to night school and Chris used to come in and get in bed with me and watch television."

She admitted there were minor problems between Suzanne and Chris, but nothing serious.

"There was name-calling and tattling and things like that, but nothing physical."

Sueanne spent several additional minutes telling the jury how she and Chris had been friends and how his grades had been improving. She talked about the happy birthdays and Christmases they had spent together, the clothes, toys, and records she had bought him, and their plans to redecorate his room.

All the while, Moore sat quietly at his table, making notes and waiting for his turn. What Douglass had told him earlier seemed true. Sueanne did think she was smarter than everybody else. But it was one thing to be self-assured and portray everything in its best light when she wasn't being challenged. He was anxious to begin his cross-examination.

But Sueanne still had plenty of things she wanted to say to the jury. Scott switched to questions of Jimmy's motivation for killing Chris.

"Jimmy had got in trouble and he felt like he was going to prison for the credit cards and the drugs and things like that," she said. "He said 'the hell with it' and he left. I beg your pardon," she commented to the jurors, "but that's what he said."

Her attempt at gentility didn't work. Several spectators groaned in disgust. It was the first outward sign during her testimony to indicate many people in the courtroom weren't buying her approach. She ignored the reaction and looked toward Scott for his next question.

"Did he tell you that he thought Chris narked on him?" Scott asked.

"Yes, he did. He was very upset and angry toward Chris because he felt that Chris narked on him. He thought the fact that he was in trouble was Chris's fault."

"Was it true that Chris snitched on him?"

"No."

Satisfied that he had at least laid the basis for doubt in the jury's mind, Scott moved on to another critical issue: Jimmy's repeated accusations that Sueanne had told him she was going to buy him a car as payment for murder.

Sueanne calmly explained that she and Ed had told Jimmy they would buy him a new car, but that had been before he had gotten into trouble and left home. She further explained about her child support lawsuit against Jimmy's father, and how that money was earmarked for a car by the teenager.

Scott moved to the issue of Chris's bedroom and of their plans to remodel it. For the first time on the witness stand, she showed anger when discussing Margie's accusations that the furniture she had given her came from Chris's bedroom.

"The dresser and shelves were in the basement and had been for about three months," she said sarcastically. "And we had always given her Chris's outgrown clothing because she had two little boys. What she said was not true."

Scott was systematically going through all the evidence that was damaging. In each instance, Sueanne had a plausible explanation.

He turned to the most damaging evidence: her own statement to the detectives the night she was arrested. Again, she thought she was on safe ground. She anticipated the questions and was ready with the answers.

She admitted asking Jimmy to talk to Chris about spreading rumors about Suzanne, and she admitted talking to Jimmy the night Chris disappeared.

"During this conversation, did you remember using any language—"

Sueanne interrupted before Scott had finished the question.

"You're referring to 'get rid of,'" she said, as several spectators again grunted their disapproval. Sueanne was too anxious and too well-prepared, and it showed.

"That's one of my favorite expressions," she continued without hesitation. "Yes, I did say that. I said, 'We have to get rid of it.' I did not mean Chris, I meant get rid of the problem."

It was an obvious mistake. No one seemed to buy it. Although the jurors did not outwardly respond, several squirmed uncomfortably in their seats. Her answer seemed too pat.

When Scott questioned her about why she had asked Jimmy to talk to Chris and not Ed, she said Chris had looked up to Jimmy and she thought Chris might listen to him.

"Was there ever any conversation between you and Jimmy about killing Chris?" Scott asked.

"No," Sueanne said, responding emotionally for the first time. Her eyes started to water and she looked straight at the jury during each ensuing question.

"Did you ever offer Jimmy or Paul anything to get rid of Chris?"

"No, I did not."

"Did you have any idea after you left Jimmy's apartment on April seventeenth that he would kill Chris?"

"Oh, no. He was just supposed to talk to him," she said as she slowly began to cry and wipe away the tears.

With each question, she continued to look straight at the jury. The seven men and five women stared back unemotionally. If they were sorry for her, they weren't showing it.

Scott moved closer to the witness stand. He picked up a junior high school picture of Chris and handed it to her.

"Who is that?"

"That's my . . ." she said in a halting voice as she held her face in her hands. "That's Chris, my son."

"Sueanne, I want you to look at the jury and I want you to tell them, have you had any involvement in Chris's death?"

"No, I have not," she cried.

Now the tears flowed freely. She explained how she found out about the murder the next day from Jimmy. She said she had been frightened by the tone of Jimmy's voice. She said she not only had been saddened by Chris's death, but also had been fearful for her family and felt a motherly need to protect Jimmy.

"He called me late in the afternoon—I'm sorry," she said, apologizing to the jury for her tears. "Jimmy said Chris was dead and that he didn't do it. He said he was scared and he was crying and that I had to help him. He said Paul had gone berserk. It was Paul. It was Paul. It was Paul."

She dropped her face in her hands, unable to continue.

"Would you like a glass of water?" Scott asked.

"No," she said haltingly, trying to regain her composure.

Sueanne said later that day Jimmy had come over to the house. "He swore to me that he had nothing to do with it," she said. "And he begged me to help him. I had to help him. I believed him. He convinced me that he didn't have anything to do with it."

Sueanne said Jimmy had gone down into Chris's bedroom and gotten the boy's wallet from his desk. Her answer seemed to startle Moore. It was the first he had ever heard that version of the story. In every other statement, Sueanne had claimed that she had taken the billfold from Chris's room and dropped it off at Metcalf South to protect Jimmy.

Scott asked her why she had earlier told the police she was the one who had taken the billfold from Chris's room the day after he disappeared.

"Now, I want the truth, Sueanne," he said. "How did the billfold get to Metcalf South? I want the truth."

"Jimmy took it there," she said as she began crying again. "He told me he was going to put it up there because he didn't want to get caught, he didn't want to be implicated because he had nothing to do with it. I told the police I did it because I was trying to protect Jimmy."

Scott asked her why she hadn't told Ed what Jimmy had done.

"Because my husband has a terrible temper and he would have killed Jimmy," she said, her face contorted in anguish. "He would have killed him and there would be no husband, no child, no nothing. I had also been told not to say anything."

"By who?"

"Jimmy. He told me that Paul said if I didn't help and if I opened my mouth that he'd just make it a package deal and get rid of us all."

Scott stopped, letting the emotion of the moment dissipate. Sueanne was no longer the cool, ice queen. She was a mess. She dabbed at her eyes, smearing the mascara across her face. Eerily, her appearance had changed: she looked old, hard, and frightened.

———

Sueanne had survived the first test, barely. Her direct examination had been an orchestrated presentation. She had been demure, sorrowful, and adamant on cue. She had made a few errors in timing and delivery, but overall her performance had been satisfactory. But now came the crucial test. Could she react appropriately to Dennis Moore's expert cross-examination? Could she withstand his microscopic inspection of her life without responding in anger? She thought so.

A tactical move by the Kreamers had caught Moore off guard. He had anticipated another evening to prepare, expecting Sueanne to be their last witness. But when Scott announced Sueanne would be his first witness, Moore was shocked. Throughout Sueanne's ninety-minute direct examination, Moore spent more time preparing his cross-examination than he did listening to her direct testimony. When the court took its afternoon break, Moore raced upstairs, where he reviewed her testimony with Tatum.

Luckily, Moore had spent several days preparing for this moment. He had talked to Douglass and his top assistant prosecutors about her demeanor, what she would try to do, how she would act and what he could do to rile her. He had reviewed her statements to police. He had listened to her public tirades. One thing about her readily stood out: she thought she was smarter than everyone who was trying to convict her of murder.

Moore also realized Sueanne had a short fuse. On the surface she appeared confident, with a great deal of self-control. But if he could rile her, get her angry, then maybe the jury would see the real Sueanne who had become so frustrated and angry with Chris that she had ordered his murder. His goal was to peel away the exterior and expose the real Sueanne.

When the jury filed back into the courtroom, Moore was standing patiently at the podium, a few feet in front of Sueanne. She had already taken her place on the witness stand. She had regained her composure. Her eyes were dry and her makeup repaired to perfection. She sat erect and poised. Clutching a Kleenex in her hand, she stared at Moore.

Moore had decided to be forceful, to go right at Sueanne. He started by asking her about Jimmy and why she hadn't seen him for several years after the divorce.

"What attempts did you make to find him, you personally," he said, walking toward her.

"I went over to his aunt's several times with my father," she said.

"How many times?"

"Five, six times."

"What else did you do, ma'am?" Moore said, emphasizing the last word.

"My folks hired detectives to try and find him," she answered, her voice already rising in disgust.

"No," Moore said, again emphasizing the word. "I want to know what you—you personally—did."

"I personally asked my parents to hire them because I had no funds," she said.

"What else?"

"I think that was all," she said. "I don't recall anything else."

"So, for a period of eight years you went over to his aunt's house five or six times, is that correct?"

Sueanne began to hesitate. She confused dates. Finally, she said that it was only six years, not eight.

Although the exchange was inconsequential as far as evidence went, it was important to Moore because it set the ground rules for the remainder of her testimony. It would be hard, tough questioning and he would demand specific answers.

Sueanne breathed deeply as Moore continued. He asked her about her family life, specifically her parents. She admitted she hadn't seen her parents for almost five years, because "we had a little disagreement over family problems."

"So you totally broke off communications with your parents for four years?" he asked.

"Yes, sir."

"And you didn't care about Jimmy enough to find

out where he was for six years, is that correct?"
Moore asked rhetorically.

Sueanne didn't answer and Moore went on to
another area. He had established what he wanted:
she was a person who could spend years without
seeing her immediate family.

Moore walked back to the podium, where he continued to question her about her divorce from her
first husband and her relationship to Jimmy. A pattern emerged. If Sueanne's answers weren't respon-
sive to Moore's questions, he would simply ask the
court reporter to repeat the question. Occasionally
Sueanne would become flustered. More often than
not she would become defiant.

The battle over who was going to control the
questioning had started. Moore thought he could
crack Sueanne's poise and expose her as a phony
through tough, demanding questioning. He was
about to learn that, like her daughter, when
Sueanne was backed into a corner she came out
fighting. She might not have appeared to the jury to
be a vulnerable, loving wife and mother, but neither was she cowed into submission by his aggressive line of questioning. In all his years as a
successful prosecutor, he had never met a tougher
opponent than Sueanne.

"You said Chris had some problems. What were
Chris's problems?" he asked.

"Insecurity for one," she said firmly. She hadn't
given up by any means. She was prepared to fight.
"The loss of his mother, a feeling of rejection. He
had a fear of the dark, but he got over that."

"How do you know that he was afraid of the
dark?"

"He told me, and one night—we have an all-
electric home—the electricity went out in our
house and he came running downstairs and sat in
my lap and was scared to death."

The image of Chris alone and frightened in the

dark just before he was murdered flashed into Moore's mind, catching him off guard for a moment. Then he continued. He quizzed Sueanne about the term "primate schizoid." Sueanne said she had never used the term and had no explanation for why both Jimmy and Margie would testify that it was what she had called Chris.

Moore then switched to the relationships between the members of her family. Sueanne seemed to relax a bit. The tension eased, but the underlying feeling was that it could resurface at any moment. She explained the relationships in detail, revealing little new information. Sueanne seemed to be gaining confidence. Moore had backed off and Sueanne sensed it.

"What kind of problems did you have with Chris?" Moore asked.

"Not doing his homework, being lazy as far as school was concerned," she said. "I knew Chris was bright, but that he didn't apply himself. He was sloppy. He disliked soap and water and things like that, you know. He did not go around breaking up furniture and slapping people, if that's what you mean."

"I don't mean anything, ma'am," Moore said, his voice again rising. "I'm simply asking you a question."

"And I'm trying to answer it," she said.

Sueanne said Chris also had difficulty completing some of his household chores.

"Did you get upset when he didn't put the dishes up and line them up the right way?" Moore asked.

"Sometimes, but not any more angry than I did with Suzanne," she said defensively.

"You heard your husband testify about that, didn't you?"

"If you are talking about lining them up like little soldiers, yes I did," she said. "Yes, I did."

Moore stopped his questioning as a freight train

passed by the courtroom, making it difficult to hear. The respite gave each person a chance to collect themselves. Moore thumbed through his notes, while Sueanne righted herself in her chair, daintily brushing the wrinkles from her skirt.

During the next few minutes, Moore questioned Sueanne about Jimmy and his problems. She gave the same responses she had given earlier, and Moore could do little to shake her story: Jimmy had problems with drugs, stealing, and lying. Sueanne had tried to help him, but it was difficult. She said he had moved out in early 1980 because he was having too many problems and those problems were disrupting their home.

Moore had laid his first trap. He allowed Sueanne to continue.

She explained the difficulties she and Ed had had with Chris spreading rumors about Suzanne being an alcoholic and taking her clothes off at Skateland. She said they both talked to Chris and the problems seemed to cease. But a few months later Chris started spreading rumors about Suzanne again.

"What did you do then?" Moore asked.

"I asked Jimmy to talk to him," she said, adding that she hadn't told Ed.

"Why not?" Moore asked.

"Because I chose not to," she said, her voice rising as she sensed Moore's challenge. "No particular reason. Jimmy had talked to Chris before and it had worked and I knew it would work again."

"We are talking about April seventeenth?" Moore asked.

"Yes."

Moore smiled to himself. He had laid the trap and now Sueanne had fallen into it. However, it would be one of the few.

"So, during all this time that Jimmy was causing problems in your family, you were also asking him to solve the problems in your family, is that your testimony?" he asked.

Sueanne stopped for a moment. If she did realize the importance of what she had just said, she didn't show it.

"I asked him to talk to Chris," she said, down-playing her answer.

"Ed couldn't handle the problems, so Jimmy was going to do it for you?"

"Well, I asked him," she said. "Jimmy had helped me before."

"My question, ma'am, is this," Moore said, once again demanding control of the exchange. "Ed couldn't solve the problem, so you talked to Jimmy about solving the problem?"

"Yes, I did."

"Very good," Moore said, looking at Sueanne.

Sueanne looked tense. She wanted to say more, but she couldn't because court rules wouldn't allow it. She could only answer the specific questions that Moore asked. She looked toward the defense table where Hugh and Scott sat quietly.

Moore was able to get Sueanne to concede that she knew Jimmy was coming to her house that night with a friend to threaten Chris. She admitted telling detectives that "Jimmy and someone else were going to take Chris out to scare him that night." She admitted using the term "get rid of it," but said she only meant in the sense of "get rid of the problem."

The testimony was damaging, but Sueanne had not faltered. Moore asked Sueanne when she had learned that Chris was dead.

"My son had told me what happened," she said, reiterating what she had said during direct questioning, that Paul had killed Chris, not Jimmy.

"Why didn't you tell the police?" Moore asked.

"I couldn't," she said, "because I was afraid to. And because I was protecting my son."

"Did you ever tell anybody, namely Ed Hobson, that Jimmy had threatened to hurt you and Suzanne if you told anyone?"

"Yes, sir," she said, this time catching herself before Moore could lay a trap. "Now, Jimmy didn't threaten me. He said Paul threatened us all."

Moore walked toward the witness stand, holding a newspaper photograph taken a few days after Chris had disappeared. The picture showed a distraught Ed examining some clothing as Sueanne stood by his side. She admitted knowing that Chris was already dead when the picture had been taken and conceded she hadn't told anyone about his death. Again she said she was afraid because her son had told her not to go to the police.

"But you also continued to take Jimmy clothing and presents, didn't you?" Moore asked.

"I took him an ironing board, some clothes, and some old dishes," she said.

Moore moved on to another area: the billfold. Sueanne said again that Jimmy had taken the billfold from Chris's room the day after the murder and had dropped it at Metcalf South. Sueanne admitted lying to the police, but said she had told the Kreamers the truth the day after she was bonded out of jail. She said Suzanne and Jimmy were wrong when they said she had dropped the billfold at Metcalf South the night Chris was killed.

"That is simply not true because my husband found it in his room the morning of the eighteenth," she said firmly.

Moore knew she had thought about every conceivable question and answer about the billfold. He knew the jury had heard all the testimony about it. There was no reason to belabor the point.

Moore was now controlling the questioning, and Sueanne knew it. For the moment, at least, she quit trying to alter her answers to fit her own agenda. She was smart enough to realize that it wasn't benefiting her. She listened and responded directly to his questions. Her anger was under control. Moore asked about the hunting trip.

Sueanne said she had told Chris not to tell Ed about it because she wanted to tell him herself. She also angrily denied Jimmy's accusation that she had been upset when Chris returned home alive that night. She said Jimmy also had been lying when he said she had put Quaaludes in Chris's ice cream.

As the afternoon wore on, Sueanne and Moore continued to do battle. He spent the next several minutes asking her about various statements she had given to the media since Chris's death. Often her comments in the media contradicted what she had said earlier to police or during her testimony in the courtroom. Moore wanted to show the jury that Sueanne's stories were self-serving and changed to suit her audience.

Moore returned to Jimmy and the conversation she had had with him the day after Chris's murder.

"Didn't you feel you had an obligation to Chris and Ed to tell the police what had happened?" Moore asked.

"Yes, sir."

"But you didn't see fit to carry through on that obligation?"

"It's not a matter of seeing fit to carry through on the obligation," Sueanne said defiantly. "I had lost one boy. I didn't want to lose another one, and I didn't want to lose my husband. And if I told the police, I would have ended up losing both of them."

Moore studied Sueanne for a minute.

"Mrs. Hobson, did Ed Hobson love his son?" Moore asked.

"Oh, yes."

"Did it ever bother you to see Ed Hobson wondering what had happened to Chris during those two weeks that he didn't come back?" Moore asked. "Did it"?

"Yes, sir, it did," Sueanne said, using the tissue to dab the corners of her eyes. "Very much."

"Thank you, Mrs. Hobson," Moore said. "No further questions."

They had wrestled for control the entire afternoon. At the end, Moore realized she was a stronger, tougher person than he had anticipated. She was a fighter. Although her testimony had been damaging, it had not been a gut shot. She still was clinging to her story. A few times Moore thought he had shown what he perceived as her evil, devious side to the jury, but he wasn't sure how effective he had been in exposing the lies and inconsistencies in her story. He looked at Sueanne disgustedly, then turned and walked away. Her dark eyes followed him back to his table.

Scott quickly returned to the podium for one last question.

"Sueanne, Mr. Moore asked you whether you kept pictures of Chris in the house," he said, referring to a brief exchange in which Moore had insinuated that there were no pictures of Chris in the Hobson home. "Do you still carry a picture of Chris with you at all times?"

"Yes, sir," Sueanne said, again looking straight at the jury.

"Would you find in your purse the picture of Chris you carry with you every day of your life?" he asked.

Sueanne rummaged through her purse and pulled out a rumpled, worn picture of Chris. She handed it to Scott as she wiped back tears.

"Have you always carried that with you since his death?"

"Oh, yes," she said, quietly sobbing. "You can tell it wasn't put in there last night."

"No further questions."

Scott handed the picture back to Sueanne, who continued to wipe tears from her eyes as she stepped from the witness stand. Sueanne walked to

the defense table and sat down until the courtroom
emptied. The energy that had consumed the courtroom for days evaporated. Everyone had anxiously
awaited her testimony, and now that it was over,
they rushed outside into the evening air.

Sueanne spoke to no one. It was a few minutes
past five P.M. and she had been on the witness stand
for almost three hours. She was exhausted. Scott
and Hugh stood next to her, expressionless. She
had survived, but that was about all, they thought.
It was now up to them to build on her story through
the other witnesses they intended to call.

23

"I saw my wife and son have a good relationship.
He kissed her before he went to school every
morning and I saw her put her arms around him
every night."

—ED HOBSON

MAY 4, 1982 Although Sueanne had
defiantly offered explanations for most of the lies or
inconsistencies that Moore exposed, her credibility
was still in doubt, and Scott knew it.

On day six of her trial Scott called several witnesses who portrayed Sueanne as a dear friend, a
good mother, and a loyal wife. More than one witness described Sueanne as "a very warm, compassionate, and loving person." Some, who had known
both Chris and Sueanne, described their relationship as loving and affectionate.

When cross-examined by Moore, the parade of
defense witnesses said they couldn't believe
Sueanne would lie, but even if she did, they would
stand beside her.

"I'd be hard-pressed to believe that she lied," said
Kandy Sams, a friend and former coworker of
Sueanne's. "I would be more inclined to not believe
the person who was saying that she lied."

Another former coworker, Sara Beth Clarkson,
described Sueanne as "a very honest and truthful

person, a very loving and caring person. She is a very thoughtful person," Clarkson said. "She is very honest. She would not lie. I would let her raise my children. What can I say? She is an excellent mother. I am very impressed and very proud to have known her, and I am impressed how she raised her children."

During cross-examination Moore asked Mrs. Clarkson whether it would change her mind to know that Sueanne has admitted to lying about this case on several occasions.

"No, it would not," she said defiantly.

While those witnesses were credible, the last witness called by the defense wasn't. Near the end of the day, Scott called Sueanne's elderly mother to the stand. It was a mistake, and Scott knew it almost immediately. What he hoped would be a simple statement from a loving mother turned into a disaster. She was simply not believable.

"Goofy," was how Scott later described her.

She pathetically provided the court with detailed, handwritten notes of conversations she had had with Jimmy just before Chris's murder and again after Jimmy's arrest. Her testimony was even more rehearsed than Sueanne's.

Holding her handwritten notes, Mrs. Sallee testified that Jimmy came to her house in February 1980 and told her that he was going to kill Chris for telling on him about the stolen credit cards.

"He was in a highly emotional state," she said. "He threatened to kill Chris. He said, 'I'm going to kill that kid, you wait and see.'"

She said Jimmy had called her from the Miami County jail after his arrest and told her he had been lying to detectives about Chris's murder. According to Mrs. Sallee, Jimmy had admitted to her that he and Paul "already had our stories together way ahead of time in case we got unlucky and got picked up."

Her credibility was weak, but her intentions were honorable. Mrs. Sallee said she loved her grandson, but couldn't believe the lies he was telling about her daughter.

"One minute I had an adored grandson, the next minute I had a boy who was charged with murder," she said.

During cross-examination she openly admitted that she and her daughter did not talk to each other for a four-year period because of a "piddly little disagreement." Although she did not say what had caused the estrangement, she was adamant that it was her fault, not Sueanne's.

"I have very Scotch blood," she told the jury. "I had a stiff-necked Scotch pride and I would not give in."

Throughout it all, Sueanne sat quietly at the defense table. She appeared relaxed and happy to have witnesses defending her and her honor. She seemed pleased at the day's end.

MAY 5, 1980

The last defense witness was enigmatic Ed Hobson. Scott believed he was the last and best chance they had of convincing the jury of Sueanne's innocence. Ed's ardent support of Sueanne had to give the jury some doubt about her guilt.

When Ed appeared in the courtroom, he was a ragged bundle of nerves waiting to explode. The seven days of trial had frazzled him. Not only was he having to relive the saddest days of his life, but he was having to do it without his wife. She had spent most of her days in court and her nights in Johnson County jail. He longed for her. He had spent his time at the trial smoking cigarettes in the witness room, roaming the halls, and listening to the media's reporting of the case.

Deputies and plainclothes policemen were scat-

tered throughout the courtroom when Ed ag-
gressively stormed to the witness stand to defend
his wife. It was obvious he felt immense hatred for
Moore. Trembling and glassy-eyed, Ed stared pen-
etratingly at Moore, who sat at a table a few feet
away.

During questioning by Scott, Ed furiously defended his wife and called Jimmy a liar. He said
there was no doubt in his mind that Sueanne had
loved Chris and would not harm him in any way.

"I saw my wife, I saw my wife," he said, pointing
to himself for emphasis, "I saw my wife and son
have a good relationship. He kissed her before he
went to school every morning and I saw her put her
arms around him every night.

"And I saw that," he said, his hands now trembling. "I didn't have to ask my wife whether or not
she loved him, I could see it. I could see the things
she did for him and the things he did for her."

"No further questions," Scott said, confident Ed's
love and belief in Sueanne was evident to the jury.

Ed remained on the witness stand, trembling and
defiant, almost daring Moore to rise and ask him a
question.

The courtroom atmosphere was electric. Everyone stared at Ed sympathetically, but ques-
tioningly.

Finally, Moore stood up.

"Mr. Hobson, your wife knew that you loved
Christian very much, didn't she?" he asked.

"Sure."

"But she didn't tell you that she knew Chris was
dead for a period of two weeks after he disappeared, did she?"

"I could understand that."

"My question is, did she tell you?"

"No."

"Thank you."

Scott immediately stood up, but he, too, did not
move to the podium.

"What would you have done, Ed, if she had told you that she knew Jimmy—"

"I would have killed him," Ed interrupted, in a voice that chilled the courtroom. "I would have killed him."

Ed kept staring at Moore while Scott walked toward him.

"The defense rests," Scott said, as Sueanne wiped tears from her dark, wet eyes.

Ed turned and faced the judge, his hands trembling and tears welling in his eyes.

"May I go get a cup of coffee?" he asked Jones, his anger melting into sorrow with the knowledge that it was over.

"You certainly may, sir," Jones said sympathetically.

MAY 6, 1982

The crowds, which had grown steadily throughout the trial, were almost unmanageable on this final day. Spectators from as far as seventy-five miles away had began lining up in the dark outside the courthouse at five-twenty A.M. When the courthouse opened at eight A.M., they pushed to the third-floor courtroom to stand in line.

Sueanne and Ed walked into the courtroom holding hands as usual, at about eight-twenty. She looked tired and nervous. She was wearing sunglasses and had a white coat pulled tightly around her. At this point in the trial she was helpless, unable to fight back any longer because her time on the witness stand was over. She wouldn't be able to counter Moore's accusations as she had during cross-examination.

Ed and Suzanne sat in the front row. It was the first time either one had been allowed in the courtroom outside of their testimony on the witness stand, and they were anxious to hear what would be said. Ed wanted to be there, but Suzanne didn't.

She had been forced to come by her mother, who said she needed her support.

Each side had been given seventy-five minutes for closing, and the Kreamers had decided to split theirs. Moore would speak first, using half his time, then Scott and Hugh would follow one another, using their allotment. Moore would then return for his summation.

For the first time during the trial, Sueanne looked frightened and frail as she nervously sat at the defense table, waiting for Moore to begin.

After a few perfunctory remarks, Moore began his attack, hoping to provoke at least a facial reaction in Sueanne.

"There are two sides to Sueanne Hobson," he said, facing the jury, his back to her. "You may or may not have seen them both in court. Obviously, she has some friends who are willing to come into court and testify to her character, her honesty, and who will stand by her even when confronted with the fact that she's lied to numerous people on various occasions.

"But there is a darker side to Sueanne Hobson. A side that can plan and execute, through her own son, the murder of her thirteen-year-old stepson—the boy who called her 'Mom.'

"Sueanne is intelligent and Sueanne Hobson is masterful at deceiving, at deception, and at manipulation of others for her own ends.

"Sueanne Hobson would have you believe that she's a warm, caring person, a good mother. But does a good mother abandon her son for seven years? Does a warm, loving person abandon her parents and not talk to them for four years, no matter what the dispute?

"By her own admission, she is a self-confessed liar."

With each word, Sueanne's face turned redder and her expression angrier. She was trying to remain calm, to present a self-assured face to the jury, but she couldn't.

"You heard Sueanne Hobson's testimony during cross-examination when she said, 'But Mr. Moore, I meant get rid of the problem, not get rid of the boy,'" Moore said. "Consider that very carefully, because I think you're going to find that the problem for Sueanne Hobson was Chris Hobson, and she did a good job of getting rid of the problem."

When he finished, Moore turned and looked at Sueanne. She stared angrily back at him, her dark eyes penetrating and hateful.

During Scott's closing argument, he concentrated on Ed Hobson's belief in Sueanne's innocence.

"If there is no reasonable doubt in your minds, consider Ed Hobson," he said. "Chris Hobson is not with us. The living victim is right here, and it is this man, the father of the dead boy. Knowing everything, he remarried her.

"He told you she didn't do it, that she didn't arrange for the murder of his own flesh and blood," Scott said, turning and looking at Ed. "Are you folks going to say, 'Ed, you don't know what you are talking about. We've been with the case for seven days, you've been with her for two years, but we know better than you'?

"Ladies and gentleman, Suzanne Hobson and Ed Hobson are here seeking the return of their mother and wife. Please let them go away together."

Sueanne occasionally dabbed her eyes with tissue.

While Scott had been relaxed and prepared, Hugh used his old style: stomping around the courtroom, demanding explanations, throwing out questions to the jury and casting doubts on the testimony and credibility of all of the state's witnesses.

"I am pretty well schooled in the prosecution of

criminal cases, and this is one of the strangest cases I've had the misfortune of being involved in," he said. "I've seen lots of murder cases, but I've never seen one where the murderer said his mother was involved. What this case boils down to is who do you believe: Sueanne Hobson or her unfortunate son. And I say unfortunate because I do feel sorry for him."

Hugh's compassion for Jimmy was short-lived. He said Jimmy's reason for killing Chris was simple. Chris was receiving the love and attention from Sueanne that Jimmy thought he deserved.

He rhetorically asked the jury how they could believe a boy who testified that he often drank a fifth of whiskey a day, took every kind of drug imaginable, and even admitted to being drunk the night he gave police the original statement incriminating his mother.

"There's no evidence that Sueanne Hobson has ever been intoxicated. There's no evidence she ever took drugs, and there's no evidence she stole, because she is not that kind of woman."

Hugh admitted Sueanne had lied, but said there was a simple explanation for her inconsistencies. She was simply trying to protect her family.

"Yes, she has lied," he said, standing behind Sueanne. "But she had so much fear of what could happen to her, to her little daughter, to her husband, the whole family circle, that she did what she thought best, and that was to save them and try to help her son."

Hugh also asked the jury about a motive.

"If they had a fifty-thousand-dollar life insurance policy on this kid you might have a motive or a reason for it," he said. "To kill somebody, you have to have an awfully good motive. I ask you to find a motive for this lady to kill this young man. If you can't find a motive, then you can't find her guilty of anything.

"The victim of this crime is dead," he said. "But Ed Hobson isn't dead, and he has stood by Sueanne's side in every respect and told you in every way, shape, and form that this woman had nothing to do with this killing.

"The killing was done by two young boys that got loaded up on dope," he said. "They were drunk, stoned out of their minds and maybe hallucinating."

Moore was quick to react during his last turn at the podium.

"Motive?" Moore asked angrily. "The state is not required to prove motive, it's not even mentioned in the instructions. But the motive is here, anyway. And the motive is probably the oldest motive in the world for murder. She didn't like Chris. She hated Chris. Sueanne wasn't happy in her marriage and wanted out, but she didn't have the money to support herself."

Moore also refuted Hugh's attack on Jimmy's credibility.

"If it were just Jimmy here testifying, you might very well disbelieve him," he said. "But it's not Jimmy alone. Listen to Suzanne as she tells you about the conversations she overheard.

"Maybe she didn't stand there by those two boys that night with her hands on their shoulders," he said, his voice rising in anger. "But the presence of Sueanne Hobson was very real that night."

He accused her of playing on her son's troubled past, a past she had helped to create by her own selfishness.

"She used his desire for material things, his desire for her love and approval," he said. "She used him to insulate her from anybody else connected with the crime. She never talked to Paul Sorrentino, and that was by design.

"And it almost worked except for a couple of fatal flaws. The body was found by those two boys fishing. Had that body not been found, Chris would probably still be listed on the police books as a runaway.

"And the second fatal flaw in her plan was that Sueanne Hobson never thought her curious little thirteen-year-old daughter would overhear the conversation between her and Jimmy and later tell the police."

Moore stopped, letting his words sink in. He again turned toward Sueanne, hoping the jury would instinctively follow him.

"Sueanne Hobson has lied to you," he said to the jurors as he pointed at her. "Her lies and her deceptions are intolerable. There are two sides to Sueanne Hobson. Chris Hobson knows the dark side only too well."

Moore's hands were trembling as he gathered his notes from the podium.

Sueanne seemed relieved that it was over. Unlike Moore, she appeared devoid of any emotion. She left the courtroom quietly with Ed and Suzanne by her side. She would go to Hugh's office and await the outcome.

———

What Moore had hoped would be a quick, resounding verdict turned into a painstakingly torturous process. The jury was slow and deliberate.

Upstairs, Moore and his staff waited nervously. They rehashed the trial, moment by moment. They discussed the reasoning behind the jury's request for Suzanne's tape. They examined every possible scenario that could be occurring inside the jury room.

Across the street, Hugh and Scott also waited. Initially, whether because of the adrenaline still flowing from their closing arguments or their belief that they had provided the jury with a reasonable doubt, their confidence grew. Maybe they had achieved a question of doubt. Maybe the jury had looked past Sueanne's inconsistencies. Maybe they didn't believe Jimmy. They were hoping for an acquittal, but realistically believed it probably would be a hung jury.

Those who had diligently watched the trial were also anxious. Many had remained in their courtroom seats. Like Moore, they anticipated a quick verdict. Most of them thought Sueanne was guilty.

Three hours of jury silence was broken when the foreman asked to hear Suzanne's original statement. Moore was excited. He thought her statement was the most crucial aspect to his case.

Sueanne was devastated by the request. The Kreamers were also worried. From the beginning of the case, more than two years ago, the Kreamers had told Sueanne her daughter's statement would be a difficult hurdle for the jury. The Kreamers could explain Jimmy's accusations, but Suzanne's statement was that of an innocent child speaking truthfully about what she had heard and seen.

Suzanne knew the enormity of it, too. As soon as she heard of the jury's request, she began to cry. Hugh, sensing her agony, pulled Suzanne aside and tried to comfort her.

"No matter what happens, young lady," Hugh whispered, putting his arm around her shoulder, "you are not responsible in any way. You did nothing wrong. You have nothing to be ashamed of."

Court was re-convened to replay the tape for the jury. When Sueanne, Ed, and her attorneys came back to the courthouse, the halls were lined with people and the courtroom was overflowing. There was an eerie silence. Everyone stared at the jurors, trying to read their faces for a sign of what had been going on behind those closed doors. The jurors sat stone-faced, revealing nothing of their inner feelings. It was obvious the enormity of their task weighed heavily upon them. When the tape ended, they walked solemnly out a side door and into the jury room a few feet away. It was three-thirty P.M.

At five P.M. Judge Jones called the jury back into the courtroom and asked if they wanted to go home for the evening or continue deliberations. The foreman requested a few more minutes. It appeared they were close to a verdict.

The silence had been replaced by a frenzied buzzing of a hundred different conversations. The electricity inside the courtroom was frightening. Everyone was on edge. Television crews, anticipating a verdict for their evening newscasts, now had to scramble. Courthouse employees who normally dashed from the building at five lingered in the hallways.

At six-twenty P.M. Jones called the jury back into the courtroom to determine whether they wanted to continue. Their weary faces told the story. It was going to take longer than the foreman had anticipated. Jones ordered them to return the next morning.

It was a sleepless night for all the parties involved. The only one who seemed pleased at the end of the day was Ed. He was happy because Sueanne was returning home. Jones had told Sueanne she didn't have to spend the night in jail. The trial was over and Jones didn't have to worry about Sueanne causing another delay. No matter what she did, the jury's deliberations could continue.

Moore began the next day by receiving an unexpected offer: the Kreamers offered to plead Sueanne guilty to a misdemeanor charge related to the billfold, if Moore would drop the murder charges.

"I would rather lose the case than take it out of the hands of the jury," Moore responded. "I can live with the jury's decision, either way."

The jury returned its verdict at 3:45 P.M. after thirteen hours of deliberations over two days. Shortly before the verdict was announced, a smiling Sueanne walked self-assuredly into the courtroom accompanied by Ed. Suzanne was not with them. She had told her mother she didn't want to be there, regardless of how it turned out.

Sueanne confidently surveyed the jurors as they walked single file into the courtroom. They kept their heads down, avoiding eye contact with Sueanne.

"Have you reached a verdict?" Jones asked the foreman.

"Yes, we have," he firmly replied.

"Would the defendant please stand while the bailiff reads the verdict?" he asked.

Dressed in a cream-colored dress, Sueanne stood straight and tall with her attorneys at her side. Ed, sitting in the first row, clutched his minister's hand in his, his eyes fixed on the floor.

"We find the defendant guilty of murder in the first degree," the bailiff said, "and we find the defendant guilty of conspiracy to commit murder in the first degree."

Sueanne closed her eyes, but remained expressionless as the verdict was read. Ed threw his head back and stared at the ceiling as tears began to stream down his face.

Then, while the jurors were polled individually, Sueanne began to cry. Her cries turned into sobs as she threaded her way through the crowded courtroom. She was free on bond until sentencing.

"I can't believe it," she cried to a friend, who rushed to hug her. "It's awful."

Outside the courtroom, in the glare of television cameras, Sueanne and Ed were hustled by deputies to a side door and across the street to Hugh's office. Sueanne, sobbing uncontrollably, was supported by Ed and several friends.

It was a different story outside the courtroom a few minutes later as a jubilant Moore embraced Tatum and then addressed the media.

"I feel it was a just verdict," Moore said. "I feel kind of empty right now. It's not a tragedy for us, but it is a tragedy for Ed Hobson and Suzanne Hobson. And for Chris Hobson."

Moore said the jury told him the deliberations had been lengthy because they wanted to go through every piece of evidence thoroughly.

"They were very conscientious," a relieved Moore said, indicating some jurors had been crying when he met with them. "It was obvious in talking to them that the defendant had a great impact on their decision. They said they were especially able to evaluate her while she was on the witness stand."

At his home in Overland Park, Ed sat outside on the front steps, crying.

"They've won the first battle, but they haven't won the war," he said.

JULY 7, 1982

Two months later Judge Jones imposed a mandatory life sentence upon Sueanne. Wearing a white lace dress, she showed no emotion. She was as impassive as Jimmy had been at his trial.

Ed, however, was angry.

"I'm not in the mood," he screamed at reporters upon leaving the courtroom.

Two days later Moore received a tearstained letter from Ed Hobson. In this letter, Ed chronicled the many and various tragedies suffered by him and his family. His stepdaughter had been beaten and raped in 1970. Later that same year, his mother died of cancer, followed by his father's death two years later.

In 1973 his stepdaughter died, and the police ruled it a suicide. Over the next three years his wife slowly wasted away with cancer. "The pain in my heart and head," Ed wrote, "was unbearable." In 1978, after his wife's death, Ed met Sueanne, who understood his suffering. But tragedy struck once again when his son was murdered.

"You see, Mr. Moore, my wife knows all the pain I have been through. She would not do anything to hurt me, even in fun."

Ed bitterly continued that Moore was an ill man, as well as a liar. He had obtained justice for no one. Instead he "got blood . . . My blood and my family's blood." Ed called Moore a "fool," but promised to pray for his forgiveness by God. "I will keep on praying," the letter closed.

Epilogue

> "Every kid believes that their parents are great, wonderful and all-knowing. Then, when you find out your parents aren't what you think they are, it hurts really bad."
>
> —SUZANNE HOBSON

AUGUST 15, 1991 Ed continues to visit Sueanne weekly at a Kansas prison, still maintaining her innocence. She has already been denied parole once.

At that parole hearing in October 1989, a weary and sad-looking Ed pleaded for her release.

"Guilt or innocence doesn't matter anymore. She has served enough time," he said. "Chris would want her released."

Ed has also had legal problems relating to his son's death. He pled guilty in federal court in 1985 of illegally obtaining and using his dead son's Social Security benefits. Instead of notifying authorities of his son's death, he continued to deposit checks totaling $7000 in a bank account that was set up in his son's name after the boy was killed. Ed was placed on probation.

Jimmy and Paul remain in prison. Jimmy won't be eligible for parole until 1995. Paul has already been denied parole twice.

Ed, Jimmy, and Paul were victims of Sueanne's domination, but they were also victims of their own choice. Jimmy and Paul made conscious decisions to kill Chris. Ed chose to support Sueanne throughout the years.

Suzanne had done nothing but love her mother. She was as innocent as Chris. At thirteen years old she, like Chris, became the victim of a woman who would stop at nothing to satisfy her own needs.

Suzanne's life has been a guilt-ridden battle to survive. Now twenty-three, she has changed her name and has communicated with neither her mother nor Ed for five years. She bears scars as deep and long-lasting as Jimmy's. Shortly after her mother's conviction, she was institutionalized for alcohol and drug abuse. She spent two years meandering through foster homes and state hospitals, alternately trying to deny then admit her part in Chris's death.

Three years after Chris's murder, Suzanne finally was able to admit the truth: her mother was guilty. On a sunny day in February 1983 she finally broke away from her mother's domination. A counselor at a state hospital befriended her. The horrible lie began to unravel. The lie had been slowly devouring every aspect of her life for years, and she was finally able to admit what happened.

"You have to understand that I still loved my mother," she said during a recent interview. "Just like Jimmy. Even though she made him commit this horrible crime, he still loved her. Even though I felt so guilty about Chris's death, I still loved my mother. I finally acknowledged the truth when I was sixteen. I was completely protected there at the state hospital. I didn't have to talk to my mother. And I didn't have to see Ed anymore. For the first time in years I felt free. You can't believe how good it felt to finally admit the truth. My counselor understood me. She listened to me.

"In a way, Jimmy was lucky. Even though he is serving a life sentence and he had to go through all the trauma of a trial, once he said, 'Yeah, I did it,' it was over. He could begin to forget. I had to keep everything inside me. In my world, the world of Sueanne Hobson, the lie became the truth. For years I could never admit the truth to myself or anyone else. Even though deep down I knew she had done it.

"To think I am still alive sometimes amazes me. I had two of the craziest parents [Sueanne and Ed]. It's a miracle I didn't die by their hands. It's even more amazing I didn't die by my own hands, which I almost did. The fact that I don't have brain damage or liver damage—that I'm not a big vegetable—gives me hope that maybe someday my life will turn out to be halfway decent."

She received a two-year degree, counsels children, and is working on a four-year degree in computers. She communicates regularly with her father, James Crumm Sr., and brother Jimmy.

"We're not as close as I would like, but maybe that will change someday."

Does she want to marry and have children?

"I don't know. I worry sometimes that I'll turn out like my mother. And I don't know if anyone would want me to have their children, knowing my history."

Although she has admitted lying at the trial, the guilt remains. She still believes she could have done something to prevent Chris from being murdered. She often finds herself wandering out to Chris's grave on a hillside a few miles from where they all used to live. She stands alone, often crying, as she tries to come to grips with the guilt that has burdened her since the day she saw Jimmy and Paul drive away with Chris.

"He wasn't a bad kid. He didn't do anything wrong. He was just a teenager like every other teenager. The only difference is, they didn't live with my mother."

Even today Suzanne can't understand why it happened.

"You can fill a room with volumes of information about what happened; what was brought out in court; interviews with people who were around. But you will never get the full picture, ever. You'll never know what it was like to be there. To live in that house with that woman. To listen to her, to hear every innuendo, every indirect threat, every lie. I have tried to understand it, to explain it to other people, but I can't. There are no words to explain it."

Does she still love her mother?

"Yes and no. It's really hard to say. I love the woman I knew before Chris was killed. If they called me up tomorrow and said she was going to die, would I go see her? Probably. Because I've always wanted to ask her to just admit the truth and tell me why. That's all I want from her now. To know why."

ANN RULE

New York Times
Bestselling Author of
SMALL
SACRIFICES

There was
only one way
to please her father:
murder his wife.

IF YOU
REALLY
LOVED ME